When science
surrenders to man's
darkest impulses,
who will protect
the innocents?

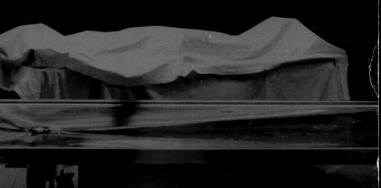

"High-concept storytelling,
non-stop action, terrific plotting.
Philip Hawley is the real deal."
John Lescroart

*STIGMA by Philip Hawley, Jr.,
is no ordinary debut novel,
and its protagonist, Luke McKenna,
is no ordinary hero.*

"We were lifting some woman out of the L.A. River—her car had skidded and gone over a bridge," the pilot of the Sheriff's Search & Rescue 'copter said. "McKenna and me are in the chopper, the other crewmember is on the end of the cable with this woman. As we're pulling them up, the cable on my hoist gets tangled around some rebar. All of a sudden we're tethered to the bridge and I'm having trouble controlling my bird. But I can't use the cable's safety release because my guy and this woman are already fifty feet above the ground."

The creases around his eyes deepened, as if pulled taut by the memory. "Before I know it, that crazy-ass McKenna shimmies down the cable with no safety harness and works it free. Then he climbs back up the line like he's some kinda monkey—we're talking a good thirty feet or so in the downwash of chopper blades." He shook his head. "Once he's back inside, he gives me this no-big-deal look like he'd just gone out for some air."

Susan had a silly grin on her face. "Whoa."

The pilot said, "I still don't know how the hell he did it. But I'll take him along on a rescue any time."

**Who is this man?
What secrets does he conceal?
Meet Luke McKenna . . .**

PHILIP HAWLEY, JR.

STIGMA

HARPER

An Imprint of HarperCollins*Publishers*

This is a work of fiction. Names, characters, places, and incidents are products of the author's imagination or are used fictitiously and are not to be construed as real. Any resemblance to actual events, locales, organizations, or persons, living or dead, is entirely coincidental.

HARPER

An Imprint of HarperCollins*Publishers*
10 East 53rd Street
New York, New York 10022-5299

Copyright © 2007 by Philip Hawley, Jr.
ISBN: 978-0-06-088744-5
ISBN-10: 0-06-088744-3

First Harper paperback printing: March 2007
First Avon Books special printing: August 2006

HarperCollins® and Harper® are trademarks of HarperCollins Publishers.

Printed in the United States of America

Visit Harper paperbacks on the World Wide Web at
www.harpercollins.com

10 9 8 7 6 5 4 3 2 1

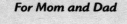

For Mom and Dad

Acknowledgments

During the writing of this novel there were many who came along at just the right moment, like stepping-stones appearing suddenly and unexpectedly just as the literary quagmire threatened to swallow me whole. They include:

My wife, Janelle, who read the early drafts without giggling (well, most of the time) and offered insights that allowed me to understand more fully the characters in this story. She doggedly sifted through a great many words to help me find those that should remain, encouraged me through the difficult times, and remained ever hopeful, even when I doubted myself.

My son, Ned, and my daughter, Sara, for their patience and love. I am truly blessed.

Paul Guyot and his wonderful wife, Kelly, who were to my creative efforts like rainfall on parched soil. Without Paul's friendship, keen literary eye, and expert guidance, my unpublished manuscript would have remained just that—unpublished. I owe Paul and Kelly a debt that can only be acknowledged, never repaid.

My teachers, most notably Bill Barnett (who aptly nicknamed me "Neb," for my nebulous and evasive answers while a high school student in his English literature class), and Shelley Singer (who taught me the importance of precision in both thought and word).

The many readers who suffered through early drafts, including: Will and Brenda Langdon, friends in the truest sense; my brother, George, who knows more about arcane subjects than I would have ever imagined; my brother, Ned, who revealed to me his considerable literary talent; my brother, Victor, who has a peculiar affection for really nasty villains; my sister, Erin, who has a keen literary eye, and also offers great family discounts for her cleaning services; Bruce Johnson, who can shoot the stem off an apple at three hundred yards; Bob and Maryann Hussey; Edgar Hussey; Tammy Sparks; John and Marilyn Maher; and Gayle Robertson.

Deborah Schofield, MD, and Lawrence Ross, MD, who generously offered their expert advice about medical issues central to this story.

Ed Stackler, the enormously talented editor who taught me the finer points of storytelling and showed me how to turn a rough draft into a finished novel.

Lyssa Keusch and the entire staff at HarperCollins, who have worked so tirelessly supporting this book. And Erin Brown, who was its earliest champion.

My agent and friend, Simon Lipskar, who has one of the most challenging jobs in the world and performs it with equal measures of insight, tenacity, patience, and humanity.

John Lescroart, Ridley Pearson, and Tess Gerritsen, whose storytelling talents provided inspiration for this effort, and whose early endorsements brought my goal within reach.

Elmer Crehan, MD, and John Thom, MD, two pediatricians who set a high and noble example for those who will follow them.

Chapter 1

Calderon figured that, on this night, he had to be the only chauffeur at Los Angeles International Airport who was picking up a dying boy.

A TV monitor above one of the airport luggage carousels flashed, announcing the arrival of Flight 888 from Guatemala City. It was 6:18 P.M. The plane was a half hour late, but Calderon was on time and that's what mattered. He'd never been late for a job.

He slid a finger down the lapel of his coat and surveyed his black uniform. Not a stray crease, not a single mark or stain—the boy and his mother deserved at least that much. He ignored the stench of spent diesel from a bus passing behind him as he stood outside the glassed-in baggage claim area and watched for his passengers. Inside, a swarm of travelers sluiced down the escalator and streamed around an eager clot of livery drivers who were jouncing like nervous puppies. No skill, no finesse.

Calderon was a professional. His passengers wouldn't have to find him. He had their description; he'd find them. When they emerged from the last Customs checkpoint, he would appear nearby—a respectful distance away, unobtrusive, but clearly visible to the persons in his charge. He'd immediately conform to their attitude and manner, gregarious if he needed to be, silent and inconspicuous if they preferred. He was especially good at his work, and he knew it. Recognizing the inescapable patterns that define people, anticipating their next thought—these things came naturally to him. He had a knack for this work.

And he usually enjoyed it, but not tonight.

For the young boy and his mother, this was probably their first-ever trip away from home, and almost certainly their first time on a plane. They'd be frightened after being locked away with strangers in a strange metal tube with wings, herded through narrow passageways, hammered with noisy directives, perhaps even stripped of a belonging or two along the way.

Weary and apprehensive, the mother would nevertheless hide behind a mask of stoicism when Calderon greeted her. She would be surprised and pleased to discover that a Guatemalan driver, someone from her homeland, was waiting to welcome them to America, but she wouldn't dare show her relief. He understood; it was their way.

Calderon would befriend her by telling stories about his own journey to America twenty-five years ago. He could still summon the memories of his illegal border crossing: he and his mother crammed into a crowded compartment under the bed of a box truck, the decrepit transmission assaulting his ears until he couldn't hear anymore, the rancid odors of a dozen unwashed bodies, and his mother choked with fear.

Once he seated the boy and his mother in the town car, Calderon would smile warmly into the rearview mirror, lift his shoulders, give them a gentle laugh, and point out the similarities of their journeys. However you come to America, you're certain to be crowded into a tight space with strangers.

The boy's mother might not even smile, but she would

appreciate the story. Perhaps her shoulders would relax as he distracted her from her worries for one brief moment.

Calderon imagined the mother's dread. Her son was a sickly boy, a medical mystery. American doctors would try to unravel the diagnostic puzzle. America's prodigious wealth and know-how were poised and standing ready, all for a four-year-old boy from a tiny village in the Guatemalan rain forests.

Only in America.

Josue Chaca and his mother had no idea that Calderon would be there to greet them. He would explain that it was a small welcoming gesture, another gift from the hospital waiting to receive them, University Children's Hospital.

Josue was one of the chosen few, emblematic of American generosity, plucked in a seemingly random way from among millions of children around the globe who endure their deformities and ailments simply because that's the only world they know.

A loud horn sounded inside the baggage claim area and a red light flashed atop one of the carousels as the machinery groaned to life.

When Calderon and his mother had arrived in America, flashing red lights were the enemy. Back then, America's considerable resources had been a constant threat, fuel that fed his mother's never-ending fear of deportation. They were happiest when they received no attention at all, wanting instead to be left alone to eke out their meager existence. A strong and healthy twelve-year-old boy, Calderon had been tossed into an immigrant labor pool that casually discarded those who couldn't keep up.

All of that had changed when he became an American citizen on his eighteenth birthday. It was the same day he enlisted in the Army. Life had begun on that day.

Seven years later his dreams had died when the U.S. military tossed him out like so much garbage. His stomach knotted as he remembered the night he returned home to his mother's ramshackle apartment and spent the night staring at her bedroom door, which was too rotted to hold in the muted sounds of her weeping. She was probably still thinking about her son's disgrace when, a few months later, the Northridge earthquake trapped her under a two-story pile of rubble. The government bureaucrats could have saved her, but instead they let her suffocate to death.

Now, the same America that had for so many years hovered over Calderon and his mother like a storm cloud, the same America that had excreted them as if they were bilious waste, that same America was giving aid and comfort to this woman and her boy. Josue Chaca and his mother were tasting the American dream, if only for a short time.

Calderon's assignment was simple: to make sure the boy never reached the hospital. Josue Chaca and his mother would be discovered later, perhaps in some dank alley—newly arrived visitors who fell victim to random gang violence. It was a distasteful assignment, made necessary only because of his client's lax attitudes about security.

His cell phone sounded. It was a unique ring tone assigned only to Mr. Kong, his "spotter" at the gate. "They here?" Calderon asked.

"We got a problem," Kong said. "Something's happening up here . . ."

Chapter 2

"Will she have any scars?" the woman asked.

"Nothing that anyone will notice," Dr. McKenna lied. He knew her girl had the worst kind of wounds—hidden from view, out of reach—the kind that fester for a lifetime. "She'll have a small scar here, just behind her ear, but in a few years you probably won't even be able to see it."

"Her fourth birthday is next week. We were talking about her party when . . ." The woman's words gave way to a muffled sob.

McKenna gently lifted the edge of the wound with forceps. "When what?"

"When we fell down the stairs."

"We?"

"I was carrying her." A heavy sigh. "It was dark. I guess I didn't look where I was going."

He gave her a sidelong glance. "What did she hit her head against?"

"I didn't notice." She fidgeted nervously, leaning forward in her chair. "You're sure she's going to be okay?"

"It's a superficial wound—she was lucky. It could've been a lot worse." *And next time, or the time after that, it probably will be.* The bruises flashed in his mind, yellowish-brown marks he had found when he removed the girl's blouse. Fading echoes of violence. They were too old to have happened a few hours ago, and with a little imagination, they formed the outline of a hand. A large hand.

Luke McKenna let the conversation evaporate while waiting for the social worker to arrive. It seemed a complete waste of time to lob lies back and forth. He was growing frustrated with this woman, and annoyed at himself for being irritated with her, so he returned his thoughts to the girl.

Surgical drapes covered the child's head. Except for a small exposed area around the wound behind her right ear, the only trace of her was a tendril of curly red hair peeking out from under the edge of a sterile drape. She was breathing heavily, slowly, nearly asleep now, having spent herself during her first hour in the emergency room. Like most children her age, the girl had fought every step of the way. That is, until two nurses wrapped her body, flailing arms and all, in a Velcro papoose designed specifically with combative toddlers in mind.

An occasional sigh was the woman's only assurance that her daughter was still breathing under all those bloodstained towels and drapes.

Luke adjusted the overhead light with his elbow and picked up a clamp. "As soon as I finish with these stitches, we'll send her over for some X-rays just to make sure that she—"

"She doesn't need any X-rays."

Of course. You've been through this before—you know the routine. No X-rays, no chance that we'll find old healing fractures. Her voice was thick, but not from alcohol or drugs. It was difficult to speak clearly with her lower lip protruding awkwardly.

McKenna put his instruments down and shifted his gaze to the woman. She had the face of a boxer—the one who lost the fight. Her cheeks were a latticework of contusions and raw abrasions, her left eye was clamped shut, and her lower lip had swelled to the size of a small walnut. Dried blood matted her short brown hair in spots. Passing her on the street a month from now, he probably wouldn't recognize her.

A flashing red light invaded his peripheral vision. The intercom unit on the wall called out, "Dr. McKenna, the Trauma Unit wanted me to let you know—the airport transport is on its way in."

Luke worked a jaw muscle. "Tell 'em I'll be there."

He knew that the frustration creeping into his voice wasn't helping. Looking back at the woman, he said, "For your daughter's sake, it's important that we get those X-rays. Without them, I can't be certain about the extent of her injuries. If this was caused by a fall—"

"*I told you,* we fell down the stairs." Her face was an equal mix of defiance and fear. "That's how it happened."

"Okay," was all he could think to say. What he wanted to say was, *But I don't believe you.*

"That's what happened. We fell," she whispered to no one in particular.

Tears began running down her bruised cheeks. She looked about his age, thirty-six, but life's afflictions probably added ten years to her face.

He reached over and placed a hand on her arm.

She recoiled with a shudder.

Luke drew back as if yanked by a rope. "Sorry."

He was clumsy at this, he realized. What did he expect—that she'd collapse onto his shoulder and admit that some cretin had beaten the two of them?

"I just want you to understand that I'm concerned

about you," he said. "I'm concerned about both of you." The words felt awkward and cumbersome.

They shared several seconds of uncomfortable silence before McKenna settled on a different approach. He glanced at a side table, rechecking the patient's chart to see that the woman's last name was the same as her daughter's. "Mrs. Erickson, you sustained some fairly significant injuries yourself. I'll say it again. You should be seen in an emergency room—tonight."

The woman exhaled heavily. "Can't one of the doctors here just take a quick look at me, maybe give me some bandages?"

He shook his head. "I wish we could, but this is a pediatric hospital. Unless it's a life-threatening emergency, we have to send you to an adult facility. There's a hospital just a few blocks away that—"

"Never mind, then."

Adjusting the needle to start another suture, Luke went back to work on the girl's wound. Time for brass tacks. "I'm sorry if what I'm going to say offends you, but your injuries don't look like they happened falling down a stairway."

"It wasn't a stairway like in a house. We were outside." She squirmed in her chair, as though she were sitting on a hot griddle. "The steps outside our back door are concrete. It was dark. I slipped."

He looked up just as the woman pulled back a strand of hair hanging over her swollen eye. Her hand was shaking.

"Then do you mind if I swab a few areas on your daughter's scalp?" he asked. "We can test it for traces of concrete." He had no idea whether such a test even existed.

She didn't respond.

As he snipped the ends of the last suture, he heard the

woman weeping again. He slowly removed the surgical drapes.

The girl's head did not move. She was asleep.

Luke and Mrs. Erickson both turned to a metallic sound—curtain hangers scraped along an overhead track. A tall, thin man, his graying hair pulled back neatly into a ponytail, peered at them from behind the half-open privacy curtain.

It was Dennis, the social worker. Luke waved him into the room.

If anyone could connect with this lady, it was Dennis. He had more experience with child abuse than anyone else in the hospital, and his skills were particularly useful when dealing with an abused spouse who was afraid to talk.

Of course, it was now considered more "correct" to refer to these incidents as nonaccidental trauma rather than child abuse, to remove the supposed bias conveyed by the word "abuse." Luke still favored the term "child abuse."

Seeing the question on Dennis's face, Luke shrugged his eyebrows. No, he hadn't made any progress.

In a relaxed motion, Dennis crouched to meet the woman's downward gaze. He smiled, introduced himself, and said, "A police officer is on his way to the hospital. He has some questions for you. Once Dr. McKenna is finished—"

"No police!" she snapped.

Her daughter startled with a loud cry.

The woman reached over and stroked the girl's forehead with an unsteady hand. She showed both men a pleading expression. "Really, we'll be fine," she said in a weak and unconvincing tone. "I don't need to talk to anyone. I just wanna go home."

Luke and Dennis exchanged glances.

The woman's gaze swung back and forth between her daughter and her trembling hands.

The intercom unit lit up again. "Dr. McKenna, they're calling *again*. They say they need you in Trauma One." The red light blinked off.

"Mrs. Erickson, we're here to help you," Dennis continued. "When we see injuries that aren't easily explained by an accident, we have to notify the police, as well as the county's Department of Children and Family Services. It doesn't mean that we've decided anything, only that we believe the injuries *could* have been caused by another person. Do you understand what I'm saying?"

"Yes."

"I hope you also understand that we're doing this out of genuine concern for both of you. We need to be sure that you and your daughter are safe, which I know is also what you want."

She nodded without looking up. The shields were coming down.

"We can help you deal with this," he said.

"There's nothing to deal with."

"I think there is," Luke broke in.

Dennis shot a glance at Luke. The message was clear: Let me handle this. But Luke knew they were battling the same frustration. For reasons a man could not easily understand, this battered woman would probably retreat into the clutches of her captor. She seemed to shoulder the feelings of shame and worthlessness as though she'd come to accept them as part of her core identity.

Everyone in the room shared at least one feeling— helplessness. Luke watched the woman knead the palms of her hands with nervous thumbs. He wondered how she endured the cruelty in silence. He wondered how she could surrender herself to the creature that had beaten her child.

But this woman *had* come to the hospital. At least part of her was begging for help.

A man's angry shouts interrupted Luke's thoughts—an enraged parent launching into a tirade down the hall.

Moments later there was a deafening *smack*—someone's fist slamming against a wall or countertop.

The woman flinched, her breathing quickened, and her face bloomed with fear.

Calderon stood at the curb outside the terminal and watched the ambulance blast its way through a phalanx of traffic. Brake lights veered to each side of the street in a modern day version of the Red Sea. A duet of sirens faded to a low-pitched yawn as the flashing lights shrank into the distance.

"What do you mean, you lost him?" asked the voice in his earpiece. The encryption technology built into Calderon's cell phone shaved some of the subtle inflections from his client's digitally reconstructed words, giving them an unnatural quality.

Calderon spoke into the tiny boom microphone hanging from his right ear. "A medical team took the kid away on a stretcher. There was no way to grab him—cops and security were all around him. Nothing I could do."

He unbuttoned his black coat and pressed a hand against his left ear to muffle the street noise. The coat collar rose awkwardly on his steeply sloped shoulders. His flexed arm swelled like a tire filling with air. Calderon had always been big, favoring the genes of the German banker in Guatemala City whose home his then-teenage mother had cleaned for the equivalent of fifteen U.S. cents a day.

After a seven-second delay during which Calderon's phone ciphered the encrypted code, his client's voice came back: "He was alive?"

"Yeah, but it looked like he was struggling to breathe." Calderon stepped away from a noisy Chinese couple who were barking at each other in what sounded like Cantonese. He was careful to stay beyond the reach of three security cameras tucked into the ceiling over the baggage carousels. "Airport security had cordoned off a path. I couldn't see much."

During the commotion, he had joined a crowd of spectators who stood gawking as a medical team—dressed in blue coveralls with incongruously cheerful rainbow insignias—trotted alongside the stretcher carrying his mission objective. Calderon had caught only a fleeting glimpse of the boy grimacing through an oxygen mask as the stretcher raced through the baggage claim area.

"You're sure it was our boy?" asked the flat voice in his earpiece.

Encryption technology didn't explain everything that Calderon was hearing, and not hearing. The pitch of his client's voice was oddly high, and his words were stripped of the intonations that gave human speech its texture. His client was using embedded software to camouflage his voice.

"My man at the gate got a good look at him. It was our boy," Calderon said. "His mother was right there too, walking alongside the stretcher—she matched the picture you sent me. One of the medical people was firing questions at her."

He raked his upper lip with his teeth. His paste-on moustache was beginning to itch. The rest of his disguise was minimal: implants stuffed inside his cheeks to soften the lines of his face, red-tinted eyeglasses, and a wig. The wig was just long enough to cover the lower half of his left ear, which was missing.

His mother had always wanted him to get that ear fixed. Now, he wished he had—for her.

A small throng of camera-toting tourists spilled out the exit, luggage in tow, passing on either side of him. Calderon turned to avoid the lens of a trigger-happy woman for whom the taxi stand sign held some profound photographic interest.

Just as he turned, a swarthy young man brushed up against him. Rap music leaked from headphones that were hanging loosely around the man's neck.

The would-be chauffeur's right hand instinctively twitched toward the shoulder holster that wasn't there. The weapon was tucked away in the trunk of his rented town car.

After another several second delay, the voice in Calderon's earpiece said, "Do you know where they're taking him?"

A chorus of horns sounded.

"The logo on the side of the ambulance says University Children's Hospital," Calderon said—too loudly, he realized. He glanced to either side.

The swarthy man was crossing the street, walking toward the parking structure. Something about his casual gait seemed exaggerated, like that of a stage actor who wasn't yet comfortable in his role.

A gust of wind whipped up a sooty air funnel. Calderon reached down and rebuttoned his blazer.

Something didn't feel quite right. His body had always perceived the smallest things, things that were imperceptible to others. The left side of his blazer was too light, a few ounces of drag missing when he drew the lapels together.

His wallet was gone.

His eyes shot across the street.

The swarthy man was walking into the parking structure.

Chapter 3

Megan Callahan challenged the thick metal doors with a heavy stare, willing them to remain shut until she was ready—which might be never, she realized. Her blank expression and clouded blue eyes were a message to the other members of the trauma team: *I'm preparing; leave me to my thoughts.*

University Children's Hospital was the third largest pediatric hospital in the United States, and one of only a few medical centers in southern California equipped to deal with critically ill children. The first stop for every patient arriving by ambulance was the Trauma Unit.

Each team member had an idiosyncratic habit that erupted like a nervous tic during the final moments before a patient arrived. Susan, the charge nurse, fiddled with instruments and medication vials until they were just so—lining them up on the stainless steel tray like little soldiers at parade rest. The other nurse, sporting an oversized nose ring that almost made his spiked orange hair a nonevent, stepped on every moment of silence with idle chitchat. The respiratory therapist checked and rechecked her equipment, her demeanor grim, as always. And Megan, third-year pediatric resident, stood motionless, staring at the well-worn swinging doors, her gloved hands joined at the chest.

Gloves and goggles were the only common element of dress among the four persons standing in Trauma One. They were otherwise a motley crew. Megan was wearing a threadbare yellow smock over well-worn jeans and a green blouse, Susan favored loose-fitting floral scrubs, the other nurse a purple tie-dye creation, and the respiratory therapist wore dark blue scrubs.

Megan's mouth felt dry. At its best, trauma medicine was an edge-of-your-seat display of exquisitely choreographed action and reaction. At its worst, it was bedlam. She didn't care much for either image. After all, she was training to be a general pediatrician, not one of those emergency medicine types who suffered from adrenaline-seeking behavior.

A siren suddenly invaded her thoughts, and pulses of red light pierced through the room's casement windows. A knot formed in her stomach—and then just as quickly uncoiled as the ambulance raced past their hospital.

She let out a heavy sigh, and hoped that no one noticed.

"Megan, what do you know about this kid we're getting?" asked Susan. The charge nurse's tone, as usual, bordered on interrogative.

"Not much. A four-year-old boy—his white blood count is off the charts, mostly lymphocytes. He showed up at our clinic in Guatemala and—"

Nose Ring turned to Megan, his eyebrows lifted. "Aren't you going there next month?"

"I leave in a couple of days," Megan said. "Can't wait to get on the plane."

Like other senior residents nearing the end of their training, Megan had the option to spend four weeks at the northern Guatemalan clinic in lieu of a second month in the E.R. She had jumped at the opportunity, but for reasons that differed from her overworked colleagues who simply wanted a break from the hospital routine. Her reasons had more to do with healing her ragged spirits. She needed to get out of the E.R. and its daily reminders of her shattered romance with Luke McKenna.

She didn't know much about the clinic, which was located in northern Guatemala and staffed by volunteers from University Children's. Each year, at least a dozen patients from the Guatemalan clinic arrived at University Children's, usually for specialized surgical procedures. The patient arriving tonight was different; he was a diagnostic conundrum.

"Lotta short people down there," Nose Ring said to Megan. "Except for the blue eyes, you'll fit right in."

"Yeah, well, I've always wanted to go someplace where short and muscular were considered chic," Megan said. Despite her trim body—the only benefit of a work life that encroached on meals—she couldn't disguise her natural muscularity, accentuated by a hyperkinetic nature that her father had channeled into gymnastics when she was a young girl.

Susan twirled her hand impatiently. "So about this kid . . ."

"Nobody's really sure what's wrong with him," Megan explained. "They're thinking he probably has leukemia, but the lymphocytes don't look typically leukemic."

"What do you mean?" Susan asked.

"They didn't find any blasts—there were no leukemic cells in his blood. But who knows how good our lab is down there?" Megan shrugged. "Originally, he wasn't scheduled to come through the E.R. He was supposed to be stable, a routine admission going straight to the ward, but he started having trouble breathing during the flight up here."

The respiratory therapist looked up from connecting her oxygen line to a valve recessed in the wall. "How much trouble?"

"Not sure. Apparently, the pilot called ahead to the airport, the airport called us, and we decided to send a transport team to pick him up. The team called in as they were getting ready to leave the airport, said he was on oxygen but still breathing on his own." Megan glanced at the large, round clock on the wall—it was 7:03 P.M. "That was about twenty minutes ago."

Susan grimaced. "I'd like to know what genius decided this kid was healthy enough to fly up here." She turned to Megan. "By the way, are you *it* tonight?"

Megan hesitated a beat, irked by where Susan had placed the inflection in her question. "Yeah, just me. I'm the only senior resident on duty."

Her voice cracked on the last word, rising a few octaves.

Damn. Her voice had always had a husky, two-pack-a-day quality. What bothered her most, though, was its tendency to crack when she was nervous or upset.

Susan squinted at a sheet of paper taped to the far wall. "Who's the trauma Attending tonight? If we have a kid coming in that we know next to nothing about, I want an Attending here."

Megan didn't have to look at the schedule. She knew that McKenna was the Attending—the supervising physician. He did the scheduling for the E.R., and she was sure it was no coincidence that, whenever she had trauma duty, he was the Attending covering the unit. The message seemed clear:

He didn't think she could handle the challenge of trauma care.

"It's McKenna," Megan said finally.

"McKenna," Susan echoed, as if trying the thought on for size. "Good."

"Ahh, the Iceman cometh," the therapist clucked.

Iceman. The stories abounded, and most centered on Luke's ability to think clearly and act decisively under extreme conditions that caused even his testosterone-endowed peers to wilt. McKenna did this, McKenna did that, McKenna inserted a chest tube using only his pinky finger, McKenna wrestled a giant gorilla while doing a heart transplant . . . blah, blah, blah. It was one of those silly macho things.

She thought the nickname more strange than praise-worthy and sensed that Luke didn't much care for it either, but then how would anyone know for sure? During the entire eight months of their now-broken relation-ship, he had rarely shared any feelings deeper than a rain puddle.

"That's three times this week—you and him on trauma duty," the therapist added. "Maybe a tiny flame still burns for the Iceman."

The nurses' heads jerked toward the therapist, then at Megan. An instant later they buried their faces in busy work.

Megan opened her mouth to respond, but just as quickly gave it up. Nothing she could say would dissuade them from imagining whatever they wanted.

But, God, I am sooo over him.

Looking back, it had been a foolish idea from the be-ginning. He was an Attending, she a lowly resident. Then there was the seven-year difference in their age, though

Luke's military career before medical school left a narrower gap in their professional lives. He had been an E.R. Attending for just two years.

And as it turned out, none of that mattered.

What did matter was that Luke had never given himself to their relationship as she had. He seemed unwilling to return the trust and emotional intimacy that she had offered to him so freely. The man was a jigsaw puzzle of conflicting images: decent, kind, but also distant and difficult to penetrate.

Three months earlier, while struggling through a difficult time, she had finally surrendered her hopes.

But because her female counterparts at the hospital were so . . . so . . . enthralled with him, from time to time they'd remind her of the relationship that she wanted only to forget.

Another siren. Megan glanced at Susan, who was attaching strips of tape to the edge of the treatment table where she could easily grab them when needed. The nurse didn't look up from her work.

The siren abruptly stopped sounding, turned off because the ambulance had reached its destination.

A woman's voice squawked through the loudspeaker above the door. *"Ambulance in the bay, ambulance in the bay."*

Megan took in the room and winced as an uneasy feeling visited again. *Where is Luke?*

A minute later she heard the gurney's clanging wheels. Muffled voices. Her stomach tightened.

Whoosh. The heavy metal doors opened and a small platoon of blue jumpsuits—each sporting a rainbow insignia and the letters UCH—trotted into the room with their stretcher and its diminutive cargo.

Blankets covered all but the patient's head. The transport team's gear was strewn along the edge of the gurney: beige monitors spewing green squiggly lines, bright orange fishing tackle boxes stuffed with drug vials, and a pair of green tanks lying on their sides.

All that Megan could make out was the boy's brown hair, the oxygen mask covering his face, and two dark eyes darting around the room.

Transport personnel were just beginning to disconnect their equipment when the trauma team went to work. Susan peeled off what was left of his clothing. The other nurse, a loop of IV tubing draped around his neck, searched for a vein. The therapist slapped on a fresh set of self-sticking "leads" for her monitoring equipment. Their work slowed for just an instant when they lifted the boy onto the treatment table.

That was when Megan got her first glimpse of the boy. His features were Indian—a rounded face, high cheekbones, and straight black hair—and his limbs were emaciated. Whatever his illness was, it had been ravaging his body for many months.

Susan called out, "Orders, Doctor?" even before Megan could get close enough to examine the patient.

Megan squeezed in closer to the table and reached over someone's stooped shoulder to place her stethoscope on the boy's chest. Everyone was jockeying for position. A tangle of arms crisscrossed the table as instruments, tape, syringes, IV bags, tubing, and cords passed back and forth at a furious pace.

Behind her, the transport physician had already started into a highly regimented account of his team's assessment and therapy. It yielded no clues that pointed to a diagnosis and was revealing only in what they had *not* found—the boy had no fever, and no abnormal breath sounds.

"A few minutes after I called you from the airport," the transport doctor continued, "the patient's O-2 sat dropped to eighty percent. We increased his oxygen—it's now running at ten liters a minute—and gave him nebulized Albuterol to open up his airways. But his sat's are still hovering around eighty-five percent."

The boy's oxygen saturation—O-2 sat—merely quantified what she already knew by looking at him. He was oxygen starved. The question was, why? Pneumonia was an obvious possibility, but she'd have expected to hear wheezes or crackles in his lungs, and she didn't.

Megan's head turned to the transport physician. "You start antibiotics?"

"I wanted to, but our IV came out and we couldn't get a new line into him."

Susan interrupted them. "*Doctor,* orders?" This time the request sounded more like a command.

Megan saw the nurses connect with a glance.

It didn't help that everyone in this room had more experience than she did, and would instantly jump in and take over if they sensed the slightest hesitation on her part. Working to keep her voice even, Megan called out a long list of blood tests and ordered "shotgun" antibiotics to cover a broad spectrum of possible infections. She glanced back at the transport physician, who shrugged his indifferent agreement.

"And call radiology, *stat,*" Megan added. "They were supposed to be here when the patient arrived." Remembering that the radiology technician on this shift was known more for his napping skills than his punctuality, she added, "Remind him that *stat* means *now.*"

"Be sure to let us know if he turns out to have some

exotic infection," a transport nurse said. "We were in pretty tight quarters on the way over here."

Susan said, "I've heard enough. Everyone puts on a mask and gown." She opened a cabinet and started tossing the infection control gear into waiting arms.

"O-2 sat is slipping—now at seventy-eight percent," the respiratory therapist called out. "He's working way too hard to breathe. I'm starting full-strength Albuterol."

As she slipped on her mask, Megan swept the length of the boy's body with her eyes, looking for some physical sign that hinted at the cause of his illness. The skin over his ribs was drawn tight from exertion, skewing a crude crescent-shaped tattoo on his upper chest.

But what seized her attention was his face, which was turning ashen. *Oh, God.*

"Put him on a non-rebreathing mask," she said. The specialized mask's one-way valves and balloon reservoir would allow them to deliver eighty percent oxygen, twice as much as a regular mask.

"Already working on it." The therapist held it up for Megan to see as she dug into one of the drawers of her portable cabinet and came up with a connector of some type.

Susan grabbed for the wall phone. "I'm calling to find out where McKenna is."

Megan wasn't listening. "What's the boy's name?" she asked.

"Josue Chaca," the transport nurse called out.

Megan looked into his eyes, enormous brown eyes teeming with fear.

She laid a hand on his forehead. *"No se preocupe, Josue. Vamos á tomar el buen cuidado de tú,"* she said, using the passable Spanish most residents learned while working at University Children's. "Don't worry, Josue.

We're going to take good care of you," she repeated to herself.

The boy locked eyes with Megan. He didn't say anything. He couldn't say anything. He was too busy gulping air.

It was happening too fast. She was losing this patient.

Chapter 4

As soon as McKenna emerged from the treatment room, his eyes fixed on the hulking figure standing over the E.R. check-in desk.

SMACK. The man's fist slammed onto the desktop. "Where's my wife? Goddammit, I wanna see my wife and kid. *Now*." His voice was as gargantuan as his bulk.

A nurse standing off to the side grabbed a red wall-mounted phone—Security.

Luke walked toward the desk. A nervous crowd of on-lookers edged in the opposite direction.

Chewy Nelson, a skinny young intern to McKenna's left, plopped a handful of M&Ms into his mouth and mumbled through a mouthful of chocolate: "Jesus, that's Lloyd Erickson."

Luke recognized the name. Anyone who had even a passing familiarity with professional football had heard of the NFL linebacker. His career-ending tackles on the field drew almost as much media attention as his erratic, violent behavior during the off-season.

Erickson stood at least six-foot-four and had a thickly sculpted physique that reeked of steroids. He was big for a linebacker, even an NFL linebacker, and his blazing red hair sat on a head that was three sizes too small for his body. The veins in his oversized neck bulged as he shouted across the counter at the desk clerk.

When McKenna reached the desk, he gestured with his eyes and signaled the clerk to leave. She rocketed out of her chair and disappeared around a corner.

Erickson was sputtering with rage, his words unintelligible. He leaned into McKenna's face, his massive torso dwarfing Luke's wiry six-foot frame. The linebacker was an explosive torrent of fury, shaking his arms wildly in convulsive spasms.

Luke just stood there, staring back at the man, trying to restrain his own swelling rage.

This he was able to do until Erickson grabbed his white coat.

Reflexes took over.

McKenna discharged like a coiled spring. His left hand clutched the linebacker's wrist as his right forearm came up from below and slammed into Erickson's locked elbow.

A snapping sound echoed off the walls and Erickson let out a thunderous groan. His grip on Luke's coat loosened for an instant.

It was long enough. Luke stepped inside, spun around, and arced his flexed elbow behind him and into the linebacker's jaw.

Erickson's eyes bulged from their sockets as he registered the sound of his teeth shattering. He shook his head and spit a bloodied tooth onto the floor, then let out a roar and lunged at McKenna like a frenzied lion going in for the kill.

Luke sidestepped the attack and unleashed his cocked leg in an impossibly fast motion. His right foot went through the linebacker's face like a wrecking ball.

The impact lifted Erickson off his feet. He landed on his back with a dull thud.

He wasn't moving.

It was over. The skirmish had lasted less than three seconds.

People rushed out of exam rooms. A plump security guard rounded the corner, panting from what probably had been a very short jog. When he saw the hulking mass on the floor, the guard froze for a moment, then slowly tiptoed toward Erickson as if approaching an unexploded bomb.

Another doctor joined the guard. They knelt at the linebacker's side, checking the enormous body for signs of life. "He's breathing," shouted the doctor, sounding out of breath himself.

McKenna wasn't paying any attention. He studied the floor around him, looking for the stethoscope that had flown out of his pocket during the clash. He glanced down at his white coat. There was a tear in the lapel.

The swarm of onlookers grew. The E.R. director, Dr. Keller, vaulted out of a room and took in the scene. *"What the hell?"* he yelled. "What *happened* to that guy?"

Still staring at his lapel, Luke said, "He'll be okay."

A moment later McKenna looked around, first at Erickson and then at Keller, who was staring at him, slack-jawed.

Suddenly remembering the intercom page, Luke turned and started toward the Trauma Unit.

As he trotted away, he called back over his shoulder, "I'd slap some restraints on Godzilla once you figure out how to lift him onto a gurney. He may be a little restless when he wakes up."

Calderon scanned the parking structure for a spotter, someone with overly attentive eyes marking pigeons for the pickpocket. No one fit the profile.

He watched as the pickpocket collided with a harried traveler who was pulling luggage from the trunk of his car. Calderon admired the thief's skill. The hapless victim had no inkling that his wallet was gone.

"So what about the boy?" he asked his client. Calderon poked the air with a finger and shook his head as he walked along a parallel row of cars. To all the world, he appeared a man absorbed in his phone conversation, oblivious to everything around him, even as his eyes fixed on the pickpocket. Calderon realized he had been the perfect mark: a chauffeur standing near a crowded exit, looking for his passengers, desensitized by the occasional brush with a bag-laden traveler; his loose-fitting black coat, unbuttoned, assumed to be holding a wallet bursting with tips from wealthy clientele; his mind elsewhere, displaying the telltale signs of distraction.

"Let me worry about the boy," his client replied.

The pickpocket, now forty feet in front of him, glanced occasionally to each side—probably watching for tails as he hugged a row of cars on his way to the rear of the structure. The money was of no significance to Calderon, and the driver's license and credit cards described a nonexistent person. But that could also become a problem. False IDs were designed to stand up to visual scrutiny, not investigative inquiry. The police, responding to some overeager Good Samaritan trying to return the wallet to its rightful owner, would discover that the driver's license with his picture belonged to a nonperson.

Questions might arise, his picture circulated and studied. He couldn't have that.

"But I am worried," Calderon said. "This is the second time I've had to go chasing after test subjects that—how shall I put this?—strayed from the herd."

He didn't need to remind his client of the girl who was

still missing. After a moment, he added, "Maybe it's time you let me deal with this problem, yes?"

The pickpocket glanced back, but not quickly enough. Calderon had crouched behind a van—a woman pushing a stroller paid little attention to a man retying his shoe.

"Perhaps you're right," his client said. "I'll give it some thought."

When Calderon rose to his feet, the pickpocket was gone. An exit sign flickered over a concrete archway.

Calderon rushed to the exit just in time to hear a muffled *crunch*—a footfall. He stood to one side and surveyed the darkness outside. A twenty-foot walkway led into an adjoining parking structure; to either side, wide unlit alleys. He looked up and saw no security cameras.

He moved through the exit noiselessly.

Another sound, more distinct—a shoe stepping on a shard of glass—came from behind a trash container on his right. Then the faint beat of rap music. An Adidas shoe peeked out from the corner of the large metal container, tapping to the music.

He edged along the bin.

"The important work is going well," his client offered. "In another two weeks, the project moves to full-scale production. There're always problems. We'll deal with them."

Calderon stepped around the corner of the bin, making no effort to conceal his movements.

The thief was sitting there, thumbing through Calderon's wallet. Another one was waiting on his lap.

"You mean, I'll deal with them," Calderon said to his client.

The swarthy man looked up. Oddly, his dark eyes showed little surprise, even as he sprang to his feet and unfurled a butterfly knife in one, smooth acrobatic move.

The man had very good reflexes, but not nearly good enough to react before Calderon's iron-like fingers speared his throat.

The pickpocket's grip loosened, his knife clattered on the pavement, his eyes finally showing the shock and bewilderment that Calderon had expected.

Calderon placed a finger to his lips and silently mouthed *Shhhh*, but it wasn't necessary. The man couldn't raise a whisper through his crushed windpipe.

The thief started clawing at the deep depression where his Adam's apple had once been, desperately trying to reopen his airway. He began to wobble.

Calderon grabbed the thief's neck in a vise-like grip and steadied him.

The man's eyes bulged. His feet thrashed the ground wildly.

Calderon's right hand lifted the unlucky thief by the neck and held him against the concrete wall.

"I have a flight back to Guatemala in the morning," Calderon said. "You can reach me at the project site."

"Cancel your flight."

The swarthy man's feet floated just off the ground. His legs twitched and spasmed, and his eyes soon drifted in different directions as his muscles went limp in death.

"Why?" Calderon asked.

"Tartaglia. She's become a problem. I need you to take care of it—quickly."

Chapter 5

Luke berated himself as he jogged toward the Trauma Unit, knowing that, on some level, the only difference between the football player and himself was a thin veneer of discipline. In both men, a malignant capacity for violence simmered just below the surface.

He told himself every day—he wasn't that person anymore—but it was a lie. Cutting short his military career and following his father into pediatrics hadn't changed who he was. Burying his past in a dense grave of gray matter hadn't put the *warrior* out of reach.

The pneumatic doors swung open with a loud hiss just as Luke reached the entrance to Trauma One. A transport physician appeared in the doorway, dragging a gurney behind him.

Luke pointed inside. "How're we doing?"

The man waggled his hand and launched into a clipped summary.

Luke listened while looking over the doctor's shoulder, taking in the scene. Susan, syringe in hand, stabbed the patient's right arm repeatedly, a hint of frustration playing on her face. The other nurse tapped the patient's left foot, searching for a vein. Megan was hunched over the table, her back to Luke, moving her stethoscope across the boy's chest.

"Any unusual rashes?" Luke asked.

He was hoping he wouldn't have to call in his father, who, as the head of Infectious Diseases, was the go-to person for tropical diseases. The man already worked too many hours.

The transport physician shook his head while continuing his report.

Luke cut him off in mid-sentence with a "Thanks" and walked into the room, taking a position well behind Megan. From ten feet away nothing jumped out at him other than the boy's wasted form and a crude tattoo on the left side of his chest. It was dark blue, about an inch across, and shaped like a crescent moon.

Only Susan, who was facing Luke, seemed to notice his presence.

"Patient's moving air well," Megan said, her tone a swirl of confusion. "A few faint wheezes, but otherwise his lungs are clear."

The respiratory therapist angled her eyebrows downward, her expression bemused.

Apparently, everyone shared the same question. What would normally have been good news was anything but. Despite good airflow into his lungs, their patient was oxygen starved.

Susan showed Luke a peevish frown while fingering the stethoscope around her neck.

Luke waved her off. There was no reason to usurp Megan's role as team leader—at least not yet.

"Is the blood gas ready?" Megan asked the therapist.

"Just drew it. Have it in a moment."

The blood gas results would give them far more information than the oxygen saturation alone. It would reveal if the patient's body was retaining carbon dioxide, and if so, whether his blood was becoming dangerously acidic.

But it wouldn't tell them why.

Luke hoped that Megan didn't spend too much time thinking about the unknowns—questions for which she didn't have answers. She needed to focus on what she knew and could act upon.

"Someone call X-ray again," Megan said, "and while you're at it, call Admitting and tell 'em to get an ICU bed ready."

"Megan, we're not having any luck getting an IV started," Susan said, her eyes aimed at Luke. "His perfusion's poor—he's clamping down."

The boy's body was doing exactly what it was designed to do, diverting blood flow from the muscles and skin to more vital organs. *Come on, Megan, it's time to move on this.*

Susan shot another frustrated glance at Luke.

Luke held out a palm.

The nurse rolled her eyes, shook her head.

A split second later the acoustic rhythm of the heart monitor broke its stride and played a few erratic beats. Luke's eyes went to the electrical tracings and jagged lines. The boy's heart was racing at 180 beats per minute, and his blood pressure was dangerously low.

Megan said, "Get me a central line setup, and pull an endotracheal tube in case we need to intubate him."

Placing a central line into one of the larger, deeper blood vessels would allow them to deliver substantial amounts of fluids quickly. Luke wondered how many times Megan had placed a central line, if ever.

The respiratory therapist handed a strip of paper to Megan. "Here's your blood gas," she said. "We're going nowhere fast. O-2 sat is hovering in the low seventies and his CO-2 is climbing. I'm switching to an ambu-bag."

The therapist ripped off the patient's oxygen mask and

replaced it with a thicker one attached to the ambu-bag, alternately compressing and releasing the rubber oxygen reservoir.

Luke glanced at the boy's face when the therapist removed the oxygen mask. The fear that had been there a minute ago was gone. He had a glazed, stuporous look. He no longer felt anything.

Whoosh. The doors swung open. Five sets of eyes turned in unison.

A high-pitched whir invaded the room when the X-ray technician guided the motor-driven X-ray machine into the room. Luke held out an outstretched arm, signaling the tech to stay put for the moment. The technician returned a tired look of acknowledgment, as though he was used to the hurry-up-and-wait routine.

"Blood pressure's dropping," Susan announced. "And his pulse is thready."

"Someone get McKenna," Megan shouted. *"Drag him in here if you have to."*

"Right here." Luke stepped up beside her.

Megan's eyes showed a blend of puzzlement and irritation. "How long—"

"Let's divide and conquer," he said while stepping over to the surgical tray. "Go ahead and intubate the patient. I'll put in the central line."

Megan said, "I was about to—"

"You comfortable intubating the patient?" Luke asked. His gaze had settled on the instrument tray, but he could feel Megan's stare.

After a long moment, she said, "Yeah . . . sure."

Luke quickly scrubbed the boy's upper thigh, found the femoral vein, injected an anesthetic, made a quick stab, and inserted the line.

Megan said, "As soon as Dr. McKenna has that line

secured, give the patient a three-hundred-cc bolus of normal saline, as fast as it'll run. Call out the blood pressure every minute until it's back above ninety."

Luke glanced at the boy's face. He'd slipped into unconsciousness. They had no time to give the drugs normally used to sedate and anesthetize a patient undergoing intubation. He hoped Megan realized that.

Holding the laryngoscope in her left hand, Megan called out, "Ready."

The therapist removed the ambu-bag from the patient's face and stood back.

Megan inserted the laryngoscope into the boy's mouth, taking a deep breath as she did so. "Hand me the tube."

The therapist passed it to her, and Megan immediately slipped the endotracheal tube down the patient's throat.

The respiratory therapist connected the ambu-bag to the end of the tube and began squeezing and releasing it with her left hand, her movements practiced and rhythmic.

Megan ran her stethoscope over both sides of the boy's chest.

"Tube's in position," she said, exhaling heavily. "Let's hyperventilate him for a few minutes."

They were now breathing for Josue.

Megan told Susan, "As soon as you draw the blood work from the line, start antibiotics. Give him eight hundred milligrams of Unasyn and"—a pause, then—"eight hundred of Cefotaxime."

Luke nodded at Susan and hoped that Megan hadn't noticed the nurse waiting for his confirmation.

Megan turned to the X-ray technician. "We're ready now." She waved her arm in a circle as if directing the man through a busy intersection.

The tech sauntered over to the table with his film casings, displaying the same energy and enthusiasm as someone standing in line at the post office. He said, "By the way, folks, there's a whole bunch of commotion at the other end of the hall. Some guy got into it with one of our docs. I heard maybe one of them's dead."

"No one's dead," Luke said. "Let's focus on our work here."

Megan glanced at him, or more specifically, the tear in his lapel.

Dr. Henry Barnesdale, chairman of University Children's medical staff, sat at the antique burled-walnut desk that dominated one end of his cavernous office and stared at a list of E.R. patients on his computer screen.

Patient number 134—Josue Chaca—stared back at him.

"He's in the E.R.," Barnesdale said into the phone. "What do you want me to do?"

"Nothing," the Zenavax CEO said.

"But—"

"I said leave it alone." A heavy breath came through the phone. "But in the future, stay away from my test sites. It's a big world out there—your hospital can find another place to do its charity work."

Barnesdale's oblong shadow jiggered on the far wall of his office, swimming in a pale green halo of light seeping from the banker's lamp on the credenza behind him. He was usually the one wielding the power, and didn't like playing serf to this man. Henry couldn't help it that the boy and his mother had marched fifty miles through mountainous terrain to reach the hospital's clinic. But he wasn't about to say that to the Zenavax CEO.

The man didn't like hearing that Henry had no control over the Guatemalan clinic. For that matter, neither did Henry, but he had no say in the matter. Caleb Fagan, the head of Immunology at University Children's, had funded the clinic using outside donations since its inception five years ago. It was the only clinical budget item outside of Barnesdale's reach.

The clinic seemed to be part of some mid-life crisis for Fagan, who had taken up the mantle of healthcare in developing countries with the same zeal that had propelled him to near celebrity status in the field of immunology. Despite his seeming conversion to humanitarian causes, Henry didn't trust the man's motives. Caleb was a self-important jerk.

"We have another problem," the CEO said. "It's Tartaglia."

The starch in Barnesdale's shirt collar began to give way to the warm moisture forming on his neck. "Oh, Christ."

"Tartaglia's not giving up. It looks like she's going to tell her fairy tale to people outside the company."

"Is it a fairy tale?"

During the long silence that followed, Barnesdale felt as if someone had lit a road flare inside his stomach.

When the CEO finally spoke, his voice was like molten steel. "There's nothing wrong with our vaccines. It concerns me, Henry, that you doubt me."

Barnesdale pulled a handkerchief from his breast pocket and wiped his forehead. "Forget I asked."

"You see," the executive continued, "in exactly two weeks, we cross the finish line. I'm not letting anything—*anything*—get in our way."

Barnesdale wasted no time bringing their discussion back to Tartaglia. "How do you know that she's talking to people?"

"Not people—person," the man said. "I have someone monitoring the situation. Two hours ago she sent an e-mail from her home. There's a photograph attached."

Barnesdale ran a hand through his gray hair. "Who— Who did she send it to?"

"Someone at your hospital—Luke McKenna." A pause, then, "Any relation to Elmer?"

"That's Elmer's son."

"Why would Tartaglia send the information to *him*?" the CEO asked.

"Luke McKenna's one of our E.R. doctors." Barnesdale pulled up the staffing roster on his computer screen. "He's working Trauma tonight, which means he's probably downstairs with the kid right now."

Another heavy breath came through the phone. "So, unless you believe in coincidences, Tartaglia knows about the boy. She knew he was coming to the hospital."

"What are you going to do?"

"You mean, what are *we* going to do? We both have a problem, here," the man said. "And I think you know what needs to be done."

The phone line went dead.

Henry's eyelids fell closed. *What did I get myself into?*

When Zenavax had approached him four years ago, Henry was in no position to turn down the company's "business proposition." Several years earlier, a drunk driver had decimated not only his wife's brain, but also their meager savings. Once the cost of her skilled nursing facility care had reached the lifetime limits of their insurance plan, it wasn't long before he spent through his financial reserves, and then the proceeds from a heavily leveraged second mortgage. When the Zenavax CEO had made his offer, Henry was despondent and on the brink of bankruptcy.

And the bastard knew it.

Life being what it is, his wife had died just one month after he traded his integrity and self-respect for a hefty bribe. He hadn't had a decent night's sleep since.

The intercom on his desk sounded. "Dr. Barnesdale, I'm sorry to interrupt, but you're needed on the phone."

"Tell them I'm busy."

"I already have, sir. It's the Emergency Room and they say it can't wait. One of our doctors just got into a scuffle with someone."

"Blood pressure is coming back," Susan announced. "Systolic is now eighty-eight."

As in most battles, the momentum tends to work for you or against you, and the tone of the nurse's voice told Luke that she too could feel the tide turning in their favor.

Megan pulled her mask off, wiped a moist sheen from her cheeks with a four-by-four gauze, then shot a glance at Luke.

He gave her a nod.

She suppressed a small grin that looked as if it was straining against the urge to become a full-fledged smile.

Luke had never thought of Megan as classically beautiful—except, that is, when she smiled. Her agreeable face would suddenly become strikingly pretty. In the past three months she had rarely shown him anything but a resolute and dogged temperament. God, he missed her.

Megan said to the therapist, "Let's get another blood gas."

Luke sidled up to her. "So what do you think?" Seeing the question on Megan's face, he elaborated. "We have a four-year-old boy, apparently breathing well a few hours ago, who suddenly decompensates. What are the most likely causes?"

"A chronic lung disease like cystic fibrosis might look like this, but not if he was breathing fine a few hours ago. It wouldn't happen that fast." She tapped the edge of the table a few times, staring at the boy. "Leukemia could explain this. Leukemia would set him up for sepsis, which in turn might lead to acute respiratory distress syndrome. That would explain most of his pulmonary and cardiovascular symptoms."

"Am I hearing a 'but' somewhere in there?"

"Maybe." Her eyes flitted toward his. "Well, yeah. There're a few things that just don't make sense. Why don't his lungs sound worse? And if this is all due to leukemia, why didn't they find any blasts in his blood?"

Luke had the same questions.

"Anything else you'd do right now?" Megan asked.

"I'd add something to cover him for the possibility of a fungal infection. We have a patient we know very little about, from a place we know even less about."

The respiratory therapist handed Megan the results of another blood gas.

"Blood pressure is dropping again," Susan broke in, the pitch of her voice a notch higher.

Megan ordered another bolus of IV fluid while checking the blood gas. "He's still not ventilating. He's becoming more acidotic." She passed the results to Luke.

He scanned the monitors. "Susan, give him twenty milliequivalents of bicarb." He turned to Megan. "Call the ICU. We can't deliver the types of pressure he needs without a ventilator. Tell 'em they can either bring us a vent—immediately—or they need to take this patient right now." He pointed at a computer monitor across the room. "And try to pull up his X-rays."

He looked back at Josue. The boy's left arm hung limply over the side of the table, and his near lifeless form was quickly taking on a grayish hue. Only his chest was moving, rising and falling in rhythm with the respiratory therapist's compressions.

Luke took the ambu-bag from the therapist, to feel for himself how much pressure was required to push oxygen into the boy's lungs. The patient's lungs were becoming stiff.

Megan, a phone cradled on her shoulder, was talking to someone in the ICU while feverishly working a computer keyboard to pull up the boy's chest X-ray. A moment later the black-and-white picture popped onto the screen.

Luke studied the X-ray for several seconds, leaning closer to see that the name in the corner of the screen matched the patient on the table. He looked back at the boy. His confusion swelled.

Megan still had the phone against her ear and didn't look overly pleased to be playing the role of messenger.

Gesturing toward the computer screen, Luke said to her, "Take a look at his X-ray and tell me what you—"

The blare of an alarm interrupted him. All eyes turned toward the monitor.

"Patient's in V-Tach," Luke called out as he felt the boy's neck for a pulse. "No pulse. Susan, charge the defibrillator to forty joules . . . Megan, start chest compressions!"

Chapter 6

As the staff elevator rumbled toward the first floor, Henry Barnesdale replayed in his mind the breathless voice of the nursing supervisor who had called him from the E.R. From the sound of things, it seemed that McKenna's altercation had nothing to do with Josue Chaca. His head shook at the irony of using the bizarre antics of his medical staff—*my doctors are brawling with parents, for Christ's sake*—as a pretext for coming to the E.R. to probe his real crisis, the one disguised as a small boy.

Barnesdale choked back the acid taste in his throat. He didn't believe the Zenavax CEO for a moment. He was certain that the vaccine had triggered the Chaca boy's illness.

If the boy lived—if somehow, someone discovered the cause of his illness—fear and panic would spread across four continents like a cataclysmic eruption. The after-shocks would ripple for decades.

His shoulders shuddered. Whatever the problem was, he had to hope that Zenavax had already discovered the cause and corrected it.

When the elevator doors finally opened onto a first-floor corridor just outside the Emergency Room, Barnesdale jinked back like a moth singed by flame. It was chaos. Foot traffic was at a standstill. A growing clot of people filled the hallway. Three security guards in ill-fitting blue uniforms, one on the near side and two on the far side of the crowd, had their arms extended outward—marking the perimeter of the group but accomplishing little else.

Barnesdale stepped out of the elevator and pushed his way through the maze of unkempt humanity that stood between him and the E.R. A mother pleaded with him in Spanish, holding up her sick child and gesturing toward the Emergency Room. He didn't understand a word.

He was reminded why he hadn't chosen emergency medicine. As a practicing surgeon for the first twenty years of his career, he was used to the order and precision of an operating room. It was more like a battlefield down here. *Maybe that's what happens—E.R. doctors start to think of themselves as combatants, and before you know it . . .*

When Henry emerged on the other side of the crowd, he was just in time to see the ambulance attendants struggling to raise a gurney that was holding—*Christ*—some sort of man-mountain.

The behemoth's shoulders spilled over the stretcher like a lava flow. He wasn't moving. A woman stooping next to him had a badly bruised face and her left eye was swollen shut. A girl with a bandaged head—she was bug-eyed with fear and oddly quiet—was stuffed under the woman's arm like a bag of dirty laundry.

Why hadn't anyone mentioned the woman's injuries? What the hell had McKenna done?

Just then, a squat woman with tired eyes—the hospital's night nursing supervisor—marched up to him. Before she could speak, Barnesdale said, "Where's McKenna?"

"He's in Trauma One," she said. "They just got Mr. Erickson onto a gurney. We were waiting for an ambulance—it arrived a few minutes ago. He's being transported to—"

Barnesdale brushed past her in mid-sentence and started toward the Trauma Unit. When he turned the corner onto an adjoining hallway, he found Caleb Fagan fifteen feet ahead of him, passing through the doorway into Trauma One.

Henry was surprised to see the man who had just last week lunched with the U.S. Surgeon General slumming in their E.R. on a Friday night. It served him right. After all, it was Caleb's volunteers who had arranged to transport the boy from Guatemala. The man had no inkling that his rat-hole clinic just triggered a cascade of events that had Henry's career—and life—teetering on a precipice.

Henry followed in Fagan's wake. When he stepped through the doors into the trauma suite, a cacophony of alarms and high-pitched squeals hammered his ears. Monitors blared and metal wheels clanged as nurses slammed equipment into position. A respiratory therapist was shouting over the din.

In the eye of the storm, McKenna was standing over the Chaca boy, calling out orders in a clipped tone.

Crash.

An IV pole fell to the floor as a young doctor leapt onto the table and straddled the patient. Probably a resident, judging by her age and dress. And athletic, judging by her movements and taut figure. She started thrusting the heel of her hand into the boy's sternum, shouting the numbers one through five over and over again, in cadence with her chest compressions. Her voice cracked on the second "Five," jumping an octave.

One of the nurses screamed, *"Defibrillator charged to forty."*

The resident jumped off the table, grabbed the paddles, and placed them over bright orange conductive pads on the upper-right- and lower-left-hand corners of the boy's chest.

She shouted, *"Clear,"* and sent a jolt of electricity through the boy.

Henry expected the boy's body to heave convulsively. Only his chest and shoulders moved, and then only slightly. Everyone turned to the monitors.

The female resident yelled, *"Still in V-Tach,"* and sprang onto the table in a motion as fast and graceful as a jaguar. She seemed possessed by an otherworldly force as she repeatedly drove her tightened fist into the boy's chest.

One of the nurses was yanking syringes and drug vials from drawers in a red crash cart. Another nurse, with spiked orange hair and an idiotic nose ring, injected something into a central line, the next syringe held between his teeth.

Just then, McKenna's glance swept past Barnesdale without acknowledgment and came to rest on Fagan. "Caleb, what do you know about this patient?"

"Less than you do, I'm afraid. The clinic called me, told me they were sending the boy up here. They said he was stable."

Barnesdale glanced at the wall clock behind him. It was a large analog type, like an old schoolhouse clock but with an extra hand—a red one used to measure the elapsed time in a resuscitation attempt. It was approaching the *3*. Fifteen minutes had elapsed since the patient had coded.

When he turned back, Fagan was staring at him.

"Henry, what are you doing here?" Caleb said.

Barnesdale lifted his chin in McKenna's direction. "Ask him. That mess in the hallway is his."

Fagan's eyes narrowed in a question, then anger. "Maybe you hadn't noticed, but the boy on that table is fighting for his life. Whatever you're here about, it can wait."

Barnesdale stared at Josue Chaca, feigning an acquiescent expression.

A concealed wave of relief washed over him.

The boy was dying.

Barnesdale was already halfway to the door when the intercom unit sounded: *"Dr. McKenna, I know you're busy in there. I'm just letting you know—a Dr. Tartaglia has called twice since about five o'clock. Says it's important and she needs to talk to you . . ."*

Megan was engulfed by a sense of gloom. She glanced at McKenna. He showed no hint of surrender, no hint of anything.

She saw it in the others, though. Following orders, doing what they were told. But their intensity was waning, the adrenaline leeched away, their movements becoming repetitive and tedious. A monotonous cadence had replaced the raw energy she'd felt earlier.

No single event ever brought these things to an end, just the eventual recognition that nothing was working, and nothing was going to work. Someone had to make the decision, difficult as it was.

"How long has it been?" McKenna asked.

Susan glanced at the clock. "Twenty-seven minutes, but I didn't start the clock until a few minutes after he arrested."

"Anyone have a suggestion, something they'd like to try?" Luke asked.

Megan already knew the answer, but this era of litigation demanded that the question be asked. The threat of malpractice lawsuits had changed most things about medicine. Doctors had to worry that someone—someone on their own team—might later have second thoughts. Maybe they could have done more; maybe they should have tried something else. Just the type of breach a lawyer could chisel away and expose, until it was wide enough, and deep enough, to bury everyone connected with the case.

She followed Luke's gaze as he looked to each person. The nurses looked down in resignation. The respiratory therapist shrugged her shoulders. Dr. Fagan shook his head.

When Luke's gaze reached her, Megan looked between Josue and the monitors, hoping for inspiration and knowing that it wouldn't come. Finally, she shook her head.

Susan didn't hesitate. She immediately came around the table and turned off the alarms.

Megan fought back the moisture seeping into her eyes. She was *not* going to cry. Maybe later, but not now.

Susan patted her on the arm and mouthed the words, *Good job.*

An uncomfortable silence filled the room as they removed tubes and lines from Josue's body and rolled back equipment against the wall. Someone mumbled, "We did everything we could." It didn't seem to be a comment directed at anyone in particular.

Luke offered to "talk about things."

Megan turned him down.

One by one, people slowly filed out of the room while she stood next to Josue's body.

After several minutes, she realized she was alone. The boy had taken on an eerily pale cast and one of his arms hung awkwardly. She took his hand in hers and held it for a long moment before placing it alongside the body.

Then she covered him with a sheet.

The moisture in her eyes turned to tears. She began to shake, and grabbed the edge of the table to steady herself. The tears grew to a stream, and she wept inconsolably.

Megan realized she was crying as much for herself as for Josue, and pitying herself only made her feel all the more deficient and miserable. Whatever made her think she could save lives?

"Megan?"

She whirled around and ran a sleeve under her moist nose.

It was Luke.

"You okay?" he asked.

Megan wiped her eyes with both hands and tried to raise a smile. "Oh yeah, don't I look great?" she said in a wet, hoarse voice. She could see that he was studying her.

"Someone needs to talk to the family," he said. "Are you up to it?"

"Family?"

"The boy's mother. She flew up with him. She's waiting in the conference room."

Megan grabbed her lower lip with her teeth and clamped down until it hurt. Still, tears welled in her eyes.

"Why don't I do it?" Luke offered.

She held up a hand. "No, I will."

"Are you—"

"*I'll do it,*" she snapped.

He raised a hand in submission. "Okay, whatever you want." He glanced over her shoulder at Josue's body. "Take your time."

Luke turned to leave, but stopped abruptly when his eyes passed by Josue's chest X-ray. He stepped closer to the screen.

She watched him study it. After almost a half minute, a feeling of unease swept over her. "What do you see?"

His eyes stayed on the X-ray. "I forgot to mention, let the mother know that we'll be doing an autopsy. We don't have a cause of death, so it automatically goes to the coroner."

A wave of nausea hit her. "What are you looking at?"

"Not enough to explain what happened," he said finally. Luke drew back a step, still looking at the X-ray. "There's obviously something going on in the airways. See, here, the entire bronchial tree is involved. That's what struck me when I saw this before, during the code. But now that I'm seeing this up close, what's striking is the lung tissue."

"I must be missing it. What do you see?"

"That's my point. Not much. The lungs themselves don't look bad enough to explain what happened." He paused, then said, "I'm going to run this by Ben Wilson. Tell the front desk that I'll be downstairs for a few minutes."

Luke was almost out the door before she could acknowledge him. "Sure."

Megan brought herself back to the task in front of her. She gathered herself, wiping her cheeks again and combing her hair back with her fingers. As she crouched to retie her running shoes, she muttered to herself, "Megan Callahan. Grim Reaper."

"It can't be done that quickly," Calderon said into the cell phone headset while driving east on the Santa Monica Freeway in his black town car.

"Find a way. It *has* to be tonight," his client said. "She's been leaving messages at the hospital. She's trying to arrange a meeting with the boy's doctor. For tonight."

Calderon glanced to his right while working a cheek muscle, thinking. Mr. Kong was in the adjacent lane, driving the rented green van with their equipment. The Asian was expressionless, as usual, eyeing cars on the freeway as if he were some kind of weapons targeting system.

"I know where she's going to be at ten o'clock," the client added. "That gives you a little over two hours to work out the details. I don't care how it gets done."

His client made it all sound so easy. Obviously, he had no military training.

"What about the boy?" Calderon asked.

"That's being handled."

Calderon tapped the steering wheel a few times with his thumb. "And who's this doctor that Tartaglia's supposed to meet with?"

"One of the E.R. docs. The one that took care of the boy."

"What's his name?"

"Don't worry about him. He's not connected to—"

"If I'm going to do this, I need to know everything that you know—*everything*."

"Okay," his client said after a moment. "The doctor's name is McKenna. Luke McKenna."

Calderon's eyes suddenly fell out of focus. His face flushed with heat.

Chapter 7

Light spilled from an open door at the end of the basement corridor, painting the opposite wall with a yellow rectangle. The distinctive sound of Johnny Cash's baritone voice grew louder as Luke approached the door. When the music reached the final line of the chorus, another voice, loud and off-key, joined in and sang, "Because you're mine, I walk the line."

Ben was still in his office.

Dr. Ben Wilson, Chief of Pathology, hadn't given back so much as a sliver of his thick drawl since coming to Los Angeles twenty years ago. Luke sometimes wondered whether Ben accentuated it just to make a statement. Jewish by heritage and Texan by birth, he had opinions on almost every subject and was quite willing to share them.

Luke tapped on the doorjamb as he entered the pathologist's office. The place carried a vague scent of formaldehyde. Two walls were lined floor-to-ceiling with unfinished bookshelves that held an equal mix of textbooks and cowboy memorabilia. On top of Ben's desk sat a fifteen-gallon dry fish tank, home to Charlotte, his pet tarantula.

Ben was sitting over a microscope when he looked up and waved Luke into the room. "What brings you down here?"

"Just lost a patient upstairs, a four-year-old boy from Guatemala. Respiratory failure—at least that's what it looked like. I want to ask you about an autopsy."

The pathologist scratched at his fifty-year-old temples, not a single gray hair marring his bushy brown mane. "Anything else you can tell me?"

"The boy was first seen in our clinic down there about a month ago. His white count was fifty thousand, mostly lymphocytes."

Ben reached over and turned off his CD player. "No doubt you've already thought about leukemia. Any blasts?"

"None."

"Well, I know I'm old-fashioned, but did anyone actually look at a blood smear under a microscope? Most of those automated cell counters are dumber than dirt. They're notoriously inaccurate when it comes to blasts and other abnormal cells. Wouldn't surprise me if this turns out to be lab error."

Luke came around and helped himself to the computer sitting at one end of the desk. He pulled up the boy's chest X-ray. "Maybe, but look at this."

Ben reached for his glasses and peered at the screen. He grabbed one of his eyebrows and began twirling it into a cone-like shape. The unruly growth seemed to be a point of pride with him. "And you say this boy came in with respiratory failure?" he asked.

"That's right."

The twirling gained speed. "Well, I'll be damned. A focal bronchial pattern, and not overly impressive at that. You'd think the lungs would be all shot to hell." Ben looked over the rim of his glasses at Luke. "What did his chest sound like?"

"When he arrived here, his lungs were clear as a bell.

At the end, just before he coded, I heard a few crackles and rales but he was moving air in and out."

Ben looked back at the X-ray. "I'll be damned." He was twirling his eyebrow at a furious rate.

"I was hoping I could get you to do the autopsy." Luke slid into the chair next to the tarantula tank. Charlotte was nowhere in sight.

"If I understand what you're telling me—this boy lands on our doorstep, dies in our E.R., and we don't know why—then this is a coroner's case. You know that."

"Would the coroner let you do this case? That is, if you asked?"

Ben snapped his fingers. "In a New York minute. They got the same problem I do. Too much work and too little staff."

"I want to know why this boy died, Ben. If you do the case, I *know* I'll get an answer."

Ben cleaned his ear with a finger. "Are you planning on taking a bite out of me after you finish butterin' me up?"

"Thanks."

"Whoa, partner, I didn't agree to anything."

"But you're going to."

Ben massaged his chin. "Ah, hell. Have someone bring the body down here. I'll call one of the M.E.'s and tell 'em what we're doing."

"You doing it tonight?"

"Hell no. I got a life, you know, and last time I checked, I was busy enjoying it. But there're a few things I wanna do before the body cools."

"Like?"

"Like grabbing some bone marrow," Ben said. "Those cells are sensitive little critters, and the marrow might look a lot different by Sunday."

"Sunday?"

"We're having friends over tomorrow, and next week's gonna be busy, so I guess that leaves Sunday for the autopsy. If you wanna stop by, I'll be here bright and early."

"Thanks."

"Don't mention it." Ben took off his glasses and rubbed his eyes.

As Luke was turning for the door, Ben asked, "You see the article in yesterday's paper, the one about Zenavax issuing stock on the New York Stock Exchange?"

Luke showed him a disinterested look.

The pathologist didn't seem to notice and went on: "They're doing an IPO, selling shares to the public. Burns my butt, the way those people are getting rich off your daddy's work."

In a very real sense, Luke's father had given birth to Zenavax Corporation. Its products, vaccines based on an entirely new concept of immunity, were derived from breakthrough work by a research team at University Children's—a team led by his father, Elmer McKenna. The elder McKenna's creation, a radically different type of influenza vaccine, represented a quantum leap forward.

Unlike other flu vaccines, the one his father had developed protected against almost every strain of the virus that killed hundreds of thousands of people around the globe each year. And due to the vaccine's unique properties, a single immunization provided recipients with lifetime immunity against the pervasive disease.

"Did you know that Zenavax has a market value of nearly *three billion dollars*?" Ben said. "Get a copy of the article. You may find it interesting."

Luke tapped the tarantula's tank. "I doubt it."

"It lists the company's officers and shows what each of

them'll be worth when their stock options vest in a few weeks." Ben slapped the desk with both hands. "Guess how much *that woman's* gonna be worth?" He didn't wait for an answer. "Two million bucks."

That woman was Kate Tartaglia, the same woman whose phone calls Luke had yet to return. She was also the microbiologist who had abandoned his father four years ago, taking what she had learned from the elder McKenna and trading it in for the lofty salary and stock options that Zenavax had offered her. At the time, she was a little known contract employee on Elmer's research staff. Few had taken notice when she resigned her position.

But that soon changed. Unknown to anyone at University Children's, Zenavax was working at the time on a new vaccine technology nearly identical to his father's. Over the next several months, while the hospital prepared its patent applications at the glacial speed common to most academic institutions, Zenavax paid several visits to the U.S. patent office, submitting applications that incorporated lessons the company had learned from its new employee, Kate Tartaglia. In doing so, Zenavax effectively preempted University Children's and captured for itself complete ownership rights to the new vaccine technology—all because Luke's father had never gotten around to having Tartaglia sign one of the hospital's standard employment contracts, which included nondisclosure provisions and would have given University Children's exclusive ownership rights to her work.

Ben shook his head. "How do I say this? Your daddy's an awfully bright fella, and like you, I'm fond of the man. But he needs—what's the word?—a handler. Someone's got to keep an eye on him, keep him from stepping in manure while he's busy thinking those big thoughts."

His father's administrative lapse had cost University Children's a financial windfall that would have funded all of the hospital's financial needs for the next several decades.

Luke had also paid a price. Kate Tartaglia had been his girlfriend—that is, until she betrayed his father.

Ben seemed unaware of Luke's connection to Kate. In fact, few at the hospital had ever known about his relationship with her. University Children's research activities had long ago outgrown their facilities, and Kate had worked in a laboratory at the university campus on the other side of town. Occasionally, her work brought her to the hospital, and it was during one of those visits that his father had introduced them.

Luke figured he'd been lucky to learn where Kate's priorities lay before their relationship had gone any further. Apparently, loyalty and fair play were not part of her ethos.

He wasn't sure his father had learned anything from the fiasco. Things like contracts, intellectual property, and patents were more distant from his father's mind than the moons of Jupiter, and always would be. That his father had managed to retain his position as head of Infectious Diseases at University Children's was a testament to the sovereignty and dominion of academic tenure.

Luke could almost hear an audible click in his mind, as though tumblers had suddenly fallen into place. The reason for Kate's earlier calls to the E.R. now seemed clear. She probably wanted to "clarify" the newspaper article for him, assuaging her guilt with some tortured logic.

Ben pursed his lips, as if another thought was forming. Luke preempted him. "I have to get back to the E.R."

"Go on, then, git." Ben flapped his hands in the air and

turned back to his microscope. "And make sure you get that body down here—soon."

Another boy played in Luke's memory as he walked back to the E.R., a teenage boy who would be a man today, had he not died on Luke's watch. The boy occasionally released his grip on Luke's mind, sometimes for days at a time, but he always came back. Luke had a lifetime to replay the events of that night, which, no matter how much time passed, refused to fade to a distant memory. All the things he could have done differently, all the things he could have done more quickly, all those things that—had he simply been better—would have spared the boy's life.

When the Pentagon recruited him for Proteus fifteen years ago, he was just six months out of the Naval Academy and one of only three Navy SEALs drafted for the program. It was all about proving he was good enough. It was all about the achievement. It was all about being one of the twenty-four most elite warriors in the world. It was the kind of thing that restless and adventuresome young men leap into without thinking about where the journey would take them, and how it might forever strip the calm from their souls.

Luke entered the stairwell leading back to the first floor. The pain was coming now, as it often did when he thought about the boy. It was barely a twinge—a faint throb just above his right eye—but it would build swiftly.

He had entered Annapolis as a fresh-faced seventeen-year-old, filled with the dreams and ideals of a youthful imagination. But somewhere along the way, *honor* and *service* morphed into an irrational zeal and he crossed over to a darker reality. He became an unholy weapon—a Proteus warrior. When he came out the back end of that journey seven years later, they took back his uniform and weapons, but they couldn't reclaim the killing skills or psychic residue that clung to him like a caustic resin.

Luke slowed his pace, counting the steps to distract himself. The metallic echo of each footfall on the steel-grate treads pounded at his skull. He climbed another step, gripped his forehead and squeezed with all the strength he could summon. Suddenly, a sharp stabbing pain pierced his skull. He grabbed the handrail to balance himself.

Just a few more seconds . . .

His right eye exploded, shattering his senses, emptying his mind. His back arched, the muscles in his face convulsed. Then, just as suddenly as it began, the pain was gone.

He leaned heavily over the handrail, his grip slipping as cold sweat seeped from his palms.

"Dr. McKenna, are you okay?" a woman's voice asked.

Luke strained to focus his vision. "Yeah. I'm fine." He pointed to his stomach. "Must have been something I ate."

When he finally looked up, he recognized the woman. She was a stair climber, like himself, part of that small subculture of hospital workers who eschewed elevators.

She looked doubtful, but after he straightened, she stepped past him.

He followed her with his eyes as she walked down the stairs. When she turned back toward him, he said. "If you're going to the cafeteria, don't order the lasagna."

Chapter 8

"She blames us for her boy's death," Caleb Fagan said. "Josue Chaca's mother is a quiet sort, but I can see it in her face."

Luke lifted his gaze to the immunologist, whose dyed-brown hair was too dark for his vein-streaked alabaster skin.

They were sitting in the E.R. doctors' room. Luke had been filling out a Suspected Nonaccidental Trauma report for the Erickson case while listening to Caleb describe his brief visit with the Guatemalan boy's mother.

"She tell you anything—anything that might point us to a cause of death?" Luke asked.

The immunologist shook his head. "I assume there's going to be an autopsy."

"Sunday."

"Call me when you get the results back." Caleb slapped his thighs as if to signal his legs that it was time to leave. "Our folks in Guatemala are going to want to know what you find."

Luke nodded while looking out the door. It was nine-thirty, and the E.R. was taking in wave after wave of children whose illnesses had either been relegated to benign neglect or gone unnoticed by distracted parents slogging through their workweek. Friday nights during the winter months were always hectic, but tonight had turned into a chaotic mess—courtesy of his brawl.

Across the room, Chewy Nelson fished blindly into a bag of Cheetos while eyeing the jean-clad posterior of a young blond woman standing just outside the door. The reed-thin intern looked as if he'd turn to salt were he to take his eyes off the woman.

Just as Luke was about to turn back to his report, Barnesdale appeared in the doorway. The man opened his mouth to say something as soon as his eyes found Luke.

But Chewy's mouth was faster. "Whoa, the Big Kahuna himself. Doctor B, did you hear about the fight? I'm tellin' ya, it was unfrigginbelievable what Dr. McKenna did to that jumbo burger."

Barnesdale pitched his head slightly in the manner of someone trying to decipher a linguistic puzzle, then turned to Luke. "I expect to see you in my office as soon as your shift ends at ten. And you'd better have a damned good explanation for what happened here this evening."

"This about Erickson?" Luke asked.

"Unless there are any other parents you've assaulted tonight—yes, this is about Erickson." He tapped his watch. "And remember, don't keep us waiting."

"Us?"

"The law firm that represents this hospital in litigation. One of their partners is in my office."

Barnesdale was turning to leave when the desk clerk poked her head through the door and held up two fingers. "Dr. McKenna, line two's for you. A woman named Tartaglia. This is the third time she's called. Says it's urgent—she really wants to talk to you."

Kate Tartaglia considered the risks to her career as she passed under the Hollywood Freeway, driving east on Melrose Avenue.

But she had to do something. Another child was dead, and no one was searching for an explanation because, as far as she could tell, no one else at Zenavax even acknowledged the problem.

It wasn't supposed to be like this. When she joined the company four years ago, Kate brought with her a key discovery from her work at University Children's. Zenavax's flu vaccine, like Elmer's, consisted of an inactivated alphavirus into which they inserted a portion of the influenza virus's genome. When injected into vaccine recipients, the alphavirus produced copies of a flu-virus-like protein. She had shown Zenavax's research staff how to amplify the body's immune system's response by modifying the alphavirus. The result was a vastly more effective vaccine.

That contribution had given her immediate stature in the company, something she never would have had if she'd stayed at University Children's. The hospital would have sold or licensed their work to some large pharmaceutical company. And yes, it was *their* work, not just Elmer McKenna's. She had made important contributions to his research, but if the hospital had sold the rights to the flu vaccine, the best she could have hoped for was a position in some bloated and slow-moving research department at one of the big drug companies.

At worst, her contributions would have been overlooked and she would have gotten a pat on the head and a pink slip.

So instead, she had joined Zenavax, a small entrepreneurial company that put her in charge of its clinical testing programs. The influenza vaccine turned out to be a stunning commercial success and quickly became the best-selling flu vaccine on four continents, including the world's largest and fastest growing market—China.

Zenavax's flu vaccine threw off an avalanche of cash that the company was using to develop new vaccines and broaden its product line. Wall Street had rewarded their efforts—her stock options were worth over $2 million—but it hadn't been only about the money. She had wanted her career to mean something. She had wanted, one day, to look back on her life and know that she'd made an important contribution to her field, that she had been an agent for change.

Lately, though, she had come to feel more like an agent of death.

The faint alarms had first sounded several months ago while she was analyzing blood samples from a group of human test subjects in Guatemala. Zenavax was testing a prototype malaria vaccine on human volunteers who had earlier received the company's flu vaccine. Blood from several of the test subjects had revealed a similar immune reaction, one that she recognized from her work on the earliest flu vaccine prototype at University Children's—one that had destroyed an entire colony of laboratory mice.

Immediately, she had told her boss. He listened attentively, perused her data, and assured her that he would look into it. "Let's not jump to conclusions" was his self-evident and pontifical counsel to her at the time, before reminding her that even unsupported rumors could decimate the value of Zenavax's stock.

But at least he had examined her data and talked to a few outside experts, or so he said when he later shared the "good news." He told her that the test results were more easily explained by other causes—probably an autoimmune reaction to one of the many parasitic diseases endemic to Central America. In any case, he said, it didn't appear to have anything to do with their vaccines.

He had told her what she wanted to hear, and for a few months after that Kate had all but ignored the lingering questions. It was so easy to do when she could throw the data onto a CD and toss it into a desk drawer.

Then, four months ago, when she traveled to the Guatemalan village where they were testing the vaccine, her life had imploded. The fragile shell of her world had broken open and a lifetime of self-seeking choices spilled out like a putrid sludge. What had been data elements suddenly became pairs of sunken brown eyes, test subjects became cadaveric young faces, titer levels became heartbeats pounding against the ribs of bodies ravaged by . . . whatever this was.

People were dying, and the only connection among the victims was Zenavax.

She had tried to do something, she reminded herself. One family, a nine-year-old girl and her parents, had been willing to leave their village. She had given them enough money to buy their way into Mexico. She'd worked out a plan to meet the family in Tijuana and, somehow, smuggle them across the border and arrange for medical care. But two weeks later, when she met them at a ramshackle hotel in the Mexican border town, the parents had pleaded for Kate to take their daughter and leave them behind.

Death was already visiting the parents. She had seen it in their graying skin, in their gasping breaths.

Her body shuddered as a wave of guilt swept through her. She had placed the decrepit child in the trunk of her car and crossed into the U.S., a light-skinned woman waved through by an Immigration agent scanning an ocean of vehicles for stowaways. Once across, she removed the girl's wasted body from the car's trunk and laid her on the backseat. The drive to Los Angeles was a lost memory, wiped clean by the terror and dread that had gripped her.

But Kate remembered the gurgling sounds. They started just as she was driving through East Los Angeles on the Santa Ana Freeway. That was when the girl's breaths slowed to agonal gasps. She was close to death, and both of them knew it.

Kate had panicked. She had left the girl near the Emergency Room entrance of a small community hospital along some frontage road, knowing that the child's death was certain.

In the final minutes of that child's life, Kate had treated her as if she were of no more consequence than an afterbirth. She had abandoned her promise to the girl's dying parents. Now, she could no longer push aside the nightmare.

She drove along the front of University Children's without giving it a passing glance. Her eyes were aimed at Kolter's Deli, across the street from the hospital. She peered through the plate-glass window that spanned the restaurant's entire length, but the interior was too dimly lit to spot Luke.

A dry swallow stuck in her throat. *Please, be there.*

Would he help her? Would he put aside his bitterness toward her, would he listen without condemning her? It would be in his eyes. After a few minutes alone with him, she'd know.

Whatever happened, it was too late to turn back now. Earlier that evening, when Luke hadn't answered her first call, she had e-mailed the photograph to him. He hadn't mentioned it when they spoke. Obviously, he hadn't seen it yet. It was better this way—she wanted to talk with him face-to-face.

Soon, it would all be out in the open.

She was risking everything—everything—but what choice did she have? She couldn't hold onto the secret any longer.

Kate rubbed a palm against her linen slacks. Moisture seeped through to her thigh.

She made a quick left turn onto a side street, then pulled into an alley and drove along the rear of a string of retail shops before passing the back entrance to the deli. A canister light hanging over the service door flickered to the rhythm of the wind gusts. Funnels of soot rose like fingers grabbing at the swaying telephone lines.

It was 10:09 P.M. when she pulled into a small open-air parking lot in the middle of the block, about twenty-five yards beyond Kolter's.

Her cell phone rang.

"Hello?"

Oh, God. Her mother.

"Yeah, Mom. I know I haven't called this week . . . Yes, Mom, I know you worry about me when I don't call . . . Yeah, you're right, I'm sorry . . . Mom, listen, I can't talk right now. I'm meeting someone . . . Who? . . . Well, Luke McKenna, but don't . . . No, Mom, we're not getting back together—that's ancient history. This has to do with my work . . ."

Why did I answer the phone?

"Okay, Mom, believe what you want, but I'm telling the truth. It's about work . . . Listen, I gotta go. He's standing right here."

Not quite true, but close.

"Okay, Mom, I'll tell him you said hello . . . What? . . . Yes, Mom, I'll tell him you miss seeing him. I've gotta go . . . Yeah, I'll call you tomorrow . . . I promise. Love ya."

Her body twitched nervously when she saw the dark form in her peripheral vision.

A white lab coat. He was walking toward her, hand over his eyes, dust and debris swirling around him. Even in the dim light she recognized the athletic stride.

Luke. He looked like he had gained some weight.

She groped for the unlock switch on her door.

I thought I'd told him we'd meet inside the deli . . .

Chapter 9

At 10:45, Luke was sitting in a crescent-shaped booth along the front of Kolter's Deli, turning a coffee mug in his hands while staring up at the helipad atop the hospital. Air-5, the Sheriff's helicopter he used to fly on as a physician volunteer with the department's Search & Rescue team, sat motionless under the wash of a floodlight. For a long time, that stint had been important—like a bridge straddling two incongruous identities—but when he relinquished it two years ago, it felt as though he'd reached another milestone in his private twelve-step program.

Luke glanced at his watch again. Kate was a half hour late.

What was going on? After all this time—they hadn't spoken in over four years—what was so important that she needed to meet with him tonight?

Barnesdale was probably apoplectic, pacing his office with that attorney. Henry would get to have his tirade. Luke was simply postponing it by an hour or so.

The bell on the front door tinkled. A red-bearded indigent man poked his head inside and sniffed the deli's aromas like a foraging animal before a busboy shooed him out the door. Moments later an older couple who were dressed for a night at the opera entered the restaurant. For seventy-three years Kolter's had fought an unresolved struggle for its identity.

The same could be said for University Children's. Across the street a warm glow glimmered through the enormous stained-glass windows that stretched across the facade of the original hospital structure. Closer scrutiny revealed a medical campus that looked like the architectural equivalent of a Rube Goldberg invention, a new addition having been added every twenty years or so, each time in a seemingly haphazard fashion. The only unifying design concept was concrete.

University Children's was similar to Kate in that way. Both lacked a defining character. The forces of life seemed to reshape her beliefs and values to accommodate her goals. It was something that had initially attracted him, her openness to different points of view. But gradually it became an irksome divide in their relationship, brought to a head when Zenavax offered her a "once-in-a-lifetime" opportunity, one that seemed to override any loyalty she may have felt for his father.

But it wasn't her decision to join Zenavax, or the problems she created for his father, that had ended their relationship. It was the way she had justified her decision. Kate seemed to reverse-engineer her principles to justify her ambitions. Her opinions shifted around like sand dunes. She seemed to have no moral center, no fixed positions that guided her decisions.

Tonight, though, he sensed something different about her. When they had spoken on the phone, her voice betrayed a fear. There was a vulnerability that she had never revealed in their relationship.

It was like the fear he'd heard in Megan's voice that night three months ago, after some goon had tried to rape her while she was walking home from the hospital. Luke's grip tightened around his coffee mug as he recalled the moment when Megan had called him from the Rampart police station.

The fear—no, the terror—had burned in her eyes for weeks afterward. That son of a bitch had stripped away her innocence, stolen the sanctuary of a mind untouched by violence.

But Luke knew it was *he* who had ravaged their relationship. In the aftermath of that night, he had done everything wrong. And not being able to explain his actions, to either Megan or himself, ripped at his gut.

A chorus of horns sounded on the street.

Luke's head jerked back. Several cars screeched to a halt outside the deli. He craned his neck and saw a small cluster of people moving clumsily across the street, carrying someone in their arms while plodding toward the hospital. Friday night was bringing the usual mix of gang- and drug-related cases to their hospital.

Moments later, traffic began moving again.

Where was Kate?

Megan looked at her watch—10:48 P.M.—seventy-two minutes until the end of her shift. The second hand was taking its sweet time completing each circuit.

God, I hate trauma duty.

Tomorrow evening was her last E.R. shift. One more night and she'd be done with trauma duty and done with Luke McKenna—forever.

And in exactly forty-eight hours she'd board her flight to Guatemala. The Central American rain forests seemed the perfect place to toss aside the emotional upheaval that had dogged her for the past three months. The perfect place to make a new beginning.

She and Susan were sifting through equipment and

supplies strewn across the Trauma Unit as the sheriff's Search & Rescue crew recovered and secured their gear. The three-year-old girl flown in on Air-5 had been pulled from a car that careened off an unlit forest road. She had suffered only minor injuries and was already tucked away upstairs for overnight observation.

One of the pilots, dressed in a green flight suit and carrying a beige helmet under his arm, was standing near the door talking with another resident. In typical male fashion, they were jabbering about Luke's fight with the football player as though recounting an epic battle that had global significance.

Megan looked at the name stenciled on the pilot's breast pocket: R. STEVENS.

"That guy's one strange dude," the pilot said.

"Whatta ya mean?" the resident said.

"I mean, McKenna's not your everyday guy. He saved my bacon big-time during a rescue a few years ago."

Susan shot a glance at the pilot.

Apparently, her face told him that she wanted more, so he explained: "We were lifting some woman out of the L.A. River—her car had skipped over the guardrail and gone over a bridge. McKenna and me are in the chopper, the other crew member is on the end of the cable with this woman. As we're pulling them up, the cable on my hoist gets tangled around some rebar sticking out of a gash in the side of the bridge. All of sudden we're tethered to the bridge and I'm having trouble controlling my bird. But I can't use the cable's safety release because my guy and this woman are already fifty feet above the ground."

The creases around his eyes deepened, as if pulled taut by the memory. "Anyway, before I know it, that crazy-ass McKenna shimmies down the cable with no safety harness, no nothing, and works it free. Then he climbs back up the line like he's some kinda monkey—we're talking a good thirty feet or so in the downwash of chopper blades." He shook his head. "Once he's back inside, he gives me this no-big-deal look like he'd just gone out for some air."

Susan had a silly grin on her face. *"Whoa."*

The pilot said, "I still don't know how the hell he did it. But I'll take him along on a rescue any time." He looked at each of them in turn. "He around?"

"His shift ended an hour ago," Susan said.

"Well, tell him Handlebar says hello." His eyes brightened and he pulled on one end of his moustache. "He'll know who you're talking about."

A scream came from behind the heavy metal doors. The nightmare did not bloom, though, until the doors opened with a *whoosh.*

A nurse pushed her way into the room, followed by three men carrying a woman's body, her crimson torso dangling just above the floor. One man was carrying her by the arms, his hands drenched in blood, his grip slipping. The other two—teenage boys—each held the woman by one of her legs. A stream of blood trailed behind them. The woman's head was lolled back, and a rivulet of blood streamed from a pucker in the middle of her forehead. Pulsations of thick crimson oozed from her chest—her heart was still pumping.

Megan shouted at Susan: "Call Surgery and tell them we have an adult female with multiple GSWs—head and chest."

The man holding the woman's arms slipped on some blood, and the woman's shoulder hit the ground. A wavy smear of red marked the spot.

Megan turned to the pilot. "Help me lift this woman onto the table." To no one in particular, she yelled, "Get me something I can use for pressure bandages. And someone call upstairs—we need six units of O-negative whole blood . . ."

Luke felt a mix of frustration, fatigue, and disgust as he left Kolter's at 11:00 P.M. He looked up at the hospital's third-floor administrative wing while trotting across the street. The lights were dark. Apparently, Barnesdale had given up on him and left.

As he jumped onto the curb, two black-and-whites sprinted by, passing behind him with lights flashing. They turned at the end of the block—probably racing to the emergency entrance that was just around the corner on a side street. At this time of night it was a good bet that a gang banger had landed in their E.R. after catching a knife or bullet.

Did Kate decide to back out of their meeting? That wasn't like her. Timid, she was not—at least not when he had known her. So where was she?

Twenty-five minutes later Luke pulled his Toyota 4Runner into the driveway of his duplex apartment. The air was soaked with the sweet scent of night-blooming jasmine, and an aging oak tree on his neighbor's front lawn flickered like a silent movie as fast-moving clouds crossed in front of a full moon.

He leased the upper unit of a two-story Spanish-style duplex, nestled in the Los Feliz area on the south side of Griffith Park. The duplex sat at the base of a tall hillside, and his living room window looked out over the red tile roofs of his neighbors' homes, and beyond that, the L.A. basin. He'd had sweeping views of the city when he first moved there, but the century-old trees along his street hadn't been pruned in several years and his vista had shrunk to a few bare spots left by irregular growth patterns.

He wasn't thinking about the view as he climbed the red tile stairs to his entry door.

A light came on in one of the first-floor windows. Walter, the owner and landlord, lived in the ground floor unit, but they rarely saw one another. In fact, they talked only when Walter inserted his sizable nose into their neighbors' business and felt the need to share his discoveries with Luke.

As he came through the front door, Luke glanced at his answering machine on the entry table. The NEW MESSAGES display was flashing the number *1*.

He pressed the playback button and kept walking. He was halfway to the kitchen when he heard the background hiss of a cell phone, then: *"Luke . . . it's Kate. I . . . I know it's been a while, but I need to talk to you. I've been calling the Emergency Room—I hope you're not ignoring my messages. It's a little after nine and I'm going to try you again at the hospital. If you're hearing this message and we haven't talked yet, call me at home. I don't care what time it is when you get this message. Please, we need to talk . . ."*

There it was again, the fear seeping from her voice.

". . . Check your e-mail. I'll explain it when I see you."

Luke walked into the living room and flipped on his computer. He grabbed a Mr. Goodbar from the desk drawer and bit into it as the hard drive groaned at him. A minute later he clicked on a small icon at the bottom of the screen. Two messages showed in the mailbox for his personal e-mail address. Both were advertisements.

He logged onto the hospital's e-mail server. Four days worth of e-mail popped into his inbox. Most were junk mail, hospital-wide announcements about everything from retirement parties to carpooling opportunities. None was from Kate.

He checked again. Nothing.

Where was her e-mail? Kate was anything but careless about such things.

Again he asked himself why she hadn't shown up for their meeting. The explanation he had settled upon earlier—that she simply changed her mind, stood him up for her own selfish reasons—now left too many unanswered questions.

Luke grabbed his jacket on his way out the door.

He took the stairs three at a time.

Chapter 10

It was just after midnight when Luke turned onto Bronson Avenue, a quiet tree-lined street just south of Paramount Studios in Hollywood. The night air was wet, and the canopies of the jacaranda trees that lined Kate's street were hidden in a mantle of fog.

Her home was a one-story bungalow, and Kate had always parked her car under the driveway overhang. After four years, he didn't know what make of automobile he should be looking for, but it turned out not to matter. When he pulled up in front of her house, there was no car under the overhang.

A light was burning in one of the rooms along the side of her house. Kate was into saving trees and whales, and small insects that he would sooner squash. She had never been one to leave a light on, even for security. She was naive in that way.

Kate was also a creature of habit, and Luke wondered why the living room drapes were drawn. He couldn't remember her ever having closed them. It occurred to him for the first time that she might not live there anymore.

On the other hand, it had been several years. People change, habits change.

He got out, went to the front door, and knocked. Nothing.

He walked around to the driveway and peered into a side window.

A reflected image showed in the glass—a silhouette on the neighbor's lawn eclipsing a street lamp.

He spun around and a flashlight beam hit him in the face. Below the light, a hand on a holstered gun.

"Police. Hold it—hold it right there," the male voice said.

A second heavyset cop in an LAPD uniform moved quickly up the driveway, flanking Luke. "Hands on your head. *Now,*" he yelled.

Luke did as he was told.

The beefy cop patted him down, then cuffed him.

"Dispatch, this is One Adam Fourteen," the first cop said into his radio. "We're Code Five on the four hundred block of Bronson Avenue and may have a fly in the trap. Put me through to Detective O'Reilly."

Luke spotted their black-and-white down the street, behind one of those large Dumpsters used by construction companies. They'd been watching her property from there.

Something was terribly wrong.

The cops asked no questions and answered none of his. Luke's temper was flaring by the time a blue unmarked sedan pulled into the driveway five minutes later. The license plate bore the letters CA EXEMPT across the top—government plates, like those used on unmarked police vehicles.

A sloppy looking man got out of the car, his right shirt collar hanging outside the lapel of his camel's hair sport coat. A large notepad protruded from his jacket pocket. He introduced himself as Detective Sergeant O'Reilly, LAPD Homicide.

Luke's stomach went hollow.

Five minutes later he knew that Kate had been murdered and that it had happened right under his nose, in a parking lot less than fifty yards from where he'd waited for her in Kolter's Deli.

Detective O'Reilly hadn't told him any of this, and would not confirm it, but the cop's questions concerning Luke's knowledge of her, his whereabouts between 10:00 and 11:00 P.M., and Kate's physical description, left no doubt. It also told him that they were probably working from her vehicle registration and hadn't positively identified the body.

O'Reilly flipped between two pages of notes he'd taken. "When Dr. Tartaglia called you at the hospital, you said she sounded upset."

Luke was slow to respond. He was remembering the limp figure being carried across the street as he had looked on indifferently from inside the deli. "That's right."

"And you didn't bother to ask what was upsetting her?"

"I *did* ask. Kate told me she'd explain it when we met." Seeing a persistent wariness in O'Reilly's eyes, he added, "Listen—it didn't sound like she was in physical danger. It was more like something was troubling her."

The detective scratched his ear. "I'm a little confused here. If her concerns didn't seem like such a big deal to you, why drive out to her house in the middle of the night?"

"When I got home, there was a phone message that she'd left earlier. Kate wanted me to get ahold of her, no matter what time it was. There was something in her voice that worried me. She also mentioned an e-mail that she'd sent—I couldn't find it."

If O'Reilly thought that Luke's last observation was significant, he didn't show it. Instead, the detective looked him up and down while tapping his upper teeth with a pencil. Then he said to one of the patrol officers, "Take the cuffs off."

A watchfulness lingered in O'Reilly's eyes, but he seemed to conclude that an unarmed man wasn't a threat to three armed officers.

Luke gave them no reason to think otherwise.

O'Reilly asked several more questions about Kate's personal habits—was she the type to drive without a purse or license, how much cash did she usually carry, did she wear expensive rings or jewelry? Whoever had killed her probably took her purse, together with her license and keys. The police had staked out her address on the chance that Kate's killer might be brazen enough to try and ransack her home.

"Anything else you can tell me?" the detective said. "Anything that I haven't asked you about?"

Luke looked back at the house, then at O'Reilly. "Two things you should know about Kate Tartaglia. She never left a light on—ever. And she never drew the curtain over that front window that I can remember."

The cop's right eyebrow arched, as if Luke had just offered his first useful tidbit. If this was a simple robbery-homicide, the thug had gotten to Kate's house before the police unit.

Had some two-bit punk snuffed out Kate's life for a petty haul he'd sell on the street for a few hundred bucks?

For all of Luke's disillusionment with the choices she'd made, the thought that her life had ended in this way sickened him.

"Dr. Tartaglia's phone message," the detective said. "Did you save it?"

"Yes."

"Don't erase it." He handed Luke a business card. "And when you find that e-mail, I'd like to see it."

Calderon's muscles were beginning to burn from crouching in the rear of their green van. He ignored the pain and adjusted the focus of his Kowa TSN-821M spotting scope. The man in handcuffs was a block and a half away, but he filled the lens.

"Bang bang, McKenna," he whispered. "You're dead."

"You say something?" Mr. Kong asked from the driver's seat.

"Just thinking out loud."

What had it been—eleven, no, twelve years—since he'd been this close to the spineless cockroach. He could take him out now, and the cops around him, but that would draw too much attention to Calderon's work.

Killing McKenna would have to wait. Besides, when the time came he wanted McKenna to know that it was he, Calderon, who was annihilating him. The right time would come, and anticipating the kill would make it all the more satisfying. After everything that McKenna had taken from him, Calderon deserved whatever small pleasures he could squeeze from the moment.

McKenna had never belonged in Proteus. He was an Annapolis boy who couldn't stomach the work and got in the way of those who could. The shitty little coward had blindsided him—Calderon could still hear his ACL snapping, his knee a crumpled mess—all because McKenna didn't have the spine to let him do what was necessary to pry information from one of their captives.

Just like that, Calderon was damaged goods, no longer a perfect physical specimen. After seven years of giving everything he had to the U.S. military, he was out and that was that. *Thank you for your service to our country, Staff Sergeant. Now get lost and don't let the door hit you in the ass on the way out.*

He had kept the incident a private matter. It seemed the smart thing to do. But then, how could he have known that two months after the cockroach ruined his military career, the ripples from McKenna's gutless cheap shot would take the only other thing that mattered in his life— his mother, Rosa Valenzuela Calderon.

His mother, always the worrier, had taken on extra cleaning jobs when he returned home with a limp, and no job. She didn't know that he already had plans to put his specialized skills to work in the private sector.

Oh, Mamacita. Calderon kissed his thumb and traced an X over his heart.

At a time in her life when she should have been slowing down, his mother had added two overnight shifts to her already exhausting forty-eight-hour-a-week daytime schedule. Thanks to that miserable cockroach, she was in the basement of an industrial park office building when, at oh-dark-thirty one night, the Northridge earthquake brought down the structure and buried her alive under a pile of rubble.

Rescue teams had decided that it was too dangerous to attempt an extraction in her building. At least, that's what the scrawny little FEMA bureaucrat had told him. The structure "was judged to be too unstable." So they had left *his* mother to suffocate and die in the collapsed wreckage, left her there like some piece of garbage.

Calderon rubbed his knee as he worked to control his breathing, quiet his rage. A year after his military discharge, the knee had completely healed but not his heart. Never his heart.

McKenna had killed his mother, just as if he'd stuck a knife in her.

Even after doing what needed to be done to avenge his mother's death, the pain had stayed with him like radioactive waste. He had learned to recycle the pain, to use it in his work. He stoked it like a flame, kept it burning like a hellfire, knowing that the right time would come. He had waited twelve years to settle up with the son of a bitch. It was time.

The only reason that Calderon had taken the job of managing security for the Guatemalan project was its connection to McKenna. As soon as his client had mentioned the name McKenna during their initial discussion—albeit a reference to the cockroach's father—Calderon had known that he would accept the assignment. Of course, the client knew nothing of his connection to Elmer McKenna's son. Telling his client would only have raised unnecessary questions and concerns.

Calderon grabbed the cell phone. After a minute of pulsing tones and hissing, the encryption code synced and his call connected. "I have the items you asked for."

"Good," his client said.

"What do you want done with it?" Calderon surveyed the objects strewn across the van's scuffed floorboard: Tartaglia's laptop computer, a box filled with CDs and zip disks, a digital camera, and enough jewelry and stereo equipment to make it look like an unfocused robbery. While he had been busy eliminating the woman, his assistant, Mr. Kong, had swept her house. Asians were good at that sort of work.

"Save the laptop and the data files," his client said. "I need to determine what she knew, and what she didn't." A pause, then, "Destroy everything else."

"Any other loose ends?"

"None," his client replied. "She was all alone in this. We're sure of that."

Calderon had come to the same conclusion while interrogating the Tartaglia woman in the final moments of her life. Her eyes never moved from the sound suppressor on his handgun, her voice choked off in fear. Her terror was complete, her honesty virtually assured. She had nodded at his reassurances—if she told the truth and gave him what he wanted, he would let her live. She probably hadn't believed him, but people grabbed at straws in the face of death.

In any case, the truth was what he got from her. He knew the inflection of truth, he knew its gestures, he knew its cadence. More importantly, the information she gave him matched what he and his client already knew. She told him about her visit to the village, about the serum samples she had collected, about talking to her boss.

She told him where to find the data files, and she swore that she hadn't spoken to anyone outside of Zenavax.

And she promised she wouldn't tell McKenna about any of it. She was right about that.

"By the way," Calderon said, "Tartaglia confirmed what I suspected. It was someone at the malaria lab that told her about the boy going to the clinic."

"The University Children's clinic?"

"Yeah. She called the clinic, pretended to be from some relief organization. She found out when the kid was coming up here. I'm telling you, that clinic is a problem."

"We may have to do something about that."

"Don't wait too long to decide." Calderon watched as one of the cops removed McKenna's handcuffs. "What do you know about Luke McKenna?" He said the name as if it meant nothing to him. He wasn't about to tell his client that he knew the man.

"He's Elmer McKenna's son," his client said. "Like I told you, he's one of the E.R. doctors at the hospital. He took care of the boy, that's all."

"Tartaglia knew him."

"The woman worked for his father. They probably met at some point."

"No, it's *more* than that. He's connected to her, somehow."

Oh please, Luke doesn't know anything. Those were her words. She had called him *Luke*.

"Don't worry about Luke McKenna," his client said. "He doesn't have anything to do with this."

"Then maybe you can explain what he's doing at the woman's house?"

The silence stretched for several seconds. "Where are you?" his client asked.

"Watching her house. The police are talking to McKenna right now."

"Oh? Then shouldn't you be someplace else?"

"I *should* be in Guatemala," Calderon said, "but I'm here, taking care of your problem. Remember?"

"Why linger near her house? Why take the chance?"

"You should know the answer to that by now—looking for loose ends."

"Seen anything that worries you?"

"Nothing," Calderon said. "Nothing at all."

Chapter 11

"All in favor?" Barnesdale asked.

Ben Wilson watched six of the eight Medical Executive Committee members—all of whom had been hand picked by Barnesdale for their obsequious nature—raise a hand into the air. In a tiresome display of chicken-hearted solidarity, the hens sitting around Henry's conference table had just voted to place Luke McKenna on suspension.

"Opposed?"

Ben and Caleb Fagan waved their hands in a flimsy gesture that underscored its futility.

Barnesdale swiped at an unseen speck of dust on the corner of the conference table. The hens strained to catch a glimpse of the offending particle, as if to conjure its significance.

The meeting—in fact, the entire day—had grown long in the tooth. Ben had awoken that morning to a call, summoning him to this emergency meeting that for some god-rotting reason couldn't wait until Monday. So here he was, at seven o'clock on a Saturday night.

Henry hadn't even shown the courtesy of telling them the purpose of the meeting. After hearing the scuttlebutt about Kate Tartaglia's murder, he had initially wondered whether there might be some connection. It seemed odd that her name hadn't even come up during their meeting.

Barnesdale said, "Anyone have something they want to add?"

Ben knew there was nothing left to say, but he reached inside and found something anyway. "Only a buzzard feeds on its friends."

The outside attorney that Barnesdale had invited to the meeting said, "Let's not forget that Dr. McKenna is being suspended *with* pay, and only for three weeks—just long enough for this committee to do a proper investigation of this incident."

Ben stared at the attorney, which wasn't easy. The man had a wandering eye that was distracting as hell. Supposedly, the attorney was there "to clarify any legal issues that arise." Instead, Henry had used his legal henchman to frighten the committee, which, Ben conceded, was not a particularly difficult feat.

Any support for Luke had quickly wilted after Wandering Eye dropped his bomb on them. If the football player, Erickson, sued the medical group, every physician in the group would be personally liable because the group's malpractice policy did not cover this type of situation.

A portly stenographer, courtesy of the attorney's law firm, noiselessly punched keys on a small black steno machine that sat wedged between his thick legs.

Ben turned to the stenographer. "By the way, 'buzzard' is spelled B-U—"

"We're giving Dr. McKenna every consideration under the circumstances," Henry snapped. "He's lucky we're not terminating him, especially after the arrogance he displayed last night—leaving the hospital knowing that we were waiting for him in my office." Barnesdale glanced at his legal lapdog, who nodded obediently.

Ben leaned into Caleb's ear and whispered, "Can you imagine that? Those two idiots just sitting there all evening like a coupla cow patties?"

Henry was glaring at Ben when he turned back. "You have something to say?"

Ben sat forward and slapped the table with both hands. "Henry, don't pee down our backs and tell us it's raining. The truth is, McKenna acted in self-defense—you know it, and I know it. I only wish I'd been there to see McKenna beat the cowboy crap outta that guy."

The attorney's left eye drifted toward Ben. "After spending all day on the phone with Erickson's lawyer, I can assure you—they have a different view on this. They're ready to go to war."

Ben shot back: "You seem to be missing the point. McKenna is a damned good physician who has never been accused of anything but doing his job. And now he's being suspended because Henry's decided to knuckle under to some bastard who deserved what he got."

The attorney put a hand on Henry's arm and said, "Let's remember what happened here. Your doctor took it upon himself to be judge, jury, and executioner. Think about it—even *if* the wife's and daughter's injuries resulted from a physical assault, how could anyone know whether Erickson was the one who did it? The only thing we know for sure is that Mr. Erickson showed up in your E.R., upset. His wife and child had been injured. That's reason enough for any man to be upset."

Ben rubbed his forehead. It was pounding. "Am I the only one who sees what's going on here? Erickson is a wife and child abuser. His attorney sees an opportunity to discredit the accuser. He's throwing up a smoke screen, and we're playing right into his hands."

"The Emergency Room is a stressful place," the attorney offered. "Maybe Dr. McKenna just lost his senses for a moment."

"What a load of crap," Ben muttered.

"Or maybe it's a genetic trait," Barnesdale said as he lifted a piece of lint from his sleeve with the wary concentration of someone handling toxic waste. "Luke McKenna seems to have a screw loose, like his father."

Caleb Fagan spoke up for the first time. "Leave Luke's father out of this."

"Why should I?" Barnesdale said. "The man makes it his life's work to ignore every rule in this hospital. He's an embarrassment to this institution, and now his son appears to be following in his footsteps."

Henry never missed an opportunity to snipe at Elmer McKenna, head of Infectious Diseases, and administrative derelict. To say that Elmer wasn't the archetypal professor of Pediatrics was like saying that the Hunchback of Notre Dame lacked a certain something when it came to good looks.

"If Elmer paid half as much attention to administrative procedures as he does to his poker games and betting pools," Henry added, "this institution would be flush with money."

Ben hated to admit it, but Barnesdale was right. Rather than a pot of gold, University Children's had ended up on the losing side of a legal shootout over the flu vaccine—draining its coffers in the process—all because Elmer had failed to get that Tartaglia woman's signature on an employee contract.

"Henry, give it a rest," Caleb said while looking at his watch. "It's late, and we're off topic."

As the recipient of grants that comprised fully one-fourth of the entire research budget at University Children's, and

with a reputation that opened doors in the rarefied domain
of international healthcare policy, Caleb was one of only a
few medical staff members with the stature and inclination
to confront Barnesdale.

He was also Elmer's longtime friend and research partner. Caleb had contributed much of the immunological
groundwork for Elmer's flu vaccine. If anyone had a right
to be angry about the Zenavax debacle, it was Caleb.

But the angry blush on Barnesdale's cheeks had little
to do with Zenavax. Apparently, it galled Henry that
Elmer was too oblivious, and Caleb too powerful, to submit to his will.

Barnesdale really was a pompous ass. And living in a
glass house. Once a pediatric surgeon whose skills were
on the mediocre side of ordinary, Henry was the last person at their table who should be sniping about someone
else's professional competence.

Even so, Ben's feelings for the man vacillated between
disdain and pity. Henry hadn't always been a schmuck. It
wasn't until a few years after his wife was devastated in
an automobile accident that Barnesdale seemed to abandon his better angels.

But then, the world was full of people who had faced
similar tragedies without giving in to bitterness. Ben
glanced at Caleb, whose only child had died from a genetic disorder. On those rare occasions when the man spoke
of his son, Caleb's pain was as plainly visible as a cattle
brand. But unlike Barnesdale, Caleb didn't foist his personal anguish onto others.

The intercom on Henry's phone sounded. "Dr. Barnesdale, excuse me for interrupting," his secretary said, "but
there's a phone call for you."

"Tell them I'm busy," Barnesdale fumed.

"I explained that you're in conference, sir. They told me you had instructed them to interrupt you if you were in a meeting."

"Who is it?"

"The Guatemalan Consulate, sir."

Chapter 12

Luke reached his office and was unlocking the door when a surgical resident came barreling around the corner. The resident sidestepped him in an agile move and raced into Trauma One, which was just down the hall.

Luke's altercation with the football player and Kate's murder were tonight's topics of conversation in the E.R., and he was using his dinner break to escape the chatter. Once inside the office, he dropped into his chair without bothering to close the door.

The gossipmongers had settled on a comfortable consensus that Kate was the victim of a random robbery-homicide. Luke was still trying to convince himself that they were right. Was he overthinking it? Were his feelings toward Kate—the untidy blend of onetime affections and vexing disappointments—clouding his judgment?

Whatever the case, between Kate's murder, his scuffle with Erickson, and the Guatemalan boy's peculiar death, the past twenty-four hours had taken on a chaotic rhythm. Perhaps he was searching for existential order where there was none to be had.

His windowless room wasn't much bigger than a cubicle, which was fine with him because he was almost never there. His routine was to stop by on Mondays and Thursdays, and then only to pick up his mail, check his phone messages, and wade through whatever paperwork the hospital bureaucrats had thrown at him.

He looked through his e-mails, going back over the messages he had already seen on Friday night. Then he checked the computer folder that held deleted messages. There was nothing from Kate. Where had her e-mail gone?

He'd spoken to one of the hospital's computer programmers earlier that afternoon. The guy had agreed to search the hospital's e-mail server for any incoming messages with a sender's address that contained all or most of the letter sequence T-A-R-T-A-G-L-I-A, but he told Luke that his backlog of work orders would keep him from getting to it until Monday or Tuesday.

Luke had also called Zenavax. The officious operator who seemed unaware of Kate's fate had been exceedingly unhelpful. If he wanted to talk to someone about an e-mail, he would have to call back on Monday. And no—she would not disturb Dr. Tartaglia's secretary at home over the weekend.

He sat forward and punched the voice-mail button on his phone. There were three messages. Two were from hospital staff members wanting to hear more about his fight, though they couched their meddlesome curiosity in expressions of concern. A third was from a drug rep who wanted to know if Luke was interested in coming to a drug symposium. He wasn't.

There were no messages from Kate.

"McKenna."

Luke cocked his head to the side. Barnesdale and another man were standing in the doorway. The second man took in his office with one eye; his other eye remained fixed on Luke.

Barnesdale pointed down the hall. "Come with us."

Luke followed the two men into a small meeting room. He didn't know the second man, but the sheen on his suit marked him as trouble.

Once in the room with the door closed, Henry came right to the point. "The Medical Executive Committee has voted to temporarily suspend your clinical privileges, pending an inquiry."

Barnesdale waited for Luke's response. When he gave him none, Henry continued, "Your suspension is effective immediately and will last for three weeks, assuming our inquiry doesn't require us to take further action."

Luke said nothing.

"Do you have anything you want to say?" Barnesdale asked.

"That question usually comes *before* someone is suspended from their job."

Henry's jaw tightened. "You had your chance—last night. You didn't take it."

Luke glanced at The Suit, then back at Barnesdale. "Touché."

The Suit said, "Our law firm represents the hospital in certain matters. Dr. Barnesdale has asked me to act as counsel to the committee that will examine this incident. You'll have every opportunity to present the facts as you see them, and I want you to know that we'll do everything possible to deal with this issue quickly and fairly."

Luke couldn't tell whether the attorney was looking at him, or the door behind him. He nodded at the man's nose and said, "While you're busy looking out for my welfare, who's looking out for the child?"

"The child?" asked Barnesdale.

"Erickson's daughter. The one that looks like a punching bag. The girl that might just turn up dead someday."

"That's up to the case workers at the Department of

Children and Family Services. DCFS is perfectly capable of doing their job. Maybe you should take a lesson from them, and stick to doing your job."

Luke fought to control his anger. "Anything else?"

The attorney said, "I hope you'll take some time to think about the hospital's position in all of this. Of course, we want what's right for the girl—just as you do—but the hospital is in a delicate position here, and further provoking the Erickson family isn't going to help your position, or the hospital's."

"What are you talking about?"

"Perhaps you were mistaken about Erickson. Perhaps there's another explanation for what you saw." The attorney's eyes jogged to Barnesdale. "I don't want to get ahead of ourselves, but—"

"I'll tell you what," Luke said. "Let's pretend that you weren't about to ask me to withdraw the DCFS report on that girl. That way, we can keep a civil tone to this conversation."

Henry glared at Luke.

"Like you said, Henry, we should each stick to our own jobs." Luke turned and walked out of the room.

Luke was halfway back to his office when Megan sidled up to him in the corridor.

"Do you have a moment?" she asked.

"This isn't a good time, Megan." He slowed his pace but kept walking. "If you're wondering about Josue Chaca, I don't know anything yet. The autopsy's tomorrow."

"It's not about that." She gave his elbow a gentle tug.

It was the first time in almost three months that she'd touched him in a familiar way, and the gesture stopped him in mid-stride.

Megan came right to the point. "About Kate," she said. "I didn't say anything earlier because there were others in the doctors' room and it just didn't seem like the right time. But . . . well, I wanted you to know how sorry I am about what happened."

Her eyes flittered away from his.

She rarely held his gaze anymore. He still wasn't accustomed to her reticence, the searing reminders that he'd lost her affection.

"Thanks," he said. "I'm fine, but thanks for your concern."

A nurse stepped past them. They both followed her with their eyes.

When they were alone again, Megan lifted her shoulders an inch and said, "Well, that's all I wanted to say."

She started to walk away.

"I heard she was still alive when they brought her in," Luke said.

Megan turned back. "We did everything we could to—"

"I know—I didn't mean it that way," he said. "What I'm wondering is—was she conscious, did she say anything?"

Megan shook her head. "One of the bullets shattered her skull, went straight through. She wasn't moving."

"The people who carried her into the E.R.—did any of them mention whether they'd seen it happen? Did anyone see the killer?"

Her expression suddenly changed, her eyes seeming to search his.

Finally, she answered, "No."

Luke's gaze fell and he nodded at the floor. "Okay." A moment later he turned to leave.

Before he took a step, she said, "Let the police take care of this, Luke. Don't do anything stupid."

When he looked back, a bright red flush was crawling up the side of her neck like a rash.

They both knew that her admonition was three months too late. He had already revealed a capacity for colossal stupidity that had cost him her trust—and her love.

"Megan, I'm just asking about what happened. That's all."

"The sad thing is, I don't know whether to believe you. The last time you asked me questions like this—"

"Megan, there were a lot of things I could've handled better." He dipped his chin to hide a swallow. "Let's just leave it at that."

Wanting to say more, and knowing that he wouldn't, left him drifting in a desolate sadness.

Chapter 13

S o anyway, that's my theory," Chewy said.

Megan pretended to listen to the intern's prattle as they left the E.R. together. They lived in the same apartment complex a few blocks from the hospital, and Chewy's nonstop chatter seemed an acceptable price to pay for an escort service at midnight.

"What theory is that?" Megan asked.

They walked down the corridor and entered the hospital's foyer. Everyone entering or leaving the hospital passed through the enormous two-story entry that was built during the Great Depression. It was part of the original hospital and had survived the endless renovations, saved from the wrecking ball by preservation groups that fought to protect the aging structure and its tiled cathedral ceiling, nymph-like gargoyles, and stained-glass windows.

Chewy rolled a slice of pizza he'd scavenged in the E.R. and put the last three inches into his mouth. "What'm I—talking to myself here?" he mumbled. "My theory about McKenna, that's what. I think he must be gay."

"Chewy, that's the dumbest—"

"No, hear me out. The guy's a babe magnet, right?"

"I'm not interested in—"

"But he doesn't do anything about it. Oh, sure, he dates women—girl-next-door types, ya know, like you. But when's the last time you saw him put the moves on some hottie in the E.R.? I mean, like, *never*." He spread his arms like an umpire. "Oh man, if I was him—"

"I think you just spotted the flaw in your logic."

As they neared the exit and passed a gallery of physician portraits, Megan's eyes went to the painted likeness of Dr. Kaczynski, a prominent geneticist who had died five years earlier. The shape of the man's head regularly drew stares from passersby, and the hospital staff had irreverently labeled the portrait "Mr. Potato Head." Something about it always drew her gaze.

When they stepped through the exit doors, a gust of cold air hit her in the face. Megan pulled up the lapel of her white coat and hugged herself with both arms.

It didn't help. The thin lab coat was useless against the biting cold. Chilled air found its way up her sleeves, down her back, and into every buttonhole.

"I've been thinking about this since last night, when McKenna clocked Mount Vesuvius. I think all that kung fu stuff is just his way of compensating." Chewy bobbed his head, as though pleased with his reasoning. "He's awfully neat too—I mean, for a regular guy. Ever notice the way he's always straightening things up in the doctors' room?"

They stopped at a crosswalk and waited for a stream of cars to pass.

She could sense Chewy's stare and braved a glance in his direction.

"The short hair," he said. "That's a good look for you."

The last time her hair was this short, she was eight years old. She remembered sitting on her bedroom floor and looking into the mirror that was mounted on her closet door, inspecting the damage. Her father had just cut her hair, apparently struck by a sudden urge to display his latent hairstyling skills. The result was a disaster that earned him a what-were-you-thinking rebuke from her mother. She'd give anything to have him cut her hair one more time.

Chewy turned and looked up toward a low-pitched *thwacking* sound. A helicopter was landing on the hospital's helipad.

Megan used the moment to shut out his chatter and summon the image of her father's face. The detail was gone, the vividness of his features faded. Her dad, a Boston firefighter like his father before him, had been a strong and rugged-looking man. Too strong to die in a fire. She had tried to explain that to her mother the night he didn't come home from the firehouse. She had tried to convince her mother that the men sitting in their living room were wrong.

Just as Chewy's feet started moving again, so did his mouth. ". . . so I'm guessing the world will end when some humungous asteroid hits us . . ."

Twelve years later, during her last year in medical school, fate served up another harsh lesson, when it became clear that her mother was losing a three-year battle with breast cancer. Her mom died just ten days later from a fulminant infection, months sooner than anyone had expected, and an hour before Megan reached her bedside.

The Callahans made a habit of leaving the world too early, and without a good-bye.

With no siblings to share her grief, Megan had begun her residency feeling very much alone in the world. Even a work schedule that knew no weekends or holidays hadn't filled the void. The people missing from her life found their way into her thoughts with the regularity of a tidal pattern, if only to remind her that they were no longer there.

Chewy continued his conversation with the night air. ". . . and a lot of asteroids hang out between Mars and Jupiter—don't ask me why they're not, say, floating around Pluto, but . . ."

It was during an especially lonely period that Luke had entered her life. His small attentions to her during an E.R. rotation had come at just the right moment, and before long he became more than just a pleasing distraction.

For the first time in many years, she had found herself hoping that a casual relationship might grow into something more. Luke's quiet strength reminded her of her father, which was probably why—even now—she had an irksome need for his respect.

From the beginning, Luke's hold on her was vexing, and even more so because of how closely he guarded his own emotions. It was as if Luke's deeper thoughts and feelings lay hidden behind a sealed door.

For many months she had held onto the hope that his reserve would eventually give way to a greater openness. She'd been a fool, she realized.

". . . and we're talking huge," Chewy thundered. "The big dino-killer? That sucker was about six miles wide. I wonder what Fred and Wilma must have thought when they looked up and saw that thing getting ready to whonk them on the head . . ."

Megan and Chewy rounded the corner onto a residential avenue. Across the street was the overgrown hedge where her attacker had lain in wait. A familiar shiver in her right shoulder, at the spot where the would-be rapist had grabbed her, sent a shudder down her arm.

The screams had woken the entire block, a homeowner later told police.

But not her screams. It was her attacker's yelps that they had heard—his reaction to having a pair of fingers locked between her clenched teeth.

She didn't remember his shrieks, but recalled him pulling away and leaping over a fence when a nearby porch light came on.

The first few hours after the attack remained a patchwork of disjointed memories. Her first distinct memory was of Luke appearing in the doorway of an interview room at the police station. It had loosed in her a torrent of tears she'd been holding in check.

But what she remembered most was the rage in his eyes. His eyes had frightened her even then.

". . . It makes you wonder"—Chewy looked up at the sky—"all those cosmic chunks of iron banging around out there. It's like a giant game of Pong . . ."

The rage in Luke's eyes had continued to burn for days. When what she wanted most was to feel normal again, to feel safe again, his eyes had been a constant reminder of her trauma.

Megan was only the first of three victims, and the other two women didn't escape the rapist's perverse savagery. But that was where the assailant's streak had ended. One week after his third attack, a police patrol unit apprehended him five blocks from the hospital.

It wasn't a difficult arrest. He was tied to a tree, naked, and beaten half to death.

That was when the calm had returned to Luke's eyes. It was only then that she had thought back to his questions about the rapist. The queries had seeped into their conversations after the second attack. Luke had done it subtly, extracting details that at the time seemed a natural part of their cathartic late night talks.

The police had questioned everyone connected to the case, including Luke. Their inquiries—likely commensurate with their concern for the letch—were perfunctory.

Megan's weren't. Luke never admitted that he had done it, but he didn't deny it either. He simply would not talk about it. Apparently, he didn't trust her to know the truth.

She chafed at the thought that he had kept his torments secret. If he'd shared his feelings, rather than erupting in a fit of vengeance, they might still be together.

He was a good man—in many ways, a very good man—but she could not abide his hidden penchant for violence. It frightened her, and his unwillingness to talk about it only widened the chasm between them.

Damn you, Luke.

Chewy was yammering about extraterrestrials when they passed between two squat palm trees that stood like guards at the courtyard entrance to their apartment building. After two and a half years, the U-shaped 1950s style structure was beginning to close in on her.

She couldn't wait to leave for Guatemala tomorrow.

Barnesdale hung up from his call with the Zenavax CEO, got up from his desk and started pacing. He massaged his palms in a hand-washing motion, trying to rub away the tremor as he made a track around his office.

Jesus, these people are lunatics.

They didn't have to *murder* her. They had the perfect trump card.

He had given it to them. He had the original copy of Tartaglia's employment agreement with University

Children's—signed by her—the one that supposedly had never been executed.

They could have dangled that contract in front of her indefinitely. She never would have talked—not when it would have meant prosecution for what had grown into a *$3 billion* theft.

All they had had to do was use their leverage. *That* was what he thought he had agreed to. What had the Zenavax CEO said? "I think you know what needs to be done."

How the hell was he supposed to know that they were planning to murder the woman?

And now, on the phone, the man talked about her death as if it were simply part of some karmic outcome. "It's an escapable truth," he had said, "Misfortune tends to follow those who make the wrong choices in life."

The warning seemed clear: *Step out of line, Henry, and . . .*

He could barely hold it together. Those qualities he had always used as a shield—his resolute bearing, his authoritative demeanor—were starting to crack open like thin-shelled eggs.

Henry seethed at the thought of Caleb and his goddamned clinic seeding the clouds that were raining terror onto his life.

He grabbed the wall, closed his eyes, and tightened his face into a knot.

What the hell have I gotten myself into?

Chapter 14

There's not gonna be any autopsy." Ben Wilson emptied a small bottle of dried insects into the tarantula's aquarium. "It's cancelled."

Luke dropped into a seat. "Why?"

"One of the M.E.'s called over here last night and told my staff to release the body to the family. No one called me, or I would've saved you a trip to the hospital. Looks like both of us missed an opportunity to sleep in late on Sunday morning."

Luke glanced at a wall clock that read 6:21 A.M. "How can they do that?"

"The Coroner's Office can do most anything they damn well please. Fact is, it's usually the other way around. They usually hold onto bodies that no one wants 'em to keep."

"So what happened?"

"Apparently, the family ended up making a stink about us keeping their son's body. Well, one thing leads to another, the Guatemalan Consulate gets involved, and before ya know it we have one less cadaver in our cooler."

"It's gone?"

"We released it a few hours ago. Seems the family was in a hurry to get their son's body back."

"Why the rush?"

"Have to admit, I might feel the same way if it was my son. It usually takes a day or so to arrange things—you don't move a cadaver around like a crate of cantaloupes—but we can do it faster, and we do from time to time, for one reason or another."

"Like?"

"A few months ago we had to drop everything and make arrangements to ship the body of a Portuguese diplomat's child back home."

"We're not talking about a diplomat's child here. This family lives in rural Guatemala. They're probably dirt poor. When's the last time you did it for someone like that?"

"Luke, I just work behind a plow—I only see the mule's hind end. If they tell me to hurry it up, I hurry it up."

"Did the medical examiner say why the consulate was involved?"

"It's not all that unusual in cases involving a foreign national. Last night someone from the consulate called Barnesdale when I was in that committee meeting with Henry and his gang of half-wits. He shooed all of us out the door—probably didn't want us to see him licking the dust off some diplomat's boots."

"Wait a minute—Barnesdale sent you out of the room?"

"I wouldn't read anything into that. The business of the meeting"—Ben cocked a finger and aimed it at Luke—"was done by that point, and Henry was killing time whipping his favorite piñata—your daddy."

"Something still doesn't sound right here. I didn't think the coroner rolled over that easily."

"They don't when there's a possibility of foul play. But look at it from their point of view. This is a Guatemalan citizen who none of us believes was murdered." Ben picked up a tiny scissors and started scraping under his fingernails. "When there's a foreign national involved, they generally won't hold the body unless there's"—Ben held up his fingers and painted quotation marks in the air—"'some compelling public necessity.' That's coroner-talk for suspected homicide, child abuse, a serious public health risk . . . that sorta thing."

"Who signed the death certificate?"

"Until we started this conversation, I guess I figured you had. Probably someone else from the E.R. signed it."

Luke shook his head. "I was the only Attending there. Would the coroner release the body without a signed death certificate?"

"They sure as hell would not."

"Do you have the death certificate here?"

"Nope. It'd be with the chart, and we'd have already sent that back to Medical Records."

"Let me use your phone."

Luke called Medical Records and asked one of their clerks to bring Josue Chaca's chart to Ben's office, all the while trying to calm his anger.

"We still don't know why this patient died," Luke said. "Our E.R. staff may have been exposed to a toxin, or an infection. What am I supposed to tell *them*?"

Ben shrugged. "We'll know soon enough. I'll be looking at the slides later today."

"What slides?"

"Remember? Last night I got a section of rib from the cadaver so we could look at the bone marrow. We sent it over to Oncology Friday night so we could get some quick answers for my good friend, Dr. McKenna."

"You still have the marrow? It didn't go back with the body?"

"I've already checked. All the tissues are still here."

"All?"

A conspiratorial smile took shape on Ben's wide face. "Seems I also snipped a piece of lung while I was getting that rib. While I was in the neighborhood, I figured why not get some lung tissue? Maybe it'll explain what we saw on the chest X-ray."

"That Ben Wilson's a pretty sharp guy."

Ben appeared to think about that for a second, then nodded.

"So we can settle the question about leukemia?" asked Luke.

"Yep, and we can look at some other possibilities if it turns out this boy didn't die of leukemia and sepsis. We've already sent a piece of the lung for culture. And they're making some slides of the lung tissue as we speak."

"I checked the boy's labs this morning. His amylase and lipase were sky high."

"Hmmm," Ben said. "So his pancreas was involved."

"Sure looks like it."

The phone rang.

"Wilson here." Ben grabbed a big chunk of eyebrow and started twirling it. His eyes darted toward Luke. "Thanks." While setting the phone down, he said, "That was Medical Records. Seems your boy's chart is checked out to Barnesdale."

"Barnesdale?"

"That's what the lady said."

"Why would he have the chart?"

Ben reached for the phone again. "While you're thinking about that, I'm gonna see if we can get someone to look at that marrow today."

After calling the operator and paging the on-call on-cologist, Ben reached into the aquarium, uncovered the tarantula's shallow hideaway, and grabbed Charlotte by either side of her dark brown torso. He turned the spider over, stroked its belly, then held it out toward Luke.

Luke patted himself on the stomach with both hands. "Thanks. I've already eaten."

Ben's lips curled into a smile as he rubbed the furry creature.

Five minutes later they were on the speakerphone talking to the head of Oncology, Adam Smith. "Already looked at that marrow," Smith said. "Did it myself, yesterday afternoon. I'm on call this weekend and Henry asked me to do it. Something about the coroner wanting to release the body."

"Well, I guess that explains why Henry has the chart," offered Ben.

"It doesn't explain anything. This wasn't his patient," Luke said. "Adam, what did the marrow show?"

"About thirty percent lymphoid blasts, L2 morphology, diminished erythroid cell lines."

"Would one of you care to translate that for me?" Luke asked.

"It means the boy had A-L-L—acute lymphoblastic leukemia," Ben clarified.

Luke said, "That still doesn't explain the lung findings—the chest X-ray."

"What lung findings?" Adam asked.

"A focal bronchopulmonary pattern," Ben said. "Something was going on in the airways. They lit up like a Christmas tree. But the lung tissue looked almost normal—certainly not enough pathology to explain respiratory failure."

Luke jumped in: "One more question, Adam. Do you know who signed the death certificate—was it you?"

"Henry signed it."

"How do you know that?" Luke asked.

"When I told him about the bone marrow results, he said something about being able to sign off on the death certificate so he could return the body to the family. Sounded like the whole thing was one big headache and he wanted to be done with it."

"Where the hell does Henry come off signing a death certificate for a patient he knows nothing about?"

"Henry told me he saw the patient in the E.R."

"*He was a bystander*, for Christ's sake. He wasn't there more than a minute or two."

After a brief silence, Adam said, "Luke, would you pick up the phone?"

He glanced at Ben, who responded with a beats-me expression.

When Luke picked up the receiver, Adam said, "In case you didn't know, you made the morning news. There're two TV news crews in front of the hospital doing stories about that incident in the E.R."

Luke closed his eyes and brought a hand to his forehead. "How bad?"

"The only good thing I can say is, they didn't mention you by name. You were—quote—'an unnamed hospital employee.' It sounds like they're still checking their facts. If the story develops legs, it's not going to help your situation. And word has it that Barnesdale has gone ballistic over this thing. He's acting strange, even for him." A moment later he added, "My point is, I certainly wouldn't make an issue of the death certificate right now."

When Luke hung up the phone, Ben asked, "What was that about?"

Luke shook his head. "Take a guess."

"The Erickson thing?" It didn't come out sounding like a question. "I've been meaning to ask you—how is it that you sliced through that big ol' boy like he was warm butter? I hear that that bubba was *enormous*."

Changing the subject, Luke asked, "Do you think the coroner would talk to you about this case?"

Ben placed Charlotte back in the tank. "Yeah. Why?"

"Seems like someone with a lot of juice stepped in. I'd like to know who that was, and why they pushed everyone to move so quickly."

"You thinking there's a conspiracy, here?" asked Ben. "Tell me—where do you stand on that grassy knoll thing?"

"Henry signing the death certificate, the consulate getting involved . . . I think there's something we haven't been told."

"Ya know what I think? I think the biggest trouble-maker in your life watches you shave in the mirror every morning. That's what I think."

"That'll be my thought for the day."

"Ya know what else I think?"

"Do I have a choice?"

"I think you got far too much time on your hands," Ben added, "and I'm being made to suffer for it."

Luke got up to leave. "Humor me."

He was almost to the door when Ben said, "You hear about Kate Tartaglia getting shot in that robbery?"

"Yeah, I know about it."

"Strange the way life is. I mean, we're sitting here talking about her the night before last, then"—he snapped his fingers—"just like that, she's dead."

Luke turned to leave. "Yeah, strange, isn't it."

Chapter 15

Luke was thinking about death as he sat in the crescent-shaped corner booth at Kolter's Deli and waited for his father to walk through the entrance.

The incongruities of Josue Chaca's death plucked at him. If, as Adam Smith had explained, the boy's bone marrow provided a clear-cut diagnosis of leukemia, then why had they not found any blasts in the boy's blood samples? Why hadn't the chest X-ray revealed any signs of the respiratory failure that were so evident on the boy's exam? And how had a family of meager means marshaled the forces of their consulate so quickly, and over a weekend?

Luke had seen death often enough to recognize its methods. It operated with a certain logic and natural order that were missing from this case. There was no pattern here—no fulcrum that would yield to reason.

The same elements were missing from Kate's death. It wasn't the violent method of her murder that resisted logic—this was Los Angeles, after all. It was the dissonant quality of her final hours that churned in his mind. Zenavax's IPO and her imminent wealth should have been cause for heady exuberance, not the trepidation he had heard in her voice. She should have been popping the cork on a champagne bottle, not rushing out to a hastily arranged late-night meeting with someone she hadn't seen in four years.

A disquiet that felt out of proportion to his questions gnawed at him. Something was pulling at him, something he couldn't see or hear.

But he could feel its pulsating rhythm. What was it?

"Dr. Luke, you want I pour you some more coffee?"

Luke turned and nodded at Antonio, the deli's owner, who was resting a coffee carafe on the slope of his thick Italian midsection.

Antonio and his wife, Bianca, were Sicilian-born immigrants who seemed content to follow Kolter's mixed ethnic tradition. Depending on the time of day, one of three distinctly different personalities seized control of the deli. Breakfast had a quiet energy about it, patrons taking in the blended aromas of freshly baked pastries and strong coffee. By lunchtime its origins as a delicatessen dominated, with long lines of customers shouting their orders across the take-out counter. At sunset, Kolter's transformed itself into an English pub, its stingy antique wall sconces barely illuminating the dark wood paneling and burgundy leather seats.

After filling Luke's mug, Antonio stood back and smiled at the front window. "Ah, another beautifuls sunrise for the childrens."

Across the street, a small trickle of early birds had grown to a steady flow as hospital staff arrived for the 7:00 A.M. change of shift. Few showed any interest in the TV news crews standing near the hospital entrance—the same crews that Luke had skirted by leaving from the rear loading dock.

A bell on the front door tinkled and the second customer of the day, an Asian man, walked through the front door.

He was followed almost immediately by a disheveled man with unruly white hair who was wearing a lab coat that was creased in a dozen places it shouldn't be.

Luke waved his father over to the table. Ever since Luke's mother had died in an accident twelve years ago, breakfast at Kolter's was an everyday event for Elmer.

Just as poker with the residents was an every-Saturday-night event.

The dark circles under his father's eyes told Luke that last night had been no exception. The venue for Elmer's card games changed from time to time, depending on the schedule and whereabouts of certain hospital administrators. Management had made it clear: Poker was not an activity for which their hospital had been licensed, and though many of the residents might not be able to control their illicit urges, the senior faculty should know better than to participate in an unlawful pastime.

Luke was certain that his father *didn't* know better—after all, Elmer organized most of the poker sessions—but by moving the location of the games around the hospital campus, sometimes on short notice, his father probably thought he was showing proper respect, much like the mouse pays to the cat.

The elder McKenna slid into the booth. "Help me fatten up my son, Antonio. He's too skinny."

"You want I make-a you a nice omelet, Dr. Luke?"

Luke lifted his cup. "This'll do."

As soon as his father ordered and Antonio left their table, Luke said, "I take it you haven't heard about Kate Tartaglia."

Elmer cocked his head.

"She was murdered Friday night." Luke threw a thumb over his shoulder. "It happened just down the street."

"Oh, my Lord."

Luke wasn't surprised that his father hadn't heard the news. Elmer had gotten to the point in his career that he rarely worked weekends anymore, and a stranger's murder wasn't likely to work its way into a poker conversation among residents inured to the more-than-occasional gunshot and knifing victims who showed up in their E.R.

"She was coming here to meet with me," Luke said. "I think the police figure some punk robbed, then killed her."

Elmer brought a hand to the side of his face.

"Kate called me late Friday," Luke continued. "Out of the blue. I don't know what she wanted, but she seemed upset." He took a swallow of coffee. "Have you talked to her recently?"

Elmer shook his head slowly, as though half lost in a private thought. "Kate was so young, so . . ."

Luke couldn't remember his father ever expressing an angry thought about Kate. Ironically, Elmer seemed to be the only person who hadn't held a grudge.

"Dad, would you check to see if you received an e-mail from Kate?"

"An e-mail?" Elmer's eyes suddenly came back into focus. "Why?"

"She sent me something, but I never got it. Maybe she addressed it to you by mistake."

"Knowing Kate, that's not likely, but I'll check."

Luke reached for a spoon and starting playing with it. "There's something else you need to know about." He recounted his discussion with Barnesdale and the attorney.

"He *what*?" Elmer said. "How could Henry suspend you? As far as I'm concerned, that Erickson fellow finally got his comeuppance. It's as simple as that." He dipped his chin to put an exclamation point on his opinion.

"No, it's *not* as simple as that. I had a choice—I

could've tried to defuse the situation," Luke said. "Instead, I let loose on the guy."

"Uh-oh. I can hear all those gears cranking away in your head. Ya know, sometimes you have a way of over-thinking things."

Luke gave a tired roll of his eyes.

Antonio's wife, Bianca, marched over and laid a plate in front of Elmer. She was a matronly woman who looked uncomfortable when she tried to smile, so rarely did.

Elmer seemed to be studying him. "Do you remember Jimmy Yazzie?"

Luke's eyebrows rose in a question. Jimmy was his best friend in the first grade. In addition to reading and arithmetic, Luke learned about child abuse during that year. Jimmy had slept at their home more often than his own for reasons that Luke understood only after witness-ing a beating he wasn't supposed to see.

"What does Jimmy Yazzie have to do with any of this?"

"A lot, I think. What you learned about Jimmy's home had a profound affect on you. Remember your night-mares? They went on for months."

"Dad, why don't we talk about this another time?" He started to slide out of the booth.

"Sit still and let me finish." Elmer showed his son an uncharacteristically somber face.

After a few seconds, his father continued, "The choices you've made in your life—going to Annapolis, becoming a SEAL, your decision to become a pediatrician—all of it. From a young age, you seemed to have a need to protect the innocents of the world. That's not such a bad thing, Luke."

A pair of men walked into the restaurant and handed

Antonio their business cards. Luke recognized one of them: Detective O'Reilly. The three of them stood by the cash register near the front door and started into a conversation.

"Let's change the subject," Luke said.

"Okay, then. How's Megan doing these days?"

Luke continued to look past his father at the detectives, trying to hide his annoyance at the question. "She's doing better, I think. She's a strong person."

"She's more than that."

Luke looked from the detectives to his father.

Elmer made a show of lifting his crumb roll and examining it from various angles. "You know, Luke, some things in life are just too good to do without."

His father's expression betrayed nothing other than a keen interest in his pastry.

The detectives turned and swept the room with their eyes.

O'Reilly locked on Luke. A minute later he was standing next to their booth. "Dr. McKenna, sorry for the intrusion. We're here tying up some loose ends and I have a few more questions for you. Would you mind stepping outside for a minute?"

The other detective, if that's what he was, eyed Elmer. The man's scrutiny irritated Luke.

"This is my father," Luke said. "He knew Kate. You can ask your questions in front of him."

O'Reilly seemed to weigh the issue for a moment before saying, "When we spoke, you said you didn't see Dr. Tartaglia the night she was murdered. Is that right?"

"Right."

The morning sun climbed over the heliport atop the hospital. Luke squinted as a blinding glare cascaded down the window.

"You sure you never saw her that evening, even for a moment?"

"Yes, I'm sure."

"You find that e-mail message?"

Luke shook his head.

"But you still have the phone message from Dr. Tartaglia, the one you told me about?"

"Yeah."

"Good. Would you allow us to make a copy of it?"

Luke shrugged. "Sure."

"I'll give you a call. We'd like to do that sometime today."

Inside the green van parked across the street from Kolter's Deli, Calderon adjusted his headphones and listened through the static while studying McKenna from a side porthole window.

"Dad, would you check to see if you received an e-mail from Kate?"

"An e-mail? Why?"

"She sent me something, but I never got it. Maybe she addressed it to you by mistake."

Calderon swung his tripod-mounted spotting scope toward the booth along the restaurant's rear wall where Mr. Kong was sitting. The man was bent over his plate, shoveling eggs into his mouth. Why did Chinese people eat that way?

Even though he was right-handed, Kong held the fork in his left hand. Cupped in his right hand was a miniaturized directional microphone, pointed at McKenna's table.

Calderon had spent most of the previous day acquiring the surveillance equipment. He didn't like doing things this way—it was too rushed—but his client's carelessness had left him no choice. Fortunately, he knew the town and its sources, and had used Kong as an intermediary for the purchases. He wanted his trip to Los Angeles to remain dark, untraceable.

He clicked back the magnification and took in the two detectives talking to a man at the cash register. Calderon recognized one of the cops from the woman's house.

Eventually, the detectives turned and started walking toward McKenna's table.

With any luck, Calderon thought, he would be back in Guatemala in two days. He hadn't planned on being away from the project site this long.

Calderon was fiddling with a knob on the radio receiver when he heard:

"But you still have the phone message from Dr. Tartaglia, the one you told me about?"

"Yeah."

"Good. Would you allow us to make a copy of it?"

Calderon slammed the side of the van with the base of his fist, then grabbed the cell phone and called his client.

Chapter 16

When Luke arrived home thirty minutes later, there was a voice mail from O'Reilly. The detective left his number and said he'd stop by that evening to retrieve Kate's phone message.

Luke pressed SAVED MESSAGES and replayed Kate's voice mail.

Again, the trepidation in her voice swirled around him like unsettled air.

Outside his front window, the morning mist had burned away and it was a perfectly crisp January day, so he did what he had always done to untangle his mind. He changed into baggy navy-blue shorts and a loose-fitting gray sweatshirt, and went for a run.

Griffith Park was his backyard, over four thousand acres of hilly terrain covered with California live oak, sagebrush, and chaparral. The hills were speckled with bare spots, and from a distance they had a moth-eaten appearance. The craggy park was the botanical equivalent of a mutt.

But it was his mutt, and his haven. After years of almost daily eight to ten mile runs, he knew virtually every rut in the fifty miles of crisscrossing dirt trails. He let his thoughts drift as he climbed to the summit of Mount Hollywood and then ran down the backside of the mountain.

As the sweat started to flow from his pores, so did an undercurrent of feelings that he'd been holding at a distance.

The memory of Kate's life filled him with a poignant sadness, for what her life might have been. But the deep ache he felt was for Megan.

He had soaked up her affection, laid claim to her trust, and then shattered them in a stupendously self-destructive impulse. His self-indulgent need to punish Megan's predator had ruined any hope of a future with her.

He didn't deserve her, he knew, but that didn't stop him from wanting her.

Luke tried to empty his mind on the return leg of his run. He slowed to a jog as he ran along Griffith Park Drive, then accelerated as he came up the hill on Los Feliz Boulevard. By the time he turned north onto Commonwealth Avenue, his hair was soaked through with sweat.

He was three blocks from his home when the Lexus coupé that had been following Luke for the past mile pulled up alongside him.

"How's it hanging, Flash?"

For reasons that Luke couldn't cipher, people seemed to have an inexplicable need to tag him with a nickname—but only one person had ever called him "Flash."

When Luke looked inside the car, there he was. Sammy Wilkes.

Sammy's coal-black skin was a little less tightly drawn around the jaw than when their lives had first crossed fourteen years earlier, but his smile was as big as ever. His overly large teeth had a way of taking over his face when he grinned, which was often.

Luke leaned onto the passenger-side window frame.

"Yo, Flash. Don't ju be leanin' against my wheels with yo sweaty ass."

"You can cut the cornball ghetto talk," Luke said. "I know you, remember?"

Sammy Wilkes was as much a part of the black ghetto experience as the Prince of Wales. Educated at Cornell with a degree in electrical engineering, he had grown up in an upper-class neighborhood on Chicago's north side, the son of an investment banker.

Wilkes had been the only member of Proteus without a military background. They had found him at the National Security Agency, where he'd cultivated a unique portfolio of electronic surveillance skills.

"By the way," Wilkes said, "things are fine with me. Thanks for asking."

"What's it been, Sammy, five years?" Luke looked down the street. "Do I have to guess, or are you going to tell me why you've been following me?"

It wasn't just Sammy's background that distinguished him from his fellow Proteus members. He didn't have the same pensive and brooding nature that others had worn like an overworked habit. Sammy and his pearly white teeth smiled mischievously at life. He'd been a cocky and talkative kid who glided past the questions that had tormented Luke. Covert operations that had played out as lopsided massacres, killings made to look like they were done by other groups—for Sammy, it all had seemed as inconsequential as an insect under his boot.

Sammy had had other things on his mind. He'd always talked about how he would turn his talents into something big. In fact, he had, parlaying his specialized skills into a thriving corporate security and surveillance business that operated at the furthest edges of legality—and sometimes, Luke suspected, beyond.

The black man studied the street around them. "Sammy usually gets paid to follow people. I may have to start a tab here. You owe me big-time for this one."

"Other than the fact that you've always started *every* conversation by claiming that I owe you a favor, what exactly are you talking about?"

"Breaking the code of the brotherhood. That's what I'm doing by talking to you. We'll just put it on your tab, Flash."

"You want to speak English?"

"Yours truly, the footloose and fancy-free Sammy Wilkes, was asked to conduct a super-secret clandestine investigation of one Luke McKenna. 'Course, I turned 'em down, which is lucky for you because I happen to be unmatched in my field."

"Someone is investigating me?"

"Think nothin' of it. And I do mean nothing. In fact, forget I'm here. If word gets out that Sammy makes a habit of calling ducks and letting 'em know that hunting season has started . . . well, that'd be bad for business."

"Who is it?"

"Judging from his pictures, he's more of a *what* than a *who*." Sammy eyed a passing car in his side mirror, then came back to Luke. "But I hear you recently served him up a big 'ol can of whoop-ass."

"The football player? Erickson?"

Sammy's head started bobbing. "His lawyer called me yesterday. They gonna make you look like a crazy-ass loon—at least, that's the plan." His mouth erupted in a grin that looked like his face had suddenly cracked open. "If only they knew how crazy you are, Flash. If only they knew."

Luke ran a wet hand over his head. "I can't believe this is happening."

"Oh, believe it, Flash. A blue Ford Mustang, old two-door model. It's parked up the block from your house. Check it out."

"You sure about this?"

"You kidding, right? Countersurveillance, that's Sammy's specialty. You wouldn'ta seen me earlier if I dint want you to."

Sammy waited for a response. Apparently, he could see that Luke wanted more. "Sammy decided to look in on things, see who they put on you. When I spotted the snoop, I walked up to him and asked what he was doing there."

"That was subtle."

"Best way to do it. He thinks I'm a local, looking out for my neighbors, so he gives me his cover story. Tells me he's a broker, scouting properties for his clients. Holds up a Multiple Listings book that's sitting on his lap, lets me take in the Open House placards on his dash."

"Maybe he *is* a broker."

"You kidding, right? When's the last time you saw a broker driving a two-seater—not exactly what you'd use to drive clients around in. Besides, the camera sitting on his passenger seat has a telephoto lens that'd need wheels if it was any bigger."

Luke glanced up the hill in the direction of his home. His jaw muscles hardened.

Sammy seemed to read his thoughts. "Keep it loose, Flash. Don't make trouble for yourself."

Luke looked at the ground, then back at Sammy. "I guess I *do* owe you. Thanks."

"There's times we gotta look out for each other. We're off the books, remember?" Sammy handed Luke his business card, saluted with two fingers, and then punched the throttle.

By the time Luke finished reading the card, Sammy's car had disappeared onto a side street.

Luke started walking toward his home.

Off the books. It had been years since Luke had heard that phrase. Proteus had been created to deal with national security threats that, by classified presidential order, were deemed too sensitive and imminent to disclose to the intelligence committees on Capitol Hill. The brainchild of a President frustrated by congressional leaks and a maverick Secretary of Defense, Proteus was the darkest special ops unit ever conceived. It was completely "off the books," answerable to the President alone, and known to only a handful of White House and Pentagon staffers.

It survived through just two presidential terms. When the other party won the White House, Proteus was dismantled. The outgoing President saw it for the potentially lethal political liability that it was, and almost overnight all traces of Proteus disappeared. At the time, Luke still owed the military one more year for his Naval Academy education, but the President's need to bury Proteus made that issue mute. Luke had jumped at the offer of an early discharge.

When he turned the corner onto his block, there it was. The blue Mustang was parked about seventy yards beyond his duplex under the overhang of an oak tree. With the car draped in shade, the outline of a large camera lens barely showed behind the windshield.

He felt the heat rise in his face. Each step was a battle against primal urges. When he reached the edge of his driveway, he took a deep breath and willed himself to turn toward his front door.

Keep it loose, Flash. Don't make trouble for yourself.

He made it through the door, wended his way to the kitchen, and came out onto the elevated redwood deck that sat over his driveway. A trellis overgrown with jasmine shielded him from the Mustang's view.

Luke thought about Erickson and his attorney putting him under a microscope. He was seething.

He started into his ritualized workout—abdominal crunches, inverted push-ups, fingertip pull-ups—but gave it up before he finished the first rep and sat on the deck, sweating.

Erickson's investigator would probably dredge up his "official" military record. It was nothing more than bland fiction—no more threatening than a gnat with a broken wing. His real file, the Proteus file, was buried under so many layers of security that no single individual acting alone—not even the President—had the authority to access it. His file was off the books.

But having some private detective shadow him, invade his life, and threaten the seclusion he had so carefully guarded, stirred an unfamiliar discomfort. Luke knew how to hunt a target, how to disappear into shadows, and how to stalk his prey. He didn't know how to be the prey.

There was something dreamlike about the turmoil building in his life.

He dragged himself back into the living room and dropped onto the couch. Suddenly, he was very tired.

Chapter 17

*M*oist ocean air collided with a warm offshore breeze, creating a one-hundred-meter band of mist that clung to the shoreline. Slow-moving streams of wet fog crept over the deck of the pier and meandered around its enormous concrete pilings.

For once, Luke thought, intelligence had gotten it right—near perfect weather conditions for their mission, with the fog giving them cover for their ingress onto the pier that stretched a quarter mile into the darkness. Their target was at the end of the concrete platform.

"Omega, do you have the bogey in sight?" Alpha, the team leader, spoke in a whisper.

Alpha hadn't yet labeled the man Luke had in the crosshairs of his nightscope as a hostile. For now, the unknown figure remained a bogey, someone in the target area who was putting their operation at risk.

Luke made a clicking sound with the back of his tongue, inaudible even from a few feet away but sufficient for his throat mic to send an affirmative "click" to Alpha.

Three seconds later Alpha's voice came through again. "Gamma, Zeta—can either of you identify the bogey?"

"Negative," Gamma whispered.

That was followed by two quick clicks—a negative—

from Zeta, who was in Zone One with Luke and too close to the hostiles to speak.

Darkness heightened the Proteus team's advantage. Luke's nightscope pierced the fog and turned warm bodies into luminous greenish-gray images. Poorly equipped North Korean security forces were blinded by the mist. Meanwhile, he captured every twitch, every distracted scratch, every casual gesture by their adversaries—men who at that moment were probably thinking about little else than keeping warm.

The bogey was approaching Proteus's most forward-positioned team member, Kappa, who had already reached the pier. The bogey was small and thin, and young judging by his light gait. He had no rifle; in fact, Luke saw no weapon at all.

After ten seconds of silence, Alpha said, "Bogey nearing Kappa's position, fifteen meters and closing."

Kappa was tucked into a shallow inset between two large warehouses. The mission planners had identified the structures as seafood processing plants, placed there to camouflage the military installation.

The three remaining members of the insertion team, including Luke, had only three minutes to take their positions on and under the pier, then five minutes to get to the perimeter of the naval supply station. Once at the perimeter, they had exactly four and a half minutes to breach perimeter security and place explosive charges on the hull of the submarine, which, if not destroyed, would soon transform North Korea into a nuclear naval power.

He clicked the magnification setting of his rifle scope one notch higher and trained the crosshairs on the bogey, who was nearing Kappa's position. A plume of bright green light, emissions from a heat-exhaust pipe, turned the bogey into a wavy mirage as he passed through it.

The bogey moved to within five meters of Kappa. The unidentified man was now in the mandatory kill zone.

Alpha said, "Omega, the bogey is now your target. Take him out." His voice revealed no hesitation, no emotion.

Luke was full of hesitation. His target had no weapon. Was the target a soldier, or a civilian who'd wandered into the wrong place at the wrong time?

"Anyone have an identity on the target?" he asked.

"Omega, I say again, take out the target. Now!"

The blaring siren came out of nowhere.

Luke shot up onto the edge of his sofa, his chest heaving, his face drenched in sweat.

An instant later the phone rang and a bolt of pain speared his right eye. His spine arched and he flung himself back onto the couch.

Then, just as suddenly, the pain was gone.

He hoisted himself up and threw his feet onto the floor while grabbing for the telephone. Its ring had invaded his dream, his mind transforming it into a siren.

"You're not gonna believe what just happened," came Ben's voice without preamble.

The afternoon sun painted a ribbon of orange across the far wall.

Luke rubbed the sleep from his face. "What?"

"Barnesdale marched into my office 'bout an hour ago with some big shot from the Guatemalan Embassy—"

"You mean consulate?"

"Embassy, consulate, who gives a rat's ass? The point is, Henry marches in with this muckety-muck and his attorney, telling me to hand over the tissue samples from our boy." The pitch of Ben's voice rose. "Henry's all swole up in the face, acting like I was some kinda ax murderer or something."

"Hold on, Ben. Tell me exactly what happened."

"I just told you. They demanded that I give 'em all the organ tissues, so that's what I did. Except for the bone marrow—apparently, they'd already gotten that from Oncology."

"How'd they even know you had it?"

"I'm guessing the mortician. They gotta embalm the body before transporting it out of the country. The idiot musta said something to the mother—told her a piece of the boy's rib was missing. What do they think we are, a buncha ghouls who go around collecting body parts?"

"Did anyone explain why they wanted the tissues back?"

"The consulate fella said something about religious burial rites and how important it was for the family to get back all the remains. Seems their tribe has some fancy burial ritual that gets the spirit from this life to the next. If we desecrate the body, the boy doesn't get to go to heaven—or wherever it is that Mayan Indians go."

"Did Barnesdale or this guy say anything else?"

A heavy breath came through the phone. "That's about it. I wasn't real eager to pursue the discussion."

"So we're back to where we started."

"Not exactly."

"What do you mean?"

"They didn't ask me for the slides," Ben said. "Just the tissues."

"What slides?"

"I made some slides from the lung tissue," A short beat, then, "I musta forgot to tell 'em."

Luke allowed himself a small grin.

"These folks were very particular about what they wanted," Ben said. "They didn't mention anything about slides."

"Then they probably didn't want them," Luke threw in.

"Probably not."

"So what do they show?"

"Can't tell you until I look at 'em, now, can I? And I don't plan on doing that until I get home. Henry's already taken enough of my weekend."

"Fair enough."

"Glad you think so," Ben said. "By the way, the Wilson clan is barbecuing some steaks tonight. Nothing fancy, but you're welcome to join us if you want. I'll probably get a look at those slides before dinner."

"For a lot of reasons, I think I'll take you up on that."

"Steaks'll be ready around seven."

The knock on Ben's door came as he was hanging up the phone with Luke.

"It's open."

Two workmen in gray uniforms gave Ben a deferential smile when the door opened. The larger one, a well-muscled Hispanic who was missing part of his left ear, pointed at the ceiling. "Your phone wiring?" When he didn't get a reaction from Ben, he added, "I assume someone told you we'd be working in your office today?"

"Nope."

"Third time this has happened." The worker scratched the crown of his head, glanced at his Asian partner, then Ben. "Whoever's supposed to let you people know isn't doing their job."

"Does that surprise you?" Ben asked. "If it does, you haven't worked around this place very long."

The Hispanic blew a pocket of air out from the side of

his mouth. "It's a capacity problem—the hospital's maxed out and we're reconfiguring the trunks to add more lines. Believe it or not, we're trying to stay out of everyone's way while we're doing it. That's why we're here on a weekend." The man gave him an expectant look.

Ben waved them in. "How long you gonna be?"

"Not long at all."

Fifteen minutes later the Asian worker was still on a ladder with his shoulders and head buried inside the ceiling. A labyrinth of wires hung down through the hole where he had removed two ceiling tiles.

"You guys about done?" Ben asked.

The Hispanic said, "We should have it wrapped up in another few minutes. Sorry we're taking so long."

"Don't worry about it." Ben grabbed his briefcase and tossed in some papers. "Will you be needing to get back in here again?"

"No. You won't be seeing us again."

Chapter 18

Luke had been to Ben Wilson's home only once, for a holiday party a few years earlier, but he immediately recognized the distinctive two-story Craftsman structure. Ben lived in an older area of the city known as Windsor Square, and his home made a statement with its bold red and brown tones and bright yellow trim. It looked like the type of house in which Hansel and Gretel might live.

The Lakers game was playing loudly in the background when a teenage girl answered the front door.

"I'm Dr. McKenna."

She gave him an empty stare and smacked on a golf-ball-size piece of gum, then turned her head inside and screamed, *"Dad, it's someone for you."*

The door swung open and her arm shot out as if it were spring-loaded, pointing down a mahogany-paneled hallway toward the rear of the house.

As Luke stepped through the doorway, a gigantic bloodhound charged through the entry hall and raced out the front door.

From the back of the house, Ben's voice called out: "Don't let the dog out."

The girl shrugged at Luke, swung the door closed, then trotted up a broad stairway.

He found Ben in the kitchen, standing against the island counter mashing potatoes and wearing a ridiculous lavender apron. The pathologist said "Howdy" with a drawl that stretched the word into a lengthy greeting.

Luke had met Ben's wife only in passing at that holiday party and couldn't remember her name. "Where's your wife?"

Ben pointed through the wall with the potato masher. "Lakers game. From the sound of things, it ain't going too well."

As if on command, a woman's voice pierced through a mahogany door at the far end of the kitchen. *"Wake up and get into the game. You guys are playing like a bunch of wusses."*

Ben's daughter charged through the kitchen with two other gangly teenagers in jeans and halter tops. "Tell Mom—I'm taking her car."

A tangle of bony elbows and knees scurried out the screen door.

Ben opened his mouth as if to say something, then shrugged instead.

His wife's voice called out again. *"C'mon, you morons! You're leaving the lane wide open."*

Ben's head retreated into his shoulders. "We best leave Charlie alone in her misery."

"Your wife's name is Charlie?"

Ben grabbed a pair of barbecue tongs and led Luke out the back door. "Short for Charlotte."

"Ah, I see."

Ben turned on him. "I know what you're thinking, and you're wrong."

Luke spread his palms, brimming with innocence.

"I like tarantulas," Ben insisted. "They're beautiful creatures."

"Of course they are."

"So I named one after my wife. What's wrong with that?"

"Not that this discussion isn't important in its own right," Luke said as they stepped over to a brick-mounted barbecue grill, "but did you get a look at those lung slides?"

"Yep." Ben scratched his nose with the tongs, then pointed them at Luke. "Like that little girl Alice said, it's gettin' curiouser and curiouser. That boy's airways, particularly the smaller airways leading into the lung, looked like a tornado hit 'em."

"Sepsis?"

"Doubt it. The epithelial cells lining the smaller airways were mostly gone. *Poof*. The few cells that were left had shriveled nuclei, as if they were in the process of dying."

"Couldn't you see that in sepsis?"

"This wasn't sepsis—at least, not bacterial sepsis. The white cells—they were all lymphocytes. No neutrophils to speak of, hardly any macrophages—none of the white-blood-cell types I'd expect to see if this was sepsis."

"A leukemic infiltrate?"

"Not likely. If this was a typical leukemic infiltrate, I'd expect to see blasts. But I didn't find any." Ben turned a steak. "But I haven't told you the kicker."

"What?"

"Like I said, the airways were all shot to hell, but the lung tissue itself, the alveoli, were virtually untouched. The air sacs looked normal. Whatever this was, it attacked just one type of cell—the epithelial cells lining that boy's airways."

"Then why couldn't we ventilate the patient? If the lung tissue was spared, how'd he die?"

Charlie erupted inside the house. *"Open your eyes, guys. Ever heard of passing the ball?"*

"Fluid and debris," Ben said while handing a tray to Luke. "Here. Hold this."

"Fluid and debris? I'm not following."

"Lemme back up a step," Ben said. "I said the alveoli looked normal. What I should've said is, the tissue *itself* looked normal. There was a thin layer of fluid and debris in the alveoli—think of it as a soupy mix lining the inside of the air sacs. Probably leftover fragments from the cells in the airways, the cells that'd been destroyed. The dead tissue probably just followed gravity and drifted down into the alveolar air sacs."

Luke rotated the platter as Ben loaded it with steaks.

"You were able to push oxygen into the boy's lungs," Ben continued, "but it couldn't get through the fluid layer that was covering the inside of the alveoli. The oxygen never got into his bloodstream. That's probably what killed him. Like putting a plastic bag over someone's head."

"Except this was inside his lungs."

"Exactly. And his body wasn't responding, or didn't have time to respond. I'd have expected to see some sort of war going on down there but I didn't. The alveoli should've been crowded with macrophages trying to haul away the cellular debris, but I didn't find many." Ben pointed at the door. "It's getting cold. Let's take our little chat inside."

Luke followed Ben into the kitchen, placed the platter on a kitchen counter, and the two of them went into the living room.

"Any idea how this ties into the boy's pancreatic enzymes being elevated?"

"Nope." Ben stooped to set some logs in the fireplace.

Luke stood at the front window, glancing up and down the street. "So, what's your best guess? What caused the boy's death?"

"I don't *have* a guess at this point. You got something attacking this boy's airways while leaving the lung tissue alone. Doesn't look like an infection—at least, no infection I've ever seen. Maybe some kind of autoimmune re-action, but again, I've never seen anything like it. That's about all I can tell you."

"So, unless the blood cultures turn up something, we're at a dead end?"

Ben stuffed a wad of newspaper under the logs. "Maybe not."

"What do you mean?"

Ben lit a match and touched the flame to one end of the paper. "You asked me to call the coroner about what happened with the autopsy, remember?"

"And?"

"I called him 'bout an hour ago, just before you got here." He stood and brushed his palms. "Turns out he's the one that was talking to the consulate. He didn't really add anything to what we already know—"

"So how does that help us?"

"Just hold on," Ben said. "So, the coroner and I got to talking about this case and I tell him about these lung findings. He's one of the brightest bulbs I know. I was in-terested in his opinion, ya know?"

Luke nodded while staring out the front window. There was a dark van directly across the street from Ben's home, and two cars parked ahead of it. Neither of the cars was a Ford Mustang.

"It turns out," Ben continued, "that the coroner had a case with similar lung findings—a Jane Doe case. It was a few months back."

Luke turned to the pathologist. "A woman?"

"A young girl."

"Did they ever identity the body?"

"He doesn't think so," Ben said. "Oh, and by the way, the only similarity with our boy seems to be the lung tissues, so don't get your hopes up. He was sure their girl didn't have leukemia. Like I said, it's a long shot, but I think I'll stop by and take a look at what they have."

"When?"

"Sometime tomorrow, probably. I have to call the M.E. who's handling the case, arrange a time."

"Good. It so happens I have nothing to do tomorrow." Luke turned back toward the street. In the relief of the dim streetlights, it looked as if the van's side doors were ajar.

Ben gave an exaggerated sigh. "I knew I was going to regret telling you about—"

"Do any of your neighbors own a van," Luke broke in. "Blue, or maybe dark green?"

"A van? What're you talking about?"

Headlight beams from an approaching car painted the van's length with a pale swath of light. The van's side doors were open—just barely, no more than a few inches. The gap narrowed to a sliver as the car passed.

Luke bolted for the entry hall, threw open the front door and ran outside.

The van had already pulled away from the curb with its lights off and was accelerating up the street when Luke reached the stoop of Ben's front lawn.

"*Son of a bitch,*" he whispered breathlessly.

Calderon was two blocks from Ben Wilson's home when his cell phone rang.

"Yes?"

"You sound out of breath," Mr. Kong observed.

"McKenna spotted me. I had to break off surveillance."

"Everything okay?"

"Yeah. Tell me about that young woman doctor—Callahan."

"A cab just dropped her at the international terminal," Mr. Kong said. "Do you want me to follow her, see if I can get on the same flight?"

"No. I need you here," Calderon said. "But call down to the project site. Send a team out to that clinic. It's time to take care of this problem."

When Luke arrived home two hours later, he drove a quarter mile past his home before making a U-turn and retracing his path. There were seven vehicles parked on his block, and he lingered as he passed each one. He knew his in-your-face countersurveillance methods would gain him nothing, but he did it anyway to vent his anger.

He had downplayed the incident with Ben, saying only that the van had looked suspicious. Ben's overly indulgent head nods had only confirmed that Luke's explanation didn't pass muster, but he wasn't ready to tell *anyone*—even Ben—that Lloyd Erickson had hired a private investigator to snoop around and meddle in his life.

Even more troubling, though, was the possibility that someone other than the football player's P.I. had been parked outside Ben's home. It was a dark van that he had seen, not the blue Ford Mustang that Sammy had described to him. And if Sammy was right—if Erickson's strategy was to paint Luke as an erratic character—why would the investigator waste his time following him into a quiet neighborhood at night?

But if not Erickson's investigator, then who was parked across from Ben's home? A city like L.A. rendered the possibilities almost endless: car thieves, prostitutes and their johns, drug peddlers, garden-variety punks, and drunken revelers made up only the beginning of the list.

The LAPD was also on that list, but the possibility that he was a suspect in Kate's murder seemed farfetched, even after his ill-timed visit to her home. In any case, homicide detectives wouldn't have cut and run when he ran out of Ben's house.

By the time Luke finally pulled into his driveway, he was no closer to an answer, and growing tired of his own ruminations.

Maybe his father was right. Maybe he *did* overthink everything.

When he climbed the stairs to this duplex, he found a card stuffed into the doorjamb.

It was Detective O'Reilly's business card. Luke had completely forgotten about the detective after Ben's phone call that afternoon. A handwritten note on the back of the card instructed him to call O'Reilly's office tomorrow, after 7:00 A.M.

Luke glanced at his entry table as soon as he opened the front door. In the upper right-hand corner of his answering machine, a red *1* showed on the SAVED MESSAGES display: Kate's message.

The NEW MESSAGES display in the lower corner was also lit. It was flashing *1*. He pressed PLAY and listened as Detective O'Reilly asked him to return the call.

If it wasn't already ten-fifteen, he would call the detective tonight. The sooner they copied Kate's message, the sooner he could erase it. For a while, at least, he didn't want to think about her death.

A burst of raindrops clattered on the roof.

It rained all night.

Chapter 19

Someone steal your furniture?" Ben was standing in Luke's entry, looking through the archway into his sparsely furnished living room. "Or is this some sort of minimalist thing you got going here?"

Luke looked at his watch: 8:33 A.M. "We're going to be late for our meeting with the M.E."

Ben's gaze moved among several paintings on the walls. "Looks like you spend all your money on art. Are these all by the same artist?"

"Yeah." It'd been a long while since he had taken the time to appreciate the watercolors that his mother had painted.

"Nice. Sorta reminds me of New England," Ben observed.

Continuing the disconnected conversation, Luke said, "Nice buckle."

Ben was wearing an enormous oval belt buckle with a raised outline of Texas and some kind of gemstone in the shape of a star. It looked as if it probably weighed ten pounds.

His friend tilted the buckle toward himself and polished it with the sleeve of his shirt.

Luke jerked his thumb in the direction of the door. "Let's go."

They rode in Ben's recently purchased gold Cadillac Deville. Loretta Lynn was twanging from the speakers when, ten minutes later, they took the Mission Road exit on Interstate 5. Luke had pulled his sun visor down and flipped open the mirror, studying the vehicles behind them for tails.

He pulled a Mr. Goodbar from his shirt pocket and started unfolding the wrapper.

"Oh, no you don't," Ben said. "Not while you're sitting on gen-u-ine calf leather seats."

Before Luke had finished rewrapping his chocolate bar, they pulled into a parking lot adjacent to a plain beige warehouse-like building at the northeast corner of the L.A. County/USC medical campus—home to the Los Angeles County Coroner.

"Who're we meeting?" Luke asked.

"Some Indian fella with a long name."

The county morgue was not a place that many people visited by choice, and they found a parking space right next to the entrance. As they walked up the front steps, sunlight bounced off Ben's belt buckle and cast a bright reflection that Luke figured would scorch any insect in its path. A man walking down the steps sidestepped the beam of light as if to avoid injury.

When they reached the information desk, Ben pulled a slip of paper from his shirt pocket, tried three times to pronounce the scribbled name, then gave up and handed the paper to the receptionist.

A few minutes later Dr. Jainarayan Majumdar was leading them down a flight of stairs to the basement level. The deputy medical examiner had dark skin and spoke with a slight British accent.

"So," Ben said to their host, "do you have a nickname that won't break my tongue?"

Luke shot a look at Ben.

Ben responded with an argumentative twitch.

"Jay," the M.E. replied without a hint of offense. "Everyone calls me Jay."

Autopsy Room B-3 was at the end of a long hallway. The last time Luke had been in a morgue was during medical school. At the time, he couldn't fathom why anyone would choose this line of work. His opinion hadn't changed. The room was about the size of a large dungeon, and filled with death. Seven stainless steel autopsy tables stretched out along its length, each with generous amounts of floor space around it. A large meat scale hung above the center of each table. Every work area had two water faucets, and one of the spigots on each countertop had a hose wrapped around it. At the far end of the room, a long row of rubberized aprons hung from wooden hooks.

Four of the autopsy tables had occupants. Thick plastic sheets covered three of the naked corpses. The fourth was being disassembled by a pathologist or technician whose expression was as disinterested as his client's.

As Jay led them into a meeting room at the far end of the autopsy lab, Luke asked, "Is the girl's body still here?"

"No, no. It was interred several weeks ago,"

They took seats around a conference table.

"On the table in front of you are copies of our report," Jay said. "I don't know how much you know—"

"Just to be safe, assume we know nothing." Ben grabbed the report and started thumbing through it.

"Then let's start with a brief summary," the M.E. began. "This is a Jane Doe case, a girl we estimate to have been about eight or nine years old, based on her bone age. The body was found just outside the entrance to a small hospital, on one of those frontage roads that runs along the Santa Ana Freeway."

Jay handed a stack of eight-by-ten photographs to Ben. "Here are the pictures from the scene. Notice the way the body is propped up against a wall, in the sitting position. There were no signs of trauma, and it may be that whoever left her there was hoping someone would find her and take her into the hospital. Note the pattern of lividity—the blood had pooled on the underside of the buttocks and legs, the distal aspects of both arms, and the chin, which was bent forward and resting against the chest. All of this suggests to us—"

"That the girl was still alive when she was left there," Ben broke in.

"Exactly. It's anyone's guess, but we think it may have been a coyote drop."

Ben's left eyebrow arched. "A what?"

"A smuggler that brings illegals across the border," Luke explained.

"What tells you that she was an illegal?" Ben asked.

"Well, to begin with, she's almost certainly not a U.S. citizen. Her clothing was made from a non fire-retardant weave that's illegal in the U.S., and her underwear was stitched by hand with no elastic bands. I'm jumping ahead here, but she also had two intestinal parasites—ascariasis and trichuriasis—as well as widely disseminated trichinella cysts in her muscles. Of course, she could have picked up any one of those in the U.S., but all three? Not likely. She probably lived in a region endemic for those parasites."

Luke said, "I don't see how that gets you to the conclusion that a smuggler brought her across the border?"

"Just playing the odds," Jay replied. "It's rare that no one steps forward to claim the body of a young child, but we've had it happen with families that entered the country illegally, families that are afraid to go to the authorities."

"Any idea where she was from?" Luke asked.

"Phenotypically, her facial contours suggest a fairly pure Indian lineage—could be almost anywhere in Central or South America."

Luke thought about Josue Chaca. "Any tattoos on the body?"

"As a matter of fact, yes," Jay said. "On the lower abdomen, three small circles. We spoke with a forensic anthropologist about that—it's described in the report."

Ben handed Luke a picture of the corpse, then flipped through the pages of the report. "Here it is," he said. "It says, 'The location and gender suggest some kind of fertility symbol. These types of markings are occasionally seen among Mayan tribes in Guatemala, as well as Inca tribes in Peru and Ecuador.'"

Jay said, "Why do you ask about tattoos?"

"The boy I saw in our E.R.," Luke said, "had one on the left side of his chest, shaped like a crescent moon."

Ben was looking at the report. "I see that you looked for toxins."

"Yes, but we found nothing. Serum analysis, tissue analysis, hair analysis—all negative. In fact, just about everything we've looked for has been a dead end. We know that the mechanism of death was asphyxia, but the disease or injury that caused the asphyxia is still a mystery."

The medical examiner opened a folder of tissue slides and slid one into a projection device at the center of the table.

An image appeared on the screen. "The interesting findings were found on the microscopic exam—specifically, in the bone marrow, lungs, pancreas, and bile ducts. As you can see on this slide, the bone marrow is hyperproliferative, primarily lymphocytic precursors, and cellularity is very high—over ninety percent."

"What does all that mean?" Luke asked.

"This marrow is unusual in several respects," Jay said. "I'm still not sure what it is or what it means, but I can tell you what it *isn't*. It's not leukemia, and it's not a toxin—at least, none that I've ever seen. It's probably not an infection—viral, bacterial, and fungal cultures of the bone marrow were all negative."

"You can't test for everything," Luke said. "There've got to be some toxins that aren't included in your testing methods."

"That's always a possibility, but unlikely in this case. Let me show you a section of the lungs, and I think you'll understand." Jay removed one slide from the projector and replaced it with another. "This is a section of the upper airways, the trachea. As you can see, it's virtually normal." Again he changed slides. "Now we're looking at—"

"I'll be damned," Ben whispered.

"—bronchioles in the lower airways of the lungs. The epithelial cells—see, here? For the most part, they're gone. They're just not there."

Ben shot a glance at Luke.

Jay aimed a laser pointer at a specific area on the slide. "Now, look here. There's an overwhelming infiltration of white blood cells into the surrounding tissues—almost all lymphocytes. I didn't believe it at first, so I took several additional sections of lung. Every section of lung looks like this."

Ben leaned forward, grabbed an eyebrow, and started playing with it. "That's not artifact. That's real."

Jay nodded. "So Luke, getting back to your question about toxins, it's difficult for me to imagine a toxin that would spare the upper airways and selectively attack the lower airways. It's more likely that we're dealing with a biological agent of some sort."

"I assume you cultured the lung tissue?" Ben said.

"Yes. Lung cultures were all negative," Jay said. "Except for the parasites that I already told you about, the only infectious organism we found was in her nasal secretions. It was a garden-variety rhinovirus."

"This girl wasn't killed by a head cold virus," Ben said.

Jay reached for another slide. "This next slide of the alveolar lung tissue—"

"Let me guess. The alveoli have cellular debris in them, but no specific damage."

"How did you know that?"

"It doesn't take a genius to spot a goat in a flock of sheep. This is a carbon copy of our boy's lungs. Tell us about the pancreas."

"It's equally impressive." Jay slipped another slide into place. "This is a high-magnification view of the pancreas. There's a heavy infiltration of lymphocytes, just as we saw in the lungs. And note the cells that were destroyed. Again, this was a very selective process, analogous to what we saw in the lungs. Only the exocrine glands of the pancreas were destroyed. The pancreatic islet cells are virtually untouched. In my opinion, this also supports the theory that we're dealing with some kind of biological agent. A toxin, a poison, would have caused a more diffuse injury."

"You mentioned earlier that the bile ducts were also involved," Ben said.

"That's correct, and the damage is analogous to what you've seen in the lungs and pancreas. Only the bile ducts themselves were destroyed. The adjacent liver tissue was untouched."

"Have you surveyed any other morgues for similar cases?" Luke asked.

"We canvassed about ten coroners' offices—the larger ones between here and Dallas."

"And?"

Jay shook his head. "Nothing."

Ben asked, "Can I get some tissue samples to take back with me?"

"I'll sign out our slides to you."

"Good, but I'd also like to have a tissue block from each organ. I may want to do some special staining, and I'll need the tissue blocks to prepare my own slides from."

"We're not doing anything on this case right now," Jay said. "It's easier for me if I just give you the entire file— all of our tissues. You can return it when you're done."

Ben nodded.

Luke asked Ben, "Anything in particular that you're looking for?"

"Nothing that's worth a discussion at this point. More of a fishing expedition."

Jay said, "The truth is, we don't have the staff to go any further on this case. I appreciate any help you're willing to give us. I'd like to know what caused this girl's death. It's just one of those cases that gnaws at you."

The M.E. reached over and turned off the projector.

"Before we leave the building," Luke said, "there's one other thing I'd like to see."

Chapter 20

How did you know her?" Jay asked.

Luke glanced across the autopsy table at the M.E., then back at Kate Tartaglia's corpse. "She used to work at our hospital." The man didn't need to know any more than that, Luke decided.

The upper half of her body was exposed, a thick plastic cover drawn back to her waist. The back of her skull was propped on a wooden block, lifting her head and tilting it forward, as though she were taking in the room.

"I'd like to know what you find on her autopsy," Luke said.

"I'll have to run your request by the homicide detectives." The medical examiner's voice carried a hint of hesitation. "I'm already stretching the rules by showing you the cadaver. I hope you understand."

Luke nodded while studying two tightly grouped entry wounds on her chest and a black-rimmed hole in the center of her forehead.

"Those look like some well-aimed shots," Ben observed, saying aloud what Luke was already thinking.

"Yes, I'd say there's not much doubt about the cause of death," Jay said as he pulled the semitransparent covering back over Kate's head. "Life is full of irony, isn't it? Just last week I was speaking with Dr. Tartaglia."

Luke shot an inquisitive glance at the M.E.

"For the past four months," Jay explained, "we've been sending her blood samples. Part of some research study."

From behind Luke, Ben asked, "What kind of study were you working on?"

"I had nothing to do with the study itself," Jay said. "She wanted serum samples from Hispanics and Indians who were non-U.S. citizens. She was looking for a comparison group for some vaccine research."

Luke asked, "Did you send her a blood sample from the Jane Doe case, the one we were just discussing?"

"She met the criteria. So yes, I'm sure we did."

"There're a few more pieces to this story," Luke said to Ben as soon as they were outside the front door of the Coroner's Office.

Luke was carrying a cardboard box containing Jane Doe's slide folders as well as plastic cassettes with paraffin-encased blocks of her tissues. He set it down onto a waist-high brick newel at the top of the steps, then described for Ben his past relationship with Kate, her calls to the E.R. on Friday night, the planned meeting at Kolter's, and the missing e-mail she'd sent to him just hours before her murder.

The pathologist's eyes bounced between Luke and the box as he listened.

"So, think about it," Luke said when he finished. "Kate calls me at the E.R. on the same night that Josue Chaca arrives. Now, her name pops up in connection with a girl whose death looks strangely similar to the Chaca boy."

Ben's head rocked up and down like a slow-moving oil derrick, mulling the information.

"Ben, she had to know about *both* of these cases. It's the only explanation that makes any sense."

"And that whole thing about a research study?"

"I think it was a ruse," Luke said. "She wanted to know about the Jane Doe case, and to do that, she needed a Trojan horse—something to get her inside the Coroner's Office—so she concocted that story about a research project."

"If you're right, the question is—what was she up to?"

"Maybe she was trying to figure this out," Luke said, "just like we are. That would explain why she asked the M.E. for samples of blood serum. She was probably running her own tests on Jane Doe's blood."

"You're ignoring the other possibility. Maybe she already knew what'd caused the girl's death. Maybe Kate was a fox in the henhouse."

"I don't think so. She came looking for me, remember? Kate was upset—she had something she wanted to tell me."

But before she could do that, someone put two bullets through her heart and one through her head.

Luke studied his friend's eyes, to see if they revealed the same question that was gnawing at him. Ben's expression revealed nothing, and Luke wasn't going to proffer a macabre theory about Kate's murder—at least not yet. He didn't want to give Ben any reason to back away from their probe into the children's deaths.

He hadn't called O'Reilly yet. Just as well, Luke thought. Now he had a lot more to talk about with the detective.

Luke lifted the box. "Let's go." He swept the parking lot as they started down the steps. Nothing seemed out of place.

Ben pulled a remote device from his pocket and aimed it at his car. The Cadillac chirped as Luke reached the bottom of the steps.

"Forget about taking me home," Luke said. "I want to stop by my father's office and ask him what he knows about Zenavax. I'll grab a cab home from the hospital."

As they were getting into the car, Ben said, "I may send some of the girl's tissue to Caleb Fagan."

"Immunology? Why?"

"I'd like Caleb to do some subtyping of the lymphocytes. Find out what type of critters we're dealing with." Ben pulled out of the parking lot and merged into traffic on Mission Avenue. "It's not too often that I run across something I haven't seen before. Seeing it twice in the same week tells me there's a connection. The lymphocytes are what connect these two cases. They weren't just hanging around to pass the time."

"So, where does this hunch lead you?"

Ben tapped the steering wheel a few times. "Does anything strike you about the organs that were destroyed by . . . whatever this is?"

"Which case—the boy or the girl?"

"Both," the pathologist said. "You got the small airways in the lung, the pancreas—"

"Cystic fibrosis?"

"Yep. And we know that Jane Doe's bile ducts were involved. There's not much other than CF that selectively attacks those organs."

"How do you explain the bone marrow findings? And the fact that Adam Smith made a diagnosis of leukemia in my patient?"

"I can't explain it. But I wish I'd gotten a look at that boy's marrow myself."

"You think Adam got the diagnosis wrong?"

"Have to admit, that doesn't seem likely," Ben said. "The girl's bone marrow looks reactive—like it was defending itself, responding to an attack. I can't imagine

Adam confusing that with leukemia. But the similarity between these two cases is too much to ignore. I'm also gonna have Genetics run a chromosome profile on the girl's tissue to look for CF."

Luke nodded, but his thoughts were drifting elsewhere. From the moment that Josue Chaca arrived at University Children's, Barnesdale had been lurking in the shadows of this mystery. The man had thwarted every attempt to investigate the boy's death.

"Don't tell anyone about our visit to the coroner," Luke said. "And if anyone in Immunology or Genetics asks why you want these tests done, make something up."

"I'm way ahead of you. This time I'm not leaving a trail for Barnesdale or anyone else to follow."

Ben slowed to a crawl when, ten minutes later, they passed Kolter's Deli. "I might as well let you off here, in front of the hospital—save you a walk from the parking lot." He let a bus go by, then made a U-turn and pulled alongside the curb in front of the hospital.

The chaos erupted just as Luke opened his door.

A battered pickup truck filled with gardening equipment swerved in front of them, burnt rubber rising from its rear tires as it screeched to a stop. The passenger door flew open and a thin Latino man leapt from the truck with a small boy in his arms.

The boy's half-naked body was drenched in blood, his head flopped back. Blood was spurting from a deep gash in his right leg.

Another man leapt from the driver's seat and ran around the front of the truck, yelling, *Ayúdenos, por favor! Mi hijo, mi hijo!* His screams came between gasping breaths.

Luke had already jumped from the car. He grabbed the

boy, clasped his hand over the gaping wound, and laid him on the sidewalk.

Ben started running toward the hospital entrance. "I'll find a gurney and let the E.R. know."

"Do either of you speak English?" Luke's gaze shuttled back and forth between the two men. "Can you tell me what happened?"

One of the men mimicked the sound of a motor while holding his hands as though gripping a chain saw.

The boy was limp, his carotid pulse thready. Luke ripped off his own shirt and shoved it over the wound. The blood instantly soaked through and began seeping around his fingers. He glanced at the truck, saw a rope with a wooden grab-handle hanging over a lawn mower.

Luke jerked his head toward the rope.

The two men ran to the truck and frantically grabbed at things to the right and left of the rope, looking back at Luke for confirmation. On the third try one of them grabbed the rope and got a confirming nod.

Luke drew the cord around the top of the boy's thigh and wrapped the free end around the grab-handle. He twisted the handle like a corkscrew and a tourniquet took shape around the boy's leg.

He glanced around, hoping to see a nurse or doctor. What he saw was a growing crowd of bystanders, their faces struggling to find the right expression for their sickened curiosity.

He also saw a black town car idling across the street, its Asian driver staring intently at him.

"Outta the way. Clear a path." Ben and a nurse appeared on either side of a gurney, with a security guard behind them.

The emergency entrance was around the corner and down the block—the boy would bleed to death before they reached the ambulance bay. They loaded the patient onto the gurney and raced toward the hospital entrance with the guard jogging in front of them to clear a path.

Several onlookers gasped as Luke pushed the gurney through the hospital entrance, his forearms covered in blood. A middle-aged man swooned, his eyes rolling back as he dropped to the floor in front of the security desk.

Luke and his ragtag team sprinted toward the E.R.

Calderon connected a thin cord from his cell phone to the recorder, then pressed the PLAY button. A harmonic flutter distorted the distant-sounding voices:

"It turns out that the coroner had a case with similar lung findings—a Jane Doe case. It was a few months back."

"A woman?"

"A young girl."

"Did they ever identity the body?"

"He doesn't think so. Oh, and by the way, the only similarity with our boy seems to be the lung tissues, so don't get your hopes up. He was sure their girl didn't have leukemia. Like I said, it's a long shot, but I think I'll stop by and take a look at what they have."

Calderon pulled the wire from his phone and lifted it to speak. "Could you make out the words?" he asked.

The laser microphone had captured the minute window vibrations caused when sound waves—even whispered words—strike glass. A computer had done the rest, reconstructing McKenna's conversation with that pathologist by feeding the laser's return signal through specialized software. It was hardly high fidelity, but it had worked.

"I understood most of it," his client said. "So, now we know what happened to that girl."

She had been the only test subject who was unaccounted for, and while it seemed obvious that she might have crossed into the U.S. from Tijuana, Mexico—where the local police had found her parents' bodies—Calderon's men had failed to pick up her trail.

"It can't be a coincidence—the girl ending up in L.A.," Calderon said. "Tartaglia probably had something to do with her getting here."

It annoyed him that he hadn't thought to ask the Tartaglia woman about their stray test subject.

After a medical examiner in Tijuana had contacted Guatemalan Health Ministry officials—one of whom was on his client's payroll—about two deceased persons with Guatemalan identifications, Calderon had dispatched a team to retrieve the bodies and search for the girl. The local Mexican officials were only too happy to release the disease-ridden corpses to the custody of his men, who were carrying IDs and paperwork furnished by their mole in the Health Ministry. Before returning to Guatemala, his team had spent a week looking for the girl before finally deciding that the trail had gone cold.

"McKenna and that pathologist were at the Coroner's Office this morning," Calderon said.

"Ironic, isn't it—that Dr. McKenna led us to the girl?"

"I'm telling you, McKenna and that pathologist are too persistent. They're gonna keep pushing this until we stop them." Calderon worked to keep the emotion out of his voice. His had to be the words of a dispassionate professional.

"I'm afraid you're right."

Calderon hadn't felt this kind of rush since he buried a knife in the neck of the German banker, the one whose house his mother had cleaned, the one whose bed his mother had shared—though not of her choice. He was twelve years old at the time, and though his mother had never told him, Calderon knew that he was killing his father.

He fingered the scarred remnant of his left ear. The piece he'd lost in that struggle had always been a source of pride—his rite of passage into manhood.

"How do you propose that we handle this?" his client asked.

His client had an unhealthy need to meddle in things he knew nothing about. "Leave that to me." Calderon clenched his fist and watched the veins in his forearm fill with blood.

"We need to do this in a way that doesn't draw attention to ourselves," his client said. "Let's give the police something else to focus on. Here's what I want you to do . . ."

"Here." Ben tossed a towel to Luke.

Luke glanced down at himself. He was a bloody mess.

He wiped a red sheen from his arms and hands while watching the trauma team finish its work.

The boy was going to live. They had poured four units of fresh frozen plasma and six units of blood into him, and in a few minutes the team would take him up to the O.R., where vascular surgeons would patch together his blood vessels.

Luke threw the towel in a corner and grabbed a green scrub shirt from one of the cabinets.

"Let's go." He pulled the baggy green top over himself as he and Ben walked out of Trauma One.

"Escort this doctor out of the building!"

It was Barnesdale, and he was standing in the corridor with a pair of hospital guards flanking him. He pointed at Luke like a monarch ordering a beheading.

Luke looked from one guard to the other. The shorter one standing to Barnesdale's left shrugged apologetically.

Ben erupted in a fit. *"Well excuse us all to hell, you jackass! Do you have any idea—"*

"Is there a problem?" someone down the hallway asked.

Everyone turned.

Detective O'Reilly walked toward them, his left hand holding out a badge for the guards to peruse. His right hand held what looked like two VHS tapes.

Chapter 21

And you're certain you left the hospital at 10:05 on Friday night?" O'Reilly asked.

"I wasn't looking at my watch," Luke said, "but that sounds about right."

The questions had started as soon as O'Reilly pulled him away from the confrontation with Barnesdale. The cop had offered to drive Luke home—he wanted to hear Kate's phone message, he said—but by the time they reached the hospital lobby, their conversation had become yet another inquiry into Luke's whereabouts and movements on the night of her murder.

There was something conniving about the detective.

"And then," O'Reilly said, "you walked across the street to Kolter's Deli where you were supposed to meet Dr. Tartaglia at ten-fifteen."

"Yes."

"And you didn't drop by your office, or stop to talk to anyone, on your way over there. Right?"

"That's right."

"In fact, you showed up at the restaurant a few minutes early." O'Reilly nodded at his own observation as they passed through the exit doors. "And that matches what the restaurant owner told us. He remembers you walking in while he was making change for a customer, and the only register transaction between ten and ten-twenty had a time stamp of ten-thirteen."

Luke stopped suddenly. "What's your point, Detective?"

O'Reilly took another step before breaking his stride and turning back to Luke. In an awkward motion the detective stuffed the VHS tapes into his right side coat pocket while pulling a notepad from his left pocket.

"Well, I walked from your Emergency Room to Kolter's this morning." The cop flipped open his notebook. "It took me four minutes and twenty-seven seconds. That leaves a little over three and a half minutes that I'm trying to account for."

"Are you telling me that I'm a suspect?"

"Just trying to account for everybody's whereabouts, Doc. Chasing after the little details—that's ninety percent of my job. I'm sure you can understand that."

"How many of the people you deal with account for every minute of their time?"

"Most people don't. That's a fact."

"You can count me among them."

Luke had already guessed that the VHS tapes were from the hospital's security cameras, but he wrongly assumed that the homicide investigator wanted to examine the video segments that showed Kate being carried into the E.R.

O'Reilly was going to use the tapes to pinpoint the moment that Luke had left the hospital.

"Detective, why don't we talk about this *after* you've looked at those tapes. That is, if you have any more questions at that point."

The cop let a small smile play at the corners of his

mouth while scanning his notes, as though acknowledging Luke's deduction.

O'Reilly asked, "What about that e-mail she sent you—you ever find it?"

"Not yet. Someone in our MIS department is searching for it."

The detective pointed at a plain blue sedan along the curb. "Let's go."

They were nearing the car when Luke tried to shift the conversation to his discoveries at the Coroner's Office. "There's something—"

The detective's cell phone was against his ear almost as soon as the first ring tone had faded. "Yes."

O'Reilly was circling around to the driver's side when he stopped dead.

"He what?" the detective shouted.

Luke turned to find the cop's eyes locked on him.

The man's imperturbable mask was gone, replaced by a scowl.

"The answer is no!" O'Reilly flipped his phone closed without saying good-bye. His stare remained fixed on Luke.

"You wanna explain what the hell you're up to?" he said.

Luke was still trying to cipher the question when O'Reilly pressed on: "At some point, were you planning to tell me about your little trip to the morgue to see Dr. Tartaglia's body?"

"Kate wasn't the reason I went there. At least, not directly."

O'Reilly showed him a doubtful expression.

"And you'd already know about my visit to the morgue if we hadn't spent the last five minutes rehashing my movements on Friday night."

The door locks popped up. "Get in," O'Reilly said.

As soon as they were seated inside the car, the detective gave him an *Okay-let's-have-it* look.

Luke gave him a brief summary of the past two days: Josue Chaca's death and its aftermath; the lingering questions that prompted Ben's call to the coroner; the eerie similarities between Jane Doe and the boy; and how, against any reasonable probability, Kate's name had turned up in connection with the dead girl.

But he didn't tell O'Reilly about Ben's planned testing of the girl's tissues, figuring the cop's first instinct would be to seize the evidence and sequester it. Until he had a better read on the detective, he wasn't going to risk that possibility.

"If I'm right about Friday night," Luke argued, "if Kate was coming to talk about one or both of those children—then I think the timing of her murder is awfully suspicious."

O'Reilly looked out at the street for several seconds. When his gaze finally returned to Luke, the detective was shaking his head.

"What are you doing, Doc? You trying to run your own investigation here?"

"I'm trying to find some answers, Detective."

"That's *my* job. With all your education, I'm sure you're smart enough to know that there're laws against interfering with a police investigation."

"I haven't interfered with—"

"It's not too often that people I question in a murder investigation ask to see the autopsy report of the murder victim. It's even less often that they tamper with physical evidence by examining the body."

"I didn't touch the body. Ask the medical examiner."

"Believe me—I will."

Luke stared at traffic for a long moment, waiting for the tension to dissipate.

It didn't.

"I'm not trying to get in your way, Detective. This whole thing started because I wanted to know why a patient of mine died. Doesn't the fact that it led back to Kate Tartaglia seem odd to you?"

O'Reilly turned over the engine. "This Guatemalan boy—"

"Josue Chaca."

"Yeah, him. Was that the kid that died about the same time you got into the fight with Lloyd Erickson?"

"What does that have to do with anything?"

The detective regarded him for a moment. "I interviewed Dr. Barnesdale this morning. He told me about your suspension."

"So?"

"Well, I understand there's a question about that boy's death—something about a delay in treatment. Dr. Barnesdale seems to think you were knocking heads with Erickson when you should've been busy saving that boy's life."

A surge of anger reached out and grabbed Luke like an unseen riptide.

"Did Barnesdale also happen to tell you—*he* signed the papers that prevented us from doing an autopsy? If he's so concerned about why that boy died, ask him why he did that."

"Ever occur to you that he may not wanna know? Maybe he was saving your ass, and his hospital, from a lawsuit."

"That's not why he—"

"Doc, unless you're ready to tell me that that kid was murdered, I don't really care why or how he died. I conduct homicide investigations—that's what I do. Whether you screwed up or not with that kid isn't my concern. Neither is the bad blood that seems to exist between you and Barnesdale. But anything you do that interferes with my investigation *is* my business."

O'Reilly glanced at his rearview mirror, and then pulled into traffic.

"Doc, you're playing in the wrong game here. Stay clear of my investigation."

"What was I supposed to do?" Barnesdale said. "Tell the detective that he couldn't have the tapes?"

"You could have put him off for a day, called your attorneys, wrung your hands about patient confidentiality—whatever," the Zenavax CEO said. "At the very least, you should've *talked* to me before handing over those tapes."

Henry wasn't going to tell the CEO how he had almost heaved his breakfast when security paged him to the lobby, telling him that an LAPD homicide detective was there looking for him.

"What did you give him?" the CEO asked.

"Exactly what he asked for. He wanted the tapes from two of our security cameras—the lobby, and a corridor that leads to the E.R. I don't understand what harm that could do."

"That's the problem," the CEO said. "There are too many things you don't seem to understand."

After Barnesdale hung up the phone, several seconds passed before the realization blew through him like a sudden wind.

His hospital's security tapes held secrets that had unsettled the CEO.

Henry had a weapon.

"So where's her message?" O'Reilly asked.

"I don't know," Luke said, "but it was here this morning. I checked."

They were standing in Luke's entry hall with the front door still open, staring down at his message machine. There was a *0* showing in the SAVED MESSAGES display. Luke pressed the playback button again.

Nothing happened.

"Did you change tapes?"

"It's a digital machine. There *are* no tapes." He showed the detective a mask of calm, but his temper was flaring. Someone had invaded his home.

"You think, just maybe, you could've erased it?" O'Reilly asked the question like a parent leading his child to the inevitable conclusion.

"That's not what happened. Somebody else erased it."

Luke walked the length of his short hallway, peering into the kitchen and then his bedroom before returning to the entry. Anyone with the inclination could easily have broken into the seventy-year-old structure, but a thief would have taken the machine—not erased its messages.

"Any sign of a forced entry?" O'Reilly asked.

"Nothing obvious."

The cop had undoubtedly noticed that his TV and computer sat undisturbed in the living room.

O'Reilly scratched his head in an exaggerated manner. "I was never very good at riddles, Doc. You wanna let me in on how you think that message disappeared?"

There were only two possible explanations, and both seemed utterly implausible. Erickson's P.I. could have accidentally erased the message while snooping around Luke's apartment, but what could the guy have been hoping to find? Given the kind of money that Erickson could afford to pay, it didn't seem likely that he'd hire an investigator who was both reckless and stupid.

The other possibility brought back the disquiet that had visited him several times in the past few days.

But how could anyone have even known about her voice mail? And why would anyone—even Kate's killer—risk burglarizing his apartment to erase a message that contained little more than a passing mention of some e-mail that never got to its recipient?

Neither explanation made any sense, and Luke's credibility with O'Reilly was already stretched to the point that it probably would not withstand the shock of another bizarre-sounding theory.

"I don't have an answer to your question, Detective. But there's one thing I'm certain of—when I left here this morning, Kate's message was still on that machine."

O'Reilly blew out a long, slow breath while staring at the voice-mail recorder. "You mind if I borrow this thing for a few days?"

"Go ahead."

Luke figured his machine was going to spend the next few days on a lab bench where forensic technicians would try to recover the erased file containing Kate's message.

As soon as the detective left, Luke was going to engage in his own search and retrieval mission. Whoever erased Kate's phone message did so without leaving any conspicuous signs of a break-in. People with those kinds of skills could also tap a phone line or plant a listening device.

Chapter 22

The microbiology lab had always reminded Ben of a temple—its rows of lab benches lined up like pews, butane flames burning like candles, techs wearing hairnets in place of skullcaps. Invariably, though, the sanctified atmosphere would dissipate as he reached the far end of the lab, where its would-be high priest, Elmer McKenna, resided.

Ben knocked on the door frame as he entered the older man's office.

"Be with you in a minute," Elmer said, his back to Ben, his tone a swirl of distraction. He was bent over his credenza, peeling away layers of paper from a sloping mound of documents, searching for something.

From the looks of things, whatever he was hunting for might take hours to find. Waist-high piles of computer printouts formed a battlement along the walls of his office, and his desktop—covered with medical journals, stacks of unopened mail, and a half-eaten crumb roll— looked like the termination point of a landslide.

"I'll come back later," Ben said.

Elmer turned suddenly. "Oh, Ben. No, no, have a seat."

Wilson lifted a pile of medical charts off a chair and sat. "What are you looking for?"

Instead of answering, Elmer pulled a Post-it note from

his computer monitor and read it. "Uh-oh. I forgot to call Medical Records."

"I'm sure they're as shocked as I am," Ben said. "Listen, I need to ask you about Kate Tartaglia."

"Oh." Elmer's eyes suddenly came into focus. "What a horrible thing that was, what a tragedy."

"Yep." Ben allowed a moment, then said, "Actually, Luke wanted to come himself and talk to you about this, but he managed to get his keister booted out of the hospital. So I'm here in his place."

Luke hadn't given him an explicit instruction to visit Elmer, but that's how Ben interpreted his friend's remark when, as Luke was walking away with the detective, he called back: "Say hi to my dad when you see him."

"What sort of a mess did my son get himself into this time?"

"It's a long story, but it'll blow over," Ben said. "Listen—we were hoping you might know what Tartaglia was involved in at Zenavax. What sorts of projects was she working on?"

"The last time I talked with Kate was the day she quit her position here. But the infectious disease community is pretty small—things get around. Why are you asking?"

"Luke and I think she may have known something about two deaths we're looking into." Ben gave Elmer a sketchy synopsis and explained how Kate's name had turned up in connection with the dead girl.

Elmer nodded. "Luke asked me to check if I'd received any e-mails from Kate. Does this have anything to do with that?"

"Bingo." Ben gave him an expectant look.

"Well, she didn't send any messages to me." Elmer scratched his nose. "You know, sometimes my son has a way of making things more complicated than they are."

"Maybe so, but I think these deaths are worth looking into. One of the cases—the boy—came from our clinic in Guatemala. Can you think of any link between Zenavax and Guatemala?"

"Malaria."

"As in malaria vaccine?" Ben asked.

Elmer nodded.

"You gotta be kidding," Ben said. "Zenavax is working on a malaria vaccine too?"

Elmer's malaria vaccine project was well known to everyone at the hospital, in part because his approach was so unorthodox—turning mosquitoes into allies by using them to administer the vaccine to humans. The idea wasn't likely to catch on anytime soon in economically privileged regions like North America and Europe, but among developing countries with small budgets and high mortality rates from ongoing malaria epidemics, the prospect of malaria-fighting mosquitoes was seen as a godsend.

The medical basis for Elmer's vaccine was elegantly simple, and scientifically daunting. He had set out to create a genetically modified version of the ubiquitous Anopheles mosquito—one that was inherently resistant to harboring malaria parasites and endowed with saliva glands that produced a malaria-like protein. The altered female mosquitoes would inject the protein while feeding on their human prey. To work, the protein had to fool the human immune system into believing that it was being attacked by the real thing—a malaria parasite.

Initially, most thought Elmer's quest a fool's errand. That is, until he, Caleb Fagan, and the now-deceased geneticist with whom they worked initially, Dr. Kaczynski, proved their hypothesis with primates.

That was five years ago. Now, after successfully completing human testing, Elmer and his Chinese partners were gearing up to produce and deploy his mosquito in quantities sufficient to meet the already vigorous demand for his creation.

"Zenavax hasn't formally announced their malaria vaccine project, but like I said, word gets around. Rumor is that they've just recently started testing it."

"Sounds like they're at least a few years behind you," Ben said. "When do you go live?"

"Another few months. We're testing the breeding cycle now, making sure that successive generations of our mosquito retain the modified genetic code. If we don't encounter any unwanted mutations—and we haven't so far—we move to full-time production at a facility in southern China."

Ben's thoughts came back to the reason for his visit. "Well, one thing I can tell ya for sure—these two children didn't die from malaria. The girl's liver and spleen were normal." Ben described the lung findings of Josue Chaca and Jane Doe. "I'm looking for something that attacks the lungs, pancreas, and bile ducts."

"Sounds like cystic fibrosis."

"I had the same thought, but CF alone wouldn't explain what happened. The pathology looks nothing like cystic fibrosis. Whatever those children died from caused a massive lymphocyte response. The tissues were saturated with lymphocytes."

"Hmmm." Elmer puckered his mouth, as if trying to shape a thought with his lips.

"What?"

"Oh, it reminds me of something that happened when I was working on the first prototype of my flu vaccine. Lost a whole batch of mice to a runaway autoimmune reaction. The mice literally devoured themselves. The tissues looked just like what you're describing, crammed full of lymphocytes. It turned out that they were Killer T-cells. My prototype vaccine activated some sort of self-destruct signal."

"Apoptosis?"

Elmer nodded.

Apoptosis. Nature's version of suicide. It was still a poorly understood frontier in medicine. In some circumstances, human cells damaged by infection, mechanical injury, or toxins announced their injured state to the body's immune system, which promptly induced those cells to commit suicide. Specialized lymphocytes—Killer T-cells—served as the messenger of death in those instances, triggering the process of self-destruction.

"Strangest thing I ever saw," Elmer said. "Eventually, Caleb Fagan and I came up with a way to down-regulate the reaction, to get the immune response we needed without triggering the self-destruct signal."

"Is it possible that Zenavax is encountering a similar problem with their malaria vaccine?"

"Hardly likely. We published our findings at the time—this was before I'd ever heard of Zenavax. The solution to the problem is available to anyone that wants to read about it."

"You're not helping me much here, partner."

Elmer shrugged. "Well, if you're looking for a connection between Zenavax and those two deaths, look for an alphavirus."

"What do you mean?"

"Zenavax built their entire company on that virus, and there's still a lot of untapped potential for using alphaviruses in future vaccines. In fact, it's an ideal vector for a malaria vaccine. It promotes the kind of immune response you need to protect against malaria. What I'm saying is, if there's a connection between Kate and those children, you're likely to find the remnants of an alphavirus in their blood. Run some antibody titers, take some tissue and—"

Elmer's gaze moved toward the door just as Ben heard the knock.

"I need to talk to you." It was Caleb Fagan, and he was looking at Elmer. "I just got out of a Risk Management Committee meeting."

What nitwit had come up with the euphemism, risk management? Ben wondered. The term was nothing more than a roundabout way of referring to litigation and malpractice lawsuits.

Caleb continued without bothering to excuse the interruption. "Henry's favorite attorney was there, the same jerk that rallied the troops against Luke. Of course, the Erickson thing came up and this guy tells us that the hospital is already negotiating with the football player's attorney. Long story short—Barnesdale's going to write a letter to the Department of Children and Family Services saying he reviewed the E.R. records for Erickson's daughter and found no convincing evidence of child abuse."

"What?" Ben said. "Why the hell's he gonna do that?"

"Because when Henry does that, DCFS will probably drop the investigation," Caleb explained. "And if that happens, it sounds like Erickson will drop whatever legal action he was planning against the hospital and medical staff."

Ben said, "I always thought that DCFS called their own shots, period."

"I'm sure they do," Caleb said, "but look at this from their point of view. The only thing that DCFS has to go on are Luke's E.R. notes describing some bruises. There's no other evidence—no X-rays, no pictures of the bruises, no statements by anyone. And supposedly, Erickson has no history of abuse in the past. Luke's the only person stepping forward on this, and his scuffle doesn't make him look very objective. If someone here at Children's— someone with credentials like Barnesdale—looks at the records and says there's little or no evidence of physical abuse, it weakens the case even further. DCFS is probably going to drop the investigation."

"Oh, Lord," Elmer said.

Caleb said, "That's not the worst of it, I'm afraid."

Luke's first instinct was to ignore the ring of his cell phone, but when he saw his father's office number on the display, he took the call.

It turned out that his first instinct had been right.

Luke took slow deep breaths as his father, Ben, and Caleb recounted Barnesdale's manipulation of the DCFS investigation.

But when Caleb said, "From DCFS's perspective, I guess it's a losing proposition," Luke's temper boiled over.

"Next time," he said, "when Erickson's daughter comes in with a crushed skull, someone will just have to explain to her that she was a losing proposition."

There was a long silence before Caleb said, "There's one more thing. The attorney told us that Erickson would probably still file a lawsuit against you, Luke, as an individual. You're not included in the deal they struck."

Ben jumped in to state the obvious: "Barnesdale and his weasely attorney are hanging you out to dry."

"If you haven't already done it," Caleb said, "I'd find yourself a lawyer."

Chapter 23

It was just after three-thirty when Luke finally pulled out of his driveway and headed down the hill. He had allowed just enough time to get to Kolter's.

His father and Ben had called back minutes after his discussion with Caleb. When the first words out of Ben's mouth were, "We need to talk about Zenavax and Guatemala," Luke had cut him off and suggested a four o'clock meeting at the deli.

He hadn't wanted to have that discussion while searching for listening devices in his apartment.

Luke's knowledge of listening devices was limited, and more than a decade old. His only advantage was that any potential adversary would likely assume him ignorant of such methods. He had first searched his apartment for signs of tampering—dust layers missing from the upper edges of wall-mounted electrical plates and picture frames, scuff marks and nicks on the screws that held together his phones and appliances, and indentations in the carpets where table legs had been moved.

After completing his visual inspection, he turned over every piece of furniture, pulled out every drawer, examined every light fixture, unscrewed every wall-mounted plate, ran his hands over the trim of each door, and removed the covers from both phones.

He had found nothing.

As he turned onto Los Feliz Boulevard, Luke was wondering if the turmoil in his life had stirred his suspicions to an unhealthy level. It was then that he spotted the vintage blue Ford Mustang in his rearview mirror. It was three cars behind him, in the right-hand lane.

Luke immediately called his father and, without giving a reason, postponed their meeting until five-thirty. Ben was grumbling in the background when Luke thumbed the END CALL button.

If Erickson's P.I. wanted something to put on film, he was going to give him an eyeful.

When Luke walked into the tae kwon do studio ten minutes later, Grand Master Kim and two other black belt instructors were stretching on the mat. After coming to America fifteen years ago, Kim had established his studio in L.A.'s Koreatown. He had come with a reputation for unforgiving standards and debilitating workouts, qualities that contributed to his coaching Korea's national team to three consecutive world titles.

Luke was a regular at the studio, training there no less than once a week. He had never bothered to test beyond a second-degree black belt, but after almost twenty-five years of martial arts, he could hold his own against any of the instructors and had a standing invitation to train with them.

The stale odor of dried sweat—an olfactory signature that he had acclimated to long ago—filled his nostrils as he walked through the rear entrance. He bowed to Grand Master Kim, receiving a curt nod in return. It was as enthusiastic a welcome as anyone ever received from the man.

Luke took his place on the canvas mat and began contorting his body into peculiar postures that most people could achieve only with the help of equipment found in a medieval prison. While stretching, he spotted the Mustang through the floor-to-ceiling glass window. It was parked halfway up the block on the opposite side of the street.

Fifteen minutes later he was several minutes into a sparring match with the younger and burlier of two instructors. Luke executed a spinning crescent kick after blocking a jab—a centrifugal spray of sweat launched from his head like water from a blowhole. A volley of kicks and punches ensued, but none landed. Both combatants backed off and eyed each other, looking for an opening between feints.

When Luke determined that he'd given the P.I. sufficient time to capture the action through a telephoto lens, he lowered his guard just long enough for the other black belt to catch the side of his head with a glancing blow.

Luke held up his hand to acknowledge the hit and bowed to his sparring partner, then lifted a cupped hand to his mouth and pointed to the back of the studio—an exaggerated thirst gesture meant for the miscreant across the street. Once in back, he tore off his sparring uniform, threw on jeans and a T-shirt, and ran out the rear door. He worked his way around the perimeter of the studio and scouted the street from behind the corner of the adjacent building. The Mustang was parked ahead of four other cars on the other side of the street.

A UPS truck drove up the street. As it passed, Luke bounded across the road, using the truck to conceal himself. He crouched behind a parked car.

He advanced one car at a time, straddling the curb, hoping the Mustang's driver didn't bother to check his passenger side mirror. He didn't.

When Luke reached the rear of the Mustang, he stood

upright. The thick-necked P.I. twitched at the sudden apparition, threw his camera on the passenger seat and grabbed for the ignition.

But Luke was already there. He reached across and grabbed the man's right wrist, twisting and flexing it in one violent motion. The man yelped, his ruddy complexion reddening like a beet.

"Ahh, shit! You're breaking my goddamned wrist."

"Tell your client that I don't like being followed."

"What the hell are you talking—"

"I don't like having to explain myself either." Luke twisted the man's wrist again, to the accompaniment of a high-pitched scream. "Just so we can move this discussion along, let's assume that you know what I'm talking about now. Okay?"

The man grimaced. *"Okay, okay, I'll tell him."*

"Tell Erickson, if he has business with me, he knows where I live." Luke's rage swelled like a tidal surge. "If I see you again, I may have to break your neck, and then I just might break your client's neck. Who knows—I'm unpredictable."

Luke reached in with his free hand and patted the man's coat. He felt the bulge and removed a 9mm Glock. He popped the magazine, racked the slide, and checked the chamber to confirm that it was empty. Then he threw the gun onto the passenger seat.

Next, he lifted a single-lens-reflex camera with an enormous telephoto lens from the man's lap. He let go of the man's wrist and fiddled with the camera until he found a button that opened a side panel. He popped out a digital memory card, then dropped the camera back onto the man's lap.

"Get out of here," Luke said.

The P.I. picked his keys off the floor with his left hand while nursing his right arm. In a clumsy motion, he placed the key into the ignition and started the engine.

Luke stepped back, tapping the palm of his hand with the 9mm cartridge.

The man gunned the engine and used his left hand to work the gears. "You're nuts, pal. Erickson's right about you. You're a lunatic." He ground the gears a few times, then peeled away.

Luke watched gray contrails spew from the Mustang's dual exhausts as it squealed around the corner at the end of the block. Just as his eyes were about to turn away, they fell on an Asian man sitting in a black town car at the end of the block—the same man he had seen earlier, outside the hospital.

Before Luke finished accelerating into a full run, the Asian had pulled away and was gone.

Megan awoke to groans from the bus's transmission as the driver downshifted through what seemed an endless number of gears.

After leaving behind the frantic street traffic of Guatemala City, she remembered the bus wending its way around miles of tightly curved roads and finally emerging onto a highway. Then sleep had overtaken her.

She checked her watch. It was just after 4:00 P.M. She had slept almost three hours.

Megan stretched her arms above her head and took in the countryside of Guatemala. Orange sunlight bathed the waist-high grasslands outside her window. The meadows were spotted with clearings, each shaded by a tree that looked as old as the land itself. Aboveground roots the size of sewer mains reached out like claws from the base of each tree, holding steady the massive trunks that stretched a hundred feet into the air and opened into rounded canopies as large as circus tents.

Beyond the grasslands, towering peaks covered in dark shades of emerald stood like a remembrance of a civilization that was once great.

When her bus rounded the next curve, the mountains suddenly gave way to open sky. They drove onto a massive steel-cantilever bridge and crossed high over a half-mile-wide expanse of river.

The bus's brakes squealed as they came off the behemoth structure and rolled into a narrow and crowded strip of bustling commerce. A barrage of painted signs announced the town's name: RÍO DULCE.

She had come prepared for the rainy season, wearing a lightweight olive-colored poncho she had hoped would blend into the local scene. Looking around, there wasn't another one in sight. Lots of Nike T-shirts and hats sporting the insignias of various NBA teams, but no ponchos.

The clinic manager's sketchy itinerary instructed her to catch any one of several buses going to her final destination, a small pueblo named Santa Lucina. When she disembarked the bus, a horde of ticket vendors thrust themselves at her, waving their hands and yelling destinations as though trying to come up with the answer that would win them her fare.

Twenty minutes later she was on the road again, heading northeast toward Santa Lucina. For this leg of the trip she sat in a weather-beaten minivan that listed heavily to the right. The owner had replaced the factory seating with four crude bench seats that left everyone's knees propped just under their chins. Nineteen passengers were crammed into the creaky vehicle, including five small children who were sitting on the scuffed metal floorboard.

Megan glanced around. No one seemed the least bit bothered by it. The women sat pensively, wordlessly, never turning to one side or the other. There was a quiet gracefulness about them. The men were as jovial as sailors returning home to port. Several appeared to take a keen but respectful interest in the only gringo among them.

As soon as the red sun dipped below the horizon, Megan noticed for the first time that there were no lights along the roads. They had left the highway about thirty minutes earlier, and the load of passengers was gradually thinning as the driver made seemingly random stops along mostly dirt roads. Megan could finally see the windshield from her seat in the center of the minivan, but almost nothing was visible in the darkness beyond the thirty or so feet illuminated by the minivan's dim head-lights, one of which flickered whenever they hit a rut in the road.

A sense of tedium set in as the bus rose and fell over a series of undulating hills. Occasionally she caught a glimpse of the thick vegetation that lined the sides of the roads. But mostly her view was of complete darkness, in-terrupted occasionally by lights from distant villages.

By 7:00 P.M., Megan and a family of three were the only remaining passengers. All of them were going to the last and final destination on this road, Santa Lucina. As the minivan rattled its way over the crest of a particularly steep hill, the driver pointed off to the right. There was a fire burning in the distance.

When they started their descent down the hill, Megan saw a few, then several, dimly lit dwellings scattered across the valley on either side of the blaze.

"Is that Santa Lucina?" she asked in Spanish.

The driver nodded, but she could see that his attention

was still fixed on the fire. He stopped the van in the middle of the narrow road, and for several minutes everyone watched in silence as the flames rose and fell to their own eerie rhythm. She thought of her father battling an inferno in his final moments.

Her chest suddenly felt heavy and her breathing quickened. It was a ritual she endured every time she saw a burning structure.

The woman made the sign of the cross and drew her daughter closer. "*Mi Dios,*" she said.

Megan asked, "What's over there?"

The husband replied, "Our church. Oh, let it not be the church."

The woman looked at her husband and said, "Also, the clinic."

Chapter 24

Calderon crouched and dug a finger into the soil, which was still wet from the previous night's rain. He scanned the area to either side while listening for sounds that did not belong on a southern California hillside at night.

His toes were beginning to cramp—the Nike running shoes were a half size too small—but the exhilaration coursing through him overrode the pain signals trying to reach his brain.

He would reach the site in another five minutes, at exactly 8:00 P.M. Everything was well within his mission plan.

He grabbed the knife from his ankle sheath, turned the bottom of his right shoe toward him, and cut two small grooves in one corner of the rubber sole. Then he stood, took two heavy steps, and looked back at the tread prints he'd left in the wet ground.

Satisfied, he started moving along the edge of the path again. There was always a chance he'd run into someone up here, but with temperatures in the low forties—far below the tolerance of most southern Californians—he doubted it. If that happened, he'd spot them long before they saw him.

In Los Angeles, it seemed that even the criminal element was soft. Violent crime plummeted whenever the temperature dipped below fifty degrees Fahrenheit. What he was about to do, though, wasn't a crime in any real sense of the word. He was exterminating a spineless insect.

He reached the spot along the ridge of the hill that he had scouted that afternoon. It wasn't an ideal perch; the scrub brush wasn't as thick as he would have liked, but it would do. Calderon's skin tingled as he studied the target area downslope from his position. It was a two-story Spanish-style house nestled against the hillside, with a deck extending from the second story. Of course, that description also fit almost every other home in the area.

He had an unobstructed view of the structure. A little over two hundred yards. Not a particularly difficult shot.

He placed his black nylon bag on the ground and unzipped it without a sound. Before touching anything inside the bag, he donned latex gloves. His customized bolt-action Barrett 98 rifle was a prototype that had "disappeared" from a gun show in Atlanta. It was one of only five in the world, and the only Barrett model that used .338 Lapua Magnum rounds. The Lapua rounds could pierce through half-inch glass or a standard wooden door with virtually no displacement of the bullet's trajectory.

When Calderon had left L.A. for a new life in Guatemala, it was the only weapon he put into storage. He wouldn't have risked shipping an experimental, unregistered weapon that Customs agents might discover, and he couldn't part with it, so he'd stored the rifle together with other specialized equipment unique to his profession. He knew this weapon better than most men know their wives. Blindfolded, he could assemble or knock it down in less than forty-five seconds, and he could put one of its bullets through a buttonhole at three hundred meters. What he liked most, though, was the penetrating power of its .338 rounds.

The stock and barrel were a bit heavy, but sturdy. The longest piece of the rifle assembly was its 27.7-inch barrel. Disassembled, the rifle and scope fit easily into a large backpack.

Calderon's cell phone vibrated. After the second pulsed vibration, he put the phone against his ear. "Talk to me."

"McKenna just pulled out of the hospital parking lot and turned north," Mr. Kong said. "Should I follow him?"

"No." Calderon punched a button and ended the call.

He crawled fifteen feet through an opening in the brush, then edged over several feet to his right, taking the position he had chosen earlier that day. Now he was invisible to anyone who might stumble onto the dirt trail behind him.

In almost complete darkness, he silently and expertly assembled the rifle, taking his time as a mental video of the shot played over and over in his mind. Calderon closed his eyes and allowed the image of a perfect shot to penetrate the rifle barrel as he screwed it into the stock. The mechanics would flow naturally if his weapon understood the job it had to do.

Next, he took the Leupold Mark 4 scope from his bag, placed it over the top of the rifle, listened again, then turned it ninety degrees and heard the satisfying snap as it locked in place.

Calderon dropped into the prone position and unfolded the bipod. He held the rifle in a firing posture and peered through the scope, pivoting from left to right, sighting targets at random: a man walking his dog on the street below; an acorn-shaped finial atop a wooden fence; an oval address plate on the front wall of a home across the street. He quartered each target in turn and waited for his finger to squeeze the trigger.

He stopped and listened before pushing the ten-cartridge magazine into the gun stock. When he was satisfied that the area was clear, he popped it into place. It gave back a metallic click.

Finally, he turned to where he hoped his prey would appear. Light streamed from three second-story windows and a French door that opened onto the upper deck. He wouldn't get an open-air shot tonight. His target would remain inside. As long as the gutless coward passed in front of a window, he was dead.

Doing it this way grated on Calderon. He wanted to see the shock and pain in his quarry's eyes. He wanted to watch the man squirm when he gutted him like a fish. He wanted to talk to the sonofabitch as he bled to death.

But his client had insisted. It had to be done this way. His client had said that there were considerations outside of Calderon's purview—*What the hell did that mean?*—things he simply had to accept for the good of the project.

Calderon pulled a clear plastic Baggie from his rucksack, used tweezers to remove a paper wrapper from it, then placed the wrapper in a sprig of weeds about six feet from his position. Then he pulled a small roll from his bag, untied the ends, and unfurled a long, thin rubber pad on the ground. It wasn't for comfort. The insulated padding would protect him from the air-ground temperature gradient that tightened muscles and caused the body to flinch at the worst possible moment.

Once everything was ready, he scanned the target area again with his spotting scope, stopping occasionally to check the wind direction and velocity.

Nothing moved in the target area. No human forms, no telltale shadows.

Calderon checked his watch. If his quarry didn't show within the next ten minutes, he would have to abort the mission.

He exhaled heavily and stretched his muscles.

At that instant headlights appeared in his quarry's driveway.

Luke ignored the sudden and narrow break in Walter's curtains as he started up the steps to his duplex. His landlord's prying nature didn't concern him.

What did unsettle him was the etherlike miasma that was engulfing his world.

He had spent the past two hours sitting in Kolter's with his father and Ben, speculating about potential connections between Kate and the dead children. They had come up empty-handed. While Zenavax's work on a malaria vaccine provided a conceivable link—it was possible that the company might conduct clinical tests in that region of the world—his father had pointed out that it was an exceedingly thin thread. Guatemala was an unlikely choice for such testing given the relatively low incidence of malaria in that country.

Luke had gotten lost in the esoteric exchange between his father and Ben about alphaviruses, but ultimately that theory led to a similar dead end. The selective tissue destruction evident in both children looked nothing like the indiscriminate and generalized toxicity that Elmer had encountered with his initial flu vaccine prototype.

Just as Luke reached the top of his steps, a rattling sound interrupted his thoughts.

He spun around and saw his neighbor positioning a trash bin alongside the curb.

Luke turned back, unlocked the front door, and shoved it open with his shoulder.

Calderon dropped onto the rubber mat and lifted the butt-stock of his rifle. He set the magnification to give him a full view of the target area, and aligned his eye with the optical axis of the scope so that his pupil was exactly two and one-quarter inches from the eyepiece.

A figure flashed across the southernmost window.

He placed the stock of the rifle back down on the mat and grabbed the infrared range finder, focusing on the window frame where the figure had appeared a second ago: 211.2 meters.

The room looked as if it had a depth of about three meters. He set the range on his Leupold to 212 meters. He wouldn't take the shot if the target was standing more than one meter from the window.

Calderon drew the stock of the rifle into his shoulder again, cinched the sling tighter, and reacquired the window with the crosshairs. He worked the windage and elevation knobs on his scope. When everything was set just as he wanted it, he ran the bolt, waggled the fingers of his right hand in a piano-playing motion, then placed his right thumb through the hole in the butt stock.

He sighted the window again, fighting to restrain the exhilaration that raced through him like an electrical current.

His breathing slowed. Rolling waves of relaxation slackened the muscles in his torso and arms. When he was calmed, he looped his index finger inside the trigger guard.

Once inside, Luke quickly checked the carpeting under all three windows along the rear of his apartment, the naps of which he had brushed smooth before leaving that afternoon. Then he went into the kitchen and inspected the mat under the door that led onto the upper deck.

There were no shoeprint outlines.

The disquiet in his world was turning into a low rumble, but he knew that part of the turmoil was of his own making. In one brief moment he had done more to help Erickson's legal case than anything the football player's minions could have plotted. Now they had a witness who could testify to Luke's aggressive nature.

He had played right into their hands.

But what troubled him even more was the realization that he had *wanted* to hurt Erickson's investigator. Old instincts—violent instincts—had overtaken him without a struggle. He had allowed it to happen, and that truth didn't sit well.

Luke walked into the living room and clicked the TV remote as he dropped onto the couch. He started flipping through the channels in search of a distraction.

The back of his quarry's head appeared in the lower right-hand corner of the window.

Calderon took slow, shallow breaths as he edged his crosshairs to the left and quartered the target. His heartbeat slowed to a crawl.

Conditioned responses took over—his finger tightened around the trigger. The neural circuit between his right eye and trigger finger had long ago fused into a reflex. He simply allowed it to happen.

It didn't happen fast enough. The head disappeared from his scope.

He blew out a chestful of air. *"Shit."*

Luke edged forward on the couch when the close-up shot of a female gymnast replaced the newscaster's image.

The camera panned back just in time to catch a perfectly executed dismount from a balance beam.

He thought of Megan, and his mind's eye played remembered images of her smile during their better times together.

Then he thought of her in Guatemala, and a vague chill passed through him.

He stood and started walking the room.

Calderon blinked away the dryness in his eyes.

What happened next seemed surreal. The sonofabitch got up from his couch, paced the room a few times, then stood at the window looking directly at him, as if to say, *Okay, take your shot.*

This he did exactly 0.8 seconds later, right after he placed the crosshairs squarely on the bridge of his target's nose.

The bullet left the end of the barrel traveling at 915 meters per second and reached its destination just three thousandths of a second after the target turned his head to the left.

Calderon felt the kick of the rifle at the same moment he realized his shot was off target.

But only by an inch. A hole appeared just above his quarry's right eye. An instant later the body slumped out of view.

He watched, spellbound. A wave of satisfaction washed over him as a thousand shards of glittering glass hung in the air for a long second. They quickly gave way to a large spatter of dark red tissue on the far wall.

Chapter 25

M egan stood along the haggard bucket brigade, passing and receiving water-filled vessels to persons on either side of her. No one was in a hurry. The battle to save the clinic had ended hours ago; the fire had won. Extinguishing scattered embers was all that was left to do.

The acrid stench of smoldering wood filled her nostrils. The memory of her father—his musty scent when he walked through the front door after battling a blaze— flitted in her mind.

She took in the town for the first time as a bloom of orange sunlight rose in the eastern sky. A sea of corrugated tin roofs reflected the first light of day, revealing the mostly squalid wooden shacks that collectively formed the pueblo of Santa Lucina. The town was an island of human deprivation floating in an ocean of lush tropical vegetation. The surrounding hillsides were thick with vines and plants that wrapped around one another in some sort of botanical mating ritual. The sounds of jungle life poured over her in cascading waves.

Villagers who had come to the clinic site were either helping to smother the last remnants of the blaze or busy clearing debris. Children hardly old enough to hold a bucket worked alongside their parents. Everyone seemed to approach their work with a quiet fortitude, as if this type of thing was simply a part of their everyday lives.

A short, stout man wearing an Atlanta Braves baseball cap walked toward Megan through the charred rubble, his shoes making wet crunching sounds with each step. It was Paul Delgado, the clinic manager.

He said, "Not much of a welcome, I'm sorry to say."

Megan shrugged while reaching out to take a plastic water jug from the man standing next to her. Their wrists collided and water splashed out, drenching her shoes. It wasn't the only part of her that was wet. Even at sunrise, the air was thick and pasty.

Paul glanced at her shoes with the impassive expression of someone accustomed to physical discomforts.

"Listen," he said, "I've already arranged transportation back to Guatemala City for everyone."

"We're leaving?"

"Not me—you." He took off his cap, ran an arm along his forehead, and looked back at the rubble. "Nancy, my wife, and I have gotta stay here and rebuild this place."

"That's it? Just the two of you?"

"Joe Whalen and Steve Dalton are making a trip out to the *aldeas*—the villages. But except for that—"

"I'll go with them." She knew both men. Joe Whalen was a second-year pediatric resident at University Children's, and Steve Dalton was one of the Attendings at her hospital.

"Listen. Normally, we don't even go to these villages. They're too far away, in the middle of nowhere. Conditions are tough out there—what you might call primitive. The only reason Steve Dalton's going is that he knows the area, and well"—he looked around at the charred timbers—"there's not much for him to do around here."

"Seems I'm in the same boat."

Paul appeared to study her. "Steve's a pretty rugged guy. He knows what he's getting into."

"And Joe Whalen?"

Megan knew Joe well. His physique bore a striking resemblance to pudding.

"Look, I appreciate your enthusiasm, I really do," Paul said. "But I don't know if we even need *two* doctors on this trip, let alone *three*."

She grabbed another pail of water from the man standing on her right and passed it to a small boy. "They going anywhere near Josue Chaca's village?"

"How do you know about him?"

"I was working in the E.R. the night he arrived at the hospital."

"Hmmm," he said. "Well, Steve and Joe are going to some *aldeas* not far from there, but not his. The people who live in Josue's village—Mayakital—they tend to keep to themselves. We've never been invited, and now I suppose it's not likely that that'll happen anytime soon."

Paul picked up a scorched metal emesis basin from the ground and slapped it against his pant leg. "Tell you what. You can stay with Nancy and me for a few days. After that, if you still wanna go out to the *aldeas,* there'll be other trips."

He started to walk away.

"I'm not going to change my mind."

He turned back to her. "Well, if your mind's made up, then grab your things and come with me. Steve and Joe are heading out in about thirty minutes."

Ben came off the elevator and plowed through foot traffic on the fifth floor hallway like a tractor in heat. He didn't want Elmer to hear the news from some cop showing up at his office door.

Sweat was running down his neck by the time he found the elder McKenna standing with a group of interns and residents outside one of the patient rooms. They were in the middle of morning rounds, the daily procession around the ward during which the house staff discussed each patient with the Attending physician.

When Ben reached the periphery of the group, he waved his arms at Elmer.

The elder McKenna held up a finger and mimed the words, *Give me a minute.*

One of the interns—his badge said CHEWY NELSON, MD—wiped the last remnants of a jelly doughnut from his lips and began his case presentation. "The next patient is a five-year-old girl, ce-e-e-eute as a button but a real crankmeister. Her illness began five days ago with the on-set of a fever and cough . . ."

Ben cleared his throat loudly.

Elmer held up a finger and nodded.

". . . the patient's X-ray showed a right lower lobe pneumonia, and we started her on IV Cefuroxime. She's been stable off of oxygen, no fever in the past twenty-four hours, and we're thinking of sending her home today."

Elmer said to the assembled group, "Let's go in and see her."

Ben reached for the back of his neck and shook his head.

The room was dark. In the near bed, a cage-like struc-ture held a young toddler who was sleeping, his diapered bottom protruding into the air. In the far bed, a young girl was sitting up, working the knobs on a handheld gadget that adjusted the tilt of the bed and controlled the TV hanging from the ceiling. She scrupulously ignored the white coats and stethoscopes encircling her.

Ben tried a whispered shout. "Elmer, I need to talk with—"

"Good morning," a woman moaned from the dormitory-style day bed located just under a window. The vinyl covering groaned as she brought herself upright and showed the group her wingspan with a slow stretch.

The young girl was now using the controller to sample TV channels, taking in a two-second glimpse of each station, then moving on to the next.

"Sorry to wake you," Elmer said. "Are you Lisa's mother?"

Nodding, she asked, "Is everything okay?"

"Everything's fine. In fact, we're thinking of sending your daughter home today."

"Mommy, the hop-sital," the girl announced.

"Yeah, honey, we're at the hospital," said the mother.

"No, Mommy. *Look*. The *hop-sital*," the girl insisted, pointing at the TV.

Heads turned casually to the TV, which showed a reporter standing on the grassy lawn in front of University Children's. The girl feverishly worked the volume control.

"*. . . and when paramedics arrived at Lloyd Erickson's home last night, they pronounced him dead at the scene from a gunshot wound to the head.*"

The in-studio announcer asked, "*Any word on suspects at this time? Have the police said anything about a possible motive?*"

The reporter in front of the hospital said, "*Our viewers may recall a bizarre incident that occurred here at this hospital a few days ago. One of the doctors allegedly attacked Mr. Erickson, and we've since learned that the doctor involved in that incident was Luke McKenna, an Emergency Room specialist here at University Children's Hospital. The police will say only that Dr. McKenna is a person of interest in the shooting death of Mr. Erickson.*"

Ben shot a glance at McKenna.

Elmer's eyes were trying to blink away his confusion.

"Does the hospital have any comment about this?" the announcer asked.

"As you know, we're still working to get the details on this breaking story. So far, no comment from the hospital. As soon as we get any more information, we'll let our viewers know. Jane, back to you in the studio."

"Now let's go to our Sky-Seven unit, which is flying over the victim's home in the Hollywood Hills . . ."

"Wonderful," Megan muttered. The lower third of her right leg had just disappeared into a mud-filled rut.

The trail they had followed for the past four hours was nothing more than a vague strip of thinned vegetation. Clefts and crevices pockmarked the path and it was still soggy from a midday rain shower. Runnels of red clay coursed around slickened rocks and settled into what were, for the most part, shallow puddles. The depression her leg had sunk into was more like a sinkhole.

Joe Whalen, the other resident, turned around. His cherubic face looked as if it was about to explode in laughter. A half second later it did just that, which is probably why he lost his footing, rolled down a small embankment, and landed face first in a mud pit. He emerged looking as if he belonged to a tribe of Aborigines.

Steve Dalton, the third member of their team, eyed Megan with an impish smile.

Megan twisted her foot, felt some give, and yanked up with all her strength. Her leg reappeared, but with only a wet sock on the foot.

"Oh, that's just *great*," she said. "My shoe's still in there."

Eddie, their Mayan guide who had a mule-like capacity for carrying things on his back, knelt down and dug both hands into the pit where Megan's foot had been. He came up with the truant footwear, poured out a quart of wet clay, and handed the shoe to her.

The guide smiled at Megan. It was a happy, contented smile in which his entire rounded face participated.

She reseated her shoe and asked in Spanish, "How much farther to the village?"

Eddie stared up the hill. "A little while more."

It was almost three hours and five water bottles later that they finally reached Ticar Norte, the first of four Mayan villages they would visit over the next three days. No one had spoken for the past hour. Only Eddie looked as if he had the energy to talk, though it seemed his habit was to speak only when asked a question.

She counted over twenty huts as they climbed the hill and entered the village. Most were thatched-roof dwellings. The sidings were made of crooked branches bound together with twine, and there were no doors or glass-pane windows—just bare openings.

Several sets of large dark eyes peered between gaps in the sides. An older woman stood placidly at the entrance of a hut, her bare feet as cracked and callused as tree bark. Two small children, one with a swollen belly that probably held parasites, peeked out from behind the woman's brightly colored skirt. Neither had a tattoo.

Chickens and roosters roamed the area freely. A pig scurried past with a stiff-legged gait while a pack of mangy dogs studied the new arrivals. They were the scrawniest dogs that Megan had ever seen, their eyes darting nervously in every which direction, with their backs arched as if poised against some unseen threat.

Eddie disappeared into a large wood-plank structure at the center of the village. It looked like some sort of meeting hall. Even from a distance of over twenty feet, Megan could hear the men speaking in a guttural language. She didn't understand a word.

"What language are they speaking?" she asked.

"Q'eqchi. It's one of the Mayan dialects," Steve said. "A lot of the villagers can't speak Spanish, or don't care to. That's where Eddie comes in handy."

Steve Dalton picked at the bark of an enormous tree under which the three of them were standing. "The ancient Mayans used the sap from these things to make chewing gum. It's called a sapodilla tree."

Megan was more interested in the villagers. A young boy, naked except for a pair of black rubber boots, stood like a stone in front of one of the huts and studied her. Standing next to him was a teenage boy wearing a *Terminator III* T-shirt. Inside the dwelling, a tiny woman was stirring the contents of an enormous black kettle over an open fire. Thick smoke billowed all around her.

For the most part, the villagers kept their distance.

"So when do we go to work?" she asked.

"I don't know," Steve said. "This is a bit strange. The villagers usually come out to greet us, give us something to drink . . . that sort of thing." He pulled at his shirt. Like hers, it was drenched in sweat. "But I've never been here before. Maybe their social customs are different."

Eddie emerged from the wooden structure. A pair of old men remained at the doorway, watching them.

"The village elders want us to leave," Eddie said in Spanish when he reached them. "They say that you have upset the spirit of the dead." He looked at each of them in turn, his expression telling them nothing. "I will show you."

He led them to the far side of the village, then down a gentle slope to a cluster of five huts. "There is an angry spirit in that hut," he said, pointing to a structure on the far right.

The small thatched dwelling looked no different from the others at first glance, but the disparity became evident as she studied it. The other huts had signs of life: the sporadic movements of children staring back at her through gaps in the siding, curls of smoke escaping from their doorways, small animals foraging for food.

The hut on the right was lifeless.

"I don't understand," Whalen said. "What are we supposed to be looking at?"

"That hut on the right looks like it's been abandoned," Steve said. "That may be where the dead person lived."

"Abandoned? Why?"

"Sometimes," Steve said, "the Mayans do it to escape a dead person's spirit. If they think the spirit is unhappy or angry, they stay away from the hut." He pointed at the hut's entrance. "See those bowls on the ground? They're probably filled with food, to appease the angry spirit. They want it to go to the next world."

"Can we go into the hut?" Megan asked Eddie.

The guide blinked nervously and looked at the ground.

Steve said, "I think you got your answer."

Megan glanced at a nearby hut. A young woman with angry eyes retreated into its interior.

It was Josue Chaca's mother.

Chapter 26

"We've been over this three times already." Luke leaned back on the rear legs of his metal-frame chair and shook his head at the water-stained acoustic ceiling tiles.

He had spent the past four hours in a windowless interview room at Parker Center, the downtown headquarters of the LAPD. The three homicide detectives seemed to study his every twitch, and the tone of their questioning had gradually shifted from conversational to interrogative. Two of the detectives, a man and a woman, sat opposite him at the metal-frame table. The third detective was standing behind the other two, leaning against the wall. It was O'Reilly.

"We just want to be clear about your answer," the female detective offered with palms outstretched. Apparently, she had taken the role of friendly cop.

Luke aimed his eyes at Lieutenant Groff, the burly man sitting across from him, who was clearly in charge. "How many different ways can I say it? From five-thirty to seven-thirty, I was having dinner with my father and another doctor named Ben Wilson at a place called Kolter's Deli. Afterward, I walked my father home—he lives a few blocks from the restaurant. I got back to my car about eight o'clock and got home about eight-twenty. The rest of the night, I was at home, alone. Ask my landlord. He probably keeps a closer watch on my schedule than I do."

"Actually, we *have* talked to him," the lieutenant said. "He can tell us only that you came home sometime before nine."

The one time Walter's meddlesome nature could have helped, Luke thought, and the man didn't bother to look at his watch.

Detective O'Reilly was mute, observing and listening as the other two detectives peppered Luke with questions covering every minute of the past two days—where he had gone, what he had done, who he had seen—pressing him to account for an endless stream of what seemed like meaningless minutiae.

Groff looked down at his notes. "Detective O'Reilly recently spoke with your supervisor, Dr. Barnesdale."

"He's not my supervisor."

Groff ignored the comment. "He says that when he told you about your suspension, you were—quote—'highly agitated.'"

"That's not how I'd characterize our discussion."

"He also says you described Mr. Erickson as a serious threat to his daughter."

"I probably said something like that."

"Did you feel you needed to protect the girl?"

"I didn't feel I needed to murder her father."

Groff looked at the other two detectives in turn, then came back at Luke. "Do you know a private investigator named Billy Sanford?"

"Probably."

"Probably?"

"Some guy was following me yesterday, taking photographs. I assume that's the person you're asking about."

"Right. Well, Mr. Sanford tells us that you physically

assaulted him. He says that your attack was unprovoked and that you threatened his client, Mr. Erickson."

"The guy was harassing me."

"How was he harassing you, Dr. McKenna?"

Luke could see where this was going. "Look, I wanted him off my back. He'd been following me. There was nothing more to it than that."

To Groff, there seemed to be much more to it than that, and he spent the next several minutes dissecting Luke's encounter with the P.I.

Throughout the exchange, Luke's attention bounced between the lieutenant's questions and the timing of the murder. From their questions, he guessed that Erickson had been murdered sometime between eight and eight-thirty. Was it just a coincidence that the killing occurred during a half-hour period for which he had no alibi? Or had the killer set him up? If the latter, there had to be an accomplice who was tracking Luke at the time of the shooting.

When Groff stopped to glance at his notes, Luke jumped into the pause. "My fight with Erickson was all over the news. Maybe your killer is using me as a decoy." Luke described his dual sightings of the Asian and how the man had run when spotted.

"So," Groff said, "this guy sees you attack Mr. Sanford, and then bolts when you start running at him." He glanced back at O'Reilly. "I'd say that sounds like a fairly normal reaction."

"He didn't look the least bit frightened, Lieutenant."

O'Reilly shifted his stance against the wall. "Describe this man."

"He was young, maybe thirty, and he was driving a large black sedan. I wasn't close enough to get a good look at him."

"Did anyone else see this man?" the woman asked. "Is there anybody that can corroborate your account?

Luke shook his head.

"Did you get a look at his license plate?" Groff asked.

"No."

The lieutenant bobbed his head from side to side in an exaggerated manner, as though wanting to make his skepticism obvious.

A moment later, as if responding to some unseen signal from Groff, the woman said, "Dr. McKenna, we'll probably have more questions for you later. Do you have any plans to leave the city in the next few days?"

"No."

Detective O'Reilly pushed himself off the wall and said, "I have a few questions."

"Be my guest," Groff said.

"Dr. McKenna, do you know what a 201 file is?"

"My military record."

"Yours arrived by fax this morning." O'Reilly picked up a folder sitting on a side table. "It makes for interesting reading. Says in here that you were a Navy SEAL."

Luke said nothing.

"Team Six." O'Reilly whistled a long note. "Isn't that one of their most elite units?"

Luke shrugged.

O'Reilly tapped his front teeth with a pencil while eyeing the report. "Seems odd that they shipped you off to the Pentagon as soon as you finished your training. I mean, I see here that you worked as an analyst in something called Naval Logistical Planning."

"If you're going to ask me about classified work, I want a military lawyer here."

Luke had no idea whether military rules trumped police investigative procedures, but it was the only card he had to play.

"No, nothing like that. I was just wondering why the Navy would go to all that trouble to train you as a commando, then stick you in an office at the Pentagon. It just seems unusual, that's all."

"Is there a question in there?" Luke asked.

Groff pinched the bridge of his nose. "I was wondering the same thing myself."

"Just curious. That's all." O'Reilly held up a hand. "I'm done."

After McKenna left the room, O'Reilly listened to Groff and the female detective compare notes from the interview. It went without saying that O'Reilly's opinion didn't count for much. He was a lowly detective second grade from Rampart Division, and they had brought him into the case for just one reason: He knew something about the only person who had made it onto their suspect list so far—McKenna. That information had bought O'Reilly a door-knocker role when Groff and his team descended on McKenna's residence at four o'clock that morning.

Word was that Groff had been a less than stellar beat cop, but he had the good sense to marry the daughter of a deputy chief several years ago. After that, it was a fast track to lieutenant in Robbery-Homicide. In the last hour, O'Reilly had seen nothing to dissuade him from the view that nepotism still ruled supreme at Parker Center.

The guy's mind was definitely a two-cylinder job. Groff had asked McKenna to submit voluntarily to a gunshot residue test. The doctor seemed only too happy to oblige, and why not? The shooter had used a rifle, which was much less likely to leave residue than a shorter barreled handgun. And unlike blood, gunshot residue was easily removed with soap and water. Even if McKenna was the shooter, O'Reilly was certain that their GSR test would show nothing. Groff had managed only to create an evidentiary record that could be used against them in court.

The lieutenant impatiently drummed the table with his fingers while the woman thumbed through her notes and summarized aloud some of McKenna's remarks.

After a minute or so, Groff said, "I know what the guy said. I wanna know what you *think*."

"The timeline's a little tight, but doable," she said. "It's about a fifteen-minute drive from the hospital to Erickson's home. Even if McKenna was with his father until 7:45 or so, he could've made it there and climbed up the hillside behind Erickson's place by eight-fifteen."

"Six minutes before the 911 call came in," Groff offered.

She nodded. "Erickson's next-door neighbor says she called a few seconds after hearing the rifle shot. So the shooting probably occurred no earlier than eight-twenty."

"How far is it from the shooting scene to McKenna's home?" Groff asked.

"About three and a half miles, due east. Depending on where he parked, it might've taken eight to ten minutes to climb back down the hill to his car, then another fifteen minutes to drive home. He could've been pulling into his driveway by 8:45, eight-fifty at the latest."

Groff plucked at his lower lip while seeming to think about the timeline. Then he said to the woman, "Tell me again about that rapist case you dug up."

"It was a few months ago," she said. "The rapist was targeting employees at McKenna's hospital. He went after young women. All the rapes happened within a few blocks of the hospital, all of 'em at night. It went on for a few weeks, until one night a patrol unit finds the guy buck naked, tied to a tree. I hear he looked like he'd been put through a wood chipper. He was barely alive. When he finally woke up, he copped to the rapes."

"The rapist—he give a description of the guy that mashed him?"

"Nope. Said he never saw it coming."

Groff said to her, "Find out if McKenna knew any of the rape victims." He turned to O'Reilly, "Whatta *you* think? You think McKenna did Erickson?"

O'Reilly came around the table and took a chair. "I don't see it. This guy's not stupid, and he's not nuts. He's not gonna whack Erickson right after getting into a brawl with him. It's too obvious. Besides, there's no shortage of people who hated Erickson's guts. There're probably a couple hundred people grinning at their TV this morning."

The detective's thoughts flashed on the football player's wife who, during questioning, had acknowledged her husband's longstanding physical abuse. O'Reilly couldn't fathom the tangled mess of emotions that she was grappling with at that moment.

Groff said to O'Reilly, "Tell us about the Tartaglia case."

O'Reilly had been waiting for the question. His answer would determine whether he remained on the Tartaglia murder investigation. Parker Center ruled by fiat in high-profile cases, and if Groff sniffed a likely connection between the murders of Erickson and Tartaglia, he'd yank the case out from under O'Reilly and assign it to one of the homicide teams at Parker Center.

"Last Friday night, Katherine Tartaglia drove to a restaurant across the street from University Children's for a meeting with McKenna. She was shot three times in a parking lot before she ever got out of her car. Someone—

probably the killer—took her purse, then went to her house and cleaned it out. Stereo equipment, TV, computer, jewelry—everything."

The truth was, O'Reilly thought his case was anything *but* a simple robbery-homicide. The shooter had tried to make it look like one, but there was one small detail that didn't fit. There wasn't a single computer CD or diskette anywhere in Tartaglia's house. She either didn't have any—which hardly seemed likely—or the killer took the time to scoop up a bunch of two-bit floppy disks and CDs used to store computer files, while leaving behind over seventy music CDs that were sitting right next to where the stereo had been.

More likely, in his mind, was a killer who knew exactly what he was doing. There was something on the floppies or CDs that the perp did not want anyone to see.

"We're still waiting on the M.E.'s report," O'Reilly continued, "but it's gonna show that she died from gunshot wounds to the head and chest, probably nine-millimeter. Nobody heard any shots, so the killer was probably using a sound suppressor."

What he didn't tell Groff was that the medical examiner had found no gunpowder residue around any of the bullet entry wounds. In fact, there was no residue at all on the body, which meant that the killer was probably standing at least ten feet away when he put two tightly grouped shots into the victim's chest and a bull's-eye in her forehead. This was no ordinary shooter.

"Does McKenna have an alibi?"

"He was in the restaurant waiting for her at the time of the shooting. The owner remembers seeing him there. I'm not done looking at that—I still have to view a security tape and pinpoint when he left the hospital. But so far, his alibi is holding."

O'Reilly hoped the omission—okay, lie—wouldn't come back to bite him. Records from Tartaglia's phone company confirmed that her mother had called her a few minutes before the murder. The mother remembered her daughter saying something about McKenna being nearby while they had their little mother-daughter chat. When pressed, though, the mother couldn't remember exactly what her daughter had said.

There was something squirrelly about McKenna— O'Reilly felt certain the guy wasn't telling them everything he knew—but that didn't necessarily make him a murderer. More importantly, he didn't have a clear motive for McKenna. At least, not yet. Tartaglia was about to come into a sizable chunk of money, but her will listed her parents as the beneficiaries.

There was one interesting lead relating to motive—at least his instincts told him so. Dr. Barnesdale had remarked that when Tartaglia left University Children's to join Zenavax, it had stirred a firestorm of controversy that proved embarrassing to Elmer McKenna. The younger McKenna had mentioned her working for his father, but not the controversy.

Similarly, Tartaglia's boss, a senior vice president at Zenavax, hadn't mentioned the rift when O'Reilly spoke with him by phone the morning after the murder. The detective wanted to have another discussion with the people at Zenavax—this time, in person—to probe that issue. He was also going to ask them about Tartaglia's research involving those autopsy cases at the Coroner's Office.

There were always a hundred loose threads in cases like this, threads that required more time than his caseload allowed. Adding to that frustration was the reality that most investigative leads ultimately went nowhere—like Tartaglia's voice-mail message, which the lab techs had determined was unrecoverable.

Things were going to move quickly now that Parker Center was involved. O'Reilly realized he had to move faster, or risk losing the Tartaglia case. He wanted to unleash their department's computer geeks to search for the e-mail that McKenna had claimed he never received. But that required a search warrant for the hospital e-mail server as well as McKenna's home and office computers, which meant coordinating his investigation with Groff.

Tell Groff too much, and the case would go downtown. Hold back, and he risked a disciplinary action.

"You think McKenna murdered Tartaglia?" Groff asked.

O'Reilly felt like a high-wire performer. "Of course, anything's possible, but I don't see a motive at this point. Tell you what—why don't I sync up with you guys on interviews and search warrants. That way, I won't trip over anything you're doing."

The lieutenant steepled his fingers under his chin in a pose that had all the earmarks of something he'd practiced in front of a mirror. "Sounds like a good idea."

The door opened and a blond-haired detective who looked like an advertisement for Gold's Gym walked into the room. "Thought you might want to hear about this," he said. "We got McKenna's prints from the medical licensing board in Sacramento."

"And?"

"The CSI team just checked it against the partial print we got from that candy bar wrapper near the shooter's location behind Erickson's house."

"Yeah?"

The blond man's mouth opened into a smile. "It's a match for McKenna's right thumb."

"So," Calderon's client said, "we can cross McKenna off our list of problems."

"If he was dead," Calderon countered, "I'd be more inclined to agree with you."

"It's better this way. So far, he and Wilson haven't found anything. It looks like they're chasing a mirage. But if McKenna was to turn up dead, it would give credence to his theories. The investigation would lead back to the Tartaglia woman, or worse—McKenna's father. We can't have that."

"What about that pathologist, Wilson?"

"For now, we continue to watch him. Thanks to your good work, he can't cough without us knowing about it."

Calderon had considered planting listening devices in McKenna's apartment, but ultimately decided against it. He didn't want to underestimate the cockroach. He knew that McKenna's suspicions would swell when he discovered the burglary and Tartaglia's missing phone message. He hadn't wanted to risk having McKenna discover a wiretap or bug.

"Tell me about the clinic," his client said.

"We still have a problem."

"Oh?"

"It isn't completely shut down. They're sending medical teams out to the villages," Calderon explained. "My men followed that Callahan woman and two other doctors to a village called Ticar Norte. That's not very far from—"

"If they get too close, you know what to do."

Chapter 27

Henry Barnesdale wiped away the moisture above his upper lip while scrolling down the list on his computer screen.

The security log for the hospital's Research Tower showed the badge number of every person who had entered the building last weekend. He was convinced that someone had gone to the bone marrow lab on the tower's second floor and substituted the Guatemalan boy's marrow with some from another patient. It seemed the only plausible explanation for Oncology's finding that the boy had died of leukemia.

That Henry had written the bogus diagnosis on Josue Chaca's death certificate hadn't mattered to him initially. All that mattered was that a diagnosis of leukemia would satisfy the medical examiner. The coroner had stopped the autopsy and released the body. A catastrophe had been averted. Zenavax's secret was safe.

But now he wanted to know how Zenavax had so easily manipulated and corrupted the postmortem investigation. He wasn't going to play the role of mushroom anymore—he had allowed the CEO to keep him in the dark for far too long.

His arms jerked like a puppet-gone-berserk when a wind gust rattled the tall arched windows behind his desk. A full minute passed before the pounding in his chest settled.

For Christ's sake, Zenavax was having people murdered. It was a good bet that Erickson's killing also figured into their scheme somehow. *I'm dealing with lunatics.*

Did the CEO really think Henry was naive enough to believe that Tartaglia's murder was mere happenstance, that the boy whose illness had caused an obvious panic at Zenavax had died of leukemia, and *not* from a lethal vaccine reaction?

What kind of idiot does he take me for?

What if the CEO suddenly decided that Henry was expendable? Now that Tartaglia was dead, Zenavax might consider him a loose end, a liability.

He needed some leverage, something he could use to protect himself. He knew how to play that game. Knowing the secrets of supporters and foes alike had served him well throughout his career.

The rules of the game were no different here, he reasoned.

He would start with the secret that was hidden in his hospital. It was *his* turf, after all, and he had the tactical advantage. He'd soon know how Zenavax had so quickly and efficiently put a stop to Josue Chaca's postmortem.

There were only two possibilities: Either the oncologist, Adam Smith, had knowingly falsified his examination of the bone marrow, or someone had switched bone marrow samples. The first possibility seemed completely implausible. Adam had no conceivable motive for participating in such a scheme. And unlike Barnesdale, who of necessity had mastered the art of feigned contempt, Adam's disdain for Zenavax had always seemed completely genuine.

That left the second alternative, but switching bone marrow samples would have required access to the lab as well as an intimate knowledge of his hospital's procedures. The bone marrow lab occupied the entire second floor of the Research Tower.

The tower was a freestanding structure, one of the newer buildings on their medical campus. Unlike the main hospital, where people could roam freely through most areas, the tower used a badge-swipe system to limit access to only hospital employees. Employees swiped their badges to gain entry into a locked front door and the security system recorded the date, time, and employee number of each person who entered the building. Once inside, employees again had to swipe their badges to activate the elevator, and the system recorded each floor they visited.

Between seven o'clock Friday evening, when Josue Chaca arrived in their E.R., and 6:00 P.M. on Saturday, when Adam Smith called him with the bone marrow results, twenty-seven people had entered the Research Tower. Henry scrolled to the column labeled FLOORS and clicked the icon. The computer resorted the rows by floor number.

Three employees had accessed the second floor during that twenty-three-hour period. The ID column showed only their badge numbers, not their names. The first person had entered the building at 11:43 P.M. on Friday, gone to the second floor, and departed at 11:57 P.M. The second person had arrived at 7:23 A.M. on Saturday, visited the second and eighth floors, then left the building at 9:30 A.M. The third person had entered the tower at 9:17 A.M., gone to the second floor, and stayed until 4:36 P.M.

Henry called Security and spoke with the senior officer on duty. As soon as the man pulled up the security database and navigated to the records that Henry was perusing, Barnesdale said, "Look at the second row—it looks like that person went to both the second and eighth floors."

He heard some key punches, then, "Yes, sir. That's what it—oh wait, no . . . that person only went to the eighth floor."

"How do you know?"

"On nights and weekends, the elevator returns to the lobby between calls. If that person stopped on the second floor, there'd be a separate entry, a later entry, showing them calling the elevator to the second floor and pushing *eight*. But that's not what it says here. It shows that employee entering the building, then pressing both numbers one minute later. The only other entry shows 'em leaving from the eighth floor. That person never got out on the second floor. Musta pressed a wrong number when they first got in the elevator."

The guard's explanation didn't satisfy Henry. Those push buttons—2 and 8—were probably spaced several inches apart. It seemed unlikely that anyone would miss the button by that distance.

"I want the names of all three employees who accessed the second floor. Can you pull up those names using their badge numbers?"

"Sure. I have to get into another database. Give me a second to write down their ID numbers."

As he waited, Barnesdale asked, "Do we have a security camera at the Research Tower?"

"Every building has 'em. The tower has just one. It's in the lobby." There were more keystrokes, then, "Okay, I have the employee names here. They're in numerical order. The first badge—number 14793—belongs to Bryant, Susan."

Henry knew the name. She worked in Pathology. She

was the first number on his list, and had entered the building at 11:43 on Friday night. Likely, she was the one who carried the dead boy's bone marrow to the fourth floor lab.

"Let's see here," the guard said. "The next is badge number 35976—that'd be Adler, Michael."

"Who's he?"

"It says here that he works in Hematology-Oncology. One of their lab technicians."

His badge number matched the third entry on Henry's screen. Adler had entered the building Saturday morning at nine-seventeen and stayed most of day—probably the tech who was called in to prepare Josue Chaca's bone marrow slides.

"That leaves badge number 57943," the guard said while punching some keys. "That badge belongs to a doctor—Dr. Elmer McKenna."

Megan reached under her hammock, felt around in the darkness and grabbed one of her trail shoes, then hurled it at the seismic rumble coming from Joe Whalen's corner of the hut.

She heard her shoe slide off the mosquito netting hanging over his hammock. A second later he erupted in another convulsive snore. *How were Eddie and Steve sleeping through this?*

She lunged at her ankles and scratched with a fury. She'd been skirmishing all night with gangs of Guatemalan fleas. Chloroquine tablets—protection against malaria—and mosquito repellent had seemed like a better idea than netting when she was packing for her trip, but no one had warned her about the fleas.

Eddie had taken most of the afternoon convincing the village elders to allow her group to stay the night. The result was a decrepit structure near the meeting hall, a late afternoon meal of corn tortillas and lukewarm chicken broth, and an admonition to stay away from the residents of Ticar Norte.

The admonishment had come after her encounter with Josue Chaca's mother. Megan had approached the woman, but each time she stepped closer to the small hut, the woman had retreated farther into its interior, eventually positioning herself behind a phalanx of other women.

Megan soon learned the reason. Josue Chaca was the angry spirit, and his mother blamed the gringo doctors for "melting his body." Whatever that meant, it was the reason Megan and her colleagues had received such a cool reception when they arrived at the village.

Later, Eddie told them that Josue's father had died several months earlier from *mal de ojo*—the evil eye.

"It's a catchall," Steve had explained. "A name the locals put on any illness they can't explain."

According to Eddie, the father's death also explained why Josue's mother had come back to the village where she was born, rather than Mayakital, after returning from the United States.

A dog yelped in the distance. Megan lurched up, threw her legs over the side of the hammock, and groped for her backpack. She was done sleeping for the night.

Three minutes later she was standing outside in the night air. There was no moon, but the sky was teeming with stars. A warm, noiseless breeze passed through her hair. The only sound was a distant hum of insects.

She swept her flashlight in wide arcs and walked to the edge of a plateau, then aimed the light downslope at a collection of huts—to the right of which stood the one holding Josue Chaca's angry spirit. She edged down the slope, toeing the ground in front of her with mincing steps.

A gust of wind noisily flapped the sleeves of her nylon jacket. She switched off the light and stood perfectly still, her face tightening into a knot of contracted muscle as she listened for movement in the nearby huts.

Nothing.

Megan relaxed her eyes and allowed the slivers of reflected starlight to wash onto her retinas. Eventually, the dark outline of a doorway emerged.

She held her palm over the flashlight and turned it on, letting a few strands of light spill through her fingers. Just to the right of the open entry, there were several cobs of corn stacked neatly next to a bowl that held several pieces of chicken. Flies swarmed over the meat.

The hut was empty except for a ceramic water jug sitting in the middle of the dirt floor. It was a glazed vessel, bright purple, and it glistened when the light shone on it.

A minute later she was inside, looking down the neck of the carafe. It was filled with . . . dirt?

As she studied the bone-dry substance, its dust-like granularity and grayish color emerged.

The gringo doctors melted his body.

She wasn't looking into a carafe. It was an urn filled with Josue Chaca's ashes.

She sat down next to the boy's remains and wondered who had cremated his body. Judging from the mood of the villagers, and the mother's reaction to her visit, they certainly had not wanted it done. The coroner? If the medical examiners had discovered something they had needed to destroy, the information would have found its way back to the clinic, and to Paul Delgado. Steve Dalton would have known about this. It didn't make any sense.

A minute later, when she crawled out of the hut, Megan was no closer to an answer.

She remained lost in her thoughts as she started back up the hill. Eventually her mind nudged her. The slope hadn't leveled off. She already should have reached the top of the hill. She painted a semicircle with her light. The hilltop was to her right, twenty feet upslope. Rather than ascending the hill, she had followed the slope around to the other side of the village.

Her bladder reminded her that she was going to miss indoor plumbing for the next several days. If she did nothing about it, the uncomfortable stretch would command her attention until sunrise, when she'd probably have to do a half-mile march into the jungle if she wanted any privacy.

Her flashlight found a path to the left, but fear competed with her full bladder. She conjured images of wet, slippery creatures lurking out there, lying in wait. Then she imagined stooping near a trail in broad daylight just as a troupe of teenage boys happened along.

Megan started down the path. Almost immediately, the overgrowth formed a low canopy above her head. She felt closed in, as if in a tunnel. Gangly fronds caught the flashlight's beam, and disorienting fragments of light bounced back at her.

She had gone about twenty yards down the path when she heard a sound to her right.

It was a snap, like a twig breaking.

She turned off the light, lowered herself into a crouch and listened—waiting for the sound to return and hoping it wouldn't.

Her bladder could wait. She felt around for vines and branches, marking the perimeter of the path, then began duck-walking backward.

After a few awkward strides, she stood and turned toward the village.

A muted *crack* sent her back into a crouch.

Seconds passed.

Her thighs began to burn. She aimed her darkened flashlight through the undergrowth, toward the sound. Her hand was wobbling when she switched the light on, then off again.

Through the brush she saw a tiny reflected glint. Water? Metal?

It didn't matter.

Megan shot up and started sprinting toward the village.

"She saw me!" a man's voice yelled in Spanish.

Then heavy footfalls. Several.

A flashlight beam shot across the trail in front of her. She lunged to her right and collided with a tree limb. The sting didn't register, but the hand reaching through the thicket and grabbing her jacket did. She twisted violently but the grip held firm.

Her teeth clamped down on a finger. She tasted blood.

"She's biting me. Come around and get her."

The man's voice—composed, in control—sent a shudder through her. His grip didn't loosen.

Megan found a thumb and bit down again, this time like a crazed animal trying to dismember its prey. The man's grip weakened for an instant. It was long enough.

She took off toward the village, her flashlight beam jerking wildly, her arms thrashing at low-hanging branches.

A beam of light came at her before she'd taken ten steps. Megan turned and plunged headlong into the jungle.

Chapter 28

*L*uke had the bogey's head in his nightscope's crosshairs when his team leader, Alpha, ordered him to kill the unidentified man.

"Omega, the bogey is now your target. Take him out."

Kappa, the lead element of the insertion team, was tucked into a shallow inset between two warehouse buildings on the far side of the pier. The unidentified bogey had come within five meters of Kappa's position. He had strayed into the mandatory kill zone. He was now a target to be destroyed.

"Anyone have an identity on the target?" Luke whispered into his throat mic while moving his rifle scope back and forth between the target and Kappa.

The target had no weapon. He was likely a civilian worker at the seafood-processing plant that North Korea used to camouflage a naval installation at the far end of the pier.

"Omega, I say again, take out the target. Now!"

Even in a whisper, Alpha's voice carried the force of an approaching storm.

Luke clicked back one magnification setting on his scope—he didn't want to see the man's face—and recentered the target's head in his crosshairs.

"Omega, do you read me?" the team leader said. "I am ordering you to take out the target."

The target suddenly turned toward him like a deer sensing danger. Luke took out the last few millimeters of slack from his trigger.

A muted spit came from his rifle.

Four hundredths of a second later, the target's head lurched back and he slumped onto the pier.

Kappa leapt from his shadowed recess and dragged the lifeless body into his small hideaway.

"Insertion team, move in," came the order in Luke's earpiece.

By the time he and the other members of the insertion team reached the pier, Kappa had taken a position farther out on the concrete platform, and Luke was crouched in the inset that Kappa had just abandoned.

Beside him, lying facedown on the concrete deck, was the target he had destroyed a few minutes earlier.

The small male figure was dressed in tattered civilian clothing and his feet were bare. His limbs were spread at unnatural angles, and the pool of blood under his head was still spreading.

Luke grabbed the dead body by a shoulder and turned it over.

Blood oozed from a single bullet hole above the right eye.

Just below the entry wound, staring back at him, were the wide-open eyes of an adolescent boy.

Luke pitched forward in his bed, his chest heaving.

The stabbing pain punched through his forehead. He spread a hand across the front of his head and squeezed. When the pain finally left, he threw his legs over the edge of the mattress and turned on his bedside lamp.

"God damn me to hell," he whispered.

Twelve years later, Luke still could not fathom how easily he had crossed over into the darkness of Proteus. He had chosen an unholy alliance with some perverse inner demon, and a young boy had paid for that choice with his life.

He had slaughtered an innocent. He carried the weight of that truth like an iron yoke. It never left him.

The clock on his bed stand read 3:07 A.M. He was done sleeping for the night.

Megan sprinted into the jungle. The trail quickly narrowed into a tunnel-like passageway, and a tangle of branches grabbed at her shoulder. The roots and vines were closing in around her.

Behind her the heavy footfalls grew louder with each stride.

A flashlight beam flickered through the latticework of thick jungle growth on her right. Then another light. Both were moving faster than she was, angling toward her. Megan tried to scream, but the sound came out as a throaty whisper. She was already out of breath.

A man behind her yelled in Spanish, "Cut her off at the clearing."

They were herding her like stray cattle through a chute. She hadn't been on this side of the village and had no idea what was ahead.

Megan painted the other side of the trail with her light, looking for a break in the path, a way out. She guzzled air but couldn't get enough to keep up her pace. Her legs were weakening, her strides shortening.

She was oxygen starved, and the footsteps behind her sounded like thunderclaps.

The trail suddenly widened and the vegetation thinned

on both sides. The flashlights to her right were clearer now, bobbing up and down in cadence with the thrashing legs and angry grunts converging on her.

The walls of jungle on either side of her path were disintegrating into a clearing!

Megan glimpsed a small break in the undergrowth on her left and dove through it. She rolled down an embankment, tumbling blindly, her arms wrapped around her head. Soon she was flipping end over end, picking up speed as the slope turned down. Branches reached out of the blackness and slashed her arms and face. While fighting to tuck herself into a tight curl, something hard punched her ribs and pushed the last pockets of air from her lungs. She fell limp and bounced down the incline until the ground below her finally gave way and she plunged into a free fall.

Thump. She hit a soggy patch of earth.

There was no pain, but her thoughts were slow to come and her body didn't want to move. Fear left her. There was only the feeling that all of this was coming to an end. The shouted commands and angry voices flitted at the periphery of her mind as though they did not matter anymore. She felt her chest rising and falling. The sound of running water soothed her.

It was a river, and soon it was the only sound she heard. A stream of unanswered questions and what-ifs—life's unfinished journey—tumbled through her mind, carried by the watery cascade.

A hand touched her face. Fingers stroked her forehead. She soon realized that they were her fingers.

Megan opened her eyes just as a flashlight beam passed over her. Her head began to ache.

The voices again, still searching for her. Who were they? Why were they chasing her?

Her head tilted back and she gazed upside down at the lights zigzagging down the embankment—first one, then two more—like fireflies jinking toward their prey.

She rolled onto her side and a groan came out of her.

She staggered to her knees and stared up the hill. Her senses slowly awakened and she turned back to the sound of rushing water. The wash of her pursuers' flashlights painted a tall thicket of jungle that stood like a barricade in front of the pulsing watercourse.

Dropping to her stomach, she belly-crawled toward the wet sounds.

More voices behind her—hunters trying to reacquire their target.

The rushing water grew louder.

A massive tree stopped her progress. Megan ran her hand over the gnarled surface of an enormous root cap that stretched upward from the tree's base like a rocket fin. She edged around the tree and propped her back against an inset between two root fins.

"Behind the tree," a voice shouted in Spanish.

The wet grass on either side of her glimmered with patches of light. The wall of jungle growth that stood between her and the water was only a few feet away, but it was so thick, it might as well have been made of stone. She was trapped.

Megan looked up. The shadow of a root fin disappeared into black sky above her. She grabbed hold, straddled the root, and began to climb using its bulbous edging as a handhold.

She had climbed about fifteen feet when the root started to disappear into the tree trunk like a pleat. She couldn't go any farther.

Her arms burned. In another minute she'd fall back to the ground.

She craned her head, glanced down. Something thin and sinewy brushed up against her head but she couldn't make it out. Everything was a mass of dark shadows.

Her right foot slipped. She clawed at the tree to regain her purchase but the noise brought to it a beam of light from below. To her left, a tangle of hanging vines glistened.

"She's going up the tree!" a man yelled.

Megan launched herself at the vines with everything she had left in her legs. She clutched at them, slipped, then caught hold with one hand. Her body spun slowly around the ropy plants, and them around her, but the force of her leap sent the twisted bundle into a lazy arc.

She struck a tree branch, grabbed hold, and curled herself up and onto the bulky limb.

Below her a faint *click*, then metal sliding against metal. She looked down just as an orange flash broke through the darkness. With it came a loud *bang*.

She had to get to the river. She rolled into a standing position, arms outstretched, and moved out onto the limb. The shouted voices pushed her into a slow trot. With each step the sound of churning water swelled. The branch narrowed and eventually started to bow under her weight.

When the second gunshot sounded, she ducked into a crouch. The limb wobbled. She joggled right, then left, and nearly recovered her balance before falling again into the darkness.

Chapter 29

Luke spent the second half of the night in his living room, sitting in front of his computer and searching the medical internet site, Medline. He had cross-referenced a stew of medical terms—lung diseases, sudden death, cystic fibrosis, tropical infections, lymphocytosis, leukemia—hoping to tease out some fragment of information that explained the deaths of two children whose only apparent link were some arcane microscopic findings.

He had come up empty, but at least he'd burned through three hours of night's darkness without having to relive torments from long ago, or roil in the nascent nightmare of Erickson's murder.

Even before a cab had delivered him home from his session at LAPD headquarters yesterday, homicide detectives had interviewed his father and Ben about their dinner meeting at Kolter's. After debriefing both of them and satisfying himself that their recollections and answers had coincided with his, Luke had called an old acquaintance from the Naval Academy who lived in Seattle—the only criminal defense attorney he knew. The lawyer agreed to help him find a defense attorney in L.A. only after berating him for talking with homicide detectives.

Luke expected to hear back from the guy this morning, but he was more eager to talk to Ben. The pathologist had promised to call no later than 9:00 A.M. with a progress report on his probe into Jane Doe's death.

The clock in the bottom corner of Luke's computer screen read 6:12 A.M.

He glanced out the front window and took in the L.A. basin—streetlights were still burning across the darkened city—then hefted himself from the chair and made his way out the front door. He was about to start down the stairway for his newspaper when he spotted it in the corner of the landing. On a good day, the *L.A. Times* landed on his driveway. It had never made it to his doorstep before. He scanned the street before picking up the paper.

Underneath the paper was a large manila envelope.

He looked back at the street, then scooped up the unmarked package.

Once inside, he tossed the paper onto a table and tore open one end of the envelope. Inside were two letter-size sheets of paper. The first page was printed and read:

From: ktartaglia@simcast.net
Sent: Friday, January 30 @ 5:12 PM
To: LukeMcKenna@uch.university.edu
Subject: [None]

Luke,

Look at the attached, then call me ASAP. Please, we need to talk.

Kate

He threw the envelope aside and turned to the second page.

It was a color photograph, and its images tightened his throat like a wire ligature.

Two men and a woman with bronze skin and rounded faces were sitting on a crude wooden bench in front of a thatched hut. In front of them, on the ground, were a boy and a girl. The children were naked—he guessed their ages at about two and four years—and they were leaning heavily against one another, as if barely able to sit upright.

The five faces stared at the camera lens with vacant expressions. They were physically wasted. His first thought might have been malnutrition—caloric deprivation would explain their hollow cheeks, protruding ribs, and wasted limbs—but this wasn't malnutrition. Of that, he was certain. The tattoos on their skin told him so. The men and boy had a crescent-shaped mark on their chests, just like Josue Chaca's. The girl had three blue circles on her lower abdomen; they looked identical to those he'd seen in the postmortem pictures of Jane Doe.

The photo's background showed forested peaks rising into an incongruously beautiful sapphire sky streaked with gauzy clouds. In the distance behind the hut, a slender waterfall streamed down the center of a massive cup-shaped rock formation at the convergence of two mountains.

Luke glanced at the footer on the bottom of the page: MAYAKITAL.JPG. He was looking at a print of a digital photograph.

Amid the avalanche of questions and puzzles that bombarded him at that moment, two inescapable facts emerged. The photograph in his hand confirmed the link between Josue Chaca and Jane Doe, and Kate's e-mail established her connection to both children.

Luke thought back to the lethal precision of Kate's bullet

wounds. What had been a nagging suspicion suddenly wailed like a klaxon. Someone had killed her before she could unravel the mystery of those children's deaths for him.

And somewhere out there was a person who had made certain that he knew the truth.

But who?

"C'mon, talk to me." Ben was sitting over the microscope in his study at home. He grabbed an eyebrow and started twirling.

It was already six-fifteen and he needed to get to the office, but he couldn't let it go. He had spent most of the night poring over nearly one hundred slides from the Jane Doe case and still couldn't match the pattern of what he was seeing to any known disease.

He picked up the last folder. It contained just three slides—the only slides produced in his lab—one each of the girl's lungs, pancreas, and bile ducts. He took the first slide from the cardboard jacket, leaned back in his chair, and rubbed it between his fingers as if hoping that a genie would appear with some answers.

He agreed with most of Jay whatchamacallit's findings. The girl's smaller airways, pancreatic exocrine glands, and bile ducts were decimated, while adjacent tissues were virtually untouched. The damage was selective and precise. Whatever had caused her death was an exquisitely orchestrated process.

But the M.E. had missed at least one finding—the damage to the girl's ovaries. It was subtle. In fact, the gross structure of the ovaries was almost entirely normal. Only when Ben examined them under higher magnification did he find that the oocytes themselves were depleted. There were very few eggs. An overworked M.E.

could easily have overlooked it or assumed that it had nothing to do with the girl's death.

Ben also wanted to write it off as unrelated to the cause of death—he already had enough puzzles to solve—but there were a few things that tugged at his curiosity. There were too many lymphocytes in the ovaries; not nearly as many as he had found in the most heavily damaged tissues, but more than he could explain. And unlike the lungs, pancreas, and bile ducts, there were almost no cells undergoing destruction at the moment of Jane Doe's death. Whatever had happened to her ovaries had occurred sometime before she died.

What was the connection between this case and Josue Chaca? Ben couldn't let go of the conspicuous similarities—the pattern and precision of the tissue destruction in both cases was unlike anything he had ever seen. But then there was the glaring inconsistency between the cases, too. Adam Smith, a damned good oncologist, had been certain that the boy had leukemia. After reviewing Jane Doe's bone marrow slides, Ben was just as certain that *the girl* did not.

He tapped the slide against his palm, then slipped it onto the microscope tray and leaned over the eyepiece. It was a section of Jane Doe's lung tissue that his lab had stained with an immunofluorescent dye, which selectively bound to Killer T-cells. After hearing Elmer describe how his prototype flu vaccine had caused the toxic reaction in those lab mice, Ben had decided to try the special staining on a hunch. He didn't like being reduced to hunches, but then, he had very few leads to pursue.

"Well, I'll be damned."

The slide fluoresced brightly. The lung tissues were bathed in Killer T-cells.

Apoptosis. Unlike other forms of cell destruction, which

were messy and chaotic, apoptosis was an exceptionally tidy process that left almost no residue. The cells lining the airways were simply gone, having surrendered to the girl's immune system, which had marked them for death.

But this wasn't anything like the normal apoptotic process, which was subtle and restrained. This was suicide on a massive scale.

Ben suddenly wanted to know more about Elmer's misadventure with the mice—and a *whole lot more* about Zenavax's vaccines.

He grabbed the other two slides from his folder, sections of the girl's pancreas and bile ducts that had been stained with the same immunofluorescent dye.

Again the slides shone brightly with Killer T-cells. As in the lungs, the destruction was precise and devastatingly complete.

"Well, I'll be goddamned."

Something had caused the girl's own immune system to attack these tissues. The question was, what? Every new piece of this puzzle added another question, another mystery. Now, at least, he had a trail to follow.

As he reached for the phone to call Luke, his beeper vibrated.

It was Caleb Fagan's office number.

Ben wasn't expecting any pages—one of the other pathologists was on call. Maybe Caleb was contacting him with the flow cytometry results. Ben had sent a sample of Jane Doe's lung tissue to Immunology for flow cytometry, a specialized technique for analyzing and quantifying the subtypes of lymphocytes present in tissue samples. It was far more precise than anything he could do in his lab.

He reached for the phone and dialed Caleb's office.

While Luke's concerns about Barnesdale had seemed a

bit overdone at the time, Ben had gone along with the secretive approach, labeling the transmittal slip with an alias and fabricating some fiction about a research project when he'd spoken with Caleb.

Ben had done the same with the tissue he sent to Genetics for chromosome analysis. He wanted to know whether the girl had cystic fibrosis, even though he wasn't sure how that information would help him solve this puzzle.

"Looks like you're up with the roosters," Ben said when Caleb answered.

"Sorry for paging you so early, but I've got a lot on my plate today. Maybe you heard—our clinic in Guatemala burnt to the ground. Night before last."

"No, I didn't. How'd it happen?"

"I don't know yet. But look, that's not why I paged you. I need you to send me another slice of tissue for those lymphocyte studies. I'm embarrassed to admit it, but my usually crack team managed to lose the tissue."

Ben could hear the irritation in Caleb's voice, and decided not to probe. "I'll get another sample up to your lab this morning."

As soon as Caleb hung up, Ben dialed his lab. He needed to call his chief technician anyway, to discuss the additional slides she was preparing from Jane Doe's tissues. Some of the special stains he had asked for were no longer relevant—not after what he'd just seen on those two slides. More importantly, a number of tissue-staining techniques he now wanted done weren't on the to-do list.

His technician answered on the fourth ring. "Margie, listen. I need you to—"

"Dr. Wilson, I was waiting for you to get here. I need to explain—I don't know how it happened. Oh, God—I just can't believe this happened."

"Slow down, Margie. Take a breath and tell me what you're talking about."

"The paraffin blocks—all of the organ tissues for that Jane Doe case. We incinerated them."

"What?"

"I really messed up here, Dr. Wilson. I don't know how, but I must've put them near the stack marked as biological waste. The night shift destroyed all of it. They said it was sitting with all the other stuff that was marked for incineration. I just can't believe I would've done something like that. I just can't believe it."

"Neither can I."

Chapter 30

Luke was dialing Ben's home phone number when someone knocked loudly on his front door. He hung up and grabbed Kate's photograph from beside the phone.

When he opened the door, Lieutenant Groff was standing on the other side of the threshold holding up a wad of folded papers.

"We have a warrant to search these premises," he said. "Please step outside."

Luke looked past the lieutenant at three plainclothes detectives with shields dangling from their neck chains. They were lined up in a tight single-file formation on his stairway. All of them wore latex gloves, including Detective O'Reilly, who was at the end of the column, eyeing him.

Two uniformed cops stood at the end of his driveway under the wash of a street lamp. It was 6:29 A.M. and the city was still dark.

"Can I put on some clothes?" Luke was wearing a T-shirt and scrub pants, and his feet were bare.

"No."

Luke didn't care about his clothing. He was stalling while deciding whether to tell the cops about the mysterious package, including the photograph that he was still holding in his left hand. If he told them, O'Reilly would almost certainly assume the worst and conclude that he'd had the e-mail all along. The detective would reason that he was telling them only to preempt the more incriminating scenario of their discovering the items during their search.

Luke thought back to the attorney's advice—*keep your mouth shut*—and decided to wait until later, when his disclosure wouldn't seem suspect.

"This is your copy of the warrant." Groff tapped Luke's chest with the papers. "Now, please step outside."

Luke took the papers with his right hand while lifting his left hand and placing the photograph against the bottom of the stack. He used Groff's body to conceal his maneuver from the other cops.

The lieutenant turned and gave a hand signal to the uniformed cops. One of them trotted down the driveway toward the backyard, while the other loitered at the front of the property with her thumbs hooked around her gun belt.

Even before Luke was completely through his front doorway, Groff disappeared inside. O'Reilly and the female detective from his interrogation session followed behind their boss.

An overmuscled detective with spiked blond hair remained on the small landing with Luke.

"Mind if I sit?" Luke asked.

Muscles let his eyelids droop and cracked a knuckle.

Luke slid down against the stucco wall and flipped through the search warrant. Some of the listed items told him things about the killer's methods: .338 caliber rounds, rifles with barreling that was visually compatible with .338 ammunition, sighting scopes, and so on. A few of the items, like "athletic shoes" and "hiking boots," suggested that they might already have some forensic evidence that could ID the killer.

Good. Maybe this would end here.

Nothing on their search list gave them a reason to examine his desk, and he remembered slipping the e-mail back into its envelope. He could tell O'Reilly about Kate's e-mail later.

Luke stared out through the decorative iron balustrade. Spanish-tile rooftops on the hillside below him crept into view as the sky turned from black to gray.

No one said anything to him for the next ten minutes. The monotony was broken only occasionally by his hardwood floors creaking under the weight of a footstep, or the murmur of clipped conversation.

O'Reilly appeared in the entry, huddling with Groff. The two men spoke in a muted tone with their backs turned to Luke.

A minute later O'Reilly came through the front door, holding up Kate's e-mail message. "This was sitting in the open, next to your computer," he lied. "Were you planning to tell me about it at some point?"

"It showed up on my doorstep this morning, in a plain envelope."

"I see." The detective looked at the paper. "Just like that, it showed up on your—"

"Chocolate fan, huh?" Groff shouted at Luke from the entry hall.

The female detective was holding a plastic bag with several Mr. Goodbar wrappers.

Luke struggled not to shiver in the morning air while wondering what possible interest his candy bar wrappers could hold for them.

"I have a whole drawerful," he said. "You can have them if you bring me a jacket."

Groff called O'Reilly back inside. For several minutes they stood in a cluster. Groff held up one of Luke's running shoes by the tongue while O'Reilly and the female cop studied the rubber sole. Their gaze went back and forth between the bottom of his shoe and what looked like a photograph that Groff had pulled from his briefcase.

Luke slipped Kate's photograph into the back pocket of his scrub pants while Muscles was leaning over the railing to sneeze.

When the three detectives came outside again, both of Luke's shoes were sitting in plastic bags. "These yours?" asked Groff.

Even in the dim light, Luke could see that his shoes were streaked with mud. Something was wrong. He didn't wear those shoes when the ground was wet; he had another pair he used on rainy days. "I'm not sure."

"Take a good look." Groff turned the bags in front of Luke's face. "Nike. Size eleven. These look like yours?"

The laces were untied. Luke always kicked his shoes off after a run. He never bothered to untie the laces.

"C'mon," Groff said. "This shouldn't be too hard. Don't make us look for DNA traces in your dried sweat. Be a sport."

Old habits kicked in. Luke studied each detective as they fanned out around him—how their eyes responded to the environment, where they carried their weapons, how their bodies moved—sizing each threat while his senses took in the smallest details of each movement and sound.

"I think I want to talk to an attorney," he said finally.

"Well, you're gonna get that chance because you're under arrest for suspicion of murder. You have the right to remain silent. Anything you say . . ."

Luke didn't hear most of it. His mind was busy fighting a war of its own.

He was being framed. Hardened reflexes screamed at

him to evade and escape. His intellect reminded him of the absurdity of that choice.

". . . you have the right to speak to an attorney, and . . ."

This was insane! Someone was setting him up and he had no idea why. He'd never find out if they locked him away in a cage.

"If you cannot afford a lawyer, one will be . . ."

Who was doing this? Did this have something to do with Kate's murder?

"Please place both hands behind your head."

Primal instincts took over. Luke's foot plunged into Groff's midsection. The detective tumbled down the stairway, carrying Muscles with him.

An instant later Luke was on his feet. He swept the woman's legs before her gun had cleared the holster—she went sprawling—then he head-butted O'Reilly. The detective melted into a puddle.

Luke ran through his front door and down the short hallway into his bedroom. He grabbed the blanket from his bed and threw it over his head before plunging through the closed window.

Glass shattered. He tried to pull the blanket off and extend his arms before the ground came up to meet him.

He didn't quite make it, and the ten-foot drop sent a bolt of pain through the left side of his body. Shattered glass rained down on him.

He expected a shouted command—or gunshot—as he came up onto his feet in the backyard. Instead, he saw no one. The uniform must have sprinted back up the driveway.

Luke hurtled toward the bushy hillside at the rear of the property.

Megan listened to the jungle awaken as she sat behind a thin barrier of reeds and ferns along the bank of the murky green river. A shaft of sunlight broke through the canopy overhead, and birds began squawking at one another in rhythmless pulses.

She hugged her legs and rested her chin on a pair of wobbly knees. A wet T-shirt sagged over her shoulders, and her shivering legs struggled to hold their purchase on the sloping riverbank.

She had remained in the river far too long. Her body was battling hypothermia. For what seemed like an hour, she had bobbed around in total darkness, bouncing off unseen rocks and scraping past low-hanging branches that reached out and speared her. Eventually, exhaustion had overtaken her resolve and she blindly clawed her way onto the river's edge.

For the second time in as many hours, she wondered whether she was going to die in this wilderness. The Callahans were cursed, it seemed, but she had always pictured her life as having some purpose. That her life, its work unfinished, might be extinguished in this alien place carried her to a desolate corner in her soul. That she might die alone, her death as inconsequential and unnoticed as a fly caught in a spider's web, uncovered a loneliness that scraped at her soul with a dreadful indifference.

The slow-moving water lapped against the silty riverbank. She had to stay silent. Her pursuers might still be searching for her, and they likely would have followed the river's path.

Megan shuddered when something small and dark skittered past her. The ache in her hand returned when she swiped at a large fern to let the creature know that it wasn't welcome. She held her palms up and examined the damage. Her skin was hidden under wet silt, but the throb told her that she had sprained her right thumb.

"*Ouch* . . . Get away from me, you little shit!"

It was a man's voice, speaking English, on the opposite side of the river.

Megan's mind melted into a pool of fear. Her body shook uncontrollably.

The sound of water thrashing, then, "Jesus, Mary, and Joseph, forgive me my sins, but I'm coming after you, you little bloodsucker . . ."

The voice was that of an older man, the accent unmistakably American. It had a brassy New York quality, like Brooklyn or Queens.

Megan crawled to the river's edge, using the man's shouts to disguise the sound of her movements. She spread two large fronds and looked across the river.

On the other side, several yards downstream, a naked man was standing knee-deep in water. He was short and had a slight build. His forearms and neck were brown, the rest of his skin pearl-white. Folds of skin sagged over his waist.

He suddenly jerked a leg out of the water, lost his balance and fell backward into the river. "That's it, you little pecker . . ." Using a leafy branch, the old man whacked the muddy water with a fury while hurling colorful epithets at the unseen creature.

Eventually he gave up the battle and stepped onto the shoreline. A small brown man appeared from behind a thicket, passed the old man a ragged towel, and stood by as his pale companion dried himself. Next, the dark-skinned man handed pieces of clothing to the man and watched as he dressed.

When he finished dressing, the old man took something from his rucksack, kissed it, and draped it around his neck.

A large gold crucifix glinted in the sunlight.

Megan stuck her head out of the brush and glanced up and down the riverbank, looking for any sign of her assailants.

When she looked back, the dark-skinned man was pointing at her. The older man turned.

She ducked behind a palm leaf.

A second later the older man called out, *"Buenos días. ¿Está bien?"*

Megan took a deep breath, then poked her head out.

"I need help," she said.

Chapter 31

Luke bounded onto the fire road in a dead run and sprinted west on the upward slope of a trail into the interior of Griffith Park. He had moved methodically through the steep and heavily wooded hillside behind his property. It had cost him time, but disguising his tracks was his only chance. He hoped the cops were still combing the area that he had marked with trampled undergrowth and broken branches. He needed a few minutes of confusion.

The charcoal sky was giving way to shades of gray-violet, but the sun was still hiding on the other side of the hill. His lungs were already on fire, but he couldn't stop to rest until he had at least a half-mile lead on the hunters. He'd spread them out, force them to expand the search area. If he could do that, his meager advantages would come into play. He knew how to use the shadows of early dawn to evade and conceal. He also knew the terrain, and how to disappear into it.

Echoes of an earlier life pounded at him as he raced up the hill. He could feel a dark core reigniting, smoldering ashes suddenly finding fuel. He fought to ignore the waves of dread that passed through him.

The *whomp whomp whomp* of a helicopter played in the distance. They couldn't have vectored a helicopter in on him this quickly, he figured, but in another five minutes the sky overhead would be swarming with aircraft.

The jagged edges of half-buried rocks slashed at his bare feet. He lengthened his stride, ignored the pain. He couldn't leave the trail until he had put more distance between himself and the hunters.

Speed and distance were all that mattered. Nothing else.

He held that thought until he came around a blind curve on the trail. A black Doberman was waiting for him, snarling, its teeth bared.

Luke dove off the trail and rolled down the slope, tumbling over sharp rock edges and scraggly dry vegetation until he finally came to a stop in tall grass on the lip of a small gully. He rolled into the depression and scanned the hill above him.

He mopped a painful spot on the back of his neck with his T-shirt. It came back dark red.

The dog stared down at him, growling and scraping at loose gravel on the edge of the trail. Small rivulets of sand streamed down the hill.

Ten feet to his right, a concrete culvert hung over the edge of a small knoll. He scurried over and tucked himself under the overhang. His chest heaved and he struggled to control his breathing.

A woman's voice yelled, "Samson . . . Samson, get back here."

More growling.

Then, the sound of loose gravel under hard-soled boots. "Samson, what got into you? Calm down, boy."

WHOMP WHOMP WHOMP WHOMP . . . The thunderous roar of a heavy chopper came out of nowhere. A moment later the air blast from its rotor wash wrapped him in a cloud of gritty sand.

"STOP RIGHT THERE!" a loudspeaker commanded.

Luke brought his hands up to shield his head from flying debris. He leaned into the side of the knoll, tucking himself under the two-foot concrete overhang. The direction of the windblast changed as the helicopter moved overhead in a tight circle.

If the police were using thermal sensors in their helicopters—and they probably were—his heat signature would look like a 500-watt bulb against the damp ground and cool morning air. The hunters had everything he didn't have—airpower, logistical support, communications—but as long as the chopper was directly overhead, its heat sensors wouldn't find him under the thermal camouflage of a thick culvert. Until and unless they backed away far enough to inspect the hillside from an angle and look under the drain, he was invisible.

The percussion waves weakened. The helicopter was climbing.

The loudspeaker again: *"We're looking for a man . . . six feet, brown hair, light green or gray clothing . . ."*

Luke tried to open his eyes. The sand stung his lids closed. The dog was yelping in the background, terrified.

"Ma'am, turn back and follow the path west. Instruct anyone you come across to do the same. If you see someone fitting this man's description, do not—I repeat, do not—approach him."

Luke sat there for several seconds after the helicopter flew east toward his property. He hadn't come as far as he wanted, and the trail was out of the question now. Worse, the orange hues of daybreak were peeking over the top of the hill. Soon, he'd lose any ability to conceal himself in the dry brush.

He had to move now, before the sun came over the hilltop, but his exertion was generating enough heat to light up any thermal sensor within five hundred yards of his position.

He cupped his hands and splashed himself with the cold muck trickling from the end of the culvert. When his body began to shiver, he stopped.

A moment later he disappeared into the hillside.

"You Indians are killing me. You know that, don't you?" The old man was leaning against a large boulder along the side of the trail, trying to catch his breath while staring at his dark-skinned companion.

The old man's name was Father Joe, and he was a Catholic missionary priest. Megan had never kissed a priest before, but that was just what she felt like doing when he offered to take her back to Santa Lucina. The priest and his helper, Paco, had two more villages to visit. After that, he promised, the three of them would hike out of the jungle.

Father Joe put a hand on his companion's shoulder. "What do you say we quit this job and take up golf?"

Paco nodded at the priest, as if he was accustomed to the old man saying things in a language as unfamiliar to him as the dark side of a distant planet.

The priest started to laugh, but it quickly turned into a wheeze. He grabbed a medication inhaler from his pocket and took three quick puffs. When his breathing settled, he turned to Megan and answered the question she hadn't yet asked. "A touch of emphysema."

The priest's smile was framed by creases that looked like etched granite. His blue eyes had a piercing quality, as though they'd easily penetrate another's thoughts.

A growing sense of guilt was nibbling at Megan, the feeling that she had abandoned Joe Whalen and Steve Dalton. It felt as if she had knocked over a hornet's nest and left the aftermath for her colleagues, and the people of Ticar Norte.

That thought was still with her when they arrived at the first village two hours later. Xical—one of almost sixty *aldeas* that Father Joe traveled among with Paco. The priest visited each village no more than three or four times a year, and that fact probably explained the festive greeting that accompanied their arrival at the village.

An hour later Megan was sitting on a bench at the back of a makeshift church watching Father Joe say Mass while a small rabble of dogs lay at her feet, licking themselves. Every time she moved, pieces of silty muck fell from her clothing as if she were a molting insect. Her wallet and passport made a soggy outline on her jeans.

She felt like a toad next to the women of Xical, who were dressed in brightly colored blouses with immaculate white trim and wraparound skirts that reached to their bare ankles. They appeared to move within some invisible pocket of air that was impenetrable to dust and grime. Only their bare feet, which looked like rusted iron, showed the wear and tear of their lives.

It seemed as if the entire village was crammed into the large wooden structure: about eighty men, women, and children; half as many dogs; a dozen free-range chickens and two roosters; and, in front of the altar, two mice sitting in a makeshift cage made of twigs and twine.

A man standing next to the altar poured incense into a hollowed-out rock filled with hot coals. Mushroom-shaped plumes of smoke rose and wrapped Father Joe in a thick white cloud. He choked out a prayer, then exploded in a fit of coughing and waved his hands in search of air. The incense handler seemed not to notice or concern himself with the priest's violent reaction, and Father Joe did nothing to stop the smoky ritual.

Over the past half hour, the same scene had played out every five minutes or so. Every time the cloud of incense ebbed, another scoop of incense landed in the bowl and the priest broke into a paroxysm of coughing.

Megan didn't understand a single word of the Mass. Father Joe was performing the entire service in a Mayan dialect.

The churchgoers suddenly broke out in song, accompanied by an enormous marimba that was manned by five young boys with rounded mallets. They stood along its length, reaching across one another and tapping parallel rows of wooden bars with the speed and precision of knife jugglers.

Father Joe came around to the front of the altar and lifted the captive mice above his head. He appeared to talk to the rodents as the room chanted verses in a singsong tempo. Next, he carried the cage down the center aisle of the church. As he passed the rows of wooden benches, men standing along the aisle spoke to the mice. Megan had stopped attending Mass after her mother died, but she was raised Catholic and knew its liturgy. It seemed that Father Joe was bending the Church's rituals into the shape of a liturgical pretzel.

When the priest reached the back of the church, he started around the back wall. As he passed Megan, he said, "The field mice are ruining their crops. We're asking the mice to move someplace else." He lifted the cage an inch. "After Mass, the elders will take the mice out to the fields and let 'em go so they can tell the other mice about the deal we struck here." He looked at her and shrugged.

Despite the sweltering midday heat, the Mass continued for another hour. She couldn't think of anything but food as she followed Father Joe and a throng of villagers out the back of the church.

Just as she lifted her face to the sunlight, the ground shook violently. On the horizon, a huge flock of yellow birds lifted skyward with a loud clatter.

A low-pitched rumble followed seconds later.

The shaking lasted almost a minute, during which the residents of Xical wore expressions of terror.

Then it was gone.

For the next several seconds, the only sound came from chickens pecking at the ground.

Megan moved next to Father Joe. "Was that an earthquake?"

The priest was looking into the distance, slowly shaking his head. "I don't think so."

Minutes later she heard the rushing water. At first it sounded like a river carrying runoff from a storm, but the flow quickly took on an unnatural quality, surging into a wet pulsating din.

A loud *crack* reverberated in the jungle.

"Father?" she asked.

"I hear it. It sounds like a tree just snapped in half."

A small group of Indians collected on the far side of the village and pointed east toward a deep gorge that was covered with tropical growth. Trees were going down like bowling pins.

Megan, Father Joe, and Paco gathered their things and followed a dozen men along a twisting mile-long trail toward the ravine.

They wended their way through the jungle, eventually coming to a precipice overlooking a furious torrent of water. The raging river—it was over thirty yards wide— engulfed the slopes of the deep canyon as it raced by them. Loud popping sounds ricocheted off the canyon walls as brushwood broke free at the water's edge. The hulking carcass of a tree, roots and all, hurtled past them.

Eddies of red turbid water swirled like demon whorls rising from the underworld.

Megan watched Father Joe make the sign of the cross. His lips moved, as if in prayer, but his voice was lost in the fury of the watery rampage.

For the next several minutes she stood there dumbfounded, watching the deluge gallop past her. A hypnotic state took hold of her.

Then, just as quickly as it rose, the floodwaters receded. In the span of just five minutes, the river shriveled to a languid stream.

She turned to the priest. His skin was pallid, and his eyes were in another realm.

"Father Joe?"

When he didn't respond, Megan followed his line of sight.

There, on the shoreline, half submerged in a knotted mess of vines and branches, was the glistening flesh of a naked corpse.

Chapter 32

Luke clung to the outside edge of a concrete wall and peered at the manicured lawns in front of Griffith Park Observatory. Jets of water angled back and forth over the section of turf closest to him, sending ghost-like swirls of mist skyward.

The Observatory sat on a flat three-acre oval of ground created seventy years ago by shaving off the top of one of the park's taller peaks. The bank of phones he needed stood on the other side of the grassy expanse, on the western side of the property.

Skirting a maze of crisscrossing hiking trails, it took almost ten minutes to work his way around the steep slope out of which the concrete art-deco structure rose. The Observatory was not yet open, and he expected foot traffic to be nil, but a small army of municipal groundskeepers were milling around the property. They moved at a lethargic pace, appearing to have no more interest in their work than the city had in their lives. They would be easily distracted, drawn to anything that might break up the monotony of their usual routine.

Word of an escaped murder suspect would be more than enough to grab their interest.

Luke studied the men. None showed any sign of heightened awareness.

Five women on the far corner of the grass promenade were stretched out on blankets, lost in the ritual of their yoga exercises.

The net hadn't extended this far yet, but the police would arrive soon.

To the east, two police helicopters buzzed the hillside behind his property like angry insects. Above them, four TV news copters maintained fixed positions. He was probably on every TV set in southern California.

Luke stripped off his T-shirt and rolled the bottom of his scrub pants into a cuff. He continued this until the pants had become knee-length shorts. It would look ridiculous to anyone who gave him more than a passing glance, but he had to do something; the green scrubs marked him like a bull's-eye.

The pay phones were twenty feet away, next to a closed food concession. Luke jumped out from his hiding spot and casually jogged to the bank of phones. While dialing the number, he shook his arms loosely and twisted his torso from side to side—as though stretching after a long run—while he waited for an electronic operator to process the collect call.

If the man he needed wasn't there, or wouldn't take his call, Luke had no backup plan. He had one shot, and even that was a dim hope.

One of the groundskeepers turned in his direction, gave an indifferent glance, and went back to raking the ground.

When Sammy Wilkes answered the phone, Luke emptied a lungful of air he didn't remember taking in. "Sammy, I need a favor."

A minute later they were still talking when a convoy of police cars exploded over the crest of the hill at a full gallop and splayed across The Observatory's promenade.

Luke plunged over the concrete wall, grabbing furiously at branches and sprigs to slow his fall down the steep hillside.

Megan climbed over uprooted trees and slogged through mounds of leafy rubble, following the flood's path. Paco led the way, forging a trail along what was left of the river's embankment. Father Joe brought up the rear, fingering a rosary as he went. The priest's brooding mood seemed to pull the rain out of every storm cloud that passed overhead.

The priest had merely shaken his head, glassy-eyed, when she asked if he had any idea what had caused this.

Her mind was a jumble of conflicting thoughts. The last thing she wanted to do was follow a swath of destruction along an unfamiliar river into unknown territory. But then, neither did she want to stay behind in Xical, just her and a village full of strangers speaking Q'eqchi. Those had seemed to be her choices because Father Joe started upriver the moment the floodwaters subsided, as if pushed toward the source of the destruction by some unseen force.

The memory of her waking nightmare in Ticar Norte, knowing that her assailants were still out there, had tilted the scales in favor of Father Joe's company. And their trio was traveling southeast, Megan reminded herself, not northeast toward Ticar Norte.

She pictured people lying injured from the flood, clinging to life in some remote corner of this wilderness. Knowing that she might be able to help them aroused in her a sense of purpose.

But her moments of resolve were fleeting. The young man's corpse that had washed onto the riverbank near Xical was a harbinger of death. She could feel it.

Father Joe's countenance told her that he felt it too.

Megan slowed her pace until the priest was alongside her. "Father, you need to rest."

The priest pulled the inhaler from his breast pocket and took a puff. "There'll be time for that later," he said with a tight throat.

Five minutes passed before they came across the second body. It was an older man, and his body lay cockeyed at the water's edge. His wide-open eyes held the gray fog of death. There was a crescent-moon-shaped tattoo on his chest.

Paco remained at a distance as Megan and the priest approached the body. Father Joe knelt by the corpse and looked skyward in prayer. His face suddenly relaxed, his expression trance-like as he whispered an indecipherable prayer.

When he was done, the priest gently folded the dead man's arms across his chest and said, "I knew this man. He's from a village about three miles upriver."

She glanced at the tattoo again. "Mayakital?"

The priest nodded without looking away from the corpse.

"When was the last time you visited Mayakital?"

"Ten, maybe eleven months ago. They're an independent sort of people. And they're not Catholics, so I wait for them to invite me. That happens maybe once a year."

"The tattoo. What does it mean?"

The priest turned to her, the question slowly congealing in his eyes. "It's part of a fertility rite. It's unique to their tribe." The priest started to raise himself. "The people of Mayakital tattoo their infants on the night of the first full moon after their birth. Boys get a crescent moon on their chest. Girls are marked with three small circles—down here on their stomachs." He pointed at his lower abdomen.

"I've seen that tattoo before, on a boy that came to our hospital. He traveled all the way to the U.S., only to die in our emergency room."

He looked back at the corpse and nodded through a distracted gaze. "The Mayans have a hard life. And their children—well, they die in greater numbers than you're probably used to in your work. I've heard that infant mortality is as high as twenty percent in some of these villages, and from what I've seen, that figure sounds about right. It's a fact of life for these people." He waved Paco forward. "These people don't ask a lot from life, and they don't get much."

The priest opened his palm and let his rosary unfurl as they walked through a thin cloud of mosquitoes.

She slapped at a prick on her neck. "What do you do when the prayers *don't* work?"

He glanced at her. "I'll let you know if that happens."

It wasn't long before they came to another body. It was a small girl with a mid-shaft fracture of her right femur and a dislocated left shoulder. Her body was wasted and shriveled. Something had been at work, stealing her life, long before she drowned in the flood.

With each grisly discovery—the next hour brought three more—Father Joe walked faster, his legs churning through the mud like pistons.

When they finally stopped to rest, he was coughing with almost every other breath.

After he caught his breath, he said, "Megan, do you pray?"

"Not . . . no, not really."

"This might be a time to reconsider." He kneaded his fingers, as if trying to rub an image out of his mind. "Mayakital is just over the next rise."

She followed his gaze up the slope.

The priest exchanged a few words with Paco in Q'e-qchi, then said, "Paco's going to stay here. He'd rather not . . . He'd rather stay here."

The Indian lowered himself onto a rock and started to remove his pack. Megan glanced back a few times as she and the priest started up the slope.

Paco followed them with stolid eyes.

She spent the next five minutes trying not to think about a growing blister that was searing the heel of her left foot. What she saw when she came over the top of the rise swept away any thought of her pain.

A wet moonscape stared back at her. She stood at the lip of a half-mile-wide lake of reddish-brown mud that looked as if it had probably been an upland valley.

Twenty feet from where she stood, a crude wood-plank table floated on the surface. No one had to tell her: There was a dead village lying on the basin floor, buried under hundreds of acres of mud.

Towering mountains shadowed the soggy graveyard on three sides. At the far end of the valley, a bulbous rock formation protruded like a kangaroo's pouch from a cluster of peaks. It was enormous, rising several hundred feet above the valley's floor. Running down the middle of it was a broad, ragged fissure at least thirty feet across.

Water poured from the bottom of the fissure.

Father Joe came over the rise at that moment. He exchanged a silent gaze with her, then raised his hand over the scene. "Eternal rest grant unto them, O Lord, and let perpetual light shine upon them. May their souls . . ."

Megan jumped at the sound of a thunderclap overhead. She looked up and a raindrop struck her in the eye. A second later, a cluster of black clouds opened up.

Puddles of water formed quickly and churned like boiling red broth.

She turned to the priest. He stood frozen in prayer.

Thunder boomed again and sheets of rain poured over her. She stumbled along the edge of the muddy lake and took cover under an overhang of jagged rock.

A minute later the rain stopped as quickly as it had started. She stepped out into the open and started around the edge of the lake, looking for survivors.

Above her, patches of dark limestone spotted the forested peaks, staring down on the wet clay like hunters' eyes taking in the fresh meat of their kill.

She passed the body of a pregnant woman who looked about her age. Megan stooped and felt the woman's abdomen. It was quiet.

By the time she reached the other side of the valley, the scale of the wounded earthen formation had grown to freakish proportions. Three peaks rose to either side and behind the massive stony pouch. A jagged V-shaped fissure ran up to the top of what looked as if it had been a gigantic earthen reservoir—a geologic oddity that collected runoff from rivers hidden beneath a carpet of green on the towering peaks above her. She was standing a hundred or so feet below the lower edge of the breach.

It appeared as though the bulbous front wall of the reservoir had ruptured, releasing a small ocean of water that carried with it the mountain's earthen slopes. The mud had probably consumed the shallow valley in a matter of seconds.

She waded through ankle-deep mud along the shoreline and maneuvered around a tree trunk snapped in half by the torrent.

When she stepped back onto firm ground, what she saw stopped her in mid-stride.

A fresh boot print.

She looked closer. A second and third print led into a

coppice of trees on her left. She glanced behind her. Father Joe was making his way around the valley with a downward gaze.

A thought tapped her on the shoulder, and then screamed at her.

Get out of here. Now!

It happened before she could scream. Her feet left the ground, her body arched by the torque of the force. A hand came up over her mouth.

"Watch out. She bites," were the last words she heard before the world went dark.

Chapter 33

I'm telling ya, Elmer, there're too many peculiar goings-on, here."

Ben Wilson had just recounted the unlikely events of that morning—discovering the Killer T-cells in Jane Doe's lungs, and moments later hearing that his senior lab tech had inexplicably mislabeled the girl's autopsy tissues for incineration.

"Margie doesn't make those kinda mistakes," Ben added.

The two men were standing shoulder-to-shoulder, staring at a ten-foot-tall Plexiglas mosquito pen in the center of Elmer's malaria lab. The only other person in the lab couldn't hear them talking; he was inside the see-through enclosure, wearing a rubberized suit and netted hood to shield him from the mosquitoes swarming around him.

Elmer ran a hand through his tousled white mane. "Maybe you should have a talk with someone in Security."

"If I talk with anyone, it's going to be the police," Ben said. "Luke is right—every time we get a lead going on that Guatemalan boy or Jane Doe, some hobgoblin pulls the rug out from under us. Something's up."

Elmer turned to him. "Have you talked to Luke this morning?"

"I tried calling—several times—but he didn't answer."

"All this stuff going on . . ." The older man's eyes drifted out of focus. "I'm worried about my son, Ben."

Both men turned back to the enclosure when the hooded man tapped on the Plexiglas.

When the man saw that he had their attention, he started removing the covers from a row of petri dishes. Throngs of mosquitoes immediately blanketed the bottom of each dish, covering the thin red layers of blood agar.

"The one person I'd most like to talk to," Ben said absently, "is lying in the morgue."

"Oh?"

"I'm thinking of Kate Tartaglia."

"You really think Zenavax had something to do with those children's deaths?"

"I have no idea, but twenty-five years in this business tells me that whatever killed them is *not* a natural biological process. Somebody's messing with Mother Nature. Jane Doe was attacked by a stampede of Killer T-cells— the likes of which I've never seen—and I'm willing to bet I'd've found the same thing going on in that Guatemalan boy if the autopsy hadn't been stopped." Ben held up a pair of fingers. "Two deaths, both with findings that sound strangely similar to your episode with those mice."

Elmer held up a hand, as if pushing back an uncomfortable thought. "But the other day, you told me that the girl's pancreas and bile ducts were damaged."

"That's right."

"Well, I can't think of any reason that a vaccine would damage those organs," Elmer said. "There's got to be another explanation."

"I'm just following the trail these children left," Ben said. "Death *always* leaves a trail, and you and I are gonna find out where this one leads."

"Sounds like I'm being recruited for something here."

Ben nodded. "The alphavirus vector you developed for your flu vaccine—how similar was it to Zenavax's?"

"Very. Some key segments of their viral genome are identical to mine. That's how the lawsuit came about."

"Would Zenavax use the same alphavirus vector for their malaria vaccine?"

"Without a doubt. It's the perfect vector for a malaria vaccine. They'd have made a few changes, but most of what's unique about their bioengineered strain would remain the same."

The man in the mosquito pen picked up a handheld light that was shaped like a gun and aimed it at the petri dishes. Mosquitoes passing under the blue swath of light sparkled like glitter.

"So, with what you know about their alphavirus strain, could you identify it, isolate it from other strains? That is, could you tell me whether someone was exposed to it?"

Elmer's head moved up and down while watching the man in the pen. "Most likely, yes. One of the things that's unique about their alphavirus vector—and mine—is its ability to replicate. Unlike other live-virus vaccines, it reproduces for about twenty generations before the body's immune system finally kills it off. That's one of the reasons it works so well—it produces enough copies of itself to generate a strong immune response."

Elmer turned to Ben. "Normally, you wouldn't find any traces of a vaccine vector in the patient—it never leaves the site of the injection—but because their virus replicates itself for a period of time, tens of thousands of copies of the viral genome get scooped up by white blood cells in the tissues and eventually end up in the circulation. Months after the vaccine is given, you can still find small amounts of the viral genome circulating in the patient's bloodstream."

"Whatta you thinking here? A PCR?"

Elmer made a clicking sound with his tongue. "Exactly. If there're fragments of the Zenavax alphavirus in the children's blood, I should be able to find them using a polymerase chain reaction. Give me a sample of blood from those children. It may take a few days, but if they received a Zenavax vaccine during the last several months of their lives, we'll know."

Ben was shaking his head even as Elmer spoke. Unfortunately, performing a PCR analysis required whole blood—unclotted blood—and they had no whole blood from either Josue Chaca or Jane Doe.

"There's no whole blood. The girl died hours before they found her—her blood had already coagulated. And the boy's blood went out the door with the rest of his remains when the autopsy was cancelled."

"What do you have?"

"I called the M.E. this morning," Ben said. "They have a frozen vial of the girl's blood serum. That's it. That's what we've got to work with."

"Serum won't help us. I could do an alphavirus titer, but any of several alphaviruses that are found in Central America would give us a falsely positive result."

"How about doing a malaria titer?" Ben asked. "There was no evidence of malaria on Jane Doe's autopsy—none. The liver and spleen were completely normal. What if we were to find that she has elevated malaria titers, that she's immune to malaria?"

"I see where you're going, but elevated malaria titers alone won't prove that she's gotten a malaria vaccine. Some people living in malaria-endemic regions have elevated titers even though they've never had any clinical symptoms of the disease."

The man in the mosquito enclosure entered a laminar

flow chamber at one end of the mosquito pen. Almost instantly a rush of air cleared the small compartment of insects.

Elmer began walking in a tight circle, pulling on his earlobe as he went.

Ben knew to leave the man alone when he was thinking.

Halfway around his third lap, Elmer stopped and asked, "The boy that died in our E.R.—did you send any of his blood for viral cultures?"

"Yeah. Why?"

"When we do viral cultures, we always split the blood specimen and send a portion to the state lab. Regulations—the state makes us send them part of each specimen so they can do their own tests on random samples to check our results."

Ben was generally familiar with controls of that type—the State Health Department exerted its influence over every department at their hospital—but he didn't know the specific regulations that applied to Elmer's lab. It was one of the myriad quality control practices that regulators thrust upon hospitals, and in this instance he wanted to kiss the bureaucrat who had devised that procedure.

"So assuming that someone hasn't made off with the blood sample at the state lab, you can tell me if that boy was recently exposed to Zenavax's alphavirus, right?

"Sure."

Ben rubbed his hands together. "I'll send one of my techs to pick up the blood specimen from the state lab. When he gives it to you, label it using an alias. I don't want *anyone* to know what we're doing." He glanced back at the closed door. "And Elmer, tell no one—and I mean *no one*—about this discussion."

A lab technician suddenly threw open the door. The sound of a TV carried from the next room.

"Dr. McKenna, you better come in here," the tech said. "It's—It's . . . there's something on the TV that you need to see."

"What about the bodies?" the client asked.

"There weren't that many," Calderon replied. "A few got washed downstream by the flood, but my men cleaned the area. Like I said, that village is now buried under forty feet of mud."

The background hum in Calderon's earpiece stretched for several seconds before his client's sterilized voice said, "What about the woman and that priest?"

"They're tucked away."

"Make sure your men understand. We need her alive, to take care of Petri." A heavy breath, then, "How's he doing?"

"Not good. Maybe my men should get him to a hospital."

"No. We've got a doctor there now—that woman. Put her to work."

"Okay." Calderon looked out his hotel room window at the helicopters over Griffith Park. "I assume you've seen the news reports about McKenna."

"Yes," his client said. "Amazing how the cops managed to botch a simple arrest. But his escape plays into our hand, makes him look guilty."

"I still think we should've gotten rid of him, *and* that pathologist."

"Forget the pathologist. He has nothing left to work with. It's over," his client said. "As for McKenna, give the police another hour or two. They may find him. But if they don't—"

"My men have the script." Calderon checked his watch. "They'll call it in to one of the local TV stations at noon."

"You think McKenna will take the bait?"

"I hope so." In fact, Calderon was certain that McKenna would take the bait. He just wasn't going to tell his client that.

"Good. If he does, then you can deal with him."

Luke was packed into the corrugated drainage pipe like an oversized bundle of cannon fodder. It was going on two hours, and the muscles under each of a dozen welts and bruises were steadily hardening into rigid knots.

But he was still outside the police dragnet.

He had glanced back when he leapt over The Observatory's retaining wall, catching a glimpse of helmeted cops with assault rifles fanning out along the eastern side of the grassy promenade. Apparently, they hadn't considered the possibility that he had already come that far west.

He had made his way to Ferndale, an eclectic little area on the southwestern edge of Griffith Park. Each day, Ferndale played host to youthful birthday revelers, hikers, philosopher-chess players, indigents, and amateur botanists. This early in the morning, it was usually deserted except for the occasional runaway teenager sleeping off a drug stupor.

A flotsam of decaying leaves and muck drifted under him in a stream of rust-colored water. He watched as it made its way out the end of the drainage duct.

He lay on his stomach, arms stretched out in front of him, breathing through his mouth to lessen the stench. In a prior life, the stink would have barely registered. Proteus warriors suppressed everything but mission.

The military apparatus had used Luke and his fellow Proteus members, collecting them like lab rats for some sort of perverse Darwinian experiment. It was elegantly simple. Bring together the fifty most capable special ops commandos in the U.S. military—each man selected for his primal alpha traits, physical prowess, and killing skills—then submit them to a training program that stretched the known limits of human performance to the breaking point. The warriors had fed on one another like a fusion reaction, the training itself costing two men their lives.

When it was done, Luke was among the final twenty-four selected for Proteus.

In his lifetime, only one goal had consumed him more fully—undoing what Proteus had done to his psyche. He had worked for years to dismantle the unflinching ferocity and lethal instincts that for a time had been his defining identity.

He shook himself free of the unwanted memories and aimed his gaze at a public restroom nestled in a copse of trees.

Where is Sammy?

When the grim reality of Luke's situation had taken hold, Sammy's smirking face surfaced in his mind, as if to say, *I knew you'd be calling. Sooner or later, everybody needs Sammy's help.* Exactly how Sammy Wilkes helped people, and the types of problems he helped them with, had never been entirely clear to Luke. When asked, Sammy would throw out the term "corporate security," but when pushed to describe what that meant—exactly— the man had always displayed an astonishing talent for vagueness.

Ex-Proteus member or not, there was something conniving about him, and Luke had always stood clear of him. That is, until today, when there seemed no viable option but to dive headlong into the dark crevasse of Sammy's world.

The sun was out, which strengthened Luke's concealment. Set back six feet from the mouth of the pipe, he
was invisible to eyes constricted by the sun.

Five more minutes passed before a tall, lanky black
man dressed in gray coveralls walked into the restroom
carrying a red metal toolbox. When he came out, he
wasn't carrying anything.

The man dusted his sleeves—no threats in site—then
disappeared from view.

A minute later Luke was in the restroom donning coveralls and ill-fitting shoes left for him in the toolbox. A
minute after that, he climbed into the front passenger seat
of the white van in which Sammy was waiting.

"Let's get out of here," Luke said.

He was studying the sleepy tree-lined road when the hard
blunt end of a rounded cylinder brushed against his ear.

"Don't make me splatter your brains." Sammy threw a
pair of handcuffs onto Luke's lap. "Put 'em on. I figure
the po-lice will want you cuffed when I hand you over."

Chapter 34

The hell you thinking?" Wilkes said. "That Sammy's gonna risk everything—help you escape after popping that football player? Now put the cuffs on."

Luke could feel a thick sighting blade at the top of the rounded barrel. A revolver.

"Slo-ow and easy, Flash."

Luke leaned forward slightly when he reached for the handcuffs.

Sammy flexed his wrist, following the forward motion of Luke's head, and shoved the muzzle deeper into his captive's ear.

It was exactly what Luke had expected. Both movements loosened Sammy's trigger finger for just that instant. An immutable reflex. When combined with the slower double-action trigger of a revolver that had to rotate the cylinder while cocking and releasing the hammer, it was long enough.

Luke grabbed the pistol before Sammy took up the trigger's slack, thrusting the barrel upward and out of Wilkes's hand in a lightning-fast motion.

He pointed the gun at Sammy's chest. "You were never very good at the close-in stuff."

"Eew-weee." Sammy's luminescent white teeth blossomed into a smile. "Flash still got the touch."

"Did you have something you wanted to ask me?"

Sammy's face became a blank mask. "You do him?"

"No."

"Well, okay then." Sammy's eyes brightened. "I guess we're cool."

Luke took in the nickel-plated finish on the Smith & Wesson .357 Magnum, then emptied the bullets onto his lap. He flipped the gun in his hand, showing Sammy the pistol butt.

Sammy took the gun and stuffed it into his belt. He let out a belly laugh as he turned over the engine and checked the rearview mirror.

"It's time to introduce Flash to Sammy's world."

The first thing Megan heard was her own voice, a long and sluggish moan echoing in the black ether.

The darkness whirled around her, her eyelids too heavy to open. She tried to lift herself into a sitting position, but fell back when the nausea struck. A projectile of vomit erupted from her. Then the vertigo.

Through the fog, she heard, "Lie still, dear. Try not to move."

The priest. *What was his name?*

She moaned again, louder this time, and then another wave of nausea hit. Her stomach convulsed with dry heaves.

"Oh, dear God"—cough—"help the poor girl."

Another voice, in Spanish: *"Shut up!"*

The shouting peeled away a layer of her stupor, and her senses edged toward wakefulness.

Suddenly, her eyelid was pulled open. A bright light brought an explosion of pain. She struggled to turn away from the beam.

"Stop it. Let her be."

The light vanished, her eyelid fell closed. A moment later she heard a sickening *thud,* and then a weak groan coming from the priest.

The other voice said, "Your friend needs to learn to keep his mouth shut."

A radio crackled. Through the static she heard, "The old man's getting worse. Is she awake yet?"

"No."

"We need her over here—soon. Let me know as soon as she wakes up."

Megan tried to count the fading footsteps before the blackness returned.

"Sammy's not into causes. Sammy's into coin, and this is gonna cost you."

Wilkes hadn't changed, physically or otherwise. He had a restless, bouncing gait that accentuated his lanky farm-boy physique. His long arms swung in undulating waves as he paced around the room.

"I can pay you," Luke said.

"Now how you gonna do that, Flash? On the run, the po-lice on your tail, no wallet. Shit. You living in a fairy tale." He gave Luke a loose-wristed wave of his hand. "You what they call a pariah—a penniless pariah."

"They ever teach you about connecting verbs at Cornell?"

"What?"

"Never mind."

They were in the living room of Sammy's condominium, facing one another across a glass and chrome coffee table. The room was a study in black leather and polished metals. It looked out over the skyline of Los Angeles from the twenty-fourth floor of a Wilshire Boulevard high rise, just west of the Los Angeles Country Club.

Living in proximity to the city's oldest money was probably Sammy's way of mocking them.

Luke said, "How does eighty thousand sound? That's what I have in savings."

Sammy cocked an eyebrow.

"You get me what I need," Luke continued, "help me figure out what the hell is going on, and you can have all of it. I get caught, or something happens to me, and you get nothing."

He figured it was a long shot. Looking around the condominium, it was clear that Sammy wasn't struggling financially. Was the pot big enough for the risks involved? Would Sammy trust him?

"Someone is setting me up," Luke added, "and they're doing a damned good job. I need your help."

"What kind of help?"

"I don't know."

Sammy slapped his thighs. "Well, that's a good start."

"There was another murder, five days ago. A woman. The two murders are somehow connected."

"How?"

"I don't know, but they are. A woman I haven't seen in four years sent me an e-mail that has something to do with a boy who died in our E.R. Just before we were supposed to meet, she was murdered. A couple days after that, I'm framed for killing Erickson."

"And why's Sammy supposed to believe you didn't murder these nice folks yourself?"

"Because you know me."

Wilkes waggled a finger at Luke. "Sammy once—as in, a long time ago—knew a guy that kept to himself, didn't say much. Come to think of it, Sammy hardly knew this guy."

"Was the guy you knew stupid enough to leave tracks a Boy Scout could follow?"

Sammy ran a finger across his chin, then gave Luke a small nod. "Okay, so let's suppose you didn't do these people—"

"I didn't."

"If that's true, the question is, why does somebody want you outta the way?"

"I don't know."

"If what you're telling me is true, you probably do know. You just don't know what you know."

Luke thought about that for a moment. "If I was their problem, they could've just come after me, taken me out."

"You haven't been paying attention. I think they just did that." Sammy came forward in his seat. "Look. Maybe killing you would draw too much attention to their problem, shine a light on 'em. Maybe this thing is closer to you than you realize."

Luke regarded his former colleague. He wondered if Sammy was even aware of the change in his phrasing and idioms. He was shifting into professional mode. The man morphed from one persona to the next as easily as a chameleon changed its colors.

"Flash, are you drifting on me, or are you just deep in thought?"

"You going to help me?"

"I'm listening."

Luke described for him the events of the past several days. After telling Sammy about the mysterious arrival of Kate's e-mail, he pulled the photograph from his pocket and handed it to Wilkes.

"This came with the e-mail from Kate," he said. "Look at the children. The boy that died in our E.R.—Josue

Chaca—he had the same tattoo as the boy in that picture. And Jane Doe—her tattoo was identical to the girl's."

"Wait a minute." Sammy made a time-out sign with his hands. "You telling me someone's feeding you stuff? Some guardian angel just dropped this e-mail on your doorstep?"

"Looks that way. But now the police think that I was holding back. I told them about the e-mail a few days ago, told them I never got it. Then this morning, they storm into my apartment and find it sitting there."

"Shee-it. Even when things go right, they don't go right for you, Flash."

The comment evoked in Luke an uncomfortable feeling: hopelessness.

Sammy glanced at his watch and then turned on a plasma-screen TV that spanned half of the wall on which it hung. "It's five o'clock. Let's check out the latest on Doctor Fugitive."

Luke was the second item of the hour on the local news channel. A head shot from his hospital ID flashed on the screen behind the brunette anchorwoman's right shoulder. A picture of Erickson appeared to her left. Most of the report centered on Erickson, including mention of the young girl left fatherless by the murder.

When the anchor moved on to a preview of tomorrow's weather, Sammy leaned back into his couch, hands clasped behind his neck. "You need to get your hands on ten thousand, up-front cash. Sammy ain't fronting expenses."

Luke gave him a nod.

"And if you're lying to me, there's no place on earth that you can hide from Sammy. I think you know that."

"I'm not lying."

Sammy framed Luke between his outstretched hands.

"First thing you'll need is a makeover. Just happens to be one of Sammy's specialties."

"... *Megan Callahan* ..." Luke heard the name through Sammy's chatter. He lifted a hand to silence Sammy as he turned to the TV.

"... *Today, University Children's Hospital is making news on more than one front. Hours ago, an armed militia group in Guatemala took responsibility for the abduction of Dr. Callahan. The group claimed that, by interfering in the customs and practices of native Mayan tribes, she and other American doctors are practicing a form of genocide. Any further interference, they warned, will lead to the captive doctor's immediate execution. A hospital spokesperson would not comment on what, if anything, is being done to secure Dr. Callahan's release.*

"*Abductions of U.S. tourists and relief workers in Central and South America have been on the rise for several years. The U.S. State Department says they have no knowledge of the group involved in this abduction. They advise U.S. citizens traveling abroad to* ..."

Chapter 35

Barnesdale settled onto the couch in his library. A single flame-colored swath of light from a torchiere floor lamp crawled up one corner of the walnut-paneled room.

He picked up the remote from his coffee table and pressed PLAY.

The TV played an image of the Research Tower's small marble-floored lobby, the tempered glass entry doors, and a small section of the walkway just outside the entrance. It looked more like a photograph than a video running in play mode. Except for the seconds counter on a time stamp in the upper right-hand corner—it read 7:12:23—nothing was moving.

Twelve minutes after seven, Saturday morning, eleven minutes before Elmer McKenna had walked through the front doors.

Barnesdale didn't fast-forward the recording. He wanted to see if anybody had been milling in front of the building's entrance around that time.

He'd had all day to think about the scene that was about to unfold on his TV screen. There had been no reports of a stolen badge, and even Elmer would have noticed if his badge had gone missing. He knew he'd see Elmer enter the Research Tower at 7:23. One of the three Infectious Disease laboratories was located on the eighth floor. Elmer had gone to his eighth floor lab on Saturday morning.

But Elmer had pressed both *2* and *8*. That was no accident. He had pushed the button for a coworker.

Barnesdale had walked the perimeter of the building a few hours earlier, looking for other points of entry. There were none. The only other doors at ground level were fire exits from stairwells on either side of the building. Neither door had an exterior handle, lock, or keypad. The only way to enter through those doors would be with a crowbar, and neither door showed any signs of tampering.

Inside the tower, people used elevators to travel between floors because the exit doors on each floor couldn't be opened from inside the stairwells. Presumably, that prevented people from wandering between floors.

But it wouldn't prevent someone from leaving the building. Anyone could leave the building without having to use the badge-swipe system, merely by walking down either of the two stairwells and exiting through one of the side doors.

Barnesdale sat forward on his couch. For the second time a pair of legs appeared briefly in the upper left-hand corner of the image. It was a man wearing gray slacks, cordovan shoes, and a white lab coat. The time stamp read 7:20:03.

In three minutes he would know who had switched the marrow samples. He pictured Elmer walking up to the front door in his usual cloudy state.

Someone he knows, probably a coworker, approaches from behind and greets him. Elmer opens the door and the pair walk inside together.

They continue chatting as they board the elevator. The Zenavax mole asks Elmer to save him the trouble and press 2. Elmer obliges.

The mole wishes McKenna a "good day" as he gets off on the second floor. Fifteen minutes later, his work completed, the mole leaves using one of the stairwells.

It seemed more than a small irony that Elmer had opened the door for the person who switched the dead boy's marrow. The eccentric old fool had thwarted his own son's efforts.

The time stamp now read 7:22:05. In one minute he'd have the leverage he needed to ensure his safety. Zenavax wouldn't touch him once they knew there was a letter in his attorney's safe—a letter to be opened in the event of his death.

The Zenavax IPO was in eight days. On that day, the shares he held in a blandly named trust—shares he received for his "special services"—would be sold into the feeding frenzy that was developing around the company's Initial Public Offering.

And he'd be done with Zenavax.

A strand of hair fell over Henry's forehead. He fought a tremor as he tried to pat it back in place.

Barnesdale forgot about the stray hair when he saw Elmer McKenna's image appear on the video.

Elmer trundled up to the front door and swiped his badge through a reading pad mounted on the door frame. He turned to his rear when a man wearing gray slacks and cordovan shoes appeared in the corner of the screen.

The pulse in Henry's neck throttled up when the man stepped into the foreground.

"You bastard," Barnesdale whispered. "I got you."

"White guys just shouldn't shave their head." Sammy pruned his face and pursed his lips. "Uh-uh, no way. Just shouldn't be done."

Luke ignored Wilkes's chatter and examined himself in the mirror.

Sammy had taken Luke's full head of hair and turned it into a one-eighth-inch crop of dyed red stubble, but what drew most of Luke's attention was the badly dimpled cleft lip scar. The scar was fashioned with a Krazy-Glue-like substance, and the jagged mark crossed through his upper lip and formed a pucker as it snaked its way into his right nostril.

They were in one of the back rooms at Sammy's offices, which were located in an industrial park complex about a mile from Burbank Airport. A makeup bench ran along one wall. The rest of the room looked like a photography studio.

"The scar won't last more than four or five days," Sammy said while handing Luke a small tube. "Hold onto this. You'll need it when you return. Don't forget what I showed you, and don't show up at a passport checkpoint without that scar."

Luke rubbed an eye. "How am I supposed to keep these contacts in? They sting like hell."

"You'll get used to them, and anyway, you won't need 'em once you get to Guatemala.

Sammy had created Luke's new identity with the same proficiency and sense of routine that other men achieve only with a TV remote. He had perused the online obituaries from several southern California newspapers and found three recently deceased males in their mid-thirties. After a call to a criminal attorney, Sammy discarded one of the names because of a criminal record that could lead to unwanted scrutiny if Luke was stopped or questioned.

Luke selected one of the two remaining names. He was now Edward Schweers.

Next, Sammy had gone to work with his contact at the DMV. Two hours later they had the former Mr. Schweers's Social Security and driver's license numbers. It would be several weeks, or perhaps months, before dutiful public servants marked Edward Schweers's state and federal records as deceased.

Luke scrutinized the ID photos that Sammy had taken. The only difference was his eye color. In one pair of photos, his eyes were their natural dark brown; in the other, they were coral blue.

"Forget the contacts," Luke said. "I don't want to have to explain to some Customs agent why my eyes are bloodshot. Use these." He tossed the two brown-eyed photographs to Sammy.

By morning one of Sammy's vendors would create a passport and driver's license from the photos.

Earlier, Luke had reached Ben Wilson in his office. The pathologist agreed to leave a package with ten thousand dollars in cash on his front porch at exactly 10:00 P.M. Sammy would drive by at 10:03 and pick it up. A third of the money had been spent already on Sammy's vendors, and Luke's journey hadn't even begun.

"So let me see if I got this plan down," Sammy said. "The one that Sammy's betting eighty gees on. You're gonna make your way to Guatemala, which you never been to, find some people you're not even sure exist, locate this woman—"

"Megan. She's got a name."

"Yeah, whatever. So when you find this woman, who may or *may not* be alive, you're gonna do a Sherlock number and figure out how two dead kids figure into the murders of some scientist lady and a football player"—Sammy took an exaggerated breath—"then come back and explain to the cops how you were framed. Is that about it?"

"It sounded better when I said it."

"And you gonna do all this while snooping around in a country where you don't even speak the language."

"I understand enough."

"Cabalgará usted el cerdo al mercado?"

Luke gave him an ambiguous nod.

"Oh, I see." Sammy's head bounced up and down like a dashboard doll. "So you *are* going to ride your pig to the market."

"Look, eighty thousand dollars should buy me more than makeup and IDs. If you have a better idea, now's the time to share it."

"I'm just saying there's a lot of pieces missing from this puzzle. You may end up chasing your tail in Guatemala."

The cell phone in Luke's coat pocket rang. It was the phone that Sammy had given him to call Ben.

"Ignore it," Sammy said. "No one has that number. That phone's only used for outgoing calls."

Luke said, "Ben Wilson has this number. I gave it to him when we arranged the drop." He flipped open the phone.

"Ben?"

Silence.

"Hello?" Luke said.

"Stay away," said a heavily accented Hispanic voice.

Luke shot a glance at Sammy. "Away from where?"

"Dr. McKenna, there is no need to insult me. I am sure you know what we are talking about, no?" There was a long silence, then, "I guess you want that we . . . how you say, make our point in a more direct way."

The phone went quiet for a moment, then a slurred female voice said, *"What are you . . . No—No more . . . please."*

"Megan!" Luke yelled.

"No . . . please . . ." Another scream.

The man's voice again: "Are we understanding each other now?"

Luke's chest heaved. "If anything happens to her, you're a dead—"

A dial tone interrupted him.

Chapter 36

"Flash, you still don't get it, do you?" Sammy shook his head while driving east on Interstate 10. "These people aren't trying to hide from you. They want you to know that they got you wired."

Luke squinted into a burst of sunlight rising over the horizon. "I don't scare that easily."

"Maybe that's what they're counting on. It looks to Sammy like they're reeling you in, using your doctor friend as bait. Think about it—they do you in Guatemala, use you as fertilizer in some banana orchard, and nobody ever hears from Doctor Fugitive again. You might be playing right into their hands."

Images of Megan, locked away in some dark hole, flashed in Luke's mind. "I'm not running from these people."

Sammy adjusted his rearview mirror. "The cell phone you used to call Ben Wilson has caller ID block. No-way no-how anyone could get that number 'less they work for the phone company. You're dealing with pros here. These people got juice—they wired Wilson's office. They heard you give him your phone number."

A thought that had been floating at the edges of Luke's mind suddenly dropped on him like a brick. "I need to call Ben. He's in their crosshairs and doesn't even know it."

"Whoa, Flash. You're not calling *anyone*. By now the po-lice probably have a fix on every person you've called in the last six months. You can bet that Wilson's on their list. You call him from a landline, they'll probably be tracing it. You call him from a cell phone, they'll have your location mapped on the cell grid in less than a minute."

"Then you get to him. Tell him to leave this thing alone."

Sammy nodded. "I'll talk to him."

"And tell Ben to get ahold of my father, let him know that I'm okay." Luke reached into the backseat and grabbed a small backpack with some clothes and travel items that Sammy had bought for him. "How much farther to Riverside?"

"We should be there in about twenty minutes."

"So you're clear on your assignments?" Luke asked.

"Give me two days. I'll have some dope on that company, Zenavax. But it'd help if you could tell me who mighta left the copy of Tartaglia's e-mail on your doorstep."

"I have no idea."

Sammy started playing the steering wheel like a set of bongos. "I'm also gonna see if I can turn up anything on your lady friend, Megan Callahan."

Luke pulled a bulky cell phone from the backpack. "Tell me about this phone."

"It's a satellite unit—uses a lotta energy. Fifteen, maybe eighteen hours between charges."

"You sure this thing is safe? They found me on your other cellular."

"Sammy burns through a lot of cell phone numbers in his work. That's a clean number—never been used." He jabbed the handset with his thumb. "And this has encryption, but it only works when you're transmitting to *me*. My unit has the same algorithm. It's smaller than most satellite phones—that's the advantage—but it's also less powerful. Unless you're out in the open, forget it."

"When will I hear from you?"

"I'll call you once a day," Sammy said, "at 1900 hours, Guatemala time. That thing has voice mail, but I'm not leaving you any messages so make sure it's turned on at seven o'clock each night."

Sammy glanced at the rearview mirror again. "Highway Patrol. Coming up on my side."

Luke affected a relaxed pose. The cream-colored sedan with no markings or roof lights passed them without a glance. The only clue of law enforcement was a shotgun mounted next to the driver, pointing up toward the rearview mirror.

"Get outta California before you go near an airport," Sammy said. "Take a bus into Arizona, or New Mexico. Then, maybe you can fly to . . ."

Luke could hardly listen through the grim desolation that washed over him. He was on the run with a rapidly dwindling supply of cash and no weapon. He didn't know whom he was up against or why they were targeting him, nor did he know how Megan's abduction fit into this nightmare. The only thing he knew with certainty was that he had set in motion the events that led to her abduction. Because of him, Megan's life had suddenly turned into a hellhole.

"You listening to me?" asked Sammy.

Luke stared at a freight train crawling along the side of the freeway. "Yeah."

"One more thing. I know someone who might be able to help you. You know him too."

"Who?"

"Calderon."

"Forget it."

"Just listen," Sammy said. "Calderon used to work for me. But he didn't really fit into corporate security. He was a little too much into bone breaking. The Guatemalan army offered him a job training their special forces, so he headed south a few years ago."

"What does that have to do with—"

"Coupla years ago he got tired of working for their army and started his own company, doing security-type work in places where the sun's a little hotter and the laws are a little more relaxed." Sammy laughed. "He hired away some of my best people. I guess he needed English speakers for some of his clients. I didn't take it personally. In fact, we do favors for one another from time to time. We each have our special skills."

"I *know* what his are."

"Just keep it in mind. Maybe he knows someone in Guatemala, someone who's connected. Hell, you don't even know where to start looking." Sammy turned to Luke. "I know there was some bad blood between you and Calderon, but that was a long time ago."

"Bad blood? The last time I saw that scumbag, he was taking the skin off a prisoner's face with his K-Bar. Calderon had his knee on the guy's throat and was cutting off an eyelid. That man was our captive—we were responsible for him."

Sammy's face puckered like a fish. "Calderon has some strange shit going on in his head, that's for sure, but he's learned how to control himself. And he's the best wet-ops guy I ever worked with—the man's a human sledgehammer. I doubt you'd last ten seconds in a room alone with him. Who knows? His skills might come in handy."

"I said forget it."

"So, McKenna's alibi for Tartaglia doesn't hold up," Groff said. "Now we got him for two murders."

The lieutenant slapped the table as though his hand were a gavel and he had just rendered his decision. He winced when the motion carried to his ribs, three of which McKenna had broken the previous day when he kicked Groff down the stairway.

O'Reilly had been summoned to the windowless third floor conference room at Parker Center to give an update on the Tartaglia investigation. They were sitting in what had become the "war room" in the hunt for McKenna.

"Lieutenant, I don't think we can say that yet," O'Reilly countered. "There are problems with the timeline."

The blond muscle-bound detective who'd gone down the stairs with Groff was sitting to the lieutenant's left, staring at O'Reilly. The man was finding it awkward to chew a stick of gum with his neck wrapped in a brace, but he was doing better than his female partner, who was laid up at home with a back injury.

Sitting on Groff's right was a drop-dead gorgeous LAPD psychologist who specialized in profiling suspects.

She was looking at the knot on O'Reilly's forehead when she asked, "What problems, Detective?"

Groff said, "Yeah. You just told us that the security tapes showed McKenna leaving the hospital at 10:07:22 on the night of Tartaglia's murder. The victim's phone call with her mother didn't end until seven minutes later, at 10:14:29."

"Give or take," O'Reilly said. "The hospital's security clock runs seventeen seconds behind Tartaglia's cellular service."

"You're splitting hairs," Groff said. "If, like you say, it only takes four and a half minutes to walk from the hospital exit to that parking lot, that means he had two and a half minutes to do her."

"Not exactly," O'Reilly said. "The owner of Kolter's Deli remembers McKenna entering the restaurant while a customer was paying his bill. There's only one cash register receipt within ten minutes of the murder. It had a time stamp of ten-thirteen."

"Which still leaves him with a minute and a half," Blondie said. "What's your problem?"

"The clock in that restaurant's register"—O'Reilly checked his notes—"runs sixty-seven seconds behind the cellular company's. That means, when McKenna walked through the front door at Kolter's, the time on Tartaglia's phone was somewhere between 10:14:06 and 10:15:06. I can't narrow it down any more than that because the restaurant's register doesn't show seconds on the printed records. But even if we use the later time—10:15:06—and we assume that McKenna murdered Tartaglia at the moment her phone call ended, that would leave just thirty-seven seconds to take her purse and keys, and get to the restaurant."

O'Reilly allowed that thought to sink in, then said, "It takes almost a minute to walk to the restaurant from where her car was parked—"

"So he ran to the restaurant," Blondie offered. "We already know the guy moves a lot faster than you, O'Reilly."

The embarrassment and anger about McKenna's escape hung over the room like a stench, and no one was hiding the fact that they blamed O'Reilly. They couldn't fathom how McKenna had sent them sprawling, jumped to his feet, swept Blondie's partner onto her back—all before O'Reilly could unholster his weapon.

"Let's just get through this." Groff aimed a finger at O'Reilly. "What else do you got?"

Shortly after McKenna's escape and the discovery of Kate Tartaglia's e-mail message in his apartment, Groff had officially taken charge of O'Reilly's investigation. The investigation and search was now a task force operation involving all four of Groff's teams—eight detectives. Three of the teams were out hunting for McKenna, which was the only reason that O'Reilly was still working the case. As soon as things settled down, Groff would reassign the Tartaglia case to one of his own teams.

O'Reilly tapped his notes with a pencil. "Tartaglia's e-mail. I'm still trying to find the attachment she sent with it, but then, I don't even know what I'm looking for. There's nothing in McKenna's apartment that looks like it belongs to that e-mail. Tartaglia's ISP has a record of the transmittal, but not the e-mail message itself—they wipe their server clean as soon as an e-mail goes through to the recipient. That leaves University Children's. That's where Tartaglia sent her e-mail, and the hospital's IT group tells us that they save everything for thirty days. But so far, our computer forensics team hasn't found any record of her e-mail on their server—nothing. Our guys say they need another couple of days before they can tell me when it was erased, and whether they can recover a copy."

"I'll get you more resources if you need 'em, but I want that e-mail attachment. McKenna didn't just lie to us about not receiving her message. He tried to erase the whole goddamned trail. I wanna know why." Groff sat forward, flinching as he did so. "What about Tartaglia's employer—Zenavax?"

"Talked to her boss, and the company's CEO. Both of them said the usual stuff. She was a good employee, she'll be hard to replace, they can't imagine why someone would've wanted to kill her."

When asked about Tartaglia's project at the Coroner's Office, they had also produced a bland memo describing the creation of a "library" of human blood serum from non-U.S. Hispanic subjects for undetermined future purposes. According to them, it was no more than a collection and storage program. In other words, it was an investigative dead end unless he wanted to slap a warrant on them and search their files, which Groff would never approve.

So instead of tilting at that windmill, O'Reilly said, "Lieutenant, it's what they didn't say that I found interesting. When I mentioned that Tartaglia was murdered on her way to a meeting with someone at the hospital, neither of 'em asked me who. I didn't mention McKenna, and they didn't ask."

"What's your point?" asked Groff.

"Well, I've already told you about the big brouhaha that happened when she first joined Zenavax. She used to work for McKenna's father, remember? So wouldn't you think they'd be curious enough to ask who she was meeting with at the hospital?"

Groff was shaking his head. "Where you going with this? I don't need more suspects—McKenna killed her. Tartaglia's mother puts him at the murder scene, and you just tore a hole in his alibi. His military file tells us that he has the skills. God knows, he had motive—in his mind, the woman stole his father's work, and maybe cost him a big inheritance."

"This is about retribution, not money," the psychologist said. "It's important that you understand who you're dealing with. McKenna sees the world in terms of good and

evil, and he has no doubt about his judgments. He's acting with absolute moral clarity."

"So he makes up his own rules," Groff said, "and
whacks anyone who breaks 'em?"

"More likely, he sees himself as enforcing time-
honored rules that society has let lapse. Ironically, people
like McKenna consider themselves strong law and order
types, but when the world doesn't live up to their expec-
tations, they snap. It may have happened when that rapist
attacked his woman friend, but whatever the trigger was,
McKenna decided that he needed to right the wrongs. He
had no other choice—people with his mind-set see weakness as the greatest sin."

Blondie used a finger to free something between his
teeth. "Typical nut case."

"Don't make the mistake of thinking he's insane," she
said. "McKenna has a firm grasp on reality, but he's chosen to deal with that reality differently than you or I
would. He's a completely rational thinker. That's our
advantage—we can use that to anticipate him."

"How?" Groff said.

"First, think about how he views his current situation.
He knows this will end badly for him, but he's committed
now. He's probably going to continue to"—she made
quotation marks in the air—" 'right the wrongs' until we
stop him. We need to examine his life, come up with a list
of people who, in his mind, deserve to be punished."

A uniformed officer across the room called out, "Lieutenant, phone call on line four."

Groff picked up the receiver while snapping his fingers
at Blondie, who handed him a pen. The lieutenant listened to the caller for almost a minute without making a
note.

Then he dropped the pen and spread a hand over his

eyes. "Oh, shit." When he hung up the phone, he looked at O'Reilly. "Henry Barnesdale."

"What about him?" O'Reilly asked.

"He's dead. Somebody crushed his windpipe, then broke his neck." Groff turned to the psychologist. "Looks like we're a little late making that list."

Chapter 37

"You sure you know where you're going?" Luke asked.

Ari, an Israeli student Luke had latched onto during his flight out of the U.S., turned the travel guide map one way, then the other, before pointing down the side street. "This way."

They had arrived in Santa Elena, Guatemala, at 2:00 P.M. Luke had been on the move for almost twenty-four hours: a Greyhound bus to Phoenix, a nearly empty plane from Phoenix to Houston, a direct flight from Houston to Belize, and then a dusty bus trip west into Guatemala.

Tomorrow, the Israeli was traveling to the Mayan ruins at Tikal. Until then Luke would use his Spanish-speaking companion as human camouflage.

"By the way," Ari said while hefting a backpack that towered over his shoulders, "your share of the hotel room comes to three U.S. dollars. In Guatemalan currency, twenty-four quetzals."

"Fine." The moist air stuck to Luke like a wet blanket, and a furious itch had taken hold under his improvised scar. "Take a look at your maps and tell me how far it is to Santa Lucina from here."

The risk of going to the University Children's clinic was obvious—his colleagues would send word back to the hospital that he was in Guatemala—but he had to act quickly. After the call from Megan's captors, Luke had no doubt that her abductors and the people who had framed him for Erickson's murder were one and the same.

And they had already shown that they dealt with their problems by killing them.

The storefronts changed as they walked along a wood-slat sidewalk. Over a distance of three blocks, Laundro-mats, convenience stores, and pharmacies became bars, dance halls, and what looked like an occasional brothel. A woman wearing a filthy yellow blouse pointed at them and whistled while strutting along the second-story colon-nade of a ramshackle clapboard structure. A string of naked lightbulbs hung over her head.

They stopped at the edge of an alley while Ari looked at his map again. Santa Elena secreted an aura that had Luke checking his pants pockets every few minutes for his wallet and passport.

A small boy holding a box ran up to them, dropped it next to the Israeli's leg and said, "You need shine, boss. Six quetzals."

Ari looked down at his dust-covered boots. "Two."

"No way, boss. Four."

"Okay, four." Ari glanced back at his map. "We're go-ing the wrong way. We need to head in that direction." He threw a thumb over his shoulder.

The boy, who looked to be no more than eight or nine years old, lifted one of Ari's boots onto the box and went to work rubbing polish into the leather with his black-tipped fingers. But he didn't seem to have his heart in his work. The boy glanced to the side every few seconds, as if already searching for his next customer.

On the third or fourth glance, the boy nodded at the air, then tapped Ari's boot.

Luke looked in the direction of the boy's nod.

Two men with oily, matted hair and clothes to match were walking toward them. One glanced down when Luke met his gaze. The man was holding his right hand inside a jacket that struck a discordant note in the sweltering heat.

Luke said, "Ari, let's go."

"What?"

"Move, now." Luke grabbed the Israeli's shoulder.

The urchin yanked on Ari's leg. "Hey boss, no move."

Ari lost his balance, stumbling under the weight of his pack.

Before he recovered, the shorter of the two men had reached them. He unsheathed a knife from his belt. His taller partner, who wore a thick white scar where one of his eyebrows should have been, pulled a 9mm Glock handgun from under his jacket and shoved it into Ari's face.

Luke allowed his arms to come up in surrender as he watched the little urchin step away in what looked like a rehearsed move.

It seemed impossible that his enemies could have discovered him this easily.

The scarred man jerked his head toward the alley. Luke and Ari stepped back into a shadowed area that smelled of urine and rotting fruit.

Ari was on Luke's left, and Scar Face stood on the other side of the Israeli, away from Luke.

Scar Face said something in Spanish while the second man circled behind them.

Ari nodded nervously and choked out some words, his tone pleading.

Whatever he said, it didn't work. Scar Face bit off an angry response and the gun barrel ended up on the side of Ari's head.

Luke tried to draw attention to himself by waggling his hip and eyeing his right pants pocket, as if to say, *The money's in there. Take it.*

The man standing behind them reached around and held the knife against Luke's neck while reaching into his pocket and grabbing his passport as well as a billfold containing three hundred U.S. dollars. He repeated the process with the Israeli.

Luke wasn't going to tell them about the nearly two thousand dollars tucked into his shoes.

Scar Face took a step back, angling away from Luke while keeping his gun trained on Ari.

Luke could hear the other man behind them, rifling through the wallets.

A moment later, the billfolds and passports flew onto the wet ground in front of Luke. A crumpled five-dollar bill landed beside them a moment later.

The urchin swooped in and snatched up the passports and money. Then he ran across the street, glancing back once before disappearing between two buildings.

Luke tried to read Scar Face's eyes, looking for some sign of intent and purpose. Was this a simple robbery? The man's eyes were lifeless caverns. Whoever this man was, it was clear that Luke's and Ari's lives were as meaningless as microbes.

Scar Face held Luke's stare for a long moment, then stepped up to Ari and rammed the butt of his gun into the Israeli's temple.

Ari slumped to the ground.

Scar Face showed his rotted teeth to Luke, then swung the Glock down and took aim at Ari's head.

Luke lunged at the man, grabbed the gun barrel and twisted it free while sweeping the assailant's feet and up-ending him.

The knife in the accomplice's hand was already swinging toward Luke's neck when he put two 9 mm Glock rounds into the man's chest.

Scar Face was coming off the ground when Luke dropped onto him with a cocked elbow and connected with the would-be killer's temple.

The man's skull gave way. His eyes rolled back and he went limp.

Luke reached for a stinging pain in his left shoulder and felt a sticky wet fluid running down his arm—blood. A moment later he saw the knife in Scar Face's limp hand, and the empty belt sheath that the man's jacket had concealed.

Luke checked the bodies and quickly retrieved more cash than the assailants had taken from them. He took the Glock and shoved it under his belt, then picked up Ari in a dead man's carry and followed the alley back into a labyrinth of twisting passageways.

"Where are we?" Megan asked, trying to shake off what she recognized as the remnants of a drug stupor.

A steady vibration came up through the floor, accompanied by the reverberating hum of heavy machinery.

"It's a storage shed of some sort," Father Joe said. "We're in some sort of walled compound with, maybe, a half-dozen small buildings. They brought us here in the back of a truck. Don't you remember?"

She shook her head.

They were sitting next to each other, leaning against the only wall space not taken up by wooden crates. Megan looked around the small wood-frame structure. The only light came in through two small portholes at either end of the ten-by-ten-foot room. The place smelled of mold.

She tried to raise herself. A wave of nausea overtook her and she fell back.

He put a hand on her shoulder. "That's a pretty big lump on your head. Try to take it easy."

She palpated a knot on her left temple.

"You must be Irish," he said. "I think you gave them more of a fight than they expected."

"How long have we been here? The last thing I remember is . . . the village, the flood. Then someone grabbing me from behind."

"That was two days ago. When we first got here, they drugged you. I heard them say the name of the drug—something like 'Bersed.' "

"Versed," she clarified. Now she understood why her connections to time and place were severed, her memory a blank. She had drug-induced amnesia.

"They seem to think you know something. They were asking a lot of questions, trying to get information from you."

"About what?"

She had no memory of the interrogation. They had used the drug to reduce her inhibitions, to get her to talk.

"I couldn't hear all of it. We were in one of the other buildings, and they had you in a separate room. But I heard them ask over and over why you'd come to Guatemala."

"They must have questioned *you*."

"They did, but they seemed a lot more interested in you. They already know who I am, anyway. I guess they didn't think I had much to tell 'em." The priest's breathing was rapid and labored.

"Are you okay?"

He patted his chest. "It'll pass."

"Where's your medicine—your inhaler?"

"They took it." Father Joe leaned back to take a breath.

The light caught his scalp. There was a deep gash on his forehead.

"Did they beat you?"

He lifted his shoulders. "I have a big mouth."

Megan startled at the sound of the door swinging open with a loud creak. Two men entered. One was Asian, the other a tall and powerfully built Latino who was missing part of his ear. Neither man was carrying a weapon, but it hardly mattered. She could barely stand, let alone put up a fight.

The Asian hoisted her by the collar and lifted her to her feet with one arm.

Megan tried to kick him but missed.

The Latino grabbed her jaw in one hand and squeezed.

The pain shot through her like a bolt. Her vision went dark.

"I don't have time for this, *puta*."

Puta—whore.

She spat in his face—a reflex that surprised her.

The Latino let go of her and slowly wiped the spittle from his cheek. A thin smile played on his lips.

Then a sharp blow to her face sent her sprawling against a pine-board crate.

Father Joe threw himself over her and yelled, *"For the love of God, stop!"*

Megan felt another wave of nausea.

The Asian lifted both of them by their arms and pushed them through the door.

The Latino man led the way through a compound that was the size of a city block. It was enclosed on three sides by walls made of stone and white mortar; the entire length of wall was capped with barbed wire. The fourth side needed no wall. It was a shear cliff of blackened limestone, pockmarked with caves, and there was a large tunnel entrance in the middle of a stony talus at the base of the mountain.

They passed between two metal-sided buildings that glistened in the sunlight. Parked alongside one of them was a tan-colored transport truck with a red caduceus on its cab door. Two workers dressed in white coveralls stepped out from one of the buildings and glanced furtively in their direction before walking quickly into the other structure.

Beyond the perimeter wall, forested slopes rose on two sides. About halfway up one of the inclines, a canvas-tarp truck passed in and out of view as it threaded its way along a mountain pass obscured by green timber.

Their destination turned out to be a long two-story wooden structure at the far end of the compound. She peered through the open doorways of several dormitory-style rooms as they walked down the first-floor hallway.

When they passed the last room on the left, Megan saw a young girl lying on a steel-legged table. The child had dysmorphic facial features that marked her as suffering from a genetic disorder. An ultrasound machine was sitting next to her, and a female technician in a white lab coat was moving a sonographic sensor over the girl's lower abdomen.

Other than a ruptured appendix, tumor, or diseased ovaries, Megan couldn't think of many reasons to do an ultrasound of the lower abdomen.

And she couldn't think of *any* reason that someone would be doing such a high-tech medical procedure in the middle of a Guatemalan jungle.

What is this place?

They climbed a flight of stairs and walked down a corridor to the third room on the right. In its only bed lay an elderly man, his head writhing as if in a delirium. Two IV bags hung from poles. A woman was injecting something into one of the bags as they entered the room. Even from the door, Megan could see that the patient was flushed with fever.

The man had a large head with graying red hair that was matted with sweat. His face looked as if he had just come in from the rain.

The Latino man motioned to the woman standing at the bedside. She immediately left the room. As soon as the door was closed, he said, "This man's life is now your responsibility."

"What do you mean?"

"What don't you understand? It's your job to make sure this man recovers from his illness."

"I'm trained to take care of children." She stared at the old man while calling back the image of the ultrasound machine. "There must be other doctors here."

"Only one," he said, "and you're looking at him."

She moved closer and studied the old man's face. After a moment she brought a hand to her mouth.

"I thought he was dead," she whispered.

Chapter 38

Luke reached over the front seat and handed the cab driver another hundred-quetzal bill, then leaned back and pulled his brimmed cap lower on his forehead.

He needed his passport, and to do that, he had to find the little urchin. For the past hour he had ridden up and down mostly unpaved streets while thinking about his encounter with the assailants. Was it anything more than a coincidence, a random robbery? He hadn't told anyone where or how he would enter Guatemala—not even Sammy.

After the robbery attempt, Luke had carried the Israeli through a half-dozen narrow alleyways separating a disorderly collection of buildings. They emerged onto an adjoining street and hailed a filthy little cab whose driver smirked knowingly when Luke used gestures to indicate that his friend was drunk. He had pointed to Ari's guidebook and shown the driver the motel that his travel companion had underlined. After stuffing a wad of money into the Israeli's pocket, Luke handed the driver three times his requested fare.

He'd watched Ari's cab disappear into traffic before hailing another cab to begin his search for the street urchin. Except for the thermonuclear headache that was waiting for him on the other side of a long sleep, the Israeli was going to be all right.

Luke tried not to think about how easily the killing had come back to him. When threatened, his humanity had fallen away like a loose-fitting robe, and the natural-born killer had revealed himself.

The late afternoon sun was glowing orange when he finally spotted the boy. The little imp was shining a pair of shoes on the sidewalk outside a tavern, just two streets over from where the assailants had snared Luke.

He trailed the boy on foot for the next thirty minutes, watching from a distance as the urchin traveled in a pattern that resembled the spokes of a wheel, always returning to the same tattered one-story building at the hub of his movements.

The boy was thick-bodied and had a protuberant belly that was oddly man-like despite his short stature. He resembled a Buddha in miniature and had an inefficient waddling gait, leaning to the side with each step like an aging dockworker with bad hips. But his physical appearance was deceptive. He had a way of disappearing like a mosquito into a shadow. Every time Luke's eyes left the boy, even for just a second, he vanished into a crowd.

It was unnerving, and he decided to seize his next opportunity to snatch the boy. That happened when the urchin emerged from his third visit to the ragged building. The boy stepped out the front door, glanced over his shoulder at the horizon, and walked toward the open-air bar where Luke was sitting behind a large clay planter.

There was only one other patron in the bar's terrace when Luke reached out from behind the planter and grabbed the boy, lifting him off his feet and pulling him over a wooden railing that encircled the terra-cotta patio. The shoeshine box fell onto the tiles and its hinged top split in two. The boy's expression told Luke that he knew what had happened to the muggers; his eyes looked like two large eggs popping out of a hen.

The lone customer sitting on the other side of the patio let out a drunken giggle as Luke placed the boy in the seat next to his own.

"Please, boss," the boy said in a squeaky voice. "I glad you got away."

"You're going to return my passport, right?"

The boy's head nodded like a piston engine at full throttle.

"Good. Let's go."

Another staccato burst of nods.

Luke scooped up the remains of the shoeshine box and held the boy's hand in a tight grip as they walked toward the building that appeared to be his base of operations. The structure had no particular character: beige stucco with rust stains running down its sides, a corrugated steel canopy across the front, and an open archway entrance that offered no protection from the elements. They entered a small atrium with white tile flooring from which several pieces were missing. Two doors at either end of the lobby opened into large dormitory-style rooms.

The boy whispered, "I give you you wallet and you money, boss. Act like you my friend. If they know why you here, they kick us out. Please, boss."

They walked into the large room on the right. A woman in a drab but well-pressed uniform sat at a small wooden desk in the far corner of the room. She looked at Luke, then at the boy.

"Frankie?"

The boy said something to her, but Luke wasn't listening. He was taking in the room. Eight metal frame beds sat along one wall. All but one had an occupant. All were women. All looked like they were young, though it was difficult to know with certainty because they lived in bodies that were ravaged by disease.

The boy walked over to the second bed, knelt down, and pulled a large green duffel bag from underneath the metal-framed fixture. He opened the zipper and buried his arm up to his elbow, pulling out a small leather satchel as Luke approached.

The woman lying in the bed seemed not to notice any of this. She was a skeleton covered by gray skin, her eyes clouded, her expression trance-like. Each breath looked as if it might be her last. Two flat purple lesions sat on the side of her neck: Kaposi's sarcoma.

The woman was dying of HIV.

"Here, boss. Here." The urchin held his hand out to Luke. In it was a U.S. five-dollar bill. "This what they gave me."

"Do you know this woman?" Luke asked, though he figured he knew the answer.

"*Mi madre*—my mother." The boy grabbed Luke's hand and put the bill into it.

Luke didn't have to ask the rest of the story. Judging from the neighborhood, it was a good bet that his mother was a prostitute or IV drug user. Maybe both.

The boy pointed to a door at the rear. "I be right back."

While the urchin rummaged through some trash in the back of the property, Luke looked around the room again. A crucifix hung over both doorways. There was a small stand next to each bed; all were vacant except for the one next to the boy's mother, which held several trinkets and a vase with one stemmed flower. The crude plaster walls were a maze of swirl lines, but the painted surface had a scrubbed look. The concrete floor had an uneven glaze from what looked like several coats of wax. It was remarkably clean, except for the shoe prints of dust that he and Frankie had brought in with them. Someone cared deeply about these people and their plight.

The boy came up from behind and said, "Here."

He was holding Luke and the Israeli's passports and wallets.

"Your name's Frankie," Luke said.

"*Sí.*"

Luke took the items from the boy, brushed off some watermelon seeds, and put them into his pocket along with the money. "Frankie, if you steal things, you're going to die someday—just like those men."

The boy seemed to think about that. "Shoeshine—not much money. Have to steal. *Mi madre* need better medicine."

The picture was coming together. Anything beyond the barest necessities probably had to come from the patients' families. For all he knew, Frankie might have been his mother's only means of support.

"How you kill la Cicatriz."

"What?"

"Cicatriz." Frankie ran a finger over his eyebrow, mimicking the thief's scar. Frankie looked to either side, then whispered, "He boss man."

"Why did he pick me?"

Frankie looked down at the floor. "He no pick you."

"What do you mean?"

"I pick you. That my job. I find touristas with money."

Luke didn't know whether to feel relieved that it was a random robbery, or furious that street thugs were using children to mark their prey. He reached into a pocket and pulled out some of the cash he had taken from the thieves. "Here. This should pay for your mother's medicine for a while."

Frankie's mouth parted. He blinked twice.

Luke took the boy's hand and placed the money into his palm.

Frankie waddled over to the nurse's desk where Luke had laid the remnants of his shoeshine box. He carried the box back and set it down, then lifted one of Luke's black leather Reebok shoes onto what remained of the top and started furiously brushing the shoe.

"I work for you," he said. "Whatever you need me do."

Luke shook his head. "Your mother needs you here."

He didn't respond. Instead, he spit on Luke's shoe and brushed some more.

"Do you go to school?"

"Someday." He glanced at his mother. "When she better."

Luke thought about the Frankies of the world while the small boy fiddled with a can of wax. "You want to earn another five American dollars?"

Frankie looked up, his eyes brightened. "Five bucks a week, boss. I work for you in you home."

"You have a job . . . here. Your mother needs you."

Frankie looked at his mother. "She not know I am here anymore."

Chapter 39

Megan looked into the man's gaunt face. His skin was white and blue-veined, his teeth crooked and yellow. Except for his full head of hair, he had a look common to many old men.

"His name is Petri Kaczynski," she told the priest. "He was the head of Genetics at University Children's Hospital. Among geneticists, he was known around the world."

"Was?" Father Joe asked. His breathing sounded like hard labor, and he was beginning to speak in clipped phrases.

"The story was that he died during a trip to Guatemala," she continued. "I'm not sure about the details. But I remember someone telling me that they never found his body. It happened a few years before I came to University Children's."

"Are you sure it's him?" Father Joe reached for his breast pocket, probably a reflexive grasp for the inhaler that wasn't there.

"It's him." She stared at the geneticist's oversized cranium—it was shaped like an inverted eggplant—and the peculiar cowlick at the front of his hairline. "There's a portrait of Kaczynski in our hospital's lobby."

"Get to work, Doc," their guard said in English. "My

boss is gonna be back any minute, and I don't wanna have to tell him that you're ignoring your patient."

Megan and the priest turned to the beefy man. He was sitting backward on a wooden chair, straddling the spine with his legs, his arms draped over the top. His right thumb was wrapped in gauze.

Megan thought back to the thumb she had bitten while escaping from her assailants at Ticar Norte. "I hope it hurts like hell."

"Hey, bitch, I'd start paying attention to Dr. Kaczynski. He's the only reason you're still alive, in case you hadn't figured that out."

Megan felt light-headed. She couldn't remember the last time she'd had anything to eat or drink. "Are you going to tell us what this place is?"

"No. Any more questions?"

She had a hundred questions, but he wasn't going to answer any of them, so she turned her attention back to her patient. The muscular Latino man—she had overheard someone call him Calderon—had allowed her to speak briefly with the white-coated lab tech who had previously cared for Kaczynski. Apparently, the woman was their closest facsimile of a medic.

The woman had explained that the geneticist's illness started a week ago with high fevers, chills, profuse sweating, headaches, and back pain. At the time, Kaczynski had diagnosed himself as having malaria and instructed the nursing staff to treat him with IV fluids and the anti-malaria drug, chloroquine. On the fourth day of his illness, it looked as if he was improving.

But two days ago—day five of his illness—the fevers had returned with a fury and the geneticist developed several additional symptoms: a cough accompanied by blood-tinged sputum, delirium, jaundice, and a rash.

Megan realized that his turn for the worse had saved her life, if only for a time.

"Get Calderon in here," she told the guard.

"I don't take orders from you. And where'd you hear that name?"

She ignored the guard's question. "If you want Dr. Kaczynski to live, get your boss in here."

The man lifted himself from the chair and called out to somebody in the hallway.

While Megan waited for Calderon, she reexamined her patient. He looked to be in his mid-sixties, but his sallow skin added several years to his appearance. He was breathing rapidly, more rapidly than fever alone could explain. His yellowed eyes were suffused with swollen blood vessels. When she palpated the upper right quadrant of his abdomen, he groaned—his liver was inflamed.

His torso and extremities were speckled with red pinpoint lesions—petechiae. His smallest blood vessels—capillaries—were beginning to rupture.

There were any number of tropical illnesses that could explain many of his symptoms and physical findings—malaria, dengue fever, yellow fever, typhoid fever—but the man's eyes pushed her toward another possibility.

Leptospirosis—an infection that occurs when humans come into contact with the body fluids of infected animals. She had seen only one patient with the disease during her residency, and it was a mild case. One of the few things that had stuck with her from that case was Elmer McKenna's colorful description of Napoleon's siege of Cairo in 1812, when an outbreak of leptospirosis crippled his forces. That and the fact that leptospirosis could be treated with penicillin.

The lab tech had not kept up with Kaczynski's fluid

losses, and Megan decided to increase the flow rate of his IVs. It was a calculated risk. If he had the severe form of leptospirosis, his kidneys would shut down and she could literally drown him in IV fluids. On the other hand, not keeping up with his fluid losses put him at risk of death from dehydration and vascular collapse.

Calderon walked into the room, followed by the Asian man.

Before Calderon could speak, she handed him a list. "Here's a list of medicines and supplies that I need."

Calderon smirked while scanning the list. "What makes you think I'm gonna get all of this for you?"

"If Kaczynski doesn't survive, then you'll probably kill me. If he *does* survive, you don't need me anymore. Either way, it looks like I'm going to die, so do whatever you want."

Calderon laughed. "Touché. Just for that, you get your supplies."

A slender woman walked into the room just as Frankie was finishing with Luke's shoes. Her deliberate gait and short gray hair reminded him of his third grade teacher. Everything else—her layered white blouse, her full-length skirt, the sash made of wooden beads with a cross hanging from it—made clear that he was looking at a nun.

She and Frankie exchanged a few words in Spanish, then the boy left the room.

The woman turned to Luke. "I'm Sister Marta Ann." She had what sounded like a British or South African accent. "Frankie tells me you're visiting from the United States."

"Yes." He held out his hand. "Ed—Ed Schweers."

She stared at his left shoulder.

He looked down and saw the bloom of red coming

through the clean shirt he had donned in the cab while searching for the boy.

"Caught myself on something sharp." He wondered how many people begin their conversations with nuns by lying repeatedly.

"Are you here for work or pleasure?" she asked.

"Neither. I'm trying to find a friend who's missing."

"Oh?"

"A young woman, a doctor. She disappeared a few days ago. She was with a priest."

"Padre Joseph." It wasn't a question.

"You know him?"

"No, but he's in my prayers. And so is your friend."

"You work for the same . . . ?" Luke couldn't come up with the right term.

"Padre Joseph and I both belong to Catholic orders, but no, we've never met. He's a Maryknoll missionary. I'm with the Sisters of Charity."

"What do you know about their kidnapping?"

"Almost nothing. I was talking by phone yesterday with my Superior in Guatemala City. She once worked with Padre Joseph in Pactumal. She mentioned the news report about their abduction." The nun shrugged. "I'm afraid that's all I know."

"Pactumal—is that a town?

"More like a small pueblo. When Padre Joseph's not traveling among the Mayan villages, he lives there with another priest, Padre Thomas. That's their *parroquia*— their parish."

"Where is it?" Luke could feel his sketchy plan shifting from Santa Lucina to Pactumal.

"Southeast of here, but I've never been there. Your friend disappeared in an area that's on the edge of civilization, you might say. It's mostly unmapped territory."

The nun showed him a doubtful expression. "Are you here on your own?"

"Yes."

"Pactumal is near the Belize border. It's a good distance off the main highway, but if you're willing to pay, we can probably find a bus driver who will take you there. You can leave in the morning."

"I have to leave tonight."

"It might be difficult finding a bus at this hour. And it's really not safe to travel at night. The bandits prey on buses, especially those with tourists. In this area, there have been six killings in the last month alone." She kissed her crucifix.

"I'm leaving now."

She glanced at a clock on the wall. "Very well, then. I'll send Frankie to the station with you. He can help you find a bus. He's pretty resourceful."

"I've noticed." Luke reached into his pocket and pulled out Ari's passport and wallet. "These belong to a friend. Would you mind returning them to him?" He gave her the name of the hotel as he handed the items to her.

She raked the corner of her lip with her teeth, studying Luke as if searching for a stray fact.

He changed the subject. "Frankie's mother—she doesn't have much longer to live, does she?"

The nun glanced back at the bed. "No, she doesn't."

"You have anything to give her, any medications?"

"We have very little. We rely on donations—surplus medicines from drug companies, that sort of thing. But we almost never have enough."

Luke turned and looked again at the boy's mother. "How old is Frankie?"

"He's nine, going on twenty."

Luke nodded. "What'll happen to him when she dies?"

"I suppose he'll stay here, if he wants to." She sounded mildly surprised by the question. "Besides Frankie, there are only three of us here. He does a good deal of the chores. He's a rascal, but he's devoted to his mother. I'm afraid more than she ever was to him."

A voice behind them said, *"Perdóneme, Hermana."*

Luke turned.

Three uniformed police officers were standing in the doorway, staring at him.

Chapter 40

Luke purchased a map at a newsstand while watching Frankie work a group of bus drivers who were milling at the station's arched entrance. The boy used the same in-your-face bluster that had seemed to befuddle the cops.

The police, it turned out, had come to the hospice looking for Frankie. They were making the rounds—conducting what appeared to be a perfunctory murder investigation—talking with known associates of the dead thieves.

Suddenly, Frankie caught Luke's eye. The boy lifted his arm and pointed at one of the bus drivers.

Twenty minutes later Luke was sitting in the back of a bus rumbling south on the Guatemala Highway. His mind replayed images of the boy standing alongside the bus until just before its departure, waving like a trained seal every time that Luke had glanced out the window.

A large yellow moon bathed the grasslands on either side of the highway, and he struggled to stay awake. It was almost nine o'clock, which meant that it was coming up on seven o'clock in Los Angeles. Luke reached into his bag and turned on the satellite phone.

Just as he was wondering whether a satellite signal would find him inside a metal can traveling at fifty miles an hour, the phone chirped. He thumbed the green button marked ENCRYPT, then pressed SEND.

"Where are you?" Sammy asked without preamble.

"North of Guatemala City." His response would have been judged unresponsive in a court of law, but this wasn't a court of law and he was still a fugitive. He wasn't going to tell *anyone* more than they needed to know. "What do you got?"

"That company—Zenavax—they have an office in Río Dulce. You know where that is?"

"No, but I'll find it."

Sammy gave him a street address and phone number for the company's Río Dulce office, then said, "I got nothing on your woman friend yet. How 'bout you?"

Luke described his conversation with the nun and explained that he was en route to the missing priest's parish. He didn't give Sammy the name of the town, and the man didn't ask.

"Seven o'clock tomorrow," Sammy said. "I may have something to tell you."

The line went dead before Luke could ask what that last statement meant.

Luke startled when the bus driver shook him awake.

"Estamos aquí. Pactumal."

He looked at his watch. It was 10:17 P.M. He jumped from the seat and hefted his rucksack over his left shoulder. A searing pain from the knife wound shot down his arm as he walked down the aisle and disembarked.

When the bus pulled away, standing on the other side of the road, smoking a cigarette, was Frankie. Dressed in a bright yellow jacket, he looked like a smoldering Easter egg.

"Hey, boss. We here."

Luke rubbed the sleep from his face while wondering at the urchin's ability to board the bus unnoticed. Commingled with that thought was the recognition that fatigue was chipping away at his vigilance.

Frankie released two perfectly formed smoke rings. "I help you. You see."

Luke launched into a blistering lecture about deception and trickery, then extracted Frankie's promise to return to Santa Elena after they paid a visit to the missing priest's *parroquia*.

"And put out that cigarette," he said.

Frankie used an ear-splitting whistle to gain the attention of a few local residents who guided Luke and his diminutive companion toward a simple clapboard structure that was indistinguishable from nearby houses except for its larger size. A cross hung on the front door.

A group of tired-looking men sat along a bench on the wood-plank porch that fronted the *parroquia*. The men seemed to regard Luke with an equal mix of curiosity and unease. A tiny woman wrapped in an orange apron was passing out glasses of juice to the men. Frankie marched up to the group as if he were their longtime companion, took a glass from the woman's tray, and started chatting with the men.

Eventually the boy turned back to Luke and said, "Padre Joseph supposed to come home three days ago. But no one see him."

"How do you know about Padre Joseph?"

"I listen to you and Hermana Marta Ann."

Luke wondered whether the boy had overheard their discussion about his mother. "Ask them where the priest was traveling to. Where was he going?"

Frankie repeated Luke's question in Spanish.

An elderly man replied, waving his arm in a wide arc and taking in a broad sweep of the horizon as he talked. He went on for some time.

When he finished, Frankie said, "Padre Joseph not here most times." He pointed in the distance. "He go to small villages. They not know where."

Luke could feel the frustration bleeding away his energy. He rubbed a bead of sweat off his forehead and turned his neck to loosen a muscle.

"They lying," Frankie added.

"What?"

"They lying, boss. They scared."

"How do you know?"

Frankie shrugged. "I just know."

The screen door swung open and a portly man emerged. He was light-skinned, and sweating profusely.

The men sitting on the porch nodded deferentially and Luke heard the word "padre" in their mumbled greetings.

After a short exchange with the group, the heavyset man looked at Luke and said, "I'm Father Tom. I understand you're asking about our pastor, Father Joe."

"Yes. I'm looking for the woman who was with him when they were kidnapped."

"You better come in."

Once inside, the priest said, "Tell me about this woman."

"Her name is Megan Callahan. She's a doctor."

"That much I know. What I want to know is, what did she do to get herself in trouble?"

"I'm not following."

"Joe—Father Joe—found her on a riverbank. She was hiding."

"From whom?"

Father Tom lifted an eyebrow. "My guess would be, the same people that abducted her."

"What do you know about their abduction?"

The priest studied Luke for several seconds. "Perhaps we're getting a little ahead of ourselves here. I'd like to know a little more about you. How do you know this woman?"

"We work together." Luke tried to hide his annoyance at the priest's interrogative attitude.

"That shouldn't be too hard to verify."

Luke pulled his passport from a pants pocket and handed it to the priest. "Here. Call University Children's Hospital. It's in Los Angeles—I'll give you the number. Tell 'em you're standing here talking to Ed Schweers. See what they have to say."

If he couldn't bluff his way past someone who was probably inclined to trust people, neither he nor Megan had any chance.

The priest handed back the passport. "No need. I'm . . . this whole thing has me on edge. Sorry."

"We're on the same side here," Luke said. "I was asking about their kidnapping?"

"A friend of mine—he saw it happen."

"Who?"

The hesitation showed on the priest's face.

"Look. I don't have time to dance around—"

The priest's hand came up. "Let me explain. Father Joe travels to the outlying villages with an Indian who's been with him for years. The man's devoted to Joe, and right now I suspect he's in as much pain as any of us. He's also scared out of his wits. He saw Joe and your friend taken away by five men dressed in camouflage uniforms—"

"Military?"

"He thinks so, but I'm not so sure."

"Why?"

"He said two of them were gringos. That's why I came on a little strong with you." Father Tom rubbed his balding pate. "I don't know how much you know, but it wasn't all that long ago that the Guatemalan army slaughtered villagers for the simple reason that they were Mayan. By most counts, at least two hundred thousand of them. Hundreds of villages were just wiped off the map. The killing went on for over thirty years—that's how long the civil war lasted. The memories stay with you, if you know what I mean."

Luke nodded.

"When Paco—that's Father Joe's assistant—when he saw those men taking Joe and your friend away, I suspect the first thing he thought was, 'It's starting again.' He's frightened."

"I need to talk to him."

"He won't talk to you. In fact, he made me promise—I can't even tell the authorities about him."

"You haven't told the police about this?"

"Oh, I told them. I just didn't give them Paco's name. But you have to understand—the local police aren't likely to be much help in this situation."

"Why?"

"They don't have the manpower or training to deal with things like this. The central government has some resources they could use, but so far they're not doing much since they think both of them are dead."

"Dead?" A pain shot through Luke's head.

"You okay?"

"Yeah. Why do they think they're dead?"

"The newspaper account describes an armed militia group that called a TV station in the U.S., claiming they'd kidnapped Joe and your friend. The police believe that story, and they think that the men I described for them—the men that Paco saw—are leftovers from the civil war. During that period, there were several resistance groups in this area, so it's not much of a stretch for the police to believe that one of those militia groups has resurrected itself. Since the kidnappers haven't made any further statements or demands, the thinking is that they may well have killed their hostages."

"Megan, Father Joe, where were they abducted?"

"It's not there anymore. The village where they were kidnapped—it was destroyed when a dam broke. None of the villagers survived and—"

"What was the name of that village?"

"Mayakital."

Luke reached into his pack and pulled out the picture from Kate's e-mail. He handed it to the priest. "Does that look familiar?"

Father Tom looked at the picture and nodded. "That's Mayakital. Where did you get this?"

"From a friend. It's a long story."

The priest flicked the picture with his finger. "Well, this is where Joe and your friend were kidnapped. That, I'm sure of. According to Paco, it happened right after the flood." Father Tom handed back the picture. "But like I said, the police seem to think they're already dead."

"So everyone's going to sit on their hands?"

"Remember, you're not in the U.S. anymore. I'm working on it, but things move slowly here."

"I need you to take me to this man Paco."

"I don't think he'll talk to you."

Frankie suddenly came back to life and said, "He talk to me. I get him to talk."

Both men turned.

Frankie made an air pocket in his cheek and showed them a bland expression.

Chapter 41

"Let me see if I understand this." Detective O'Reilly tapped his notepad with a pencil. "Last week, this Guatemalan boy dies in your E.R. Then yesterday, you get back the results of a test showing that he had little pieces of a virus—alphavirus—in his blood."

Ben studied O'Reilly as the man read from his notes. The detective's eyes were close set, as though they enjoyed each other's company. Ben didn't trust him.

O'Reilly took a sip from his mug while eyeing Elmer, then continued, "And this particular alphavirus has been modified to use as a vaccine. You can put a special protein into it—"

"It's called an antigen," Ben clarified while looking across Kolter's dining room and making a pouring gesture with his hand, signaling Antonio for more coffee. The Italian nodded at Ben through the glass facing of a chest-high pastry case into which he was placing a large sheet of cinnamon rolls.

"Okay," O'Reilly said, "so you put an *antigen* inside this virus and then inject it into people to protect them against infections like flu and malaria. In that sense, it works like any other vaccine, right?"

"Right," Ben said impatiently. He was becoming annoyed

with the detective's habit of repeating everything they told him.

"And according to you," O'Reilly said to Elmer, "those little pieces of alphavirus in that boy's blood are identical to the alphavirus that Zenavax uses in their vaccines. Is that what you're telling me?"

"Those little pieces of virus," Elmer explained, "are fragments of ribonucleic acid—RNA—and they're an exact match for Zenavax's strain of alphavirus. There's only one way that those fragments of RNA could have gotten there. That boy was given their malaria vaccine."

"How're you so sure it was a malaria vaccine?"

"Process of elimination," Elmer said. "Zenavax has just one commercial product—their flu vaccine. It's been on the market for over three years. If there was a problem with it, the world would've known about it long ago. The only new product in their research pipeline that I've heard about is their malaria vaccine. I made some calls—the rumor is that they're testing it in Guatemala right now."

Antonio walked up to their booth with a carafe of coffee and filled Elmer's cup, then Ben's. "Sir, can I make-a a question to you?" He was staring at O'Reilly.

The detective nodded.

Antonio's head began to tremble. "The police—I no understand how you be so stupid. What you are tinking?" He turned to Elmer without waiting for a response. "Why they do this to your boy. They make-a a big mistake. That's what Antonio tinks."

The Italian turned abruptly and walked away, mumbling to himself. Across the room, the deli's only other breakfast customer glanced at their table over the rim of his glasses.

O'Reilly looked into his empty coffee mug, then at

Elmer. "You're also working on a malaria vaccine, isn't that correct?"

"What's that got to do with anything?" Ben asked.

The detective ignored his question. "Dr. McKenna, tell me about your project."

"We're further along than Zenavax. In a few months we'll be in full production and my vaccine will be available in three countries. And our approach is completely different. I'm not using an alphavirus. We've developed a genetically altered mosquito that, instead of infecting you with malaria, injects a vaccine when it feeds on your blood."

O'Reilly's face curled into a knot. "How does that work?"

"We've modified the mosquito's saliva glands so they produce two extra proteins. The first protein makes it difficult for the malaria parasite to survive in the mosquito's gut, which is where it grows. The second protein looks a lot like a protein that's found in the two most common types of malaria—vivax and falciparum. That's another difference between my vaccine and Zenavax's. From what I've heard, theirs only protects against falciparum."

Elmer appeared to wait for the detective to finish writing some notes, then continued, "When a female mosquito feeds on your blood, it injects some of its saliva into your bloodstream. When *my* mosquito bites you, you'll also get a dose of my malaria vaccine, which is in its saliva. Your body thinks it's being invaded by malaria and activates the immune system to produce antibodies and something called T-cells." Elmer coughed into his fist. "The antibodies and T-cells are what protect you against the infection."

"So you're creating squadrons of flying syringes?"

"That's the basic idea," Ben said.

Antonio walked toward their booth with a carafe.

The detective held out his mug.

The Italian passed by without stopping.

O'Reilly followed Antonio with his eyes while saying, "You used the words, 'we're developing.' Who's the *we*?"

"I'm working with our Genetics and Immunology departments," Elmer said. "The original idea actually came out of our Genetics department. A doctor name Petri Kacz—"

"Detective, it seems your horse is wondering off the trail here," Ben said.

"Maybe so." O'Reilly flipped back a few pages in his notes. "Let's go back to that other blood test you told me about—the one for cystic fibrosis. What's the significance of that, in your mind?"

"The boy had cystic fibrosis," Ben said. "You don't get the disease unless you have both copies of the same CF mutation, one from each parent." He held up a pair of fingers. "That boy had two copies of the mutation. He had the disease."

"Doc, you're gonna have to make a clearer connection for me. What're you trying to say?"

"We think the vaccine caused a toxic immune reaction," Ben said, "and CF probably played a role. Whatever killed the boy attacked the same organs that the disease—cystic fibrosis—targets. And his organs weren't just damaged—the tissues literally dissolved. That's not how Mother Nature works. This wasn't a natural biological process. And the girl at the morgue—the one I told you about earlier—I think the same thing killed her."

O'Reilly's gaze shifted between the two of them before settling on Ben again. "And what would you like me to do about that?"

Ben glanced at Elmer. The two of them exchanged bemused expressions.

"Do your job, Detective," Ben said finally. "Look into Zenavax."

O'Reilly looked at each man in turn. "Your entire theory rests on a blood sample that's been in the possession of the murder suspect's father. Who, other than a moron, would believe that you didn't alter the blood, or substitute someone else's?"

"No, no, please," Elmer said. "I didn't change anything."

Ben thought back to his visit from the mysterious black man and the directive he had passed along from Luke: Drop the inquiries into the two dead children. Now, more than ever, Ben knew he couldn't do that—not if the police had stopped looking for other suspects.

"What kind of dimwit detective are you?" Ben banged his mug on the table, then shook the spilled liquid from his hand.

"Want me to keep going?" O'Reilly inspected his shirt and fingered a fresh spot of coffee. "What about the tissues you say disappeared from your lab, the ones from the coroner's case? A cynical person might wonder why you waited almost three days to tell me about that."

Ben stared at the detective for what seemed like a full minute, then said, "You don't believe a thing we've just told you, do you?"

O'Reilly tossed his notepad on the table. "Doc, you're either the dumbest cluck I ever met—or the cleverest—and I have no idea which."

Luke's climbing partners, Frankie and Paco, were slowing noticeably as the threesome neared the top of the heavily forested peak. Paco was in front, leading the group, but there was a reticence in the Indian's gait that seemed to derive from something other than the steep incline.

On the other side of the summit, they would find the remains of Mayakital, he'd been told.

Father Tom had deposited them at the mountain's base after driving three hours through overgrown jungle trails that almost swallowed his small Nissan sedan several times. He would return at sunset to retrieve Paco and the boy. Luke had other plans.

It had taken another two hours to climb the slope, and Paco hadn't said a word to Luke during that whole time. Even making eye contact seemed a struggle for the diffident man.

But not so with Frankie. Paco and the boy had an almost immediate rapport, cultivated in no small part by the little urchin's formidable storytelling skills. The night before, when the priest had delivered them to Paco's home, Frankie cooked up a fictional tale in which he cast himself as an orphan whose only hope for eventual adoption lay with Luke finding Megan, marrying her, and, soon thereafter, the happy couple adopting him.

Throughout the telling of his story, Frankie's face had been a bundle of innocence. Luke unwittingly reaffirmed the yarn, nodding like a simpleton every time the boy glanced in his direction, blissfully ignorant of what the urchin was saying. It wasn't until later that he pieced it together from some comments by the priest.

Frankie's efforts had had the desired effect, though. Paco opened up like a faucet. He described Megan's assailants. They had worn black fatigue uniforms, which, to Paco, meant that they were military. Two were Caucasian, three Hispanic, and all five wore headsets. Luke wasn't dealing with a ragtag group of thugs.

Paco had described how the black-clad men hog-tied Megan before throwing her and the priest into the back of a medium-size transport truck. He remembered the truck because he'd seen it before while traveling to some of the more distant villages with Father Joe. It was tan in color and had a pair of red snakes painted on its doors.

The Indian had twice seen the truck parked at what he thought was a military facility in a remote corner of the jungle. He described the fenced facility, which sat in a clearing and was guarded by troops with maroon berets.

The priest had explained the significance of the berets—they were part of the distinctive uniforms worn by Guatemalan Special Forces.

Paco wasn't willing to take Luke to the guarded facility—the man seemed terrified when asked—but he reluctantly agreed to accompany him as far as Mayakital. More specifically, he agreed to take Luke to a summit high above the flooded village where *los soldados*—the soldiers—would not be able to spot them.

From there, Luke was on his own.

Frankie had worked himself into the plan as a translator for Luke, and it didn't seem worth arguing about because, in fact, he needed a translator and would send Frankie back to the *parroquia* with Paco as soon as they reached the summit.

A dull throb was taking hold in Luke's left shoulder when they reached the mountaintop and he got his first view of the devastation that was once Mayakital. He gazed down at a half-mile-wide lake of reddish-brown mud a thousand feet below them.

Looking to the north, he found the cause of the flood. An earthen reservoir had fractured. It was a limestone pouch formed by the confluence of three peaks— mountains joined at the hip, the geological equivalent of

Siamese triplets. He looked through a gaping V-shaped scar into the reservoir's interior. Sheets of water from mountain streams cascaded down its darkened limestone walls.

Luke told Paco and Frankie to stay put while he searched the area. A dark presence accompanied him as he worked his way down the steep incline and around the perimeter of the muddy moonscape. By the time he reached the northern end of the valley, he was carrying a thick layer of red clay on his jeans.

Staring up at the jagged fissure on the earthen dam, he tried to imagine how it had ruptured. His eyes followed the reservoir's contours up and down, then across the top.

It was then that he knew what had happened.

It was subtle, but it was there.

Several hundred feet above him, along the reservoir's upper rim, a spatter pattern of brownish-red sediment covered the jungle's canopy for a hundred yards to either side of the fissure. He had missed it when peering down from the summit, but saw it now.

The earthen wall had been blasted open from the inside, sending an explosive cloud of pulverized limestone and clay into the sky. It dispersed and rained back down, covering the jungle's canopy with a film of sediment.

He knew about explosives and blast patterns. It was what SEALs did best.

Whoever had done this was proficient at disguising their lethal handiwork. In another few days, rain would have washed away the last traces of evidence.

A few minutes later Luke reached the spot that Paco had pointed out from the summit. The rains hadn't completely washed away the shoe prints on the shoreline. At least three different boot treads mingled with the outline of a much smaller set of shoe prints.

He stooped and ran his finger along the rim of one of the small shoe treads, thinking of Megan and the terror that must have seized her.

A raging fury choked off his vision. His chest heaved.

He let out a deafening scream that echoed across the valley.

It was the roar of a wild animal.

On the other side of the valley, Mr. Kong lowered his field glasses and reached for his satellite phone.

"He's here."

Chapter 42

Megan awoke to another of Kaczynski's delirious outbursts. She uncurled her body and threw off a collection of rags and towels she'd used to fashion a sleeping nest in one corner of the room.

Father Joe was propped in a chair next to the geneticist's bed, breathing heavily in sleep.

The guard—this one didn't speak English—was sitting next to the door. He slapped his arm, then flicked something off his skin.

It was the middle of the day, but she was taking catnaps whenever she could because the geneticist's waxing and waning condition left her little time to sleep.

A flutter of birds sounded outside. Megan stood and walked over to the screened window while rubbing the stiffness from her neck. Ten yards away, the compound's perimeter wall with its garland of concertina wire stared back at her. Tree branches as thick as telephone poles dipped over the walls, as if the jungle were trying to reclaim the land for itself.

The geneticist's utterances had initially seemed like nothing more than random salvos, but as time passed she noticed recurring words and phrases: malaria, T-cells, germ cells, ovaries, and another word she didn't recognize—Chegan.

She let his words percolate through her mind, looking for clues about the purpose of the forest compound. Her captors didn't seem to care about Kaczynski's chatter, which only underscored what she already knew. Whether her patient lived or died, they were going to kill her as soon as his fate became clear.

It was obvious that Kaczynski was important to them. They wanted him to live and had obtained everything she asked for: a stethoscope; tubing, needles, and fluids for a second IV line; two oxygen tanks and a mask; and an assortment of medications including Lasix, which she would use if the geneticist's kidneys started to fail, and penicillin.

While considered an exotic disease, leptospirosis responded to penicillin, the most common of antibiotics. What she didn't know, and wouldn't know for several more hours, was if the infectious spirochete had destroyed her patient's brain. He had signs of encephalitis—inflammation of the brain—but it was too early to know whether any damage had occurred.

"How are you doing?" It was Father Joe's voice.

She continued staring out the window. "Fine."

His chair creaked. "What can I do to help?"

She spun around to face him. "Can you help me understand why I'm working so hard to save this man's life, all the while hoping he dies?"

Father Joe suddenly leaned forward, clutching his chest.

She ran to the priest, eased him into his chair, and then grabbed Kaczynski's oxygen mask and placed it over Father Joe's face. "I'm sorry, Father. Just relax and breathe." Megan stooped next to him. "I'm such an idiot. Ignore me."

A smile formed under his mask.

A moment later the hissing of the oxygen suddenly faded away.

Megan turned.

Calderon was closing the valve on top of the tank, shutting off the oxygen flow.

"You bastard!" she screamed. "He needs—"

"This oxygen is for Dr. Kaczynski." Calderon held up his index finger. "If I catch you doing that again, the priest dies. Understood?" He waited for a response and got none. "Good. Now, tell me about your patient. How's he doing?"

"It's too early to tell." Megan bit off the words.

"So, what does he have?"

"Hemorrhagic fever," she lied.

"How bad is that?"

"It's bad," she said. "And something else you should know—every one of us is going to get this illness. It's spread by mosquitoes." If she was right about her diagnosis—leptospirosis—neither statement was true.

Calderon studied her. "I think you're lying."

She held his stare. "You've already made it clear that I'm going to die, so whether you believe me just isn't very high on my list of worries. Sooner or later—whether you like it or not—anyone that spends time in this room is going to get bitten by a mosquito that's taken a drink from Dr. Kaczynski. I couldn't care less what you do with that information."

The truth was, it was the only thing she cared about at that moment. As foolish and unlikely as it was, her escape plan hinged on getting their guards out of the room. It was a harebrained scheme, and her chances of success were minuscule, but at least it was a chance.

A bulky phone on Calderon's belt buzzed loudly. He pulled a small headset from his shirt pocket and plugged it into the brick-sized device.

After a long stretch of listening, Calderon said, "Follow

him, but keep your distance." A pause, then, "This guy is good—even without any gear, if you crowd him, he'll spot you." Calderon looked at this watch. "I'm leaving now. Don't lose him, and make sure everyone understands that they're not to do *anything* until I join up with you."

Calderon punched a button and slowly removed the headset from his ear. His eyes seemed lost in a distant thought.

Megan felt a chill on her neck in the ninety-degree heat.

Luke knew he was on the right course when he reached the river crossing. It was exactly as Paco had described it. An enormous banyan tree sat alone on an islet where two rivers converged. As he waded across the knee-deep shallows, a large squadron of birds took off from the tree's canopy in a V-formation.

On the other side, he left behind dense jungle and entered a rain forest. It was an odd combination of enclosure and openness, like the lobby of a grand old hotel. A hundred feet above him, a thick weave of branches and vines let through only a few thin shafts of dusky skylight. The forest's floor was sparse, covered by a carpet of moss and the occasional stalk of an immature seedling.

It had been almost three hours since he left Paco and a sulking Frankie to make their way back to the rendezvous point with the priest. If the Indian's information was correct, he was nearing the guarded facility where Paco had seen a truck matching the one that Megan's abductors had used.

The purple shadows of twilight were descending on the forest. It was the time of day when eyes strained to adapt to diminishing light levels, when the body's cortisol level slid—and with it, attentiveness—and when guards performing monotonous duties would be distracted by hunger. On a scale that weighed his advantages against those of his adversaries, they were grains of sand, but they were all he had.

He sat against the base of a tree and pulled the thief's Glock from his shoulder bag. It was filthy, and dry; the weapon hadn't been oiled in a long while. He popped the clip and thumbed the rounds out of the magazine. His entire arsenal consisted of seven bullets.

Luke quickly disassembled the weapon, cleaned it with his shirt, and reassembled it. Then he began moving forward in a crouch, using the shadows, darting from tree to tree, scanning in a 360-degree arc each time he stopped. Just before nightfall stole the last light, he twice saw fresh tracks in the sodden ground—neither was human.

Crickets were beginning to chirp when a distant set of lights flickered hesitantly, then swelled to an amber glow. They were spotlights, a quarter mile east of his position.

He went prone.

As he crawled through a humus-covered depression, a small multilegged creature latched onto his forearm. He stopped and waited for it to pass over him, but instead the thing slowly creeped up his arm until it reached his shoulder, where it stayed.

Luke moved forward.

When he was still two hundred yards from the facility, he spotted one man, then another, patrolling inside the two-acre compound. Three buildings were set back from a Cyclone fence perimeter that was topped with barbed wire.

One of the men passed under a floodlight. He wore a forest camouflage uniform and maroon beret.

Soldiers. Whatever this place was, it was important to someone.

The low hum of insects was everywhere. The creature on his shoulder stroked him with one of its legs, exploring him. Luke brushed off the arthropod.

Twenty minutes later, he'd circled the perimeter and reconnoitered the area. A single dirt road wound its way to a secured entry gate. Outside the entrance was a small unmanned guardhouse. Inside the compound he saw a large windowless building made of prefab aluminum siding that was flanked by two smaller wooden structures. A single canvas-tarped truck sat in the blackened shadow of an overhang along the side of the main building. It was too dark to make out the truck's color or any logos.

The compound had its own electrical generator, fueled by a large natural gas tank.

Paired cameras sat atop twenty-foot posts at opposite corners of the compound. One lens in each pair was almost certainly a visible-light camera. The other was probably an infrared night-vision lens or motion detector. He maintained a hundred foot distance and hoped it was enough to avoid detection.

It seemed unthinkable that a remote facility in the Guatemalan rain forest would use security measures beyond what he had already seen. But if these people *had* set up external security zones with tree-mounted heat sensors or ground-level vibration detectors, they'd soon be on to him.

Both of the sentries carried M-16s, cross-chest position, barrel down, their index fingers wrapped around the trigger guard. Their patrol patterns were irregular, their routes inconsistent. It was no accident. He was looking at well-trained soldiers.

They had no special gear—no sniper scopes, no head-sets, no night-vision goggles. Either they had no such equipment, or they weren't expecting an intruder. Luke hoped that both were true.

He spent the next several minutes considering his options. He didn't like any of them. He might be able to draw one of the sentries outside the compound and take him out, but no more than one. These soldiers wouldn't be duped in tandem, and whichever one remained inside would immediately raise the alarm. He had to assume that inside those buildings there were other armed men. Someone, somewhere, was probably monitoring the security cameras. And if they were holding Megan and the priest in there, he guessed he'd find at least two more guards.

Before he made his move, he wanted to know more than just their numbers. He wanted to know their positions, their capabilities, their methods.

But that would take time, and fatigue was already sapping his strength.

He wiped a bead of sweat from his forehead. The shoulder infection was worsening, the throb swelling.

Waiting was not an option.

Chapter 43

Luke found a gully deep enough to conceal his movements and belly-crawled along its path until he reached a culvert that passed under the road, about fifty feet from the compound's gate.

The entry gate, he decided, was his only way into the facility. If necessary, he'd coax one of guards outside with a ruse, but he was hoping for an opportunity that fell within the natural cadence and rhythm of their duties: patrolling the outside perimeter, or opening the gate for an arriving vehicle.

To take advantage of the moment when it came, he had to get closer. Twenty feet from the entrance the hulk of a fallen tree lay along the side of the road. From that position, he could close the distance to the front gate faster than the guards could process and respond to an unexpected attack.

Luke lay back against the embankment and mulled whether to sprint to the fallen tree, which carried with it the risk of awakening the forest and drawing the guards' attention, or to creep slowly and silently, which meant more time in the camera's lens.

He checked his Glock one more time. Given its condition, the gun probably wasn't accurate beyond twenty-five or thirty feet, but he had no plans to use it. He had quieter ways of eliminating his enemy. Using the weapon would mean that something had gone terribly wrong, that his mission had failed.

That was when he heard an echoed sound so soft that it almost joined with the pulsing hum of the woodlands.

He froze.

Behind him, in the forest, a leafy branch fluttered.

Fluttered in the perfectly still night air.

He rolled noiselessly, his eyes rising over the edge of the gulch like a crocodile breaking the water's surface. He let his eyes' focus drift, relaxing his pupils, letting in the dim shadows.

A movement on his left, low to the ground. He raised the Glock and aimed, slowly taking in the trigger slack.

The truck inside the compound rumbled to life.

"Uh-oh," a small voice squeaked. "Boss. Where you are, boss?

Luke relaxed his trigger finger. "Damn it."

The truck's headlights flashed on, its beams converging on Frankie's yellow jacket. He lit up like a candle-stick.

"Down, Frankie. Get down," Luke said in a shouted whisper.

Luke lifted his head and glanced back at the compound. A soldier was climbing into the passenger side of the truck.

"I no can see you, boss."

Luke threw himself against the opposite embankment, showing himself to the boy. "Down on the ground, Frankie. Now!"

"No mueva!" The shouted command came from inside the compound.

The boy went bug-eyed and stared at the lights as if they were a homing beacon.

Luke heard the chain-link gate fly open with a metallic shiver, then the sound of rapid footfalls and a gun belt rubbing against the coarse fabric of a soldier's uniform.

A single set of sounds—one man.

Luke gripped his handgun with his right hand, the ground with his left. An old habit, feeling for vibrations, but the ground was too soft and moist.

Frankie started jabbering in Spanish.

"Silencio!" the soldier shouted.

A flashlight beam swept over Luke's position.

"Cállate!" The sentry's clipped voice erupted in staccato bursts. *"No mueva!"*

The soldier's head, then upper body, came into Luke's field of vision. The man was sidestepping, moving in a semicircle around the boy and edging closer to Luke's position with each step.

Luke flattened himself against the embankment.

Suddenly, the soldier brought up his M-16 and fired three quick shots into the air.

Luke swung his gun around toward the man.

A fusillade of bullets riddled the soldier's body before Luke completed the arc. The volley lifted the man's body and hurled it onto the ground next to Luke.

Rifle fire. It had come from the forest. *What the hell is happening?*

Luke leapt from his hiding spot, grabbed the downed soldier's M-16, and lunged at Frankie, who was standing bolt upright, frozen in terror.

He tackled the boy, clutching Frankie to his chest as they fell to the ground and rolled behind a tree.

A burst of gunfire from the compound bit into a patch of dirt near them.

Luke reached around the tree and aimed his handgun at

the second guard, who was crouched in a shooting stance near the gate.

He fired two rounds at the man's chest.

The soldier's right shoulder exploded and he fell to the ground, screaming.

The truck's engine roared, its gears gnashing furiously.

Luke peered around the tree trunk. The truck lurched forward and made a run for the front gate. A man in civilian dress ran out of the main building and jumped into the truck bed.

A searing pain shot through Luke's left arm just as a rifle report reached his ears. The sound came from behind them, in the forest.

He grabbed Frankie with his right arm and rolled in a violent motion toward the gully. Another bullet chewed up the dirt behind them as they tumbled into the depression.

Frankie yelped as they hit bottom.

When he put his hand over the boy's mouth, Luke noticed that the sensation in his fourth and fifth fingers was gone. He straightened his arm and worked his grip. The muscles obeyed grudgingly. He palpated his elbow and winced when a jolt of electrical pain shot down his forearm. The bullet had grazed the outside of his elbow, damaging his ulnar nerve.

Frankie said, "Boss, I scared. What we do?"

"Stay down and crawl that way." Luke pointed to where the gulch emptied into the culvert. "There's a pipe that runs under a road." He drew a circle with his hand. "Get into it and stay there."

"I come with you."

"No!" Luke pointed again. "Get going. *Now*."

The boy scurried away.

Luke stayed put while struggling to reason through the

chaos. Someone had clipped him while he was lying prone behind a tree, in darkness. They had found their mark with one shot.

Someone out there had a nightscope.

An explosion of gunfire erupted from the forest again, but this time from the other side of the road. Luke slung the dead soldier's rifle over his shoulder and used the clatter of gunfire to follow the gully into the forest. He reached a spot where the depression narrowed and deepened, curving in an S-pattern around two large trees. Using the trees as a shield, he lifted his head to ground level, looking back at the compound.

The truck—now outside of the compound—had veered off the road and slammed into a copse of trees. Automatic rifle fire from the other side of the road ripped through the canvas tarp. The right side of the windshield shattered and glass shards glinted in the wash of the headlights.

He followed the deadly green tracers back to their sources. The firing positions were too distant to get a fix on. He thought about the type of men who killed from long distances, men who used nightscopes and worked in teams.

The searing pain in his elbow told him that there was another firing team on his side of the road. The assailants had set up a cross-fire solution for the compound's only exit—or perhaps, they had figured, Luke's only way into the facility.

The guards had not behaved like men springing a trap. They had reacted like soldiers defending their site. They were pawns caught in the cross fire.

Had the hunters been waiting for him? That seemed impossible. Luke hadn't known he'd be coming here until hours ago. More likely, they had followed him from Mayakital, and he'd made it all too easy. He had marched through the jungle without bothering to circle back or cover his tracks.

The gunfire stopped. In his mind's eye he saw men scanning the forest—their world alight with ghostly green images—searching for their target. The shooters on his side of the road would hold their fire, not wanting to give away their position.

Did these men know something about the man they were hunting?

A lethal darkness boiled in Luke's mind. His pulse slowed. His breathing quieted.

He let the demons take hold of him.

He rubbed his hands in the wet soil and rubbed it over his face and arms. His breaths came in a whisper as he sifted and filtered each sound, each smell, until only those made by humans would reach his senses.

The hunters probably expected him to either run or press the fight, so instead he waited, crouched in a hollow of earth between two enormous tree trunks protruding from one side of the gulch.

He didn't have to wait long. He almost missed the sound when a monkey squealed overhead.

A boot lifting from the mud.

Seconds passed before he heard a twig strain under the weight of a footfall. It was barely a wisp—the sound ending too suddenly—a skilled tracker interrupting his step in mid-stride, revealing himself with his agility.

The hunter was in the ditch, closing on Luke's position. A second hunter would be nearby, probably on ground level, moving in a parallel path.

Luke detached the bayonet from the M-16 and ran his finger along both edges of the six-inch blade.

Another footfall. Images of the takedown played in his mind, the kind of mental rehearsal he'd used in another life.

When the moment came, it felt as if he were in another place, watching it unfold on a video screen.

Luke flicked a pebble with his middle finger, sending it straight up, toward the shadowed outline of a branch.

When the pebble hit its mark, he heard the sudden movement, a few feet away.

He leapt from his earthen pouch. The killer was still looking up to the sound when Luke plunged the bayonet into the side of the man's neck. The blade disappeared under the corner of his jaw, severing his vocal cords.

A burst of gunfire left the hunter's rifle before the dying man reached for the knife handle protruding from his neck.

When the dark outline of a second man appeared at the lip of the gulch, Luke was already crouched in a shooting position. He caught the killer with a three-round burst. The orange muzzle flashes created a strobe-light effect, catching the hunter's stunned expression as the bullets punched through his chest.

When Luke released the trigger, his skin tingled with the presence of a ghost that had come back and reclaimed his soul.

Chapter 44

Luke grabbed one of the dead assailants' rifles, swung it over the rim of the gully and peered through the bulbous nightscope.

On the other side of the road, two black-clad figures retreated into the wooded darkness, alternating their movements, one man withdrawing while the other covered their egress. The smaller one moved more expertly than his partner. Luke considered taking a shot at the man who was making a bigger target of himself, but the receding figures were already at the outer envelope of what, on a good day in another life, was his effective range.

So instead, he followed the two men. Fifteen minutes later, when he was satisfied that they were not circling back, he returned to the compound.

The bullet-riddled truck was pinned against a tree. It was green and had no markings on the doors. The engine was still running, its rear tires churning the soil and digging grooves so deep that the axle had come to rest on the ground. It looked like a dying animal.

A lifeless man in a khaki work uniform hung out of the cab's open door, his body strewn with bullet holes. Luke reached across him and turned off the engine, then went around to the back of the truck where he found a second body curled in a fetal position.

Next, he checked the guards. Both men were dead. The one he had shot in the shoulder lay in a crimson pool. Blood was still seeping from two chest wounds that were too large to have been made by Luke's 9mm handgun.

A soft footstep interrupted his thoughts. He turned toward the sound.

"He dead, boss?"

Frankie had stopped several feet short of Luke and was staring at the soldier's body. The boy's eyes looked as though they were well acquainted with death.

"Yeah, he's dead."

Ten minutes later Luke had completed a quick search of the compound, flushed three men and a woman from their hiding places, and confirmed what he already suspected. Megan wasn't there.

The killers' tactics weren't those of men guarding a hostage. They weren't defending this site. Rather, they had gunned down two of its guards and abandoned the area as soon as Luke had reduced their numerical advantage.

So what was this place? Paco had been certain he'd seen a truck identical to the one used by Megan's abductors. What was the connection between this site and her kidnapping?

Another question, a darker question, swirled within the contradictions and puzzles.

Was Megan still alive?

He pushed the thought away and focused on his immediate problem—he now had four captives to deal with. After herding them outside at gunpoint, Luke had them carry the six dead men into the main building. The bodies were laid side by side on the floor of what he discovered was a large laboratory.

Workbenches crowded with titration columns and Erlenmeyer flasks ran the length of the room. Along the walls, glass-enclosed units outfitted with rubber sleeves held machines with robotic arms that moved columns of pipettes over rows of test tubes, extracting and injecting amber-colored fluids.

Floor-to-ceiling cages lined the far wall, and each cage held a monkey. The small dark primates had yowled loudly when Luke walked through the door with his entourage. It was a menacing, raspy howl that sounded like a lion's roar, and their first wail had sent Frankie scurrying out the door.

Luke seated his captives around a lab bench in the middle of room. Three of the four faces staring back at him displayed a convincing mask of terror. He did nothing to reassure them.

His fourth captive, a woman about his age, carried herself with an air of command despite a withered leg and noticeable limp that Luke guessed might be the residual of polio. She had ghostly white skin that picked up every hollow in her face, and jet-black hair that glimmered blue under the fluorescent lights. An ornate silver chain hung from the temple stems of her black-rimmed eyeglasses. Sitting sideways in her chair, she looked at him obliquely with her shoulders held back as if to prop up a flagging bravado.

When Luke stooped next to the body of one of his attackers to inspect it, the woman said, "Are you going to tell us what you want?"

He was surprised at the evenness of her voice. "So you speak English," he said with his back turned to her. "How about the others?"

"Only I speak English," the woman replied. Her stiff English phrasing gave her Spanish accent an aristocratic tone.

Luke searched the pockets of the second assailant, who, like his dead partner, was dressed in black fatigues and military jump boots. "Where are the tapes of your security cameras?"

"You will not find any tapes because our cameras are not connected to a recorder. I am sure you will confirm that for yourself."

"You're right. I will," he said. "What about telephones?"

"We have two satellite phones, but you will find that they do not work well at this hour. Something about the position of the satellites. I have already tried."

Whether she was telling the truth was unimportant. He'd be gone long before anyone could respond to a distress call.

But it reminded him—he had missed his call from Sammy.

He gestured toward the cages with his gun. "What is this place, and who are you people?"

"So, you kill people and you do not even know who they are?"

Luke ripped open one of the dead men's Velcro thigh pockets, fished out a piece of paper, and unfolded it. While looking at it, he said, "This is how it's going to be. I'm going to ask questions and you're going to answer my questions—*fully*. Do you understand?"

The woman sighed. "This is a research laboratory. We're developing a human vaccine for malaria." Her voice turned to acid when she added, "We're here because we want to *save* lives. You probably would not understand that."

"Perhaps not."

The paper in his hand was a digital photograph of himself, walking out the front door of Kolter's Deli. It was a close-up of his head and chest, but he recognized his father's jacketed shoulder in the foreground. Someone had snapped a picture of them leaving the restaurant after their breakfast meeting last Sunday. He folded it and put it into his pocket.

"Why so much security?" he asked.

"It's not so much, really, if you consider the amount of money we spend on our research. Our company wants to protect its investment."

"And the military guards?"

"You do not know much about this country, do you? We pay the government a generous permit fee to operate here. In return, they arrange for security from the army. It is a common arrangement between foreign companies and the government. The companies and their employees are targets for armed bandits. The bandits, they stay away from places that are guarded by soldiers."

Luke said, "Who do you work for?"

"The name of our company would have no meaning for you."

He jumped to his feet and turned on her. *"Give me the name!"*

She startled. "Zenavax—Zenavax Pharmaceuticals."

During the long silence that followed, she seemed to recognize the turmoil in his face. "Why do you look at me that way?" she asked.

"Tell me about Kate Tartaglia."

"How do you know . . . Who are you?"

He pointed at the dead killers. "Someone who wants to know the secret these men were protecting."

"How would I know anything about that?"

Luke stepped closer and drilled the woman with his stare. "There are two possibilities here. Number one— you already know who I am, why I'm here, and what I want." He pointed at the dead assailants. "In which case, you know who these goons are and you're stalling, waiting for their reinforcements to show. Then there's possibility number two—that you have no idea what I'm talking about. Either way, you have information I need, *and I don't have time to play games with you.*"

He erupted in a fit of rage, sweeping his arm across the lab bench. Two flasks and a tall glass tube crashed to the floor.

"So tell me what you know. Now!" he shouted.

One of the men lifted off his seat as if yanked by a cord.

The woman's hands came together in her lap, trembling. "About what?"

"Start with Kate Tartaglia. Tell me what you know about her murder."

"I heard she was shot during a robbery. That is all I know. What does that have to do with—"

"What was she working on when she died? What projects?"

"Nothing that anyone would want to kill her for." Her head wobbled in confusion. "She was in charge of our clinical trials—our vaccine testing programs."

"Tell me about that."

Her eyes hardened. "Why are you here? You don't even say who you are." She looked past Luke at the bodies lying on the floor. "I knew four of those men—they were good men. You point a gun at us like we have done something wrong. But we have done *nothing* wrong." Her lower lip trembled and her eyes moistened. "What? Are you going to kill us after you ask your questions? Is it so easy for you?"

The men sitting on either side of her looked nervously at one another.

The woman's blue eyes shone with the intensity of a

quasar, and her body language told him that she was done talking unless he terrorized her.

"No. It's not easy." He blew out a heavy breath. "I'm a doctor, and this isn't in my job description."

Her jaw slackened.

Everything about the woman's manner and words seemed genuine. Whatever Zenavax might have done, he felt certain that she wasn't involved, at least not knowingly. So he had taken a chance and revealed himself—at least partially—hoping to break through her defenses.

He didn't stop there. He told her about Josue Chaca and Jane Doe, and Kate's mysterious connection to both of them.

"Kate's killing had nothing to do with a robbery," he added. "She was murdered because of something she knew."

He took the photograph of Mayakital from his rucksack and handed it to her. "And it has something to do with this village."

The woman took the photo, glanced at it for only a moment, and handed it back to him.

"I took that photograph." She saw Luke beginning to speak and held up a hand. "And I know about the boy, Josue Chaca."

Chapter 45

I'm the one who sent Josue Chaca to your hospital's clinic in Santa Lucina," the woman said. "I don't know anything about the girl, the one you call Jane Doe. But I assure you, the rest of what you have told me can be explained without conspiracy theories."

"Tell me," Luke said.

"I see the suspicion in your eyes," she said. "Before I tell you, you need to know that there is nothing evil going on here. The only deception that I know of—one in which I willingly participated—has to do with those howler monkeys."

She looked over at the small primates. "Several years ago, while doing research as a microbiologist at the university in Guatemala City, I discovered that the howlers in this region have a unique resistance to malaria falciparum."

Plasmodium falciparum—the deadliest form of malaria.

"I approached Zenavax and they were interested in my work," she continued. "A short time later they hired me and built this laboratory. Most experts in my field thought us foolish because the primary form of malaria in this region is *vivax,* not falciparum. But then, my colleagues did not know what I had found here."

"What does this have to do with Josue Chaca?"

"You will understand in a moment." She brushed a strand of hair from her face. "Using the antigen that I isolated from these monkeys, researchers at our U.S. laboratory created our first prototype malaria vaccine almost three years ago. We have already demonstrated its effectiveness in primates, and testing on human volunteers began ten months ago. That's when Kate became involved."

Both of them turned to a rattling sound—one of the monkeys was working the latch on its cage.

"Kate was responsible for analyzing the results from our human trials," she continued. "We had identified five villages, all within fifty kilometers of here, where malaria falciparum is known to occur. Four of the villages, including Mayakital, agreed to participate."

Her gaze suddenly turned inward. "Everything went well at first. But several weeks after we administered the vaccine, an illness began to spread through Mayakital. Kate was monitoring the situation from her office in the States, analyzing the test data. Then, four months ago, she came here because she wanted to visit Mayakital herself. That was the first and only time I met her."

"She thought your vaccine was responsible for this illness?"

"Not my vaccine, specifically," she said. "Kate thought that our alphavirus vector had caused the illness."

"Explain that."

"We administered our flu vaccine to the test subjects months before they received the malaria vaccine. It was simply a goodwill gesture, a small gift in exchange for their participation. When several of the test subjects became ill after receiving the malaria vaccine, Kate had us collect several additional blood tests over a period of months."

The woman seemed hesitant to continue, but after taking a deep breath, she said, "After looking at the data from the blood tests, Kate seemed to think that our flu vaccine had primed these people's immune system in some unusual way, and that their second exposure to alphavirus—from our malaria vaccine—triggered an overwhelming autoimmune reaction. She believed that the test subjects' immune systems were literally devouring their bodies."

Luke recalled the batch of mice destroyed by his father's prototype flu vaccine.

"Did she mention Killer T-cells?"

"Yes. She thought apoptosis was to blame," the woman said. "But you must understand, no one else in our company agreed with her."

"What about you?"

"I have seen none of the data. Our company builds what you might call a one-way mirror between the research staff—those of us involved in developing vaccines—and clinical analysts like Kate who collect and study the test data. They see our work, but we do not see theirs. The regulatory agencies require that we do it this way. Supposedly, it is to lessen the probability of bias. But even without seeing the data, I think there are reasons to doubt Kate's theory."

"Like?"

"Many of those who became ill did not develop symptoms until several weeks after the initial cases of the illness. I am not a medical doctor, but it seemed that the illness was spreading, like an infection. Our alphavirus vaccine produces a simple antigen—it cannot spread from person to person. And more importantly, no one in any of the other three villages suffered an illness similar to what occurred at Mayakital."

"I saw this illness. What I saw isn't an infection."

"Well, now we will never know what it was. Mayakital was destroyed by a flood."

"I heard." Luke wasn't ready to reveal the evidence of cold-blooded murder that he'd found at the village. At least, not yet.

"You said you took the photograph, the one at the village," he said.

She nodded. "A few months ago, Kate called me. She wanted me to persuade some of the sick villagers to go to the University Children's clinic in Santa Lucina. I am not supposed to have any contact with test subjects, but she sounded desperate. I agreed to do it if she would not tell anyone. To be honest, I did not think that I would convince any of the villagers to go to the clinic. Most Mayans living in these remote villages choose to live in seclusion."

"Even when they're dying?"

"Sometimes, even then. Most have lived through epidemics of malaria and cholera." She shrugged. "But Josue Chaca's mother agreed to take her son to the clinic. Later, I called Kate, told her about the boy, and e-mailed her one of the pictures I had taken at Mayakital. From that point on I do not know what happened." Her eyes lost focus for a moment. "That was the last time I spoke to Kate."

Luke now understood Kate's contacting him on the same day that Josue Chaca arrived in the E.R. She must have monitored the boy's travels. Kate was fluent in Spanish and could have easily called the clinic in Santa Lucina, using a ruse to learn of his trip to the U.S.

"I still don't understand how this works," he said. "You say that your group, the people here, aren't directly involved in the clinical trials."

"That is correct."

"And Kate's team, the people that analyze the data, are located in your U.S. office."

She nodded.

"So who administered the vaccines in the villages? And who's doing the blood tests? I assume you have to collect blood samples to monitor things like titer levels."

"The CHEGAN FOUNDATION. We pay them a fee, and they do the fieldwork for us."

"Who are they?"

"An international healthcare foundation. They work under a United Nations charter and provide basic health-care services in several developing countries. They have a contract with the Guatemalan government to provide immunizations in outlying areas. The Health Ministry makes an effort to immunize every person, but it's just not feasible with their limited resources. Without CHEGAN, the people living in the more remote areas would have virtually no access to healthcare. They make a big contri-bution, especially to Mayan tribes that are on the bottom of the social ladder."

"Explain to me what they do, how they work with you."

"It is a straightforward arrangement. They have med-ical technicians who visit these villages on a regular ba-sis. Many of their people are trained to draw blood samples, and almost all of their technicians can adminis-ter a vaccine. I don't know the exact financial terms, but we pay them a fee for their services."

"How do they take delivery of the vaccines, and where do they send the blood samples they collect? How does it work, *exactly*?"

"We store the malaria vaccine samples here, for quality control reasons, and CHEGAN's medical technicians pick them up on their way to the villages. When they return, they deliver the blood samples here. Everything coming from, or going to, our U.S. office stops here first. Why?"

"What kind of vehicle do they drive?"

"Vehicle? I am not sure."

"Think. What type of vehicle?"

Her face was a bundle of puzzlement. "A truck, maybe. But I haven't paid any attention. Why are you asking about this?"

"Any logo on the side?" Luke pointed at the men on either side of her. "Ask them if they've seen the vehicle. Ask them what color it is, and whether there's a logo on the side."

She went back and forth with two of the men, then said, "The men from CHEGAN, they drive a tan truck. It has a red symbol on the side—from their description, I think it's a caduceus."

The medical caduceus symbol: two snakes curled around a wooden staff. Close enough to Paco's red snakes, Luke thought.

"CHEGAN—where are they located? Where's their office?"

"What?"

"Their office," he said. "Where is it?"

"Río Dulce. It's a port city—"

"Pack your things. We're leaving now."

Chapter 46

Calderon stared at the young man standing on the other side of his desk. Despite his anger over the bungled mission—McKenna would flee the forest lab long before he and his men could get there—he took no pleasure in what he was about to do.

The truth was, he had underestimated McKenna. He wouldn't do that again.

Hector was standing at attention, trembling like a frightened child. He wasn't much older than a child, Calderon realized for the first time. The young man had been one of his better students at the training center for the Guatemala Special Forces in Poptún. Most of the security force at the CHEGAN site had come from there. They were men disillusioned with their military careers and easily enticed by the kind of money that he offered them.

Developing a talent pool to draw from was the only reason that Calderon had spent two miserable years in Poptún as a civilian trainer, working alongside corrupt officers who pocketed the money that was supposed to pay for the state-of-the-art equipment his trainees lacked.

"So, Hector," he began in Spanish, "tell me again why you fired your weapon when you were instructed not to?"

Calderon didn't wait for the answer. "Didn't Mr. Kong tell you to hold your fire?"

Calderon glanced at the Asian who was standing in the corner of the room with his arms folded across his chest, his eyes indifferent and unblinking.

The young man choked out a response. "I—I thought the sentry was firing at Raoul."

"I see. So you had a good reason to ignore orders."

"No, no, I did not mean—"

"You see, I wanted you to wait for me to get there. But instead, McKenna has escaped, and Raoul and Jorge are dead. What am I going to say to their families, Hector?"

"I am sorry, sir. It will never—"

Calderon's eyes went to the Asian. "And what am I going to say to Hector's family, Mr. Kong?"

When he looked back at the young man, Calderon's hands were face up in the manner of a question. Resting in his right palm was a serrated steel blade.

But only for an instant.

Hector's eyes grew wide when the blade pierced his throat. He stumbled backward, grabbed at the metal haft, and pulled the knife from his neck.

But that wasn't going to help him. His windpipe was already severed. Pulling the knife out only meant that blood would flood into his lungs—he was going to drown rather than suffocate to death.

Calderon watched the young man slump into Mr. Kong's waiting arms, but his mind was busy replaying his phone conversation earlier that evening with Sammy Wilkes.

It was now or never, Megan realized. If she was going to have any chance of escaping, she had to make her move now. Kaczynski was improving rapidly, his temperature curve receding, his delirium clearing. He had responded after only thirty hours of penicillin, more quickly than she had anticipated.

Once his recovery took hold, the value of her life to her captors would evaporate.

As she had hoped, word of her mosquito scare had spread among the guards, and a screen door had replaced the open doorway to their room. Their guard was sitting in a chair on the other side of the screen, his head propped against the opposite wall of the corridor.

She had rehearsed the movements in her mind a hundred times: climbing onto the window ledge that was outside of the guard's field of vision; leaping to the tree branch that was as far away as any vault she'd ever done; swinging up and onto the huge limb and crossing to the other side of the compound wall; and finally, climbing the steep mountainside to a road she'd seen only once while walking across the compound two days earlier.

The screened window was on the wall to the left of the entry door. Both she and Father Joe had feigned catnaps near that window to condition the guard to their disappearing from view for long periods. At random intervals the guard would put his face against the screen door and survey the room. She and Father Joe had worked out a system of signals and taken turns working on the window's wire mesh when the guard was in his seat. They had separated the edge of the screen from its frame an inch at a time, then put it back in place. Working all night, they had freed most of three sides.

She needed the cover of darkness. They had taken her watch, and she didn't know the exact time, but based on the flow rate of the IVs and the lab technician's habit of changing the IV bag at midnight, Megan guessed it was about 4:00 A.M. The sun would be rising in a few hours.

They had come up with the plan together, communicating in gestures and coded whispers when standing together over the patient. The priest had worked excitedly, at times causing him to lose his breath. She could see the fervor in his eyes. He wanted her to escape, probably more than she wanted it.

Even though it was his idea that she should attempt an escape, her sense of guilt swelled as the moment approached. Both of them knew what their fate would be once Dr. Kaczynski emerged from his stuporous state and took over his own care. And both knew that Father Joe did not have the physical agility or stamina to accompany her.

The priest would pay for her escape with his life unless she could quickly get to the police and return with help.

Megan was standing over Kaczynski when the guard rose from his seat. He walked up to the screen door, studied the room, then sat down again.

Father Joe came up from behind and whispered, "It's time."

Megan nodded without turning. She was fighting back tears.

The priest stepped beside her, took a damp cloth from her hand and patted Kaczynski's forehead.

"I'm coming back for you," she said.

He smiled while dabbing a rivulet of sweat from the patient's neck. "Godspeed, Megan Callahan."

She stepped away from the table, opened her mouth while spreading her arms in a yawn, and shuffled over to the window. She listened for any telltale sounds from the guard as she eased back the screen.

Once she had the screen peeled back, she looked in both directions at the dimly lit compound below, grabbed the window frame and lifted herself onto the sill.

Her throat tightened. She bounced lightly a few times, shaking away the fear.

Then she sprang at the tree limb.

Father Joe coughed to cover the sound.

Megan caught the thick branch with one hand, missed with the other. She hung there, swinging by one arm, her body suddenly announcing its fatigue.

Her free arm caught hold of the bough, then slipped away.

She had almost no strength left. She knew her body. Her reserves were gone. Soon, her single handhold would give way.

Panic swiped at her like a tiger's claw.

She looked back into the room.

Father Joe was watching her. There was a smile in his eyes. They were strangely calm, like those of a parent watching his child learn a new skill.

Without a word, he turned both thumbs skyward.

Megan hadn't seen that gesture since she was a young girl. At gymnastics meets, before each event, she'd turn to her father and he'd lift his thumbs.

It was their private little ritual, an unspoken message to her. *You can do it, Megan.*

And do it, she did, speaking to her father in silent thoughts as she curled up and onto the tree limb.

She raced over the top of the stone wall.

Chapter 47

"This woman, Megan, I sense that she is more than just a friend," the microbiologist said.

Luke downshifted without replying to the woman's comment. The truck's gears ground loudly.

He had just told her about Megan's abduction by men whose description matched the killers at Zenavax's lab. He had described the tan truck with a red caduceus that her kidnappers used, and the explosive charges that destroyed Mayakital.

They had left the Zenavax lab two hours ago and were winding through a narrow mountain road. The transmission groaned every time the speedometer needle passed the fifteen-kilometer bar, and the bullet-riddled truck creaked loudly whenever they hit a pothole, which was often. It wouldn't be long before the mechanical beast died.

He was breaking every rule of evasion and countersurveillance he had ever learned. Their truck was as conspicuous as a zebra with pink stripes, and his passengers included a woman about whom he knew little, three men about whom he knew nothing, and a nine-year-old boy over whom he seemed to have no control.

The only precaution he'd taken was to bar any communications. Earlier, the woman had asked to call Zenavax's

U.S. headquarters, to tell her company about the melee at the lab, but Luke had not allowed her to make the call. There were still too many unknown risks—his enemy had already demonstrated that they could tap a phone line— and he didn't want to risk giving his adversaries any more information than they already had.

His only concession to the woman had been delaying their departure from the lab for the few minutes it took to release her monkeys from their cages.

"Our guards, Miguel and Eduardo, you did not kill them, did you?" she said. It sounded more like a statement than a question.

"Does it matter?"

"To me, it does."

"I shot one of them in the shoulder."

"That would not have killed him."

"I was aiming for his chest."

The edge of the dirt road floated in and out of Luke's view. One of the truck's headlights was broken and the other lolled to the side like an eye hanging from its socket. His only view was through a gaping hole in the shattered windshield. Insects streamed in through the opening and ricocheted off his face.

"My name is Rosalinda," she said.

"Luke." He offered his hand.

She took it. "Luke, I know the executives who run our company. They are aggressive business people, and sometimes unpleasant, but they are not killers."

It had already occurred to him that Zenavax might be a pawn in this drama. The men guarding the forest facility had displayed total surprise, and the killers had shown no regard for anyone at the laboratory—gunning down two of Rosalinda's workers in cold blood. If the company was trying to conceal something, why bring attention to itself by staging an attack on its own site?

But if Zenavax wasn't at the center of this maelstrom, the CHEGAN FOUNDATION seemed even more implausible. A healthcare organization doing relief work in remote Indian villages was hardly the profile of a violent cabal.

"What are you going to do when we get to Río Dulce?" she asked.

He'd been mulling that question for the past hour and still hadn't come up with anything resembling a plan.

"Follow the only lead I have." He pulled a piece of paper from his pocket on which Rosalinda had written the Río Dulce address for CHEGAN.

"I have no idea what is there. It is simply the address I had in my records."

"I need to see what's there." He glanced over at her. "And I'll need your help, at least to drive by and scout the place. You blend in better than me."

Frankie stuck his head through the porthole between the cab and the truck bed. "Boss, where we going?"

"Stop calling me 'boss.'" Luke reached into the foot well on Rosalinda's side of the cab, grabbed his pack, and fished out Sammy's phone.

He had missed that evening's call from Sammy, but they were passing over the crest of a mountain and Luke thought he'd try for a satellite connection while he could. He punched in Sammy's number.

A voice filled with sleep answered on the other end. "Do you know what time it is?"

Luke looked at his watch. "Three-seventeen A.M."

"Where the hell have you been, Flash?" Sammy's voice was suddenly awake.

"I need information about something called the CHEGAN FOUNDATION." He spelled it for Sammy.

"Hang on. Let me get something to write with."

Luke kept going: "Last time we talked, you said you might have something to tell me tonight. What did you mean?"

"I'm still working on it. Sammy'll let you know if—"

"Tell me now."

After a long stretch of static, Sammy said, "Okay, but don't say anything until Sammy's done talking." Another pause, then, "I'm coming up dry on your lady friend's kidnapping. Now, I know you said no-way no-how you were gonna talk to Calderon, but I got to thinkin' that maybe I should call him."

Sammy seemed to wait for a reaction that Luke didn't give him, so he continued, "I didn't tell him about you. I told him your hospital had hired me to look for her. He's got connections in places where polite folks usually don't go. I figured it's worth a try. But I haven't heard back, so maybe he's got zip."

Luke looked down at the gun tucked under his belt. It was a Colt 1911A1 semiautomatic that he'd lifted from one of the would-be killers—the same make and model that Calderon had used while a member of Proteus.

Rather than the standard .45 caliber model, Calderon had used a modified version that shot 10mm rounds—just like the one tucked under Luke's belt.

"Stay by your phone," Luke said. "I have a feeling that Calderon will be calling you."

"A feeling?"

"When you hear from him, let me know." Luke thumbed the END CALL button.

Megan looked back at the valley below her. She'd been climbing the mountainside for over twenty minutes and wondered why she hadn't reached the road she'd seen from inside the walled compound.

The complex was strangely quiet. There were no men rushing under the wash of floodlights, no flashlights on the hillside below her—none of the angry sounds she had expected to hear.

Nothing to distract her from the guilt that hung over her like a guillotine blade. Earlier, she had rationalized that they wouldn't risk killing Father Joe as long as she was on the loose. After all, they had to know that she would bring the police back with her. But there was something about the nature of these men that tugged at the logic of her argument.

Especially their leader, Calderon. There was a zeal and obsession to his cruelty. She couldn't expect him to think and act as other men might.

Megan climbed over the rotting trunk of a deadfall. Her foot came down on a dry branch. A loud *crack* split open the forest's calm.

She froze, winced. The buzz of insects filled her ears.

A moment later a grinding sound pierced the white noise of the forest.

Metal against metal. Gears scraping against one another. She looked up toward the sound. A headlight strobed on the hillside above her, about twenty yards up the hill, its beam darting between breaks in the trees.

Her legs started churning like a jackhammer. She thrashed up the hill.

The single headlight swept over her, then a truck drove past on the road that was just ten feet up the hillside.

She screamed but it came out as a hoarse whisper. Her breath was gone.

Megan clawed at the undergrowth and finally, on all fours, dragged herself onto the edge of the road.

She was spent.

The truck downshifted—more grinding—and turned

into a curve about thirty feet ahead of her. The only brake light that worked glowed red.

She guzzled air, her lungs heaving, trying to catch her breath and raise a scream.

She rose onto her knees and yelled.

As she did, an arm came from behind and wrapped her neck in a chokehold. The last thing she heard was the unearthly sound of her own smothered scream.

Chapter 48

What was that?" Luke pumped the brakes and slowed the truck as they rounded a curve on the narrow mountain road.

"Probably a predator finding its next meal," Rosalinda replied.

"It sounded human," he said. "Like someone screaming."

"In a forest full of primates, sounds like that are common."

Luke pinched the bridge of his nose and blinked his eyes into focus. Ahead of them a faint blush of moonlight dusted the timbered peaks. Outside the driver-side window, a single cluster of amber lights burned in the valley below them. The sound was too close to have come from there.

He looked into the back of the truck. Rosalinda's workers were staring at the trailer bed, avoiding his gaze. Frankie was curled up, asleep.

Luke eased off the brakes and the truck started to roll again.

They rode in silence for the next hour while he replayed the past week's events. He thought back to something that had gnawed at him for days. The person who had framed him for the football player's murder had to know that

Luke was proficient with a sniper's rifle, or the frame wouldn't have worked. Only a handful of close friends knew of his training as a SEAL, and no one but fellow Proteus members knew about his brief career in black ops.

Luke fingered the Colt 1911A1 semiautomatic under his belt. Proteus had given its elite fighters a great deal of freedom in selecting sidearms and other personalized weapons. Two of its members had used the modified 10mm Colt. Both had come to Proteus from the 1st Special Forces Operational Detachment—formerly known as Delta Force.

But only one—Calderon—held a grudge against him.

The men who had attacked him at the forest lab were highly trained soldiers who used military tactics. He thought back to what Sammy had told him about Calderon training Guatemala's Special Forces before forming his own security company, a company he would likely staff with men he had trained, and men he equipped to his own standards.

The pieces of the puzzle fell into place like pins in a lock tumbler. Calderon knew him in a way that few did, well enough to reel him in, using Megan as bait, knowing that Luke would press the fight rather than run.

Calderon would have seen through Sammy's charade and known that Luke, not University Children's, was behind Sammy's search for information about Megan.

Luke was counting on it. He *wanted* Calderon to act on his hunter's instinct. The killer had lost Luke's scent and would follow every lead to reacquire his prey.

Without knowing it, the cunning Sammy Wilkes was being played by both sides.

Would Calderon know that he'd been discovered?

Luke realized it wouldn't matter. Calderon would never run, never go underground. He'd continue the hunt.

And that would be his final mistake, because Luke was going to kill him.

You're already dead, you bastard . . .

A narrow band of violet was pushing up against a black-domed sky when Rosalinda broke his reverie and announced, "Ahead. That's Río Dulce."

A mile ahead, the port town's lights shimmered. Luke pulled off the road and cut the engine behind a cluster of trees. The truck's diesel snorted a few times before dying.

Luke decided they should break up into smaller groups, and after some back-and-forth between Rosalinda and her workers—they were concerned about her staying with the gringo—she finally convinced the men to walk into town ahead of them and find buses to their homes. The woman waved them forward as if shooing reluctant children off to school.

Chaos had shattered the workers' quiet and ordered lives. Luke understood the feeling.

Fifteen minutes later he and Rosalinda walked toward town along the same road. He carried his knapsack over one shoulder; draped over the other shoulder was a large duffel bag filled with equipment and weapons he had scavenged before leaving the forest lab.

Frankie was several paces in front of them, his horse-shoe-shaped legs bobbing back and forth.

"Can you remember anything else about CHEGAN?" Luke asked "Anything you haven't told me?"

"Nothing that paints a picture of evil." She shook her head slowly. "In fact, quite the opposite. They operate a hospital in Guatemala City, a hospital for children with genetic disorders. They do it without compensation, I am told."

They came up on Frankie, who had stopped to light a cigarette.

"Put that thing out." Luke grabbed the cigarette and crushed it under his shoe.

By the time they reached the edge of town, the sky was changing from black to muddy gray. Entrails of smoke swirled from stubby stone chimneys. Even at that hour there were men loitering in alleyways—the type of men who linger with stooped heads, glancing sidelong at the world and missing very few of the details that pass in front of them.

The smell of hot grease and burning wood wafted from an open doorway on the right side of the street. A primitive wooden sign hanging over it read COMIDA.

Luke saw that Rosalinda's limp was becoming more pronounced. "Let's eat," he said.

They sat at a bench table and Luke ate like a ravenous animal, washing down a mountain of corn tortillas with a brothy soup, in the bottom of which sat a single chicken claw.

Two ruddy-faced men with dull bloodshot eyes grinned at him from across the smoke-filled room, their heads bobbing up and down as if Luke was the most entertaining sight they'd seen in a long time.

Frankie said, "I be back," and was out the door with a fresh cigarette in hand before Luke could clear his throat of food.

Luke wiped a sheet of sweat from his forehead, then said to Rosalinda, "I need a hotel room. Can you find one that caters to tourists, someplace where an Anglo won't stand out?"

"I know of a few hotels like that."

"Good. Register under your name. Get two keys, and tell them you have a husband who'll be joining you. After that, you should leave town."

"What about the boy? He should not be with you."

"Tell *him* that," Luke said. "After you check me into a hotel, take Frankie to the bus station and put him on a bus back home."

She nodded. "Where is his home?"

"Santa Elena."

"He came with you all the way from Santa Elena?"

"He doesn't follow instructions very well," Luke said. "Stay with him until the bus leaves, and don't blink or he'll probably vanish on you." He wrote down the names of several medicines on a napkin and handed it to her. "On your way to the bus station, stop by a pharmacy and see if you can buy any of these."

The recognition showed in Rosalinda's eyes. "These drugs—they are for HIV."

Luke nodded. "I listed four medications, in order of preference. Try to buy the first one on the list—it's a combination drug. If they don't have it, try the second name on the list, and so on." He pulled a thick stack of bills from his pocket and laid them in front of Rosalinda. "Buy as much as you can get with this."

"The boy—he has HIV?"

"His mother. Give the drugs to Frankie and tell him what they're for. It'll make it easier to get him on the bus."

Luke's backpack started chirping. He pulled out Sammy's phone.

"You in Río Dulce yet?" Sammy asked.

"Yeah."

"Don't leave. Calderon just called me—by the way, how'd you know he was gonna call?"

"Like I said, I had a feeling."

"Yeah, right," Sammy said. "Anyway, you're on for to-night. Someone's gonna meet up with you at eight o'clock.

"Who?"

"Flash, understand how this works. I don't ask, and they don't tell. I told Calderon some cock-'n'-bull story about you being one of the workers at the University Children's clinic down there. What's important is, this guy that Calderon dug up has some info on your lady friend. And Flash, he's gonna wanna be paid—a thousand U.S."

"Where's this Samaritan going to meet me?"

"I don't know yet. Keep the phone with you, and leave it on. I'll call you as soon as I hear something," A pause, then, "Luke?"

Luke couldn't remember the last time that Sammy had called him by his real name. "What?"

"Sammy's nose is picking up something here. Watch your six."

Watch your back.

Sammy was sensing what Luke had already assumed. It was a setup.

Chapter 49

Rosalinda shook her head at Luke as she walked up to the taxi in which he and Frankie were waiting.

"It seems that the address I had for CHEGAN is a private postal company," she said while squeezing back into the cab's rear seat with them.

Luke looked at the plain-looking tan stucco building at the end of the block. His precautions—giving their driver a fake street number and stopping a half block from their intended address—had turned out to be unnecessary.

"So CHEGAN gave you a phony address," Luke said.

"Perhaps not. They may have what you would call a post office box there. Many businesses and organizations use these private postal services. The state-run postal service is unreliable."

Luke wasn't convinced. "An organization that uses medical supplies and trucks has got to have someplace to keep them. Why wouldn't their mail go to the same place?"

"I would not know."

She exchanged a few words in Spanish with their dusty-looking driver, who made a U-turn and reentered traffic. When they reached the other side of town, Rosalinda followed their prearranged plan and had the taxi drop them in front of a hotel that was a quarter mile past the one where she had reserved a room.

They backtracked to their hotel after watching the driver disappear around a corner. The place was away from the town's bustling hub, in an area where foot traffic was less congested and overly attentive eyes were easier to spot.

Rosalinda registered them as a family of three, and as soon as they made their way to the second-floor room, Luke sent Frankie out to buy food and supplies. Leaving the room for a meal was a luxury that Luke couldn't afford when killers where stalking him.

He sat on the edge of a bed that sagged in the middle while Rosalinda used the bathroom. He used the few minutes of silence to salve his battered psyche.

He was surprised at how well the woman was holding up. He'd seen the wheels fall off battle-hardened soldiers hours after a fierce fight, but so far Rosalinda's emotional makeup seemed to have an epoxy-like quality.

When she came back out, she walked over to the floor-to-ceiling window and took in the view, twice squeezing her atrophied thigh with a veiled grimace. She seemed the type of person who'd rather not have her leg or stamina become a topic of conversation, so he said nothing.

He looked past her, through the wooden balustrades of his room's veranda. On the other side of the road was a park, and a few hundred yards beyond that, a large stone structure that looked like a fortress from an earlier era. The rock-walled citadel sat on the shoreline of an immense lake.

"Lake Izabal," she said, as if anticipating his question. "It empties into the Río Dulce, which means 'sweet river.' The area around here is named for the river."

Luke got up from the bed and walked to the window.

She pointed at the stony fortress. "That's Castillo San Felipe. It sits at the mouth of Lake Izabal. This is where the lake empties into the Río Dulce."

She told him about the castle's history. He nodded occasionally as she went on about pirates, Spanish conquistadors, and trading ships in the sixteenth century.

What interested him had nothing to do with its history. The castle sat on a promontory, an outcrop of land surrounded by water on three sides. By land, the only approach was across the manicured lawns and open spaces of the park. From the battlements atop the castle's walls, he realized that a single lookout could spot anyone approaching the fortress.

She turned to him. "You don't look well. Why don't you get some rest? I'll call you when I'm settled in a hotel."

"I thought you were going home?"

"My home is in Bogotá, Colombia. I came to Guatemala to teach at the university, but from the time I joined Zenavax, I have lived at the lab." She shrugged. "I will need a place to stay for the next several days, but I do not think I should rent another room at this hotel—we have already registered as a family."

She was right. His enemies had probably already found the truck they ditched on the highway outside of town. They'd be searching for him, asking questions, and willing to pay for answers. Anything unusual, like a wife sleeping apart from her husband in a second room, could lead the killers to them.

She picked up her purse as though preparing to leave. "Please understand, though. I cannot sit in a hotel room forever. Sooner or later I must call my company and tell them what has happened. Perhaps I should make that call now. They can bring the authorities into this."

"*No!*"

Luke immediately raised a hand by way of apology. "Kate's killer knew when and where she was going to meet me. That means someone was monitoring her communications. If you call your U.S. office, whatever you say is probably going to find its way to the killers. Even if Zenavax has nothing to do with this bloodbath, it's still not safe to call your company."

"Then we should go to the authorities here."

"The Guatemalan Minister of Health intervened to stop Josue Chaca's autopsy. Somebody in the Health Ministry is either involved or being paid to look the other way."

"We cannot hide here forever. Eventually, we *must* go to the police."

"Not until I find Megan."

She was looking at his hands, which he realized had tightened into fists.

He grabbed the large duffel bag, pulled out two identical metal-framed cases, and handed one to Rosalinda. "We'll use these to contact each other." They were the satellite phones from her lab. "Call me as soon as you get settled. If I'm not here, leave a message for yourself at the front desk. Say your name is Julia, let me know where you're staying. Later, I'll send Frankie over to your hotel. Get him onto a bus after you get those medicines for his mother."

Her eyes were studying him. "I hope you find her. Your friend, Megan."

He returned her gaze. "Be careful, Rosalinda. I've been dealing with these people. They don't leave loose ends. And if anything happens to me, get out of Guatemala. Get to the U.S. or go home to Colombia. *Then* go the police. And don't just tell some government bureaucrat. Tell the newspapers. The more public this becomes, the safer you'll be."

"Right now, I wish not to think anymore about this." She started toward the door. "I will call you later."

As soon as she was gone, Luke pulled off his shirt and examined his wounds. There was a blistered track near his left elbow where the bullet had grazed him. The skin was burned but would heal. The deep gash in his shoulder, though, had become badly infected. A growing circle of red was spreading outward from its edges and the wound was beginning to weep.

Luke collapsed backward onto the mattress, giving in to the fever he had ignored for the past several hours.

A minute later there was a knock on the door. "Boss, I here."

When Luke opened the door, the boy was holding two white plastic bags. One was filled with an assortment of candies, two packages of corn tortillas, and a small brown paper bag. The other held three liters of beer and some bottled water. A child's version of essential food groups.

He felt Frankie's eyes studying him. "Cerveza—you like?"

"I like." The truth was, he didn't drink beer.

Luke grabbed the small brown bag. Inside was gauze, tape, antimicrobial ointment, and a bottle of antibiotic pills labeled CEFALEXINA. He swallowed one of the large orange pills, then another. He had given Frankie a list of pharmacy items he wanted, knowing that most pharmacies in Latin American countries sold drugs without a prescription. He had written "Cephalexin." He hoped that Cefalexina was the Spanish equivalent.

"What your name is?" the boy asked.

"You know my name."

Frankie shook his head. *"Es falso."*

"What are you talking about?"

"You say Edward to Padre Tomas. You say Luke to Rosalinda." Frankie fingered his lip with one hand while pointing at Luke's face with the other. *"Y esta es falso."*

Luke reached up and felt a dry edge of the "scar" peeling from the skin under his nose. "My real name *is* Luke, but you can't tell anyone."

"Why I no can tell?"

"It's complicated." He suddenly felt light-headed and a chill swept over him.

"You okay, boss? You no look good."

Luke motioned to the bed and the two of them sat.

"Frankie, don't you miss your mother?"

The boy played with his fingers. "You want I go home, yes?"

Luke nodded.

Frankie's fingers tangled into a knot. "I no want to be there when she dies."

So, the boy knew. Luke wasn't surprised.

"I need to get some sleep." Luke grabbed a section of his bedcovering and wiped the sweat from his face. "We'll talk about this later."

"What is it, Elmer?" Ben swung his front door open. "Is this about Luke? Have you heard something?"

"No." The old man's eyes had a faraway look as he crossed the threshold. "Still no word."

Elmer didn't drive, so traveling across town to Ben's home entailed either a taxi or a long bus ride. If his need was simply to talk to a friend, he would have called.

Something was up.

"Is this about Barnesdale?" Ben asked as they walked into the living room.

Elmer shook his head as he dropped onto a couch.

Not only was Elmer living with the agony of a missing

son from whom he'd heard nothing, the man had to deal with knowing glances and whispered comments that followed him wherever he went around the hospital. The news media had all but convicted Luke in absentia for both Erickson's and Barnesdale's murders. The strain showed in Elmer's face.

Elmer pulled a sheet of paper from his breast pocket and handed it to Ben. "Look at this."

Ben sat down next to his friend and studied the document for several seconds. "It's a lab printout—I can see that. Why are you showing it to me?"

"Those are blood test results for volunteers in my malaria project, all of whom work in my lab." Elmer sighed heavily. "After they're exposed to the vaccine-producing mosquitoes, we do weekly blood tests. We measure their malaria titers, but we also do a direct measurement of their antigen level—to see how much vaccine the mosquitoes are injecting into the volunteers' blood." He rubbed his forehead. "Look at the fourth line."

"I see it. It says Elmer McKenna."

"Notice the antigen level."

"You're positive. You have antigen in your blood. So what?"

"Years ago I had malaria. I can't participate in the study," Elmer said. "That's not my blood."

"You're losing me."

"You told me to use an alias for Josue Chaca's blood specimen, the one we got from the state lab," Elmer said. "So I used my name. I labeled the tube myself, then stored it with a collection of blood samples we'd drawn from the volunteers. One of my techs ran a titer and antigen level on that tube, thinking it was just another one of the volunteers' blood samples."

"There must be a mix-up."

Elmer shook his head. "I had my tech repeat the tests while I stood there and watched. There's no mistake. Sometime before he died, Josue Chaca was bitten by my mosquitoes."

Chapter 50

When Luke awoke, his eyelids opened as heavily as a bank vault door. A red shaft of light streamed through a gap in his window drapes, and the wall opposite his bed glowed with the deep hues of sunset.

He rubbed the sleep out of his eyes and looked at his watch: 6:03 P.M. He'd slept for almost five hours.

Damn. He jumped out of bed and stumbled over to the corner of the room where he'd thrown his clothes. They were gone.

A silhouette bled through the window's thin curtain weave. Someone was on the veranda.

He eased the curtain back and saw Frankie sitting in a small chair with his feet up on the railing. He was blowing smoke rings at the sunset.

Luke threw open the door. "You're gonna stunt your growth."

"Huh? What you mean?"

"Never mind. Where're my clothes?"

Frankie threw a thumb over his shoulder.

Luke looked back inside. Sitting on the dresser were all of his clothes—two shirts, a pair of pants, underwear and socks—laundered, folded, and stacked.

"*Monjas*—the sisters," Frankie said. "At the hospital,

they make me clean clothes, like a girl." He took a long drag on his cigarette. "It no right."

Luke swiped the butt from him and tossed it over the balustrade.

A drop of rain struck his wrist. Above them, a churning swarm of dark clouds reached over to the western horizon where a reddish-orange sun was dipping into the earth.

The fever was coming back and his left shoulder throbbed. He went inside, grabbed the bottle of antibiotics from the dresser top and swallowed two more pills.

When he returned to the balcony, he was holding one of the rifle scopes he'd taken from the assailants at the lab. He clicked a knob, set the scope to ambient light, and surveyed the park across the street. A stone pathway bisected broad swaths of manicured Bermuda grass. At the end of the path was a wrought-iron gate, and behind it stood a drawbridge that spanned the narrow moat around Castillo San Felipe.

The castle's entry gate was closed. Except for a man sitting on a decorative iron bench outside the entrance, the grounds were empty.

About fifty feet to the left of the castle, a small dinghy was tied to a dock.

This will work, he thought. He grabbed Sammy's phone from his rucksack and placed a call to Wilkes.

"Where you been?" Sammy barked. "I been calling you for the past hour."

Luke realized he had slept through the phone's ring.

Sammy launched into a hurried description of some rendezvous site outside of town.

Luke interrupted him in mid-sentence. "I'm changing the plans. We'll meet at Castillo San Felipe. If he knows this area, he'll know where the castle is."

"You're gonna scare the guy off, Flash. I told Calderon I'm working for University Children's, remember? And this informant thinks you're some yokel that works at the clinic in Santa Lucina. How'm I supposed to explain you changing the meeting like this? It won't smell right."

Luke ignored him. "The castle, eight o'clock. If the guy's one minute late, I won't be there." He wasn't going to give Calderon enough time to set up an ambush.

"It's your play," Sammy conceded. "Anything else?"

"Yeah. There's a bench near the castle's front gate. Have the guy sit on that bench, then light a match. If I don't see the flame, he won't see me." Luke pressed the END CALL button.

He had Frankie call the front desk for messages. There was a message for Rosalinda from someone named Julia, who left the name of the hotel where she was staying and a room number.

"That was Rosalinda," Luke explained, "letting us know where she is." He went back out onto the veranda and studied the entrance to the castle. The man who had been sitting on the bench was gone.

"Frankie, I need you to do something for me."

Chapter 51

Luke lay across his hotel room's veranda in a shooter's prone position, his legs spread behind him. His rifle rested on the lower railing of the balustrade, its barrel protruding between two posts. It was 7:48 P.M.

Privacy walls jutting from either end of the balcony shielded him from the neighboring rooms. Behind him, his room was dark. Above him, only an occasional streak of moonlight penetrated the thick cloud layer. And below him, a roadway without street lamps completed the void of darkness.

He had an elevated perch on the second floor, and more importantly, he was nowhere near where a trained reconnaissance team would look for him. Someone with a trained eye would expect him to take a position along the top of the castle's wall, behind the battlement. From that position, he not only would have had the advantage of elevation, but also an unimpeded view of the entire plaza, the protection of water on three sides, and the concealment of stone walls.

Which was exactly why he wasn't there. From his current position, men approaching the castle by land would have their backs to him. He'd have them flanked from the outset.

Earlier, he had watched Frankie tape Sammy's phone

to the underside of the wrought-iron bench, then shuffle away with slouched shoulders and an occasional glance in Luke's direction. The boy had trudged off in the direction of Rosalinda's hotel with the enthusiasm of someone walking the plank.

When Calderon or his surrogate sat down on the bench, Luke would call him using Rosalinda's satellite phone. He'd direct the would-be killer to the far side of the plaza, watching the area around the man as he moved across the park. From Luke's position, he could easily spot any accomplice within a quarter mile of his mark.

Suddenly, an explosion of light seared his eyes.

A lightning flash had blinded him. A moment later a peal of thunder rolled over him. The gallium arsenide amplifier in his nightscope had magnified the light ten-thousand-fold, creating a burst of radiance so bright that it temporarily stole his eyesight. He blinked away the pain.

Slowly, his vision returned.

His task was already difficult enough without having to deal with lightning bursts. At this range—he was about two hundred yards from the castle—slow moving objects would be difficult to detect.

Even more troublesome were the variations in lighting across the search area, which degraded his scope's optics. A light post near the dock cast a distorting glare on the eastern approach to the castle, while the western side of the fortress was in total darkness.

A fast moving object on the water interrupted his thoughts. It was a large boat, over thirty feet long, with a steering house on the foredeck, speeding up the river toward the mouth of Lake Izabal. It suddenly changed course and slowed, steering toward the fortress. He hadn't considered the possibility that they would arrive by water.

A minute later the boat neared the dock to the left of the castle.

He checked his watch: 7:57 P.M.

Luke couldn't hear the engine but he saw a froth of water behind the boat as it throttled back and gently tapped against the dock. Two men jumped from the deck, quickly moored the boat, then stepped back onto the vessel and disappeared below deck.

The clouds broke and a patch of moonlight reflected off the lake. The castle turned into a black silhouette against the water's gleaming surface.

He swung his scope across the front of the castle and swept the other side of the plaza, searching the trees for movement, then swung it back and scanned the area around the dock. He repeated the process three times.

On the third pass, as his scope moved across the castle's front wall, he caught a fleeting shadow at the edge of his lens. A man was climbing over the fortress's dockside wall.

He swung his rifle to the other side of the castle. Another black figure was scaling the opposite wall with a rifle slung across his back.

They climbed like well-practiced spiders. He found a third man crouched just inside the castle wall, along the upper rim of the parapet just above the drawbridge.

When his eyes were elsewhere, the men had probably slipped over the boat's stern and waded through shoreline waters to the castle's lakeside wall, then around its perimeter. How many other movements had he missed?

All three men disappeared into the castle's interior, searching the stony structure just as Luke had guessed they would. A short time later two of the men reappeared at either end of the fortress's front battlement, scanning the park with their rifle scopes.

Luke centered his scope on the boat and increased the magnification. He didn't have to wait long.

A dark form emerged from the boat's steering house, stepped down onto the dock, and began walking toward the castle. The lone figure moved tentatively at first, then settled into a slow and deliberate gait.

Just before reaching the castle's front gate, the person stopped and sat on the bench.

A match flared in Luke's nightscope. His lens filled with a bright green flash of light.

Luke looked away, keyed in Sammy's cell phone number on Rosalinda's satellite unit, and pressed SEND.

He reacquired the dark figure just as the first ring sounded in his earpiece. The person on the bench startled at the sound, then looked down to where Sammy's phone was taped.

He increased the magnification and quartered the target in his sights.

The second ring sounded.

The figure slowly raised the glowing match to chin level.

Oh my God!

Megan's tremulous face filled his scope, her eyes darting from side to side.

Luke's breaths came in heaving gasps.

She was mouthing a word, the same word over and over. *Rat? . . . Rap?*

"*Trap*," he whispered.

The slide of an automatic weapon clicked in his right ear. "That's right, cockroach."

Luke closed his eyes. "How'd you find me?"

"So many sloppy mistakes. You college boys don't know how to work a con. Setting up a meeting so close to your hotel, using the woman's name on the hotel register."

"What woman?"

"Let's not play games. Did you think we didn't know the microbiologist's name? Did you think we wouldn't check the hotels in this area?"

A sudden sick feeling swept over Luke.

"In case you're wondering—yeah, she's dead. We had a little talk. It seems you told her too much. I'm afraid you left me no choice."

"You son of a bitch."

Luke didn't hear the loud *clack* when his skull smacked against the concrete deck.

His world had already gone dark.

Calderon heard the clap of footsteps on the dock as he and his men were securing their human cargo below deck. He came up through one of the forward hatches, holding his Colt semiautomatic low and behind his thigh.

Standing on the dock, next to one of the mooring lines, was a small boy.

The boy said in Spanish, "You need supplies, boss? I'll run to the store for you. Ten quetzals."

"Get outta here, kid."

The boy reached into his pocket and pulled out a cigarette. "You like? Two quetzals."

"I'm gonna count to three. One . . . two . . ."

The boy turned and ran from the dock. He had an odd, swaying gait.

Calderon went below deck again. Two minutes later, just as he fired up the diesel engines, he heard a *creak* directly above him on the deck. Using hand signals to communicate, he and Kong made their way to the fore and aft hatches. Simultaneously, they charged up through the openings, their guns held at chest level.

A seagull fluttered off the roof of the steering house. Kong gestured toward the fleeing bird.

Calderon made a looping motion with his gun, indicating that he wanted the Asian to search the deck anyway.

Calderon checked the poop ladder, then walked the length of the boat's port side. He did this while Kong searched the aft section, including the fantail where an inverted lifeboat—an inflatable Zodiac with outboard motor—was secured with ropes across the backend of the boat.

In the shadowed light, Kong didn't notice the subtle tenting of the raft bottom's rubber skin.

Chapter 52

The knot on the side of Luke's head throbbed violently, and he was still drifting at the edges of a mental fog when he saw Petri Kaczynski emerge from an enormous rock-walled tunnel. Two men walked alongside the geneticist, supporting him at his elbows. The moon threw an eerie blue cast on the old man's face—he looked like a conjured spirit.

Luke and Megan lay hog-tied next to Calderon's boat on a thick timbered dock that reached out from the mouth of the tunnel into a black water lagoon. Sheer limestone cliffs rising straight up from the river's edge swept around them in a lazy curve, forming a large cove that kept out the Río Dulce's currents.

On the other side of the dock was a massive barge onto which several workers were loading crated equipment. The word TAIFANG was printed on the back of their hard hats. Armed men stood guard over the operation.

A few minutes earlier, as three of Calderon's men had dragged them from the boat, Luke spotted the running lights of a stationary freighter in the middle of the river.

Calderon was nowhere in sight, which brought back the question that Luke had been asking himself ever since he awoke: Why hadn't Calderon already killed them?

Kaczynski took a halting step. "I need to rest," he said. "Stop, here."

The geneticist's keepers lowered him onto a wooden crate, where he sat catching his breath. All three men wore shirts stenciled with the word CHEGAN.

Before arriving at the remote site, while locked away in the boat's hull, Megan had whispered to Luke about Kaczynski, the secluded cove, and the walled compound at the other end of the tunnel where she'd been held captive. Until now her words had sounded like the imagined driftwood of a bizarre dream.

Kaczynski's eyes traveled past Megan and settled on Luke. "I wish you hadn't come here. I truly do."

"I'm sure your family would be very proud of you, Petri, if only they knew." Luke recalled watching Kaczynski's wife drowning in grief at her husband's memorial service five years earlier.

"It was necessary," the frail man offered without a shred of remorse.

Luke summoned his recollections of Kaczynski. What he remembered most was the geneticist's absorption with himself and his work.

"And the killings?" Luke said. "What's so important that it justifies murder?"

An Asian appeared on the boat's deck, the same man who Luke had spotted following him in L.A. "Don't tell them anything," he said.

Kaczynski ignored the man. "I'm not sure you'd understand, Luke."

"Try me."

The geneticist seemed to take the measure of Luke before saying, "We've spent the last hundred years and countless fortunes unlocking the genetic code, and for what?

Instead of using what we know to eliminate diseases, we've let them become a yoke around the world's neck."

Kaczynski's eyes went to a pickup truck coming through the tunnel's entrance, then back to Luke. "Medical resources aren't limitless, and we're squandering them on children who, in a better world, should never have been born. Children with brains so shrunken they can't register a thought as simple as hunger, children with lungs so crippled that each breath is an agonizing test of their will to live. And we do everything possible to keep them alive, so that those who aren't infertile can pass their disease on to the next generation. It's insanity."

Megan struggled against her rope ties. "You're giving *us* a lecture on insanity?"

"Like I said, I wouldn't expect you to understand."

Luke jumped in, hoping to keep Kaczynski talking. "So what's the solution, Petri?"

"He's playing you, Doc," the Asian said. "Let's go. I need to get you to the ship."

Kaczynski waved off the grim-looking man. "The solution? These children should never have been born. They simply should not exist."

Luke shot a glance at Megan.

"It's not a difficult concept, once you understand it," the geneticist said. "Others in my field have struggled to repair the damage caused by faulty genes, and most of those efforts have failed miserably. The rare success leads to therapies that cost a small fortune—they're an unimaginable extravagance in most parts of the world."

"So you took a different path," Luke said, gently stoking the man's ego to keep him talking.

"A simpler, more direct path. Eliminating nature's blunders before they happen. We can program the human immune system to seek out and destroy a woman's flawed eggs, a man's damaged sperm, *before* they join to create a defective human."

"And how're you going to do that?"

The man started kneading his hands. "Substantial portions of the human genome exist for no other purpose than to protect the structural integrity of our chromosomes—in effect, we have genes protecting our genes. There are thousands of so-called repair genes that remove damaged segments of DNA, build new DNA, and, when repair efforts fail, signal the cell to destroy itself. But, of course, nature's repairs are often imperfect and that's where my work comes into play."

Kaczynski's voice oozed with self-importance. "What I discovered is the common starting point for that process in the body's reproductive cells. It's a gene that's present only in oocytes and sperm. I call it the Mayday gene—it sounds the alarm and initiates the repair-or-destroy response. And it's the only gene that turns on in the presence of *any* chromosomal defect, no matter what the cause."

"And what exactly are you planning to do with your discovery?"

"It's not what I'm planning to do, Luke. It's what I've already *done*. I've created a vaccine that harnesses the power of our immune system and destroys defective eggs and sperm." The geneticist's eyes brightened. "When activated, the Mayday gene produces a protein—that's the distress signal that triggers the repair-or-destroy sequence. Like every protein, it has a unique structure, and once I had determined what that was, it became a relatively simple matter to develop my vaccine."

Luke said, "You have a vaccine that goes on search-and-destroy missions in a person's reproductive organs, and you think people are going to line up to get it?"

"They won't have to," the old man said. "The ubiquitous mosquito will administer it for me."

"Oh my God," Megan whispered.

Luke remembered Kaczynski convincing his father that they could genetically alter a mosquito's saliva glands to produce a vaccine. The insect's salivary glands already produced dozens of complex proteins, so why not a vaccine? Kaczynski had argued.

"If your goal was to create a mosquito-borne genetic vaccine, why interest my father in your concept? Why bother?"

"I'm a realist. The world never strays too far from the status quo, and purifying the human genome is an idea that most would not understand or accept. But malaria—that's a problem that everyone understands. It kills over a million people every year. Governments around the world are clamoring for a vaccine. And I'm going to give it to them."

"In a mosquito that also carries a stealth egg- and sperm-killing vaccine," Megan said in a voice filled with venom.

Kaczynski shrugged.

"So you stole my father's malaria vaccine," Luke said.

"Steal?" he said. "Hardly. Your father's mosquitoes are my Trojan horse. I want the world to recognize your father's work for the stunning achievement that it is. In fact, I'm counting on it."

The man seemed to recognize the quizzical look on Luke's face, and explained. "It was never our plan to steal your father's creation, and I doubt I could have replicated his mosquitoes even if I'd tried. The antigenic structure of his malaria vaccine is far too complex. I modified colonies of his mosquito—colonies he thought were going to China for field tests—making the necessary modifications to add my vaccine, which is much simpler. My challenge was to grow a stable self-sustaining colony that produces both vaccines, and just recently I finally accomplished that goal."

"Where did Zenavax figure into all of this?"

"They're what brought me here. I'm sure you know that the earliest versions of your father's mosquito didn't effectively protect against the falciparum species of malaria. We needed a mosquito that prevented both of the common forms of malaria—vivax *and* falciparum. When we heard of Zenavax's falciparum project through our contact in the Guatemalan Health Ministry, we took a closer look at what they'd found—"

"And you decided to steal their work."

Kaczynski laughed. "Only to the extent that Zenavax's research allowed your father to improve his malaria vaccine."

"What do you mean?"

"In a manner of speaking, it was your father who stole their work. Not knowingly, of course, but he was receptive to incorporating new ideas as they came along."

"You have moles working in my father's research group?" Luke said. "Who?"

The man shook his head. "That's not important. And I prefer to call them my *colleagues*—committed coworkers that are looking out for the interests of our patrons."

"Patrons?" Luke glanced at the man's shirt patch. "CHEGAN."

Kaczynski nodded.

"Who are they?"

"People who share my vision, and collectively have the resources to make it a reality. They live in the real world, Luke, a world beset by poverty and disease." Kaczynski seemed to anticipate Luke's question and added, "The name CHEGAN derives from the first letter of our benefactors' countries—countries that are going to buy your father's mosquitoes."

"There are *governments* supporting this?" Megan said.

"Not entire governments. We need only a few enlightened minds who are well placed and have access to funds. The benefactors of our organization—a Deputy Prime Minister, two Ministers of Health, a Politburo member, an Undersecretary of Economic Planning—they understand the social imperative of our mission, even if the leaders of their countries may not."

Luke tried to quell his anger, show the man an impassive face. "These benevolent patrons—they supported your decision to murder a village of Mayan Indians?"

"That wasn't my decision, Luke, but it was the right thing to do. We couldn't allow one unfortunate mishap to jeopardize this project."

"Mishap?"

Kaczynski took a heavy breath. "Initially, I used conventional injections, not mosquitoes, to test my vaccine and validate the concept."

Luke remembered Rosalinda mentioning CHEGAN's hospital for children with genetic disorders. He didn't need to ask Kaczynski whom he had used as test subjects.

"Those injectable doses," the geneticist continued, "were much larger than anything I could hope to attain in the saliva left behind from a mosquito's blood meal. So before I recoded the genome of your father's mosquitoes to add my vaccine, we made some modifications to my antigen to boost the immune response. Ironically, it worked too well."

"What happened?"

Kaczynski lifted his gaze to the moon. "We released the first testing batch of my mosquito in the area around

Mayakital about a year ago. There's a high prevalence of a rare cystic fibrosis mutation in their tribe. It's one of the reasons we chose that area for our initial field tests. Almost sixty percent of the villagers are carriers, but it's an innocent mutation. Even those with two copies of the mutation have virtually no clinical disease. It's probably an adaptive mutation."

Luke knew that, just as the mutation for sickle cell disease protects against malaria, the cystic fibrosis mutation affords some protection against cholera and typhoid.

"My vaccine induced an immune response that was several thousand times stronger than we had anticipated. Villagers who had the disease and were bitten by the mosquito—they were devoured by their own immune systems."

"Killer T-cells," Luke said.

"Exactly."

"I thought you said your vaccine was only active against reproductive cells."

"It is, but unfortunately, Killer T-cells are not nearly as precise in their targeting as my vaccine. T-cells are programmed to respond to specific antigens, but they're also opportunistic killers and will go after any cell that secretes stress proteins—so any cell that's injured or defective is fair game. Apparently, this particular CF mutation burdens affected cells to the point that they produce stress proteins even though, to outward appearances, the cells function normally."

Luke thought back to Jane Doe, and the pieces started to come together. The cells most affected by CF—the epithelial lining of her airways, the exocrine glands in her pancreas, and her bile ducts—were producing stress proteins that were not, of themselves, potent enough to induce an immune response.

But they were sufficiently abnormal to become an inviting target for the swarms of activated Killer T-cells that were prowling around, hunting for prey. She and Josue Chaca were dead long before their hearts stopped beating.

"We realized what was happening within a few weeks," the geneticist said, "but we'd already released our third batch of mosquitoes by that time. There was nothing we could do but watch it happen."

The mosquitoes had done their work over many weeks. Luke now understood why the illness had appeared to spread.

Megan shouted, "You have killer mosquitoes breeding out there?"

"The testing prototypes were infertile females. Those three colonies were extinct within several weeks of releasing the first batch." He shrugged. "But the biological fire they left behind smoldered for a lot longer."

An image of Josue Chaca flashed in Luke's mind. "What I saw wasn't a smoldering reaction."

"If you're talking about the boy, he has his mother to blame. Leaving their village to get medical care only hastened his death. She exposed her son to viruses that his immune system had never seen before. His immune system became a raging inferno."

Luke thought of the cold virus found in Jane Doe's nasal passages.

"So Zenavax's vaccine—it had nothing to do with this?" he asked.

"Nothing at all." Kaczynski brushed a spider from his pants leg. "What happened in Mayakital was a tragedy, but we've corrected the problem. It won't happen again."

Kaczynski leaned forward and draped his hands over his thighs. The man's strength was sagging.

"You know you'll be stopped," Luke said.

"On the contrary, there will be nothing to stop. My genetic vaccine is invisible even to those whose ovaries and testicles are affected. The biological mechanism—apoptosis—leaves no trace of itself. The impact of our program won't even be seen until the next generation of children is born. Twenty-five years from now, when the effect of our work becomes apparent, we'll have already purged those societies of genetic disorders—the gene pool will have been cleansed. By then, I suspect that most will see the benefits for what they are."

"So," Megan said acidly, "women that have a breast cancer gene just won't exist in your perfect world."

Luke remembered Megan telling him that her mother had tested positive for one of the breast cancer genes before dying from the same disease. She—and in domino fashion, Megan—simply wouldn't be allowed to live in Kaczynski's world.

Everyone turned to a giant forklift coming through the mouth of the tunnel. On it was a twenty-foot-square Plexiglas cage. A large generator was humming along its side.

As the forklift passed under the wash of a portable floodlight, Luke saw mosquitoes swarming inside the clear container. Four monkeys—a source of blood meals for the insects, he figured—leapt between the branches of what looked like a miniature arboretum.

"Somewhat more primitive than your father's equipment, but equally effective," the geneticist said. "Within a few months our breeding facility in China will be producing enough of my mosquitoes to begin deploying them on three continents—all with your father's blessing and support, who will think that we're using his mosquitoes."

The clear container brushed against the side of the

tunnel's entrance. A loud scraping sound sent the monkeys into a frenzy.

Kaczynski went ballistic. "Take it easy with that pen, you fools!" He turned to one of his keepers and muttered, "Clumsy idiots almost wiped out five years of work in this hellhole."

The forklift backed up a few feet and turned to the right. When it finally cleared the entrance, a large cloud of dust was boiling in its wake.

Seconds later Calderon emerged from the dark brown haze like a ghost. He was wearing a miner's hat, its halogen light piercing the night gloom like a spear. When he spotted the geneticist, he yelled to the Asian, "Get him to the ship. Now."

Kaczynski glanced at the freighter, then looked between Luke and Megan. "I'm sorry it's ending this way for you two . . . I truly am."

As soon as Calderon reached his captives, he leaned down, grabbed Luke's neck with one hand, and lifted him to a kneeling position. "Cockroach, you're coming with me."

Luke squirmed, struggling to free himself from Calderon's grip, but the blood flow to his brain had already ceased and a dark void quickly overtook him.

Chapter 53

My mother was afraid of the dark, cockroach. She always had to keep a light on at night." Calderon kissed his thumb and traced an X over his heart.

They were deep inside the mountain, and two of Calderon's men had just finished securing Luke, Megan, and a priest named Joe to wooden support columns in the center of a cavern. The three captives faced one another like points on a triangle.

The rock-domed cave appeared to be a storage area. It was strewn with overturned cargo boxes and empty pallets—the remnants of a soon-to-be abandoned operation. The only light came from miners' lamps mounted on their captors' headgear.

The light beams occasionally flashed on the priest, who had barely spoken a word since they joined him in his prison. The man's shoulders lifted heavily with each breath, and his sunken eyes and parched mouth made clear that he'd been without food or water for some time.

Their wrists, torsos, and ankles were cinched tight with quarter-inch nylon rope, their hands wrapped in duct tape to deny them the use of their fingers. Every few minutes Luke tightened and relaxed his hand muscles to keep his fingertips from going numb.

"My mother—she died in the Northridge quake," Calderon said. "She was buried alive."

There was a reason Calderon hadn't killed him at the hotel in Río Dulce, and it seemed that he was about to find out what that was.

"She died like a rat under a pile of rubble," Calderon said. "Never been able to get that outta my mind—that she spent her final hours in total darkness, terrified."

Calderon's plan was beginning to take shape in Luke's mind. After dragging them from the dock and throwing them onto a pushcart, Calderon and his men had hauled them several hundred yards into the mountain's interior, then through a honeycomb maze of intersecting tunnels.

Eventually, they'd reached a long passageway leading into the cavern where they were now being held. There were old scorch marks on the tunnel's walls where explosives had been used to widen it, and the roof was supported by timber posts and crossbeams.

When they had passed through the tunnel's entrance, two of Calderon's men were rigging it with explosives. One man was wrapping strings of white putty—C-4 explosive—around joints where the structural members came together. The other was drilling a borehole into the rock ceiling, creating a pocket for another explosive charge.

A box with a roll of detonation cord and small pencil-thin blasting caps sat on the ground next to them.

"You're going to seal the tunnel closed, bury us alive," Luke said. "That the plan?"

Calderon stooped next to him and checked his ankle bindings. He slowly untied the knot, and then suddenly yanked the rope tighter.

Luke winced when the nylon cord cut into his skin.

"If you hadn't busted up my knee, my mother wouldn't've been in that building when it collapsed." The skin near the corner of Calderon's mouth twitched. "She would've been at home, sleeping in her bed, instead of cleaning up other people's filth."

Luke remained silent. He saw no purpose in asking Calderon to explain his warped logic.

Father Joe lifted his head, choked out the words, "This . . . this won't help your mother."

"Let the priest go," Megan shouted. "He hasn't done anything to you."

Calderon's lamp swung around and framed Father Joe's sagging head.

"She's right," Calderon said. "He probably deserves better. Too bad he's gotta die with you, cockroach."

"Killing Megan and the priest isn't going to bring your mother back," Luke said. "Let 'em go."

The fist came across Luke's jaw like an iron mallet.

Luke turned his head and spit out a mouthful of blood, holding the man's stare as he did so.

Calderon leaned into Luke's ear and whispered, "If you speak of my mother again, you'll be dead before you finish the words." He slowly backed away and stood, then whistled at his men. *"Vamanos."*

Calderon started toward the passageway, then turned and said, "Remember how your mother used to drive out to Santa Monica and walk along those bluffs above the ocean?"

Luke felt a tightness in his throat, recalling the fall that had killed his mother. After recovering her body from an outcrop on the cliffs, the police had called it an accident.

"You remember that, don't you?" Calderon said.

"Every Wednesday afternoon at four o'clock. You could set your watch by her schedule."

Luke thrashed, his body a convulsing mass of contorted muscles.

"I knew you'd figure out what I'm saying. You college boys are good at that," Calderon said as he disappeared into the tunnel.

Even after their stony tomb went black, Calderon's laugh was still echoing in Luke's ears.

Calderon stood on the dock and looked up at the starlit sky. He sucked in a chestful of night air.

A crane in the center of the barge swung another pallet over and onto the deck as its crew members were securing cargo. The last of the equipment had come through the tunnel, and in another few minutes the flatbed vessel would return to the Chinese freighter with its payload.

For the past five years the docking facilities and tunnel—several kilometers from the nearest settlement along the river—had provided an elegantly simple means of supplying CHEGAN's inland compound without bringing attention to their operation. Supply ships navigated upriver from the Caribbean coastline at night and were back out at sea before the sun rose the next morning.

Now, CHEGAN was abandoning the site, pulling up its stakes and moving the mosquito project to a permanent facility in China. The fact was, Calderon didn't care where they were going. He just wanted them to leave. This project had become stale.

A gaggle of birds took flight from the limestone cliffs just as the rumble of a diesel engine reached his ears. Calderon's boat was returning from delivering

Kaczynski to the freighter. Mr. Kong was at the helm.

The Asian throttled back, making a large wake on his approach to the dock.

He'd miss working with Kong, who was going to China to babysit Kaczynski and his team. At the beginning of the project, CHEGAN's Chinese contingent had thrust the man upon him. Calderon had bristled at first, but Kong turned out to be a good operative.

Calderon jumped onto the boat as it neared the dock. "Tell the workers on the barge to hurry it up," he said to Kong. "I want that thing loaded and on its way out to the freighter in ten minutes."

While the Asian was shouting in Chinese at the barge's crew, Calderon pulled a bulky device from his jacket pocket. It was an ultra low frequency transmitter, a blast initiation device whose signal could penetrate up to a thousand feet of solid rock. He ran his fingers across a pair of toggle switches.

Enrique and Juan, his explosives team, hadn't finished rigging the charge when Calderon and his sentries left the cavern to return to the dock.

Calderon couldn't contact them. Unlike the detonation transmitter, their radio signals would not penetrate the thick rock strata.

But he didn't have to speak to them. When the light at the top of his transmitter changed from green to yellow, he would know that the detonator was armed. Once armed, Enrique and Juan knew they had just three minutes to clear the blast area.

Kong put the boat's engines into reverse and eased away from the dock. After the Asian disembarked onto the freighter, Calderon would return to the cove one more time.

He'd make one last trip into the tunnel, to see for himself the pile of rock in front of McKenna's tomb.

"You're not going to pull free, Megan. Save your strength."

Megan hadn't stopped struggling against her bindings.

"Save my strength? For what?" Her voice cracked on the last word.

Luke stared into the pitch-blackness. He didn't have an answer for her.

Calderon wouldn't leave them alone long enough to cobble together any sort of escape plan. The blast that would seal them inside the cavern was coming at any moment.

Suddenly, Luke heard a footstep.

Then a match flared and the quivering reflection of a small flame painted the tunnel wall.

"Hey, boss, you in here?" a small voice said. Then, *"Ouch."*

The flame disappeared.

"Who's that?" Megan whispered.

"Frankie?" Luke said.

Another flame, this time closer. "Boss?"

"Frankie, we're in here."

"Who's Frankie?" Megan asked.

The boy's potbellied figure appeared at the tunnel's opening holding a lighted matchstick. "Boss, what you doing here?"

"Come here, quick," Luke said. "Use that match and burn the rope around my wrist."

He knew it would be impossible for the boy to undo the expertly tied knots. But a match flame could melt the nylon ropes in seconds.

Moments later Luke felt the flame singing the hair on his hands, and then his right hand broke free. He grabbed the tape with his teeth and tore it away from his fingers.

The rope around his left wrist gave way and he went to work on his ankle ties.

The Río Dulce was unusually calm on that night, and Calderon's boat was skimming across the water when he heard the beep in his jacket pocket.

He pulled out the detonation transmitter.

The light had changed to yellow.

He set the timer on his chronometer for three minutes and pressed START.

Chapter 54

"Forget about it, Enrique. It was probably an animal," Juan whispered in Spanish. "Let's get out of here."

They had armed the detonator and were trotting through a warren of small passages toward the main tunnel when Enrique spotted a movement in the peripheral wash of his miner's lamp. The men had separated and crisscrossed through the intersecting paths, quickly backtracking to where they'd set the explosive charges.

But they hadn't found anyone.

Juan pointed at his luminescent watch. "In two minutes this place is going to blow. We have to leave. *Now.*"

"I'm telling you," Enrique said, "I saw something. It wasn't an animal."

Just then, a small shimmer of light shone on the tunnel wall, near the entrance to the cavern where Calderon had taken his captives.

Enrique flipped off his light, then reached over an overhead joist and turned off the arming switch on the detonator.

Juan was already moving into the tunnel with his M-16 raised.

As soon as Luke and Megan had lifted Father Joe to his feet, the priest said, "You three go ahead without me." He took a long breath, his lips pursed. "I'll follow behind."

The priest could barely walk without their support, let alone sprint through darkened passageways.

"No." Megan's head was tucked under Father Joe's armpit, her arm wrapped around his trunk. "We're going out together."

Her voice carried the tone of an appellate court judge.

Luke took the priest's other arm and the three of them stutter-stepped to the mouth of the tunnel. Frankie led the way, holding a lighted match.

Their first step into the tunnel was greeted with a volley of gunfire that ripped the priest from Luke's arm and sent both Joe and Megan to the ground.

Frankie dropped his match and the passage went black.

Footsteps—at least two sets—were moving toward them.

Luke dove to where Megan had fallen and rolled her away from the tunnel entrance.

The footfalls grew louder. A shaft of light suddenly pierced the darkness, painting an oblong circle of light at the far end of the cavern. The assailants were using assault tactics: storm the enemy's position with overpowering force, give them no time to regroup.

Luke was crouched next to the tunnel entrance when the rifle barrel yawed around the corner to scan the perimeter of the room.

He shot up with the force of a catapult, slammed the rifle stock into the assailant's head, then dropped to the ground with the slumping man, using him for cover while ripping the rifle from his grip. Luke spun the weapon in a 180-degree arc and put three rounds into the second attacker before the man could bring down his aim.

The unconscious assailant was lying in the entry. Luke

used the tip of his rifle barrel to point the man's helmet light into the tunnel and jinked his head into the passageway, searching for targets.

The tunnel was empty.

He shouldered the weapon and quickly examined Megan, who was already rising onto her elbows with Frankie's help.

She was shaking, but there were no gunshot wounds.

When he turned to Father Joe, Luke's eyes went immediately to a spreading circle of red on the priest's left side.

Luke tore open Joe's shirt. There were two entry wounds in his chest.

Megan kneel-crawled around Luke and took a position on the other side of the priest.

"Oh, my God," she whispered when she saw the wounds.

Father Joe had a rapid pulse.

In a few minutes the priest's pulse would become thready, and then fade completely.

And there was nothing that they could do for him.

Megan placed his head in her lap. "Hang on, Father," she said through welling tears. "Stay with us."

The priest coughed violently and leaned to the side. His breaths came in gasps, but his face was strangely calm. He looked first at Luke and then at Megan. When his eyes reached her, he lifted his right arm and made the sign of the cross.

Then he collapsed and was still.

After a long moment, Megan began stroking the priest's forehead. She wiped away bits of dirt and combed back his hair with her hand.

"He's gone, Megan. We have to go."

She let out a wailing cry, brought Father Joe's head to her breast, and rocked back and forth.

Calderon was nearing the freighter when he glanced at his chronometer—thirty-seven seconds until detonation.

He pulled the transmitter from his pocket.

The light was green. Someone had disarmed it!

"Turn the boat around," he shouted at Kong. "Take us back to the dock."

Calderon keyed in his radio. Two sentries standing guard on the barge checked in. Neither had heard from Enrique or Juan.

Calderon grabbed a spotting scope from a compartment under the helm and aimed it at the cove. Laborers were scurrying over the barge like a horde of worker ants, securing cargo, doing their final checks. Two men using a winch tightened cables around the mosquito container.

The tunnel entrance was empty, and dark.

He rechecked the arming indicator on the detonator. It was still green.

What had happened?

McKenna couldn't have broken free—it wasn't possible. He had checked the bindings himself.

When the boat entered the lagoon, Calderon switched his scope to infrared mode and searched for heat signatures near the tunnel entrance and in the water along the perimeter of the barge.

Nothing.

He pulled the detonation transmitter from his pocket. The light had changed back to yellow.

What the hell is going on?

He blew out a heavy breath, reset his chronometer and pressed START. He hoped his men were sprinting, because he was only giving them one minute to clear the blast area. After screwing up his timetable and delaying the detonation, they'd know better than to loiter. At worst, the percussion wave would knock the wind out of them, cover them in a cloud of silt. Or maybe their ears would ring for the next few days.

They knew the rules, and the risks.

Thirty-one seconds. Calderon ran a thumb across the ignition switch.

He still wondered what had caused Enrique and Juan to disarm the detonator for those few minutes. They knew their trade, and rule one when handling explosives was never to arm the detonator until everything—explosive charges, detonation cord, and blasting caps—had been checked twice, then cross-checked by a fellow team member.

Fourteen seconds.

"Ah, what the hell." Calderon flipped the toggle switch.

His last conscious thought was the sensation of intense heat from an orange fireball.

Luke was underwater and dolphin-kicking away from the barge when the C-4 exploded. The blast wave slammed into him like a tsunami.

The world went from dark to black and the murky water suddenly felt like a viscous soup. He was disoriented, unable to differentiate up from down.

This was supposed to be his element. Nighttime water operations were what SEALs knew best, but his mind went hazy and his eyes lost focus as the last of his oxygen burned away.

He brought his legs together and dolphin-kicked, following the small air bubbles he released from his mouth every few seconds, chasing them upward. When his head broke the surface, he pointed his mouth at the sky and gulped in the night air until his speckled vision cleared.

He was almost fifty feet from the dock when he surveyed the results of his work. A large chunk of the barge's midsection was missing, as was the Plexiglas mosquito container that had sat over the section of hull where he placed the C-4 charge and detonator. The huge iron flatbed was already listing heavily, and water was flowing into the starboard side.

At the far end of the lagoon, Calderon's boat was turning in a tight circle. A man on the vessel's bow was using a hook pole to snag something in the water. When he finally caught it, it took three men to pull the limp body from the water. As they were lifting the large figure onto the boat's deck, he erupted in a coughing fit and started thrashing. The men jumped away as if from a wild animal.

Calderon.

A man in the dimly lit wheelhouse shoved the throttle arm forward, made a violent turn, and powered the boat into the river's channel.

Luke turned to a blackened cul-de-sac at the farthest edge of the cove and stared into a shallow hollow until his eyes detected the movements. Megan and Frankie were treading water behind a curtain of hanging vines.

Chapter 55

Y ou're being stubborn," Luke said to Megan. "You *have* to go to Guatemala City, to the U.S. Embassy. You'll be safe there."

"I'm not going there without *you*." She poked his chest on the last word.

He looked across the bus aisle at Frankie. The boy was lying lengthwise on a bench seat with his head propped against the window and his hands coupled behind his head, his glance bouncing between Megan and Luke as if taking in a ping-pong match.

"I can't go to the embassy," Luke said. "There's still a murder warrant out on me and I came here on a forged passport. The first thing they'd do is lock me up."

"Fine, then. So we're not going to the embassy. But we're staying together, and that's final."

Their nearly empty bus slowed for a sweat-drenched man yanking his mule across the road. Luke felt a certain kinship with the man.

Ahead, beyond a mile-long swath of grasslands, a dome of brown haze hung over the city of Santa Elena.

Returning Frankie to his mother was the only thing they had agreed on since their escape. Minutes after the explosion on the barge, four surviving crew members and one of Calderon's sentries had escaped in a small skiff they threw over the side of the sinking vessel. Calderon's boat had disappeared and the freighter was already steaming away when the river finished swallowing the barge and its cargo.

A fishing trawler had come across the carnage at first light, making two figure-eight loops outside the cove before swooping in and unloading its crew to pick over the shoreline for loose salvage. For one hundred U.S. dollars, the skipper had ferried them back to Río Dulce, where they'd boarded a bus to Santa Elena.

"Calderon's going to come after me," Luke said, "and I'm going to let him find me because this thing won't end until one of us is dead. Until it's over, I want you as far away as possible."

"And where am I supposed to hide, Luke? Tell me—where will I be safe? I've seen what these people are capable of—they slaughtered an entire village." She grabbed his hand. "Don't leave me here by myself."

He felt the tremor in her fingers, and wrapped his hand around hers.

There was no way to remove her from this nightmare, he realized. Calderon and his men had probably already regrouped and begun hunting for them. If Megan remained with him, he was exposing her to the violent fury that would inevitably converge on him. If they separated, Megan might have to run a gauntlet of Calderon's men to reach the embassy, after which some State Department bureaucrat might or might not adequately protect her while investigating her improbable story.

"Okay. Maybe you're right," he said finally. "We'll stay together, at least until we get out of the country."

The bus lurched when it started moving again, and Megan's head pitched back as if a thought had just shaken free.

"The first thing we need to do is warn your father."

She was reading his thoughts. Wounding CHEGAN had served only to arouse his enemy. Kaczynski and his knowledge were safely secured in the bowels of the Chinese freighter. Though Luke may have destroyed Kaczynski's lone colony of egg- and sperm-killing mosquitoes, CHEGAN needed only to acquire a fresh batch of his father's mosquitoes to salvage its genocidal plan.

His father was standing directly in their path and didn't even know it.

"My dad's office and home phones are probably wired. These people are thorough," he said. "Maybe I can reach him on the wards this afternoon. They can't tap *every* phone in the hospital."

The muscles in Luke's neck tightened as he considered his quandary. He was half a continent from his enemy's objective, and a fugitive hiding from both his would-be killers and the police.

Time was on CHEGAN's side. To stop them, he had to pull his father into this vortex of madness.

He knew it, and so did his enemy.

Luke closed his eyes and rubbed his lids.

Megan's palm landed on his forehead. "You're burning up," she said.

He already knew the infection in his shoulder was worsening. "I'll get something in Santa Elena. There're some things I need to get at a pharmacy before we drop Frankie at his mother's."

When Luke finally blinked his eyes back into focus, he saw that Megan's gaze had turned inward.

"If I hadn't asked Father Joe for help, he'd still be alive," she said. "Kaczynski—I should've let him die." Her voice broke on the last word.

"If he'd died, they would've killed both you *and* the

priest," Luke said. "Wherever Joe is, I'm sure he's glad it turned out this way instead."

"Glad? How can you say that? I gave CHEGAN back their leader."

"Kaczynski's a scientist, not a leader. Petri may have come up with the idea, and he probably thinks of himself as the linchpin, but he never could've organized something as big as CHEGAN. There's someone above him."

"You think some out-of-control government put this scheme together?"

Luke shook his head. "This isn't the type of thing that government types would've dreamed up. It's too outrageous, too farfetched. This idea was sold to them by someone that was involved in creating it, someone that understood the science and could sell the idea."

"Who?"

"Caleb Fagan."

"What?"

"It all fits," Luke said. "From the beginning, he's been on the periphery of the malaria project, helping my father. He was probably the one that fed my father whatever Petri learned about Zenavax's malaria antigen. Fagan was the perfect conduit, and he could've easily diverted those shipments of my father's mosquitoes to Kaczynski."

Megan showed him a face full of uncertainty.

"Caleb's the one that figured out how my father's flu vaccine killed a batch of mice. Now that same reaction shows up in Kaczynski's genetic vaccine. That's no coincidence. Remember what Kaczynski said about needing to modify the antigen for mosquitoes? It was *Caleb* who tinkered with the antigen to boost the immune response. He understands Killer T-cells and apoptosis—that's his field—and he'd know how to harness that knowledge for a vaccine. But he underestimated the effect, and the reaction got away from him."

The bus's brakes hissed as they turned into a curve.

Megan's eyes were roaming in a thought. "He started the clinic down here."

"The clinic gave Caleb an excuse to travel here without raising any questions," Luke said. "His sudden midlife interest in international healthcare was all part of the plan. It gave him an entrée to the people he needed to sell the idea to, the people who later formed CHEGAN."

"The patrons."

Luke nodded. "The night that Josue Chaca arrived in the E.R., Caleb walked into the Trauma Unit when we were in the thick of it. He was right there from the beginning, watching us."

"Do you think Caleb knows that you're on to him?" Elmer asked after listening to Luke's story and recounting the recent events at University Children's.

"I doubt it," Luke said. "Kaczynski painted *himself* as the kingpin of their operation—he never mentioned Fagan. I'm sure they've talked since my escape, and Kaczynski would've reassured Caleb, told him that his secret was still safe."

Luke was in an Internet café a half block from the Santa Elena bus station, speaking into an incongruously modern pay phone. After dialing Sammy's number and getting a busy signal, he'd had Megan call University Children's at exactly 3:00 P.M., L.A. time, the usual starting time for his father's afternoon ward rounds. Using a phony name, she had convinced the fifth floor clerk to put Elmer on a back-room phone extension.

Luke continued, "And Caleb's gotta know that I'd find a way to reach you. If he thought I knew about his role in CHEGAN, he would've come after you."

Elmer made a blustering sound full of false bravado.

"But he'd only do that if his situation was desperate," Luke said. "The last thing he wants is a police investigation that focuses attention on you and your malaria project."

"By the way," Elmer said with a sigh, "Caleb was appointed interim chairman of the medical staff after Barnesdale's murder. He pretty much has carte blanche around here now."

That drew a weary head shake from Luke.

He thought about the twelve hours that had elapsed since his escape from the river. "Caleb's probably got minions working in your mosquito lab. Could they have already taken another colony of your mosquitoes?"

"No way."

"How're you so sure?"

"For starters, our transport unit is designed for larvae, not adult mosquitoes. That has certain advantages—our container is a fraction the size of what you'd need to move an equivalent colony of adult mosquitoes—but it means they'd have to harvest the larvae, and that takes four to five days."

"Can it be done any faster than that?"

"You can't hurry along the mosquitoes' breeding cycle," Elmer said. "It takes that long to produce enough larvae for a self-sustaining colony."

"Could they do it without anyone noticing?"

"Someone could easily do the harvesting without raising an eyebrow—it's just a matter of opening the valves on some breeding tanks that are already in the pen. But preparing a transport is another matter."

"What do you mean?"

"To remove a colony from the mosquito pen, they'd have to lug a fair amount of equipment into the lab, including our transport unit—it's about the size of a small refrigerator. And even if everything was ready beforehand, it'd take about an hour and they'd need a couple of trained technicians. There's no way to do it without drawing a lot of attention to themselves."

Luke knew the layout of his father's lab and understood his point. The only way into the malaria lab was through the hospital's main microbiology lab, which operated twenty-four hours a day. The sight of technicians rolling equipment through the micro lab would attract inquisitive eyes and unwanted questions.

"How would someone load the transport unit with larvae and get it out of the lab without being discovered?"

"That's impossible."

"Nothing's impossible. Think."

There was a stretch of silence, then Elmer said, "Wait a minute. This morning my lab manager told me we're having a hazardous materials drill on Friday. He was complaining about it to me, saying he usually gets told about these things weeks in advance."

"What time Friday?"

"Six o'clock Friday evening, just before the change of shift. That's another thing he was griping about—"

"That's over seventy-two hours from now. And they could've started the harvesting process last night."

"Which adds up to just about four days," Elmer said. "Enough time to harvest a colony."

"That's it, then. Caleb's people are going to take the mosquitoes during that drill."

Mock drills of that type were common in the hospital, even more so since 9/11, and usually run by outside consultants. Caleb's operatives could evacuate the entire microbiology lab as part of the so-called drill, giving them free rein.

Kaczynski's freighter flashed in Luke's mind. He wondered how long the transit time was from Guatemala to the Port of Los Angeles.

"Would they transport the mosquitoes by ship?" Luke asked.

"If their destination is China, absolutely not."

"Why?"

"The colony wouldn't survive the time it takes for an ocean crossing. Like I said, our unit was designed for mosquito larvae. Essentially, it's a fancy bucket of water—a stainless steel container with a lot of gadgets that dispense nutrients and control environmental parameters like temperature."

"Why does that affect how you ship it?"

"If the transport unit doesn't get to its destination in two to three days, you start losing the colony because the larvae mature and emerge as adult mosquitoes. The container has very little air space and no food source for adult mosquitoes, so they die off almost immediately."

An air transport from southern California meant that CHEGAN had a half-dozen airports to choose from, and each probably had several cargo flights going to Asia every day. If Caleb's people got the transport unit out of the hospital, there would be no way to stop them.

Luke's only hope was to thwart CHEGAN's plan *before* the mosquito larvae left University Children's.

But he had no idea how he would get back to L.A., or how long the journey might take. He had no option but to drag his father into the quagmire.

Before he could state the obvious, his father said it for

him. "Luke, there's only one way to stop this. I have to destroy my mosquitoes."

"Caleb probably has people watching your lab."

"The mosquito lab is locked up every evening at seven o'clock—it's not staffed at night. Anyone lingering outside the lab after seven is going to stick out like a sore thumb. It won't be hard to spot them."

"Be careful, Dad. And except for Ben, no one else can know about this. *No one*," Luke said. "Once you destroy the mosquitoes, get out of town. Go away for a few days, and take Ben and his family with you."

"Where?"

"Remember the lodge at Big Bear Lake where we used to stay when I was a kid?" He waited for his father's acknowledgment, then said, "I'll call you there on Friday morning."

There was a long silence before his father said, "You know, sooner or later we have to go to the police about this."

"If you don't hear from me by ten o'clock on Friday morning, that's exactly what I want you to do. But give me until then."

"Why?"

"Because I don't think the police will believe you, and I don't want them to get in my way. CHEGAN isn't even on their radar screen. The cops are chasing a killer, and they think they already know who it is. They'll look for reasons *not* to believe you. I have no proof—nothing. The only way I'm going to clear myself is to go to the police with Caleb in tow. I need to get to Fagan before he buries whatever trails lead to him."

Luke threw two antibiotic tablets into his mouth and swallowed them dry as he walked out of the pharmacy with Frankie. The boy was clutching a brown paper bag filled with HIV medications.

They joined Megan in a waiting cab, and Frankie sat between the two of them for what turned out to be a silent ride across town.

It was almost as if the boy knew what he would find when they arrived at his mother's hospice.

Luke and Megan stood back with two nuns as Frankie walked up to the empty metal-framed bed. The boy rubbed the bed's frame with a hand while his eyes traveled back and forth across the bare urine-stained mattress.

Eventually, Frankie looked back at Sister Marta Ann, and the two of them seemed to exchange a private thought. Then he squatted beside the bed and pulled out his green duffel bag. He fished through it, removed a wooden box, and opened it. Inside was a yellowed photograph of a teenage girl holding an infant. Frankie stared at it for a long moment, then rubbed it against a pants leg and slipped it into his shirt pocket.

Megan brought a hand to her mouth. Her wet swallow carried across the room.

The boy zipped up the duffel bag and pushed it back under the bed. Then he stood and walked out the door.

Chapter 56

Luke tapped Megan's arm with a water bottle. "Here. Drink some more."

He stared out over the freshly harvested cornfield north of Mexico City, squinting into the late afternoon sun while Megan drank down half the bottle without stopping to take a breath.

Twenty hours earlier, they had started their journey under a starlit sky on the Usumacinta River, crossing the Mexican border into Chiapas on a boat resembling a gondola. Frankie's uncle, a truck driver and part-time smuggler with a nervous twitch in his shoulders, had agreed to deliver both of them onto U.S. soil for $2,100—half his usual price—but only after Frankie had worn him down in a hand-waving clash of wills that lasted the better part of an hour.

Luke had realized that Frankie's feisty negotiations were fueled by the boy's false belief that he would be traveling with them. When Luke explained otherwise, Frankie retreated into himself and remained there even as they said their final good-byes.

The trip's first leg had ended when Luke and Megan's furtive boatman dropped them onto a rocky shoreline just inside Mexico, where Frankie's uncle was waiting with a large garbage hauler. The pair squeezed into a false compartment on the truck's underside, joining four other sweat-drenched stowaways whose faces showed a strange mix of both terror and hope.

Megan was still retching from the stench of rotting garbage when they finally stopped at the cornfield after driving all night and most of the next day. Her legs had barely held her upright when she first climbed from their metal cell into the late afternoon sun.

Dehydration was threatening to overtake both of them.

But they had to keep moving. When Luke had called his father a second time from the hospice, Elmer told him that Caleb had sent a memo to the medical staff announcing that he'd be traveling to Beijing, China, on Saturday for a weeklong conference on international healthcare.

Luke figured it was even odds that Fagan would suffer a fate similar to Kaczynski and "die" while on that trip.

He had to intercept Caleb before he left for China.

Megan was finishing the last of the water when Luke squatted on his haunches and started pulling chaff from a severed corn stalk.

A moment later Megan stooped next to him.

"Thanks." Her voice had a dry rattle.

Luke's eyes followed a dust funnel in the distance. "For what?"

"For saving my life."

He turned to her.

Megan stared at the ground while tracing a circle in the dirt with her finger.

When she didn't return his gaze, he picked up a shriveled corncob and started bouncing it in his hand.

Without warning, she leaned into him and kissed him on the cheek. Then she rose and started walking toward the trash hauler.

He followed her with his eyes, fingering his cheek as he wondered at the mystery of women.

The truck's passenger-side door swung open and the seat tilted forward. A moment later Frankie's head appeared.

"Hi, boss."

Megan and Luke exchanged a glance as the boy hopped down to the ground.

"I help you get home," he said.

"What are you talking about?" Luke said.

The boy stepped closer. "My uncle say you no pay him enough, so he no will take you to America. But I no think that the problem." Frankie glimpsed over his shoulder. "I no think he can do it."

"*What?*" Megan shouted. "Where's your uncle? I want to talk to him. He can't just—"

Frankie held a palm up to her. "My uncle take us to U.S. border. You take me with you, and I help you get across border."

Chapter 57

Look at the time stamp in the upper right-hand corner." Detective O'Reilly pressed PAUSE and pointed at the TV monitor showing a lanky black man leaning into Luke McKenna's office door. "He entered McKenna's office at 5:57, exactly six minutes before the e-mail was erased from both McKenna's machine and the hospital's server. He left one minute after the file disappeared from the computers. You're looking at the man that erased Kate Tartaglia's e-mail. McKenna didn't do it."

O'Reilly had replayed the security tapes after getting word from the forensic computer investigators the previous afternoon. He'd been waiting for Groff when the lieutenant arrived at Parker Center that morning.

The investigators had called O'Reilly after finding an entry confirming the deleted e-mail. They couldn't recover the original e-mail—the hard drive had been written over with newer files, but investigators had confirmed that someone used McKenna's computer to delete the file from the server at 6:03 P.M. on the night of Tartaglia's murder.

Previously, O'Reilly had viewed only the later portions of the tapes because he was trying to reconcile the timeline around McKenna's departure from the hospital at ten o'clock. It wasn't until last night, when he had gone back and studied the earlier video segments, that he spotted the black man breaking into McKenna's office.

Lieutenant Groff shrugged. "So maybe McKenna had an accomplice."

"I don't think so." O'Reilly wound back the tape and played it in slow motion. "Look at the way this guy leans into the door. Someone with a key to the office wouldn't stand right up to the door like that. This guy's concealing something. I think that *something* is a lock pick, and we're watching him break into McKenna's office."

"All I see is the guy's back. I don't see a pick."

"This guy's too good to let us see it. Watch the way he moves. He knows the camera's there. Look at the way he hides his face under the brim of that baseball cap."

The lieutenant made a show of looking at the wall clock in the conference room, signaling that their meeting was about to end. "Even *if* I assume that this guy broke into McKenna's office—which I don't—how would that change anything? We found a copy of Tartaglia's e-mail in McKenna's home with his fingerprints all over it—after he told us that he never got it. Tartaglia's mother puts him at the murder scene. And now, with what we learned about Barnesdale and his dealings with Zenavax, McKenna has a clear motive for killing both Tartaglia *and* Barnesdale."

He was right. When O'Reilly confronted Zenavax with the contents of Barnesdale's safe deposit box— Tartaglia's supposedly nonexistent employment contract with University Children's, and Zenavax stock options worth nearly $3.2 million at the expected IPO price—the company's CEO had admitted to giving Barnesdale upfront cash and stock options under a "consulting agreement."

The truth was clear: Zenavax had bribed Barnesdale to

"lose" Tartaglia's contract, leaving University Children's attorneys with no choice but to drop the lawsuit. Though the CEO had denied knowing about Tartaglia's contract and characterized the stock options as reimbursement for Barnesdale's subsequent consulting services, O'Reilly knew that federal investigators would view the evidence differently.

"If the feds wanna prosecute Zenavax on some securities law violation, they're welcome to it," Groff said. "But I'm trying to capture a murderer here, and the dirty little secret between Barnesdale, Tartaglia, and Zenavax seals it—McKenna decided to go after the people who stole the flu vaccine from his father. McKenna must've found out about Barnesdale's deal with Zenavax, or maybe he knew all along. Who the hell knows, and who the hell cares. Our psychologist is right—something sent McKenna over the edge and he went off on a killing rampage."

O'Reilly had already told Groff about the fragments of Zenavax's malaria vaccine found in the dead Guatemalan boy's blood. As expected, the lieutenant was less than impressed after hearing that it was McKenna's father who had run the tests. The truth was, O'Reilly didn't know what to make of it himself, especially when, under questioning, Zenavax acknowledged the mysterious illness.

But one aspect of Groff's theory still bothered him. "Your theory is that McKenna discovered the bribery scheme," O'Reilly said. "But if this is some sort of vendetta killing spree, and Zenavax's CEO was at the center of the bribery, why didn't McKenna also go after *him*?"

The phone rang and Groff grabbed it. As he listened to the caller, the lines in his face darkened. When the call ended, he slammed down the receiver. "Goddammit."

"What?"

"That was the State Department. Someone traveling under a fake passport who matches McKenna's description just murdered the head of Zenavax's research lab in Guatemala. The killer was ID'd by some workers at the lab. So do me a favor, O'Reilly—stop wasting my time with horseshit leads about some guy breaking into McKenna's office."

"How long will this take?" Ben asked.

Elmer attached one end of the large-diameter tube to a portal on the side of the mosquito enclosure. "I should be done in another twenty minutes or so."

"I'll keep watch outside the door. And while you're finishing this, think about what I said. If you tell O'Reilly about finding your mosquito antigen in Josue Chaca's blood, it's probably only going to cause trouble for you and Luke. My advice is, don't do it."

Ben turned to leave.

Standing ten feet away, against the closed door, was the black man who had intercepted him in the doctors' parking lot several days ago with the messages from Luke.

"You—what are you doing here?" Ben asked.

"You both need to come with me."

Elmer turned. "Who are you?"

"Your escort."

"Escort?" Elmer glanced at Ben. "Where are we going?"

Sammy Wilkes pulled back his jacket and showed them a nickel-plated revolver tucked into a holster under his armpit. "Wherever I tell you."

Chapter 58

The antibiotics had brought down Luke's fever, but the throb in his left shoulder was pounding like an air hammer when they arrived in Mexicali at 7:00 A.M. on Friday. He had slept only six hours in the past three days and his body was deadlocked in its battle with the infection.

Mexicali was a tourist town on the U.S.-Mexican border, and Los Angeles was less than a four-hour drive, but he was on the wrong side of the border and had no car, no passport, no weapon, and no idea what sort of protective phalanx he would encounter when he finally tracked down Caleb.

Luke, Megan, and Frankie checked into a motel room and took turns showering under a fixture that gave up its water reluctantly. After a shave that left Luke with the beginnings of a goatee, he and Megan left the boy and walked along a boardwalk in one of the more modern, tourist sections of town. They purchased a new set of clothes and then prowled for tourists who matched their target profile: gregarious college-age American males whose brains were marinating in hormones and alcohol.

Fifteen minutes later they were seated at a sidewalk café eating chorizo and drinking beer with a trio of male

students from the University of Arizona. The thinnest of
the three, a blond kid, was so busy ogling Megan that he
hardly noticed Luke's presence. The other two just seemed
pleased to have met someone who wanted to pay for their
breakfast.

The students pasted sympathetic expressions on their
faces and nodded as Luke spun a story about how
thieves had stolen his car and belongings. The skinny
one loaned Megan his cell phone, which Luke used to
dial two numbers.

He tried calling Sammy twice, and both times got a
recorded message stating that the number was no longer
in service. The phone's battery died as he was dialing information for Big Bear Lake.

By 11:00 A.M., Luke and Megan were sitting in the
back seat of the students' blue Ford Explorer with
Megan's admirer between them. The other two were in
the front arguing about the way college football rankings
are determined.

Their SUV inched its way toward the front of the line at
the border checkpoint. Luke would have preferred a small
sedan, figuring that smaller vehicles garnered less interest
among agents who were looking for stowaways and con-
traband.

"Damn, that's a shame." The skinny one sitting between Megan and Luke shook his head. "You're never
gonna see your car again. You know that, don't you?"

Luke nodded as if he were acknowledging a sad truth.
"I never thought our vacation would end this way."

The student seemed to study Luke's profile. "It looks
like those thugs worked you over pretty good."

Luke fingered the large knot on the side of his head. "I
figure we're lucky to be alive."

"You got that right, pal. You're lucky those thieves just took your car."

Megan said, "They took our wallets too."

"Oh, man, I hope the border agents don't ask for your ID."

Luke pointed over the driver's shoulder at the third of six lanes. "Hey, this middle lane is moving faster."

The young driver nodded and moved over, right behind a large motor home that Luke was hoping would be picked for a search. As they had drawn closer to the front of the line of vehicles, Luke was watching out his window. The agents were waving most of the larger vans and motor homes to an inspection area on the side of the road. When that happened, the agent's attention was divided for a brief moment, watching to make sure the vehicle did as instructed while he processed the next vehicle. The agents had usually waved the next few cars through with only a passing glance.

Luke looked back into the SUV's cargo area. On top of the students' luggage sat a lumpy green duffel bag. After watching it for several seconds, one of the lumps moved—just barely, but Luke's eye caught it. He hoped the lump didn't cough.

Five minutes later they reached the front of the line. As if on cue, the agent waved the RV in front of them over to the side of the road. After looking at their car and glancing at the license plate, the agent started to wave them through, then suddenly held his hand out. He walked to the open driver's window and asked for the driver's ID.

While the student was pulling out his wallet, the agent glimpsed into the driver-side foot well, then looked past Luke into the rear cargo area. "You folks have anything to declare?"

The driver shook his head while handing his driver's license to the agent. "Nope."

The agent said something about driving safely as he handed back the license and waved them through the checkpoint, but Luke was too distracted to listen.

He was searching his mind for an innocent reason that Sammy's number would be out of service. He couldn't summon one.

Luke tightened his grip on the steering wheel until his fingers blanched. "I'm going to hunt down whoever did this."

His chest heaved and he slammed a fist against the dashboard.

Megan flinched.

They were driving west on Interstate 8 in an old Ford Bronco they'd stolen minutes after the students dropped them at a Greyhound station in El Centro, California. Luke had found the SUV on a tree-lined side street and chosen it for its heavily tinted glass and a wing window that he easily pried open with the screwdriver he'd bought a few minutes earlier at a hardware store. After switching license plates with a Toyota Camry parked behind it, he had broken open the Bronco's steering column, located the linkage rod, and played with it until the engine finally turned over.

"Maybe your father and Dr. Wilson decided to hide out someplace else," she said with no conviction. "Maybe they're okay."

Ten minutes earlier they had stopped at a convenience store and Luke called the lodge in Big Bear Lake. The person at the front desk explained that Drs. McKenna and Wilson had each made four-day reservations beginning yesterday, but neither had arrived. Megan's call to Ben's home found his wife in a panic, wondering why her husband hadn't come home the previous night.

Luke's mind was afire.

"They're not hiding out," he said. "Ben wouldn't have left his family. Someone grabbed them. If Calderon got hold of them . . ." He didn't finish his thought. He wouldn't say aloud that his father and Ben might be dead.

"What do you think happened?" Megan asked.

"I don't know. My father's not exactly subtle. Maybe Caleb talked to him, picked up on something."

"It's crazy. How does Caleb think he can get away with this?"

Luke had the same question. Abducting his father and Ben was a risky move, one that would draw in the police. Everything that Caleb and his cabal had done before now—framing Luke, drawing him to Guatemala—was a carefully scripted strategy to divert attention away from their activities.

If CHEGAN was acting out of desperation, if this had been done recklessly, Luke knew that his father and Ben were already dead.

There was another possibility, though. Caleb might be using Elmer and Ben as bait—drawing Luke in, taunting him, reminding him that he was tethered like a puppet. If that was Caleb's strategy, the implied message was also clear. Come alone.

That Luke had no allies in this battle was a given. He couldn't go to the police. The detectives would lock him up, at least until they had vetted his story. His father would be dead long before he could ever turn the investigation toward Caleb.

Even Sammy had abandoned him.

Or worse.

Downtown L.A. was coming into view when Luke transitioned onto the 10 Freeway at 2:47 on Friday afternoon.

Megan broke into his reverie. "What've you been thinking about for the past hour?"

In the rearview mirror, Frankie's head was bobbing in sleep.

"A guy I trusted—Sammy Wilkes. I think he set me up."

"Who is he?"

"I'm not sure." Luke described the many faces of Sammy: the cocky young soldier who, during missions, wore a countenance as dark as his skin; the man who hid his Ivy-league intellect behind an urban ghetto persona; the man who seemed to talk only about himself without ever letting you know who he was.

Then he explained: "Wilkes showed up right after that private investigator—the one hired by Erickson—started tailing me. Sammy was probably already watching me when he spotted the P.I., then approached me with a phony story about the football player's attorney contacting him. Sammy played me perfectly—like he was looking out for me. I fell for it."

"You think Wilkes is working for Calderon?"

"Probably the other way around. Wilkes is right here in L.A. and has a good-sized operation. Caleb probably hired *him* to run CHEGAN's security."

Megan pointed at a California Highway Patrol cruiser several car lengths in front of them.

Luke had already seen it and slowed. The Bronco had probably already been reported stolen, and he had to hope that the Camry owner whose license plates he was using didn't notice that someone had switched plates. Even then, the switch provided only the shallowest ruse, protecting them from nothing more than a cursory check against a list of stolen plates. Any cop who took the time to run their plates would immediately discover that they didn't match the make and model of the vehicle Luke was driving.

"Calderon used to work for Sammy and probably still does jobs for him. Sammy's probably using him as his hammer, and I walked right into it."

Luke waited for an eighteen-wheeler to pass on their right.

"When I didn't let go of the autopsies, it was probably Sammy's idea to set me up for the Erickson murder. He's clever enough to think up something like that. The bastard was two moves ahead of me. He even told me what he was doing. Just before I left the U.S., he said, 'They're reeling you in.' Those were his words. He knew because he was the one doing it."

"How can you be sure?"

"There're other things that point to him. The fact that he wanted me to contact Calderon, and did it himself *before* I told him to. He probably thought I wasn't going to take the bait." Luke shot a glance at Megan. "And the men that followed me to the Zenavax lab—Sammy could have had me fixed with a GPS transponder and given them my coordinates."

Luke thought about the satellite phone that Sammy had given him, and how easily a transponder could have been inserted into it.

"We can't fight these people alone," Megan said. "There are too many of them."

"Not 'we'—me. This is my war."

Luke stared at the traffic ahead, but he could feel Megan's gaze.

"These people want you dead," she said. "If you keep giving them chances, eventually they're going to succeed."

Her words clung to him like a spiderweb as he cut across two lanes and took the Western Avenue exit.

Chapter 59

It was 3:14 P.M. when Luke pulled over and parked along a tree-lined residential street that dead-ended into the roadway running along the rear of University Children's. Fifty yards beyond the end of the Bronco's hood was the hospital's loading dock.

Luke and Megan crawled into the backseat with Frankie. The charcoal-tinted side windows would shield them from casual glances by passersby, but they were still visible through the windshield.

"What now?" Megan asked.

"We watch," Luke said. "Caleb knows that we could've made it back to L.A. by now. His people are probably already in position, guarding the hospital."

She pointed at the loading dock. "You think they're going to just walk out the back of the hospital with your father's mosquitoes?"

"Nobody in Security will bat an eye if a couple of lab techs acting on Caleb's authority load a metal container onto a truck."

There were three trucks facing out from the concrete platform. One was a large eighteen-wheeler, a food-service truck with a logo familiar to Luke. The second was a nondescript white van without markings. The third was a medium-sized transport with loud orange and blue lettering splashed on the sides—a rental.

"Trucks come in and out of there all day long," she said. "How're we going to know if we see theirs?"

"It's not their truck that I'm looking for."

"What, then?"

"Caleb's operatives." He watched a heavyset man climb into the cab of the food service truck. "A driver who's more watchful than he should be, someone whose hands are never in his pockets, someone wearing a jacket in seventy-degree weather to conceal a weapon."

"What if they don't use the loading dock?" Megan asked. "There're doors on every side of the building—you can't cover every exit."

"I don't have to. I'm not waiting until they leave."

If Caleb's plan hadn't changed, his people would enter the mosquito lab at six o'clock. Luke knew that his best chance was to destroy the mosquitoes now—before Caleb's team descended on the laboratory. If he waited and attempted to stop them as they left the hospital, he'd face the dual challenge of a concentrated force and having to guess which of several exits they might use.

And by then, CHEGAN would have no reason to keep his father alive. *If* his dad was still alive, it was only because they were holding him to use as leverage against Luke.

To save his father, he had to strike quickly and cut off the serpent's head. He had to get to Fagan.

Of course, all of those concerns were mute if Caleb had moved up his timetable and already snatched a colony of mosquito larvae. Luke hoped that his father's calculations were right and CHEGAN couldn't risk cutting short the harvesting period.

"I just need Caleb's sentries to show themselves. I'll find a weakness in their defense."

"And what if they *don't* show themselves?"

Megan's question pushed him in a direction he was already drifting. Time was on his enemy's side, Luke reminded himself. He couldn't wait for his adversaries to reveal themselves. He had to disturb the nest, draw out the wasps that were protecting their queen.

It was a risk, but one he had to take. He reasoned that Caleb's need for stealth limited him to using a relatively small force. Luke had to pull them out of hiding, spread them out in a protective formation around the hospital's perimeter, where he could spot them.

"I need a phone," he said.

Frankie bolted for the door. "I be back."

Luke grabbed the boy's collar. "Where're you going?"

"I get you phone."

Luke considered his options, then released his hold. "Don't get caught."

Five minutes later Luke was starting to regret sending Frankie when the boy flew around the corner as if being chased but then quickly slowed and waddled over to their vehicle.

"Here," the boy said as he climbed into the Bronco and handed Luke a scuffed cell phone. "I help lady with—"

"I don't need to know." Luke studied the buttons for a moment, then said to Megan, "Let's hope this works."

The intern, Chewy Nelson, walked into Room 402 to check on a young boy recovering from a bout of asthma.

"Hey, bud. What's with all the presents?" he asked the toddler.

"It's my burfday."

Chewy picked up a black plastic telescope from the bed. "You know what this thing is called?" he asked.

The boy shook his head.

Chewy held the scope up to one eye and pointed it out the window. "A babe spotter." He peered through the front window of Kolter's, hoping to see that nurse from 3-West. As he was doing this, a small boy collided with a pair of women in front of the deli and then scrambled to help one of them retrieve the contents of her spilled purse.

"That little twerp took her cell phone," Chewy whispered to himself. He watched the urchin cross the street, then followed the boy until he disappeared around a corner of the hospital.

Chewy bolted out the door, ran down the hall, and charged into an empty patient room along the hospital's rear. When he found the pint-sized kleptomaniac in his scope, the kid was turning onto a side street where he eventually got into the backseat of an SUV. There were others in the vehicle. All of them were crammed into the backseat.

He adjusted the lens and the image came into focus.

"Holy shit," he said.

The first hospital operator whom Luke spoke with didn't flinch when he asked her to overhead page Dr. Petri Kaczynski. He left his cell phone number and asked the woman to give it to whoever responded to the page.

Twenty minutes later no one had called, so Luke dialed the hospital again. A different operator answered this time and explained that his page had not been put through because the man he was trying to reach had died several years ago. Luke explained that Kaczynski's physician-son of the same name was very much alive and visiting the hospital. The operator agreed to put through the page.

Luke worked his left shoulder while studying the area behind them through the rearview mirror. An elderly woman led by a white poodle walked out the front door of a one-story bungalow halfway up the block. He followed her with his eyes until she disappeared around a corner at the far end of the block.

In his peripheral vision, Luke suddenly detected movement on the loading dock. He caught a fleeting glimpse of a man jumping from the back end of the rental truck and trotting into the hospital. Luke recognized the man's blue hospital security uniform.

He also recognized the man's thickly muscled physique and partially severed left ear.

Chapter 60

Lieutenant Groff had mobilized the Rapid Response Unit within minutes of receiving the call from University Children's. They had arrived ten minutes earlier and set up a command unit two blocks north of the hospital. It had taken less than seven minutes for the team to take their positions.

Groff said, "Unit One, do you have the Bronco in sight?"

A woman's voice said, "I'm fifty yards from the suspect's vehicle, approaching from the rear, west side of the street. No exhaust—engine's off."

"Any movement?"

"No visual on the inside. Rear window is too dark to see through."

"Unit Five?" Groff asked.

"In position, southeast corner of the roof, in a direct line with the street." A pause, then, "I can see the subject vehicle's hood through a break in the trees, but that's it. I have good line-of-sight if he breaks to the north, toward the hospital."

"Unit Six?"

"Southwest corner. No visual on suspect, but I got a clear shot on the driver's side."

Groff chewed the inside of his cheek for a moment, then said, "All units, ready to move on my command."

* * *

Luke's arm twitched when the cell phone vibrated. He recognized the hospital's prefix on the number showing in the display.

"You look good in blue, Calderon. Want me to bury you in that uniform?"

"Ready to settle up, cockroach?"

"Luke!" Megan yelled.

The throaty roar of engines at full throttle reached his ears before the sound of the screeching tires. Luke jerked his head around and saw a small cavalry of cars through the rear window.

Groff grabbed the handhold above the passenger window and glanced back at the unit behind them as his driver accelerated into the turn and their car hurtled around the corner. The Bronco came up on them as soon as they completed the turn, and Groff's driver had to do a controlled spin to avoid the SUV.

Three plain blue sedans were already braking behind the Bronco and three-man teams jumped from each vehicle with automatic weapons in hand.

Groff lunged from his car with his semiautomatic in a two-hand grip, sweeping his gun sight across the Bronco's windshield. A black-helmeted officer at the SUV's rear plunged his rifle butt through the back window while detectives standing at the forward doors broke through the side windows.

A moment later the men were staring at Groff, the question showing on their faces.

The lieutenant lowered his gun, reholstered it, then slammed the Bronco's hood with his fist.

"Goddammit! Where is he?"

* * *

They were two blocks from University Children's and driving south, away from the hospital, when the small herd of police cars screamed past the 1970s Ford Maverick that Luke had stolen from the poodle woman's garage. Megan was at the wheel, while he and Frankie lay across the backseat.

Luke had decided to abandon their SUV after spotting Calderon, having learned what he needed from his reconnaissance. His enemy was garrisoned inside the hospital.

Calderon had broken off their phone connection just as the black-and-whites raced by their car. When Luke retrieved the stored number and dialed it, no one answered.

Their latest car was the ugliest mint-green he'd ever seen. Luke had wanted to switch vehicles before some vigilant patrol cop ran their plates. He hadn't counted on trading his Bronco for the automotive equivalent of a peacock.

The question now turning in his mind was, how had the police found him?

However they had done it, it wouldn't be long before they knew about the poodle woman's car. They were probably already cordoning off the side streets around the hospital and searching the area. As soon as the woman returned home and reported the theft, the police would have the make, model, and license number of their car.

"Drive a few more blocks, then stop the car and let me out," he said.

As though reading his thoughts, Megan said, "You can't go back to the hospital now."

"I don't have a choice," he said. "After you drop me

off, drive a few more blocks. Then ditch the car and take care of Frankie."

"You'll never get inside the hospital," she said. "The police—they're probably swarming the place by now."

"I'll find a way in."

"Wait," Megan said. "There's another way to do this."

Chapter 61

The helicopter operations of the L.A. Sheriff's Department were located at Long Beach Airport, tucked away on a small plot of land about a half mile from the airport terminal.

It was 5:17 P.M. and the sun had already set when Megan pulled into the parking lot that the Sheriff's Aero Bureau shared with a helicopter tour company. The place looked the same as Luke remembered it from his time as a member of Search & Rescue, including the security cameras mounted atop each of the installation's three buildings. The only addition was a chain-link fence topped with coiled razor wire that ran between each of the buildings.

He turned and looked at Megan, trying to decide if he was expecting too much of her.

"You know what to do?" he asked.

"This was *my* idea, remember?"

She was right—the basic idea was hers. After breaking into Megan's street-level apartment through a rear window and retrieving her hospital ID, she had called in a prescription to a Walgreens pharmacy for phenylephrine eye drops, hoping that no one would recognize the name or face of the woman who had made a fleeting appearance on local TV channels several days earlier.

No one did. While at the pharmacy, she also picked up gauze, white tape, a pair of scissors, and, reluctantly, a box of vintage "safety" razor blades that Luke insisted were necessary for their plan to work.

After Megan parked and turned off the engine, Luke stared across the parking lot at the Aero Bureau's main entrance. On the other side of glass double doors, a deputy was sitting at the front reception desk. The rims of video monitors fed by the exterior security cameras showed above the lip of the chest-high countertop.

"Remember what I told you about the security monitors," Luke said. "You have to draw their attention away from the monitors or they'll spot me."

She nodded.

"Okay, let's do it," he said.

Frankie looked nervously between them.

"This won't hurt," Megan said to the boy. "Lean back and open your eyes as wide as you can." She unscrewed the bottle top with an attached eyedropper and instilled three drops of phenylephrine into the boy's right eye.

Luke held open the boy's eyelid and watched the pupil dilate while Megan went to work with the scissors, cutting away a small, ragged tuft of hair from the side of Frankie's scalp.

Luke tightened his hand into a fist until his veins corded with blood, then turned away and used the razor blade to make a neat one-inch incision along his forearm.

Blood poured from the wound. "Put his head on my lap," he said to Megan.

Luke clenched his fist and a sheet of blood oozed over his arm, falling onto the left side of Frankie's scalp. Within a minute the boy's head was soaked in blood.

"I starting to feel si—" Frankie wretched.

"Sorry," Luke said.

The boy wiped his mouth with a sleeve. "Me no sorry. I help you, then you help me stay in America, yes?"

Luke tried to smile at the boy, but the dishonor he felt for stoking Frankie's false dream held down the corners of his mouth.

"I'll try," he said while looking at Megan, who didn't look up from taping gauze over his arm.

When she was done, Luke draped his hand around her wrist and squeezed gently.

"Time to go," he said.

Megan didn't hesitate. She was out of the car and running toward the entrance before Luke had opened the door on his side of the vehicle.

He tapped Frankie's shoulder and grabbed two of the car's floor mats as he got out of the car. Luke ducked behind the hood of a pickup twenty feet from the Maverick just as Megan threw open the entry doors.

It was a brightly lit room, and the uniformed deputy at the front desk hadn't seemed to notice Megan approaching the building in the dark. When the doors swung open, he jumped from his chair.

Megan was shaking her arms wildly and pointing with both arms toward the parking lot. The jet engines of a landing plane drowned out her screams, which made the melodrama appear like a silent movie.

The deputy was already coming around a long countertop when Megan raced out the door. A second deputy charged through a door at the back of the room and followed them only as far as the entrance, where he stopped and swept the parking lot with his eyes. His right hand rested on a holstered automatic.

As soon as Megan and the deputy reached the car, the man shouted back to his colleague at the entrance, telling him to get the paramedics.

Luke had to scale the chain-link fence, which was in plain view of anyone standing in the parking lot. He couldn't move until they carried Frankie inside the building. Their plan would fall apart if the paramedics decided to work on the boy outside, at the car.

Megan started wailing incoherently. The deputy looked between Frankie and her as if he couldn't decide whom to give his attention to at that moment. Her glance shifted to the entrance, and Luke's gaze followed. A man and a woman wearing green flight suits and carrying red tackle boxes charged out the front doors. Paramedics.

Megan seemed to recognize the problem immediately— the paramedics were going to assess and treat Frankie at the car. She lunged into the vehicle and a second later emerged with Frankie in her arms. She started trotting awkwardly toward the building. The deputy made a half-hearted attempt to stop her, then simply jogged alongside her.

The paramedics held up their hands to stop her—one shouted "Whoa!"—but she jogged past them and continued toward the building like someone who could only hear inner voices.

Luke ran toward the fence.

"I didn't see him," Megan shouted. "I was driving and he just—just came out of nowhere. *Oh, my God. Oh, my God.*"

"Lady, try to calm down." The deputy patted her back as if stroking a cactus. "You did the right thing."

She chewed on a knuckle and her feet bounced up and down as if dancing on hot coals. It wasn't difficult to feign panic.

The female paramedic lifted Frankie's eyelids and shone a penlight over them. The boy's facial muscles tightened slightly but his body remained flaccid. He was playing his part better than Megan had expected.

"Right pupil's blown," the woman said. "Probably a bleeder inside his head." She turned to the second paramedic, who was gingerly fingering the boy's scalp. "Call it in."

Unless University Children's was closed because of the police action, that's where they'd take him. There were only two centers with heliports designated for pediatric neurosurgical emergencies, and University Children's was closer.

While the male paramedic keyed in the radio, the other grabbed an IV bag, tubing, and needle. Moments later she plunged a needle into Frankie's hand.

"Ouch," the boy yelped. His eyes popped open and bulged like two hardboiled eggs, then just as quickly, closed.

The female paramedic looked at the boy with a bemused expression.

Her partner shrugged while speaking to a dispatcher over the radio.

A man with an enormous handlebar moustache came through the rear door. He had a helmet tucked under one arm and was wearing a flight suit. The name on his breast pocket read: R. STEVENS.

"Are we a go?" the man asked as his eyes traveled the room.

Megan stooped near Frankie and put a hand to the side of her face before Stevens's gaze reached her. If the pilot recognized her from their encounter in the E.R. two weeks ago, her ploy would disintegrate.

The paramedic on the radio held up a finger.

All eyes fixed on him.

"Affirmative," he said into the handset while nodding

at the pilot. "We'll call you as soon as we're in the air."

"I'll be in the Sikorsky doing the preflight," Stevens said as he disappeared through the rear door.

While the female paramedic was taping the IV in place, she said to a deputy, "Give me a hand here. Let's move this kid onto a back board."

When the deputy reached down and took hold of Frankie's feet, Megan said, "Oh my God, I left my car running. I'll be right back." She ran for the door.

Behind her the deputy called out, "Hang on. I need a statement from you."

Megan called back, "I'll be right back," knowing she wouldn't.

Luke watched from the helicopter's rear bay as Rick Stevens climbed into the pilot's seat from a side door. The blades were already spinning and the giant Sikorsky's engines sounded like unbroken thunder.

Stevens nodded to his copilot, who bobbed his head toward the rear.

The pilot turned.

"Last time we were together, you were sitting in the copilot's seat," Luke shouted over the engine noise. "Congratulations."

Stevens looked at the pistol Luke had trained on the sergeant kneeling next to him—the crew chief. The pilot glanced at his crew chief's empty holster, then back at Luke. "What the hell happened to you, McKenna? You turn into some kinda monster?"

"It's a long story. Right now, the only thing I care about is getting to the hospital."

"Go to hell." Stevens looked at his copilot. "Power down. We're not going anywhere."

"Wrong. You're going to put this thing into the air."

Luke cocked the hammer of the gun he'd taken from the sergeant and put the barrel into the man's ear. "That is, after everyone's aboard."

Through the side hatch, Luke saw Megan peering from behind the corner of a building. She caught his eye, then sprinted toward the helicopter.

Luke flipped off the lights in the helicopter's rear bay. Against the glare of the landing deck's perimeter flood-lights, the Sikorsky's interior now appeared as a black-ened cavern.

"Any problems?" he asked as she jumped on board.

Megan shook her head, panting. "I found the floor mats hanging over the barbed wired." She motioned toward the main building. "The medics should be bringing Frankie out any moment now."

And they did. Luke couldn't tell whether the para-medics were more stunned by his handgun, or the boy's miraculous recovery once inside the aircraft.

Luke donned the crew chief's helmet and plugged the headset cord into a small receptacle on his seat. He mo-tioned for Megan to do likewise with one of the para-medics' helmets. It was the only way to talk over the roar of the engine and hear Rick Stevens's ground communi-cations.

Luke instructed Stevens through his headset: "Patch me into University Children's E.R. on channel two." He turned to Megan and said, "Stay on channel one with the pilot while I'm talking to the E.R. Signal me if he says anything to warn the ground controllers."

A moment later, Luke heard the voice of Dr. Keller, his E.R. director. In a warbling voice disguised by the air-ship's vibration, Luke described a mythical head-injury case as though he were one of the paramedics. He fin-ished by inventing a story about being delayed on the ground and gave Keller an ETA of forty-five minutes.

After Luke ended the transmission, Stevens said, "Why'd you say that? We'll be there in fifteen minutes, maybe less."

"I don't want anyone on the roof when we get there." Luke knew that his E.R.'s procedure was to send a medical team to the heliport ten minutes before the helicopter landed.

"I'll need their landing lights on," Stevens shouted. "What if they don't—"

"You'll just have to manage. Now lift off."

Luke waved his weapon in a sweeping motion at the hatch door, and one of the paramedics reached over to secure it.

The door was halfway closed when a dark figure tumbled in through the gap and landed like a brick on the crew chief.

The tip of Luke's gun barrel was pressed firmly under the intruder's jaw before the man recovered from his tumble.

The familiar black man's mouth opened into a toothy grin and he spread his arms. "Easy, there, Flash. You gonna need some help, and *help* happens to be Sammy's specialty."

Chapter 62

"Whoa, Flash. Slow down," Sammy said after listening to Luke run through his litany of accusations. "I'm working for Zenavax. That's my only gig here."

After they had lifted off from the helipad, Luke had waved Sammy to the rear of the cargo bay and then thrown one of the flight helmets at him so they could talk. Luke had placed the crew chief and paramedics in front of the ex-Proteus member as a protective buffer. Megan and Frankie were sitting with Luke at the front, just behind the flight deck.

Luke was switching between the pilots on channel one—listening to their communications with ground controllers whenever Megan signaled him that they were transmitting—and Sammy on channel two.

"Flash, I don't know nothing from nothing about this CHEGAN thing. First I heard about it was from your 'ol man—"

The gun came up reflexively. *"Where's my father?"*

"Holed up in my condo with that pathologist, Wilson."

"What?"

"Protective custody—it's one of Sammy's specialties. I took 'em outta the battle zone. Had to cuff 'em to a bedroom door to keep them away from the phone—they seemed a little doubtful of Sammy's intentions. But they're safe."

"Back up. Start at the beginning and tell me *what the hell is going on*."

"I can only tell ya what I know. Zenavax hired my company to do electronic surveillance on Kate Tartaglia. She'd come up with this theory that their vaccines weren't safe. The head of the company told me she was wrong, but he said that she wouldn't let go of it. Management was worried that Tartaglia was going to spoil their big payday. They're going public in an IPO this month and—"

"Hurry it up. I don't have time for the long version." Luke glanced out a porthole as they flew over the L.A. Coliseum.

"The e-mail Tartaglia sent you—I'm the one who erased it from your computer. When she turned up dead the next day, I thought that Zenavax had had her killed. It looked to Sammy like someone was using me, and making me an accessory to murder."

"So you figured you'd use me."

Sammy shook his head. "Not at first. For all I knew, you coulda been involved. I followed you for a coupla days. But after the Erickson shooting, it was obvious to Sammy that someone was setting you up."

"It was you that left Kate's e-mail at my front door."

"Had to keep you in the game, Flash. I wanted to know who killed Tartaglia, and why. You knew the woman, and you understand 'bout vaccines and shit—you were the perfect man for the mission."

"You threw me out there like a piece of bait."

"No. *You* did that when you wouldn't let go of the kid's death. Sammy just accommodated your natural tendencies."

Luke felt the helicopter lean into a turn. Stevens and his copilot were maneuvering the aircraft onto a direct path toward the hospital.

Luke switched to channel one and told Stevens, "Go past the hospital and fly toward Griffith Park."

"What?" the pilot said. "Where the hell are you taking us?"

Luke reached forward and placed his pistol against the copilot's neck. "You're going to do whatever I tell you to do, and your copilot is going to convince ground controllers to go along with our little deviation from the flight plan."

The copilot seemed to wait for Stevens to make a decision.

"Do what he says," Stevens said finally.

The copilot's voice was convincingly dry when he radioed air traffic control and reported a rattle in the fuselage that they wanted to investigate before landing at the hospital. They'd do a few angled turns and rapid decelerations over the unpopulated park to investigate the noise, he said. When controllers didn't respond immediately, he added, "Shouldn't take more than a few minutes."

After a long pause in the transmission, ground controllers gave them clearance.

Luke switched back to channel two and said, "My father—what did you mean about taking him out of the battle zone?"

Sammy nodded, as if being brought back to a thought. "When this whole thing began, I wired Barnesdale's office. He was connected to Zenavax, somehow. I don't know exactly how and it probably doesn't matter anymore since he's dead. Anyway, the CEO thought the guy was acting a little squirrelly and wanted me to monitor things."

"So?"

"Those bugs are still in place, but now a fella named Caleb Fagan is sitting in that office. One of my people was listening to a tape and heard one side of a cell phone conversation where Fagan was talking about sending your 'ol man and Wilson back to Abraham's bosom once they, as he put it, 'finished their work.' Calderon's name was mentioned."

Luke's mind called back an image of the mosquitoes. "Did my father destroy his mosquitoes?"

"Negative. Wilson and your dad weren't exactly chatty when I first snatched 'em from the hospital. They didn't tell me how the mosquitoes figured into this until a few hours ago."

Luke pounded his fist against a strut.

"They told me 'bout you coming after Caleb," Sammy continued, "so I was waiting when you showed up at the hospital. Following you to Long Beach wasn't too hard after you stole that puke-green jalopy."

The pilot's voice suddenly came through on their channel. "We're coming up on Griffith Park. Where you taking us next, Captain Nemo?"

Stevens probably didn't think his mood could worsen, but it did when Luke instructed him to land the Sikorsky on the front lawn of the Griffith Park Observatory.

Luke ignored the pilot's shouted curses and held up three fingers to Sammy, signaling him to switch to channel three.

"Why'd you disconnect the cell phone number I was using to contact you?" Luke asked.

"The truth?" Sammy said. "I figured you were dead. When I didn't hear from you after your meeting at that castle, I called and a Latino guy answered. He was saying something in Spanish about a park bench. You're not the type to get sloppy and lose a phone."

"That doesn't explain disconnecting *your* cell phone."

"If you were dead, sooner or later the LAPD would hear about it. They'd go sniffing around to tie up loose ends. Your phone had *my* number stored in memory. I didn't know who that guy was that had your phone, and I didn't want a trail that led back to Sammy. So I cancelled service on that number. I got a guy at the phone company that purges my records as soon as I pay the final bill on a discontinued number."

"I appreciate your concern for my well-being."

"When your daddy told Sammy that you were still alive, Sammy cried like a little itty-bitty baby." Sammy's head bobbed up and down. "No lie."

The helicopter's airspeed slowed as they approached The Observatory.

Luke glanced out the porthole, then back at Sammy. "Why are you here?"

Sammy shrugged. "I figured I owe you one."

As soon as they touched down at The Observatory, Luke took the communications cord from Stevens's helmet and herded the copilot, crew chief, and paramedics outside at gunpoint. Sammy used a roll of plastic handcuffs from one of the helicopter's supply drawers to tie them to a heavy cast-iron fence. Luke took the male paramedic's coveralls and put them over his street clothes.

Sammy did likewise with the copilot's uniform before climbing into the cockpit.

When Luke jumped back into the aircraft, he said to Megan, "This is where you and Frankie get off." He pointed outside, to his right. "You can make your way down that road, over there."

At first her eyes showed confusion—that is, until her temper had time to come to a boil. *"After everything we've been through,"* she shouted, *"how can you even think of doing this?"*

"I don't have time to argue. This isn't your fight anymore."

He turned, but she moved with him. "You think I'm here because I *want* to be part of this? Sometimes, you are so dense." She shook her head. "Why do you think I'm here, Luke? Have you even stopped to think about that?"

"Megan, listen to me. I have no idea what I'm up against, and there's a good chance that anyone who comes with me will die. You've done enough. I don't want anything to happen to you."

"Good. Me neither." She thrust her thumb in the air. "Now that that's settled, let's go."

He looked at Sammy, who held up his hands as if· to say he didn't want any part of their argument.

Luke drew a long breath and rubbed the back of his neck. He stared at her for a long moment, then said, "If you're coming, you'll need a pair of coveralls."

Chapter 63

As they lifted off The Observatory lawn, ground controllers were squawking at Stevens and demanding to know why he'd disappeared from ground radar and broken off radio communications. Stevens offered a "guess" that the hilly topography had interfered with their radar and radio signals. He quickly added the "good news"— his crew chief had found a nonstructural wing nut that'd come loose and caused the fuselage to rattle. Problem solved, he told the controllers.

They vectored Stevens to the hospital but added that they'd be writing up an incident report.

Sammy craned his neck from the copilot's seat and held up two fingers.

As soon as Luke switched to channel two, he heard, "So, Flash, what's the plan?"

"We need to get to my father's lab on the second floor." Luke pointed at Frankie, who was taking everything in with a wide-eyed expression. "He should get us past the cops on the roof, and onto the elevator. We'll get off on the third floor, find a place to hide Megan and the boy. Then you and I'll take a fire stairway that will put us about thirty feet from the lab."

"And then?"

"And then we improvise."

Megan glanced up from working on her jumpsuit. She was curling the end of each pants leg into a cuff, trying to disguise the fact that it was several sizes too large.

Stevens suddenly broke into their channel and said, "So tell me something, McKenna. Why you going back into the hornet's nest? You gotta know that LAPD's got every rifle in their arsenal at the hospital. We were listening to it on a tactical frequency before you crashed into our evening. They got an army of uniforms and a coupla SWAT units looking for you. You got a suicide wish or something?"

"It's a long story."

"I already heard most of it," Stevens said.

Luke cocked an eyebrow at Megan.

Stevens had eavesdropped on their communications channel.

"So," the pilot continued, "you expect me to believe all that crap?"

"I'm not asking you to believe anything," Luke said. "Just fly us to the hospital."

Stevens turned to Sammy. "Well, for some goddamned reason, I think I *do* believe it."

Luke and Megan exchanged a glance.

"But then, I probably got my head up my ass," the pilot added. "So how do you wanna do this?"

"Just put us down on the heliport."

Luke signaled Frankie to jump onto the collapsible gurney, and Megan secured the boy's chest and legs with canvas straps.

The digital clock mounted on an overhead panel read 6:07. His enemy was already inside the mosquito lab.

Stevens exchanged some chatter with a police helicopter on their approach to University Children's and was cleared to land only after the other pilot contacted the Emergency Room to confirm the transport. The LAPD pilot informed them that the E.R.'s medical team hadn't expected them for another fifteen minutes and wouldn't be on the heliport to meet them.

The hospital rooftop was dark, and Stevens trained his spotlight on the heliport. He circled the hospital twice before centering their aircraft over the platform.

On the second pass, Luke looked out a side window and saw the rental truck sitting at the loading dock.

He spotted two sharpshooters along the roofline as the Sikorsky descended toward the helipad, but he knew there might be others hidden in the darkness.

He put his gun into a thigh pocket.

When the Sikorsky thudded down on the heliport, the only thing he could see through his porthole was flying dust.

He lowered the tinted visor on his helmet, signaled Megan to do likewise, then swung the hatch door open. A soupy mix of soot and fuel exhaust streamed into the cargo hold.

A man and a woman wearing backward-facing caps and black fatigues with LOS ANGELES SWAT patches were at the door when Luke opened it. The man had a shouldered rifle with a sniper's scope. He was holding a semiautomatic in his left hand. The woman had oversized binoculars hanging from her neck—a spotter.

"Transport from Long Beach?" the spotter yelled over the *yap-yap-yap* of the rotor blades.

Luke cracked open his visor only enough to expose the lower half of his face. "Head wound," he shouted. "I hope they're ready for us downstairs."

The sniper threw a hand up at Luke and glanced through

the copilot's window at Sammy, who saluted him with two fingers. "E.R. told us you wouldn't be here for another fifteen," the man said.

Luke shrugged in apparent puzzlement, then pointed at Frankie. "We need to get him to the E.R. Now."

The sniper's partner was already talking into a throat mic, her eyes darting between Megan and Luke the whole time. Finally, she waved them toward the elevator.

The gurney's collapsible legs sprung to life with a loud *clack* when Luke and Megan pulled it from the helicopter's belly.

When they reached the elevator, the male cop pointed to a spot where he wanted them to stand and used a key to call the car. The woman stepped back to the edge of the roofline and aimed her spotting scope across the street.

"You know the way?" the sharpshooter asked.

Luke nodded.

The Sikorsky's engines powered down and their heavy throb was replaced by a high-pitched whine. Stevens and Sammy remained in the helicopter.

The sniper eyed Megan's baggy uniform. "What's your name," he asked.

Luke eyes went immediately to the stenciled name on Megan's coveralls: E. RIVERA.

"Eleanor," she replied while holding the cop's gaze.

"So what's the deal?" Luke jumped in and asked the sniper. "Lots of chatter on the radio, but no one's saying what this is all about."

Instead of answering, the cop turned to the sound of the elevator doors opening.

A vertical band of light from the elevator's interior painted the sharpshooter at the same moment a bullet punched through the side of his neck. He slumped to the ground.

Luke's eyes darted to the cop's partner, who had turned to the sound of the gunfire. Two rounds struck her mid-chest—in her Kevlar vest—but the bullets' force sent her over the edge of the roof.

Luke threw off his helmet and lunged at the door. He glimpsed a uniformed LAPD cop lying in a heap on the elevator floor just as Calderon charged through the doorway with a 9mm Glock semiautomatic.

Luke unfurled a front snap kick—the gun flew out of Calderon's hand.

Calderon's other hand flung a knife at Luke.

But Luke had seen it coming and jolted sideways.

The steel blade flew past his face before impaling Sammy's chest as he leapt from the helicopter.

Wilkes looked down, cursing as he went to his knees.

Luke grabbed the pistol from his thigh pocket.

"Face down on the ground. Now!" someone behind Luke yelled.

He turned and was staring down the barrel of a Remington Model 700 sniper rifle. The SWAT sniper holding it screamed, *"I said down!"*

Luke spread his arms and let the pistol fall to the ground.

Calderon said, "Officer, this man—"

The sniper stepped forward and swung his rifle at Calderon.

Luke shouted, *"No,"* but it was too late.

Calderon's left hand angled the barrel skyward at the same instant his right hand plunged a knife into the man's armpit, just above his Kevlar vest.

A loud sucking sound came from the sniper's chest just

as Luke's right foot connected with Calderon's torso.

A grunt came from Calderon as he went down, and Luke followed through with a spearing jab to the man's head.

Calderon dodged it, then rolled twice and came back up onto his feet in a low stance.

Luke's left foot flew up, but Calderon caught the side-kick with crossed wrists and twisted violently.

There was a snapping sound and a searing pain sent Luke to the ground.

He scissor-kicked Calderon just as a twenty million candlepower spotlight pierced the night sky and blinded him.

"You got a positive ID on the target?" the SWAT commander asked.

The LAPD sniper sitting on the edge of the helicopter's bay door turned to O'Reilly, whose assignment was to make the ID on McKenna. The detective peered through his binoculars again and nodded reluctantly.

Something wasn't right. Why would McKenna try to fight his way into the hospital? He had to know an army of cops was waiting for him.

"Affirmative," the sharpshooter replied.

O'Reilly could hear the anger in the man's voice. One of his team members had gone over the side of the building and two others were lying facedown in the wash of the light.

"Flight suit, sheriff's colors," the sniper continued. "Struggling with . . . it looks like a security guard. Guy's holding his own."

O'Reilly watched McKenna and the guard roll toward the edge of the landing pad, locked together like crazed beasts joined in a death struggle.

A man in a flight suit suddenly jumped out of the pilot's door and ran to where a woman and small boy were trying to drag two downed SWAT officers into the elevator.

What the hell was going on?

"You're clear to take out the target," the SWAT commander said.

"Wait," O'Reilly said. "Any transmissions from the sheriff's chopper yet?"

"O'Reilly, stay off the air." It was Lieutenant Groff's voice.

The sniper cinched his strap tighter and trained his rifle on the rooftop.

Megan and Stevens had pulled Sammy into the elevator and then gone back for the two cops.

Frankie was yelping in Spanish when Megan and Stevens dragged the two men into the elevator.

Megan pressed the button for the first floor, then said to Stevens, "Keep the boy with you."

She bolted out of the elevator just as the doors were closing.

Calderon easily pried free of Luke's grip and jumped to his feet.

The blinding spotlight replaced Calderon's silhouette. Luke rolled to his left, but a boot slammed into his side, cracking several ribs.

Calderon landed on him like a rabid animal and grabbed his neck in both hands. Unable to catch his breath, weakened by pain, Luke couldn't break the man's grip.

Calderon choked off his oxygen and a curtain of red descended over Luke's eyes.

Suddenly, a scream penetrated the growing darkness.

Then something—someone—landed on top of Calderon.

"Shit," O'Reilly heard the sharpshooter whisper.

"What's going on up there?" the SWAT commander asked.

"Can't get a clear shot," the sniper replied. "A woman just got into the middle of it."

Megan's shouts sounded distant in Luke's air-starved brain.

The helicopter's spotlight angled away and an outline of her head appeared behind Calderon, her arms flailing at his back.

Her hand came around and a finger found Calderon's right eye. She dug it into his socket.

Calderon let out a rumbling growl and his grip loosened.

Luke took a gasping breath.

Then Calderon's head shot back and struck Megan in the face.

She fell away with a loud shriek.

Luke made a spearing jab at Calderon's throat that was deflected.

Then another at his eye.

The second jab connected and Calderon rolled off of him, yowling in pain.

Luke sucked in a lungful of air and wheeled in the opposite direction. He struggled onto his one good foot.

Megan wobbled on one knee near the edge of the landing pad.

Calderon was sidestepping around Luke in a wide curve, circling his prey while rubbing blood from his eye. Then, suddenly, he charged.

Luke let out a roar, leapt into the air and spun in a 360-degree arc.

His foot landed cleanly on the side of Calderon's head.

Calderon rocketed sideways as if struck by a projectile, rolling three times before tumbling over the roof's edge.

And taking Megan with him.

Her scream pierced through the police helicopter's *thwack thwack thwack*.

"Megan!"

Luke dove for the roof's edge and grabbed the large hand clutching to its rim. He worked both hands around Calderon's wrist and tightened his grip, then peered over the edge.

Megan was wrapped around Calderon, her head buried in his stomach, her legs clawing at the side of the building.

Four stories below them was the blacktop roof of a two-story clinic building that extended out beyond the rest of the structure.

"Megan, hold still!" he yelled.

Luke dug his fingers into Calderon's sweat-drenched wrist and reached for Megan with his other hand.

He was several inches short.

"I'm slipping," Megan said.

Luke's foot found a rounded metal vent or pipe. He wedged his good ankle around it to hold his weight and leaned out over the edge.

The tips of his fingers found the collar of Megan's jumpsuit. He got a small purchase, but she moved and his grip broke free.

"Megan, try to hold still." Luke squeezed tighter around Calderon's wet wrist.

Calderon looked up at Luke and curled his bloodied

face into a sickening grin. His steaming nostrils pulsed with each breath.

"This is almost better than how I'd planned it," he said.

Then he let go.

"No!"

But Calderon had already slipped through his grip.

There were no screams—just a sickening *thud* that struck his closed eyelids like a blast wave.

When he opened his eyes, the world around him went silent.

On the blacktop, forty feet below, framed by the helicopter's twitching beam of light, Megan and Calderon's bodies lay on top of each other, their limbs spread in the awkward angles of death.

Chapter 64

*S**tay where you are and put your hands above your head,"** the helicopter speaker commanded.

The words didn't register. Luke rolled onto his back and covered his eyes.

He lay there for a span of time that was lost to his senses.

Eventually he struggled to his feet and starting limping toward the Sikorsky.

"Stop. Right there. Do not move!" the loudspeaker ordered.

The sharpshooter raised his rifle. "I got you, you bastard."

O'Reilly's hand pushed the barrel aside. "No."

The sniper turned to the detective, staring in disbelief. "You just bought yourself a shitload of trouble, pal. Get your goddamned hand off my rifle."

The radio crackled. "What's happening up there?" the SWAT commander asked.

O'Reilly pulled back his arm. "I'll do it again if you aim that rifle at McKenna."

The sniper said into his microphone, "Seems we got a reluctant soldier on our team."

Caleb Fagan hurried down the second-floor hallway with Mr. Kong in tow, asking himself how one man had wreaked such havoc on what was to be his life's legacy.

For Kaczynski, their quest was little more than an egocentric testament to the man's scientific talents. The man was a narcissistic intellectual who would accept any social construct that gave his work a veneer of legitimacy.

Caleb had lived the pain of giving life to a genetic mutant. Rather than fathering the son he had imagined—the son he deserved—a spontaneous and random mutation had corrupted one of his wife's otherwise healthy eggs. During the five excruciating years that his only child had lived, he'd watched the anguish consume his wife like a slow-growing cancer.

She had never recovered. Twenty years later the woman still spent her waking hours in a darkened corner of their house, wearing a hollow mask of death.

Caleb shook his thoughts free of the torment as they neared the microbiology lab.

He had told the cops who were using his office to peruse the hospital's floor plans that he'd return in a few minutes, after checking on a patient.

Caleb and his team were out of time. If his men weren't done preparing the mosquito transport, they'd have to abandon their plan.

McKenna had survived.

And if they were going to escape, Caleb and his men had to leave now.

When he opened the door to the laboratory, he saw that the guard who had been stationed outside the malaria lab had left his post.

Mr. Kong reached under his jacket to the gun in his belt holster.

"Uh-uh, partner. Don't touch that thing," came the voice from behind the door.

Caleb spun around and looked at the large ivory-handled revolver in Ben Wilson's hand.

Elmer McKenna was standing beside the pathologist. Each man had a pair of handcuffs fastened to one of his wrists. A doorknob assembly hung from Elmer's cuffs.

"We would've been here sooner," Ben said, "but I had to stop by home and pick up my daddy's favorite pistol." The pathologist's gaze shifted to Mr. Kong. "I haven't shot it in a long while—not since I was a kid—but it's loaded. I checked."

"Where is everyone, and what's this all about?" Caleb blustered.

"Sorry, Caleb. That ain't gonna work," Ben said. "But in answer to your question, your people are tied up in the next room. That's one of the many fine things about growing up in east Texas. You get real good at tying knots."

Just as Ben said the last word, Mr. Kong grabbed the semiautomatic from his Velcro holster and dove to his right.

A gun blast shattered the silence and a red spray exploded from Kong's right shoulder.

Elmer leaned away, holding his ears.

Caleb looked down at his bodyguard. The Chinese man was writhing on his side, groaning in pain.

Ben walked over to the Asian and kicked the man's gun across the floor.

"I lied about being outta practice," Ben said to Kong. "I go target shooting every once in a while. I was sorta hoping you'd do something stupid."

Caleb heard a stampede of footsteps in the distance.

"Sounds like we're gonna have company," Ben said. "Before the cops get here, Caleb, tell us. You weren't planning to come back from China, were you?"

Caleb looked at each man in turn. "You can't stop this. If not me, then someone else, but it's going to happen. It's only a matter of time before we step outside the artificial walls we've built around our work. Eventually, someone will take us where we need to go."

Elmer was shaking his head. "Caleb, too bad you can't see the imperfection of the human condition for what it is. It's not a curse. It's filled with lessons—for all of us."

Luke pulled a coil of nylon rope from the chopper and hobbled back to the edge of the platform. He tied one end of the rope to a metal strut and went over the side.

He was already touching down on the blacktop when he heard men storming onto the rooftop four stories above him.

Luke paid them no attention. He shot a glance at the corpse lying beneath Megan. Calderon's eyes stared out from a lopsided skull.

He knelt next to Megan and his hand went to her neck. Her pulse gave back the fading, agonal cadence of death.

He lifted his head, fighting back a wave of nausea.

"Get a trauma team out here," he shouted at the spotlight circling above him.

The loud flutter of the helicopter's rotors drowned out his voice.

Luke looked back at Megan and brought a hand over her head—his palm rising and falling at first, as if withdrawing from some unseen force. After a long moment, he gently drew back the hair over her face and tucked it behind her ear. Blood dripped from her nose.

He blinked away the wetness in his eyes.

"Oh, God," he whispered. "What have I done?"

Ten feet away, a window exploded and a herd of SWAT officers streamed through the breach.

Luke reached for the side of Megan's face, wanting to feel her warmth one last time, but a furious gang of hands yanked him away and threw him onto his stomach.

As they cuffed his wrists behind his back, he stared through Megan's still countenance, damning himself for the choices he had made.

Chapter 65

Five Days Later

Luke absently ran his fingers across the etched granite headstone, tracing over the letters of her name.

"Son, you okay?"

Luke nodded, all the while knowing he'd live the rest of his life wondering about the things he could have done differently.

It had been drizzling intermittently since Luke and Elmer arrived at the cemetery, and they had taken almost five minutes to walk up the sweeping eastern slope of Forest Lawn to her gravesite. Elmer's were the first words that had passed between them in several minutes.

Luke was stooped next to the headstone and his entire body ached, but he didn't give a damn about his physical discomforts.

The D.A.'s office had finally dropped all but the assault charges stemming from his escape into Griffith Park. Luke had walked out of jail after posting bail that morning.

He had missed the funeral, but it wasn't difficult to locate her gravesite. Hers was the only plot on the hillside marked by a rectangle of freshly planted sod.

The police had held him for five days while sorting out

the mess left from two weeks of relentless chaos. CHEGAN remained the lead story in almost every newspaper across the country. The *New York Times* had quoted his father for an article that featured statements by government officials from all five countries linked to CHEGAN. The leadership of four countries had openly denounced the gene-purifying scheme and reported that investigations were under way. The fifth—China—had condemned the plot but stopped short of admitting that anyone in their political hierarchy was involved.

Caleb Fagan was being held at the Federal Detention Center in downtown L.A. The freighter carrying Kaczynski had arrived in China, and reportedly Petri was in custody and sequestered at an undisclosed location. A *Los Angeles Times* article had quoted several experts as downplaying the risk that any remnant of CHEGAN acting alone could implement Kaczynski's plan. Releasing mosquitoes across a large geographic area was an enormous undertaking, they explained, requiring a well-coordinated plan and legions of personnel. According to them, a project of that scale just wasn't feasible without the full support and cooperation of numerous governmental agencies.

Luke hoped they were right.

Zenavax's fate was more certain. Two local papers had confirmed that the U.S. Attorney's Office was preparing criminal charges against the company, and University Children's would undoubtedly file a patent infringement lawsuit. Every legal pundit agreed that Zenavax was finished.

"At least she didn't suffer," his father said. "I'm sure she died instantly."

Megan's plunge came back to Luke in a nightmarish flash.

"Just like your mother," Elmer added in a quavering voice.

Luke turned to his father, who was wiping a sheet of tears from his cheeks. The recent mayhem had dragged his father back into the wrenching memory.

The truth of his mother's death had no place among his father's recollections. Luke was accustomed to the burden of unshared secrets. He could carry another.

"Dad, we should go. Ben's waiting for us." He glanced over his shoulder at the pathologist, who was standing by his car at the base of the hill.

Ben had ferried Luke and his father to the cemetery. His friend had been waiting with Elmer amidst a crush of reporters when Luke walked out of jail that morning.

Luke winced at the sharp pain in his ankle when he raised himself.

As he started down the incline, he wondered at the perverse wickedness that commanded innocents to pay the price for wars they had no part in starting.

When he had walked halfway down the slope, Luke turned back and looked one last time at Kate Tartaglia's grave.

"Any change?" Luke asked the red-haired nurse as he walked with his father and Ben into the hospital room at Saint Elizabeth's Hospital.

"I'm afraid not," she said while taping an IV to Megan's arm.

The top of Megan's head was wrapped in a thick gauze dressing that extended down and over her right eye and ear. She lay motionless, unaware of the world around her.

Luke's heart felt as if a clamp were tightening around it.

When the nurse completed her task, she smiled weakly in his direction and left the room.

Luke came around to the side of Megan's bed and reached for her left hand. He lifted it and gave a gentle squeeze.

Her arm hung limp in his grasp. Megan had made little progress since coming out of trauma surgery the morning after her four-story fall. After stabilizing her at University Children's, a transport team had rushed Megan to Saint Elizabeth's where CT scans revealed a brain hemorrhage, collapsed lung, fractured pelvis, and ruptured spleen. A team of seven surgeons had waged a twelve-hour battle against death during which her heart twice stopped beating.

She still hadn't moved her left side—she'd had a stroke during surgery—and an EEG from two days ago had shown mostly disorganized brain wave activity. Megan had come off the ventilator and was breathing on her own, but she hadn't uttered a word and only twice had opened her left eye for a fleeting moment. The only glimmers of mental responsiveness—if he could call them that—were her occasional bouts of agitation in response to sounds and spoken words.

Her doctors had said the usual things: The outcome of traumatic brain injuries was difficult to predict; Megan was young and her body still had significant regenerative capacity; and occasionally, patients recovered most or all of their physical and mental capabilities.

Luke knew the lines. He'd said them himself, usually to parents too anguished to hear his words. He also knew that most patients with injuries as severe as Megan's never recovered, a prospect his heart was fighting mightily to push out of his mind.

Except for visiting Kate's gravesite while Megan was in radiology for a brain MRI, he had been at Megan's bedside since his release from jail earlier that day.

Sammy was at the same hospital, in the ICU on a ventilator. The knife tip had pierced his lung; half his chest had filled with blood before surgeons finally stopped the bleeding. They expected him to live but he remained heavily sedated.

The LAPD hadn't been so lucky. Two SWAT officers had died at the scene—casualties of a war they had fought simply because it was their job.

"Dr. McKenna?"

Luke turned. A neatly dressed man with a briefcase was standing in the doorway.

Elmer was already shaking the man's hand. "Come in, Mr. Sutton."

The name was already familiar to Luke. He had called his father from jail and asked Elmer to find an immigration attorney to look into Frankie's situation. To this point, all of the conversations had been between his father and Sutton.

"I'm sorry to come here like this," the man said to Elmer, "but I need to talk to your son."

After introducing himself, Luke asked, "Any news?"

"I got a judge to stay the boy's deportation pending an asylum hearing in ten days."

"And what exactly does that mean?" Ben asked.

"It means that Frankie's not going back to Guatemala immediately," Sutton said. "More than that, I can't tell you. We're just going to have to see how this plays out, but I think we have a decent case. We're claiming the boy could be targeted by leftovers of that group—"

"CHEGAN," Luke said.

"Yeah. I'm going to argue that he's at risk and should be allowed to remain in the U.S. until Guatemalan officials can demonstrate that they've purged the bad guys."

"Where *is* Frankie?" Luke asked.

"At an INS holding facility." Sutton placed his briefcase on the arm of a chair and pulled out a sheaf of papers. "As soon as you sign these papers, they'll release him."

"Where will he go?"

"That's up to you. You're his guardian now. That is, until his status is cleared up at the hearing."

"What?" Luke churned through the papers. "Me? Look after Frankie?" His eyes came back to the attorney. "Have you met this boy?"

"Your father told me that you'd accept temporary custody."

Luke shot a glance at Elmer.

The old man shrugged sheepishly.

"This order is only valid for twenty-four hours," Sutton said. "I have to get it over to INS with a signature by five o'clock today, or he's going back to Guatemala tomorrow." The attorney shrugged. "It's up to you."

Luke turned to Ben.

"Don't look at me," Ben said. "I got my hands full trying to house-break a teenage daughter."

"What were you thinking?" Luke snapped at his father. "I can't take care of Frankie—"

A soft cough came from Megan.

Everyone turned.

Megan's right hand was twitching.

Luke stepped around her bed, cursing himself for raising his voice.

"It's okay, Megan." He rubbed her hand. "Everything's okay."

Her left eye opened slightly and her head swung slowly toward Luke. She wiggled free of his grip, and in an unsteady motion raised her right arm.

"I think she's pointing at Mr. Sutton," Elmer said.

Megan's lips moved.

A moment later she made a breathy sound.

Luke glanced at his father, then leaned over Megan and placed an ear next to her mouth.

"Shut up," she whispered in a slurred voice, "and sign the papers."